PERFECTLY
NICE
NEIGHBORS

PERFECTLY NICE NEIGHBORS

KIA ABDULLAH

G. P. PUTNAM'S SONS | NEW YORK

PUTNAM
—EST. 1838—

G. P. Putnam's Sons
Publishers Since 1838
An imprint of Penguin Random House LLC
penguinrandomhouse.com

First published in Great Britain in 2023 as
Those People Next Door, by HQ, an imprint of
HarperCollins Publishers.
Copyright © 2023 by Kia Abdullah

Library of Congress Cataloging-in-Publication Data

Names: Abdullah, Kia, author.
Title: Perfectly nice neighbors / Kia Abdullah.
Description: New York: G.P. Putnam's Sons, 2023.
Identifiers: LCCN 2023028469 (print) | LCCN 2023028470 (ebook) |
ISBN 9780593713815 (Trade paperback) | ISBN 9780593713822 (Ebook)
Subjects: LCSH: Bangladeshis—Fiction. | Neighbors—Fiction. |
Suburban life—Fiction. | Racism—Fiction. |
LCGFT: Social problem fiction. | Novels.
Classification: LCC PR6101.B37 P47 2023 (print) |
LCC PR6101.B37 (ebook) | DDC 823/.92—dc23/eng/20230626
LC record available at https://lccn.loc.gov/2023028469
LC ebook record available at https://lccn.loc.gov/2023028470

Printed in the United States of America
1st Printing

Book design by Lorie Pagnozzi

For my big sis, Shopna,
without whom I would not be a writer

PERFECTLY
NICE
NEIGHBORS

PART I

Salma had always sworn that she would never end up in a place like this. "It's a bit like purgatory," she had joked when they first came to see the house in a harried half hour before work one morning. The estate agent, a hawkish woman with a watchful gaze, had herded them from room to room and Salma had murmured politely, even commenting on this or that "lovely feature" as she and Bilal locked eyes, amusement passing between them.

They had agreed to view it only because there was a gap between their other bookings and the agent had pushed this property. It was in a neat cul-de-sac on the eastern reaches of the Central Line. It was built seven years ago, said the agent, and still had the bright, bland feel of a new development. There was a dizzying amount of brickwork and even its name, the mononymous "Blenheim," felt like an artless attempt at class, like petrol stop perfume or "Guccci" shades. Upstairs, out of the agent's earshot, they had giggled about the perfect lawn.

"Do you think neighborhood watch will knock down your door if it grows above two inches?" said Bilal.

Salma fought a smile. "We're being snobby," she said but with laughter in her voice.

The agent walked in and the two of them sprang apart like children caught red-handed. She nodded at the window, her silver-brown bob swaying with the motion. "It's lovely, isn't it?"

"Lovely," Salma agreed.

That was six months ago, and after close to forty viewings, they had both grown weary. Nothing else matched Blenheim for price, condition, space, and safety and so they talked each other into it. *Four double bedrooms*, said Bilal. *And it's still on the Central Line*, said Salma. *The neat streets and perfectly nice neighbors.* If they could set aside their vanity, they could be happy at Blenheim and so they had put in an offer—and here they were, their first week in their new home.

They hadn't yet met their neighbors but, yesterday, a square of white card appeared on their doormat inviting them to a May Day barbecue. *No need to RSVP. Just turn up!* it said in jaunty letters. Salma had read it uneasily. She wasn't an introvert by any means but did find parties tiring. She far preferred to meet new people on a one-to-one basis. Still, they were new here and had to make an effort. Salma had prepared some potato salad and told her son, Zain, that he had no choice but to join them. They approached 13 Blenheim like a trio of soldiers heading into battle. Outside, Salma paused and assessed her husband and son. As she smoothed the crooked leaf of Bilal's collar, he caught her hand and kissed it.

"Here goes," she said. She rang the bell but no one answered. Music bled from the garden and Salma counted to twenty before she rang again. Zain ventured to the side of the house and pointed at the open side gate. They walked through in single file and hovered at the edge of the gathering. There were about thirty people of varying ages, laughing and milling around. Two men were tending the barbecue, both of them wearing white polo shirts paired with khaki shorts. At first, Salma thought that they were hired staff but realized they were guests. Cheers went up around them as they dished up the first tranche of meat, filling the air with a pleasantly smoky smell.

A woman spotted them and her eyes lit up. "You must be the new arrivals!" she called. She detached herself from the group and pulled Salma into a matronly hug. "I'm Linda Turner, the hostess."

"Oh, hello! I'm Salma. Thank you so much for inviting us."

"Bilal," her husband introduced himself. He saw the crease of Linda's brow and promptly added, "Call me Bil."

She brightened. "Bill! How wonderful to meet our new neighbors." She turned to Zain. "And this must be your son. My, what a handsome boy!"

Zain smiled politely. "How do you do?"

She whooped with delight. "And such manners too!" She saw the glass bowl in his hands. "You didn't have to bring anything! But thank you." She took the bowl and ushered them into the party. "What can I get you to drink? We have wine, beer, cider." She paused. "Or we have fresh lemonade and fruit juice."

Bil smiled. "A lemonade would be lovely—thank you."

"Make that three," said Salma.

She beamed. "Wonderful!" She smoothly introduced them to their next-door neighbor. "This is Tom Hutton. He can give you the lowdown on everyone here."

Tom greeted them warmly. He was in his mid-forties, muscular under a navy polo shirt, and with thick dark hair splayed beneath an orange cap. As he spoke, a young bull terrier bounded up to him. "Her name is Lola," he said, bending down to pet her. He looked up at Salma. "She was a showgirl," he deadpanned.

Salma broke into laughter. Tom nodded in approval as if she had passed a test. Lola snuffed at Salma's feet.

"You don't mind, do you?" said Tom.

"No, not at all. We have a dog too, a Lab called Molly."

"Oh, that's great. This is such a dog-friendly neighborhood. You're going to love it."

Linda cut in to hand out drinks. Bil volunteered to help with the barbecue and she happily whisked him away. Zain took his drink to a corner of the garden and busied himself on his phone.

"So what do you do?" asked Tom.

"I'm a teacher," said Salma. "Geography at a secondary school," she added, preempting his follow-up question. "What about you?"

"I work in advertising. At Sartre & Sartre."

"Oh wow. That must be glamorous."

"It can be," he said with a grin, enjoying the compliment. "And what about Bil?"

Salma felt herself tense. "He's a restaurateur," she said, despite the fact that his restaurant, Jakoni's, had shut down earlier that year.

"Restaurateur?" Tom puckered his lips in a show of approval. "You must be doing all right then, no?"

Salma looked bemused. "I mean, we're doing okay."

"Sorry if that's rude. I was just wondering how come you got this place then?" He nodded in the direction of their house.

Salma relaxed, relieved to find that he too was skeptical of Blenheim. She smiled playfully. "It's not so bad, is it? Where else would I find such a pristine collection of lawns?"

Tom frowned. "It's just that I would've thought you were above the threshold."

"Threshold?" Salma was confused.

"For social housing," he said.

It dawned on Salma what Tom had really meant: not *you're wealthy, so why would you choose to live here* but *you're wealthy, so why did you get social housing?* She shifted awkwardly. "We actually bought it privately."

"Oh!" Tom looked mortified. "I'm so sorry. I didn't mean to assume. In fact, I *wasn't* assuming. I was certain that the house next to us was part of the social housing." He cringed visibly. "I must have been mistaken."

Salma waved in a show of nonchalance. "Ah, if only! It might have saved us a pretty penny." Her voice labored with the effort to put him at ease. She groped for another topic.

"So where do you teach?" asked Tom.

"Ilford Academy in Seven Kings."

"I see. Do you enjoy it?"

Salma could feel the conversation slipping away but was keen to keep the momentum going. If they parted now, it would surely make things more awkward the next time they met. "Yes," she replied. "It's especially nice in August." She laughed at her joke but it came out forced and hollow. She didn't understand why she was being this way. She was normally poised and confident, well versed in small talk. She reached for a question but was interrupted by a woman who slid up next to Tom. Salma stared for a second. She was tall and willowy with white-blonde hair, delicate cheekbones, and a tiny gap between her front teeth that seemed to only add to her charm. She held out an elegant hand.

"Willa," she said. "Like the writer."

Salma shook it and pretended to know which writer she meant.

"Although pictures are more my trade," said Willa.

"Oh. Are you a model?"

Willa made a snap of laughter. "You're sweet but no. I paint sometimes. Mainly, I run our home."

"Oh, sorry. You look like you could be," said Salma. "You must get that all the time."

Willa rolled her eyes. "Thank you, but it's fucking embarrassing. I'm like an Aryan wet dream."

Salma nearly spat out her lemonade. She couldn't tell if Willa was simply outspoken or if she actually rather enjoyed Salma's display of shock. She looked across at Tom, who didn't react, only slid an arm around Willa's waist. Salma cleared her throat. "How did you two meet?" she asked, steering them into safer territory.

"I know what you're thinking," said Tom. "How did a brute like me end up with a girl like her?"

"Tom used to be a firefighter," Willa cut in. "Believe it or not, he ran into a burning building and saved me. I was twenty-one. He was twenty-seven and that was that."

Salma looked from one to the other. "That can't be true!"

Willa gazed at Tom adoringly. "One hundred percent."

"Oh my god. That's incredible."

Willa burst out laughing. "I'm just fucking with you!"

Salma grew still. Then she smiled and pretended to be in on the joke.

"Of course that's not what happened," said Willa, "but the real story is almost as cute."

Salma waited but Willa was speaking to Tom now.

"Do you remember how you chased me for months? Sending me flowers and chocolates. God, wasn't there even that H. Samuel bracelet?"

Tom looked at Salma sheepishly. "Willa's family are rich," he explained. "So here I am sending her a box of Milk Tray and a five-quid bunch of flowers while she's used to"—he looked over at her—"what's that poncey brand you like?"

"Charbonnel et Walker," she said smoothly. "He wasn't a fire-fighter but"—she winked at Salma—"he did let me ride his pole."

Salma chuckled politely. She, like most people, did a subconscious thing when she met someone new. She assessed whether they were part of her "tribe." Tom and Willa with their strange, abrasive humor were far too different from her. Normally, Salma wouldn't mind and would simply get on with her day, but this was a new neighborhood and she had to make an effort. "You mentioned that you run the home," she said to Willa. "Do you have kids?"

"Yes. A son, Jamie. He's sixteen." She must have caught Salma's surprise because she added, "I had him young, at twenty-two."

Salma calculated that Willa was thirty-eight, five years younger than she was. "That works out well for me," she said. "My son, Zain, is eighteen and I'm sure he'd love to meet Jamie."

"That would be lovely," said Willa. "Jamie needs to make a few friends."

They talked until a natural lull allowed them to part ways. Salma circulated and scanned the crowd for Bil. She saw that he was cornered by Linda and headed over to join them.

"What is that delicious nutty flavor in the potato salad?" Linda was asking.

"Fried pine nuts," said Salma.

"Ah, well, thank you for indulging us. For future reference,

I can handle my spice, so if you ever want to bring something with a bit more zing, you'd be more than welcome to."

Salma smiled. "Of course. I'll bear that in mind."

Linda clapped her hands twice, like an excited child. "I look forward to it." She glanced over Salma's shoulder. "Well, I should mingle. Please help yourself to the food and drink. There's so much to get through." She beamed and then left in a cloud of activity.

Bil looked at Salma. "How long do you reckon before we can leave?"

"Stop it," she chided. "We have to make an effort." She fixed on a fresh smile and led him back into the fray.

SALMA FELT HERSELF UNCOIL, THE tension leaving her muscles as soon as they left the barbecue. Blenheim looked uncanny without any streetlamps. The council insisted that lights would spoil the character of the local area, leaving it eerily dark. Bil caught her hand in his and they headed home in silence, needing total privacy before they could fully relax. Zain walked on ahead and left their front door open for them. Salma crossed the blue-black lawn, which was still a consistent one-inch tall. Their neighbor Tom had mowed it while the house was being sold. Salma kicked a few pebbles back onto the path and retrieved from the ground a palm-size banner that Zain had stuck in a plant pot. She dug it back in place and followed Bil inside. She closed the door and sagged against it.

Bil laughed. "You okay?"

"Do you think I should take Linda some *naga* next time?" she asked archly.

"Well, she *did* say she can handle her spice."

Salma covered her face and groaned.

"It's okay," said Bil more seriously. "It was just a lot in one go."

She nodded vigorously but didn't uncover her face.

Bil pulled at her wrist playfully. "Come on, it wasn't that bad."

She looked at him. "Bil, did you hear what they call people who haven't lived here from the beginning? 'Offcomers.' Not newcomers. Offcomers. It sounds like a bloody horror movie."

A smile tugged at his lips. "They were being tongue in cheek."

"And that guy—Tom." She gestured next door. "God, it was *so* awkward." She explained how Tom had assumed that they were in social housing.

Bil winced with sympathy. "Stuff like that's going to happen," he said. "But they'll get to know us soon enough."

"Oh!" Salma cut in. "And you should have heard his wife!" She relayed some of Willa's choice remarks.

Bil laughed. "She was probably just trying to impress you. People can be like that at parties."

Salma raised a brow but didn't disagree. She was more cynical than Bil and though they shared a sense of humor—dry and sarcastic—his natural temperament was optimistic and she didn't want to spoil their evening. Salma had tried hard to stay upbeat ever since Jakoni's shut down in January following a horrendous year for the industry. It was her job to keep Bil's spirits high, just as he always did with hers.

"You're right," she said as she fit herself against his chest. "They'll get to know us soon."

He rubbed the small of her back. "You okay?"

She nodded.

"You don't think we've made a mistake?"

There was the tiniest pause before she answered, "No, I don't. I think we can be happy here."

"I think so too," said Bil.

She tipped back her head and kissed him. "Right. I'm going to take a shower." She detached herself and headed upstairs. She paused briefly on the landing to listen to the click of Zain's keyboard on the top floor.

In the bathroom, she peeled off her clothes, which smelled of smoky meat, and tossed them in the laundry bin. In the shower, she realized that she could hear voices on the other side: the deep murmur of Tom's voice and the lighter pitch of Willa's. She pressed her ear to the wall but couldn't make out any words. She listened to see if their conversation had the tightness of an argument or the lightness of a joke. Were they discussing her family, just as she had discussed theirs?

Tom's words returned to her and she flushed with embarrassment. *I would've thought you were above the threshold.* Despite what she had just told Bil, she *did* worry that they had made a mistake. If they had known that they would lose the restaurant, they would almost certainly have stayed in Seven Kings, on their estate off the high street. By the time the restaurant closed, however, they had already started the process of buying their house in Blenheim and convinced themselves to take the leap. Five months later, they still hadn't sold the restaurant premises and things were getting tight. The thought brought a familiar unease and Salma had to remind herself that they barely had a choice. Not after what happened with Zain. This was the safest place that they could afford and they would make the most of it. It was true that she missed her old neighborhood—the big, messy families and rows of crowded houses, the comfort of being among other Bangladeshis—but Zain had room to breathe here: a large bedroom, his own bathroom, a balcony, and a garden too. There would be a period of adjustment of course, but they were sure to fit in before long. They had to. They had nowhere else to go.

ZAIN BLEW OUT A LUNGFUL of smoke, fanning it as he did so. If his mum found out that he smoked, well, then there'd be hell to pay. Her father had died from lung cancer and she was a full-on fundamentalist when it came to smoking. It was annoying, but Zain knew it could be a lot worse. Some of his friends were basically double agents: respectful, obedient, *seedha saadha*, with their parents, then practically feral behind the scenes. At least his mum knew what was what and allowed him certain liberties if he didn't push her limits.

He took another draw, felt it burn in his chest, and exhaled slowly. His thoughts went to the barbecue and the repetition of that dreaded question: *What do you do?*

I'm a student, he had told them, hating himself for the lie. In truth, he'd been kicked out of school last year, which meant he couldn't sit his A levels, couldn't go to university, couldn't get a decent job, and was living with his parents like a deadbeat, spending his Friday nights on Twitch, live streaming his coding. That's one thing he could do, but most tech jobs asked for degrees. The startups that claimed to overlook formal education relied on other cues—accents and expensive accessories—that Zain lacked too. Trying too hard felt worse than not trying at all and so he gave up looking.

He leaned over the balcony wall and took another drag of his cigarette. A knock on his door made him startle and he hurriedly stubbed it out.

"Hey, kid." His dad poked his head in the bedroom. "I wanted to . . ." He trailed off as he caught a residual whiff of smoke. He gave Zain a stern look. "If your mum finds out, she'll kill you first and kill me second."

"She won't find out."

"Kid, she finds out *everything*." He stepped inside but hovered by the threshold. "How are you getting on?"

Zain leaned against the balcony. "Okay." There was a time when he would laugh at his dad's late-night pep talks, filled with ironic vim. *There's nothing that can't be solved with a list*, he'd say, taking a sheet of paper from the printer to note down practical steps. Now these talks felt medicinal: delivered at regular intervals, designed to prevent or cure.

"What did you make of our new neighbors?"

"They're all right if a bit 'Borg Collective,'" said Zain.

His dad fixed him with a blank stare. "Resistance is futile," he said in a robotic monotone.

Zain smiled, briefly lifted, remembering their old camaraderie. He reached for another quip but his dad was serious again.

"I know it's been a weird time but your mum and I are feeling good about this move."

Zain raised a brow in doubt.

Usually, his dad would break ranks and admit this wasn't true. Instead, he fixed Zain with a sincere look. "Trust me," he said.

Zain nodded but looked away.

"You'll find your way, kid." He gripped the doorknob: a surefire sign he was almost done.

"Yeah, I know," Zain lied.

"Okay." He nodded firmly as if the matter was settled. "I'll see you in the morning."

"Yep," said Zain. He waited until he was gone, then reached for another cigarette. He was about to light it when he heard a cough next door. A boy leaned out from the next balcony, past the thick column of brick separating their two houses.

"Shit. Sorry, mate," said Zain, clicking off the lighter.

"Oh, I wasn't dropping a hint," said the boy. He was close to Zain's age, white, and looked like he belonged in a boy band: thick brown hair styled stiff with gel, a touch of K-pop in his delicate chin.

"Nah, it's all right," said Zain. "I'm done anyway."

"It's nice having the top room, huh?" said the boy.

Zain noticed a quirk in his speech: the s dropped from "it's." *It nice having the top room, huh?* "Yeah, it is," he replied.

The boy stretched across the column—so far that Zain worried he might fall. "I'm Jamie."

"Zain." He shook Jamie's hand and was surprised by his firm grip. There was nothing he hated more than a limp handshake.

"So . . ." Jamie lifted his chin at the garden. "What brought you to paradise?"

"The search for a better life," said Zain, matching Jamie's tone.

"Ha! Prepare to be disappointed."

Zain smiled. "How long have you lived here?"

"Um, we moved here when I was nine, so seven years now."

"What's it like?"

"It's all right."

Zain noticed that he dropped his s again—*it all right*—and wondered if he had a speech impediment. He felt a drop of affection and wondered if this was what it felt like to have a younger sibling. Relatives often joked that Zain was an old soul. They didn't understand that as an only child you ate most of your meals with adults. You listened to adult conversation, adult concerns, and it was natural to inherit them. He remembered using the word "inquisition" soon after starting secondary school and being teased no end. After that, he deliberately dumbed down his vocabulary. Sometimes he stammered not because he couldn't find a word but because he was trying to swap it for a shorter one. That was the thing about Selborne Estate. It gave you a sense of community, but it also held you back. Zain had seen this play out with his friend Amin. He had secured a good job straight after secondary school: IT support for a medical research center in the city. Every day, his old school friends would see him leave in the frayed brown suit he'd inherited, a satchel slung over his shoulder, and tease him for being a *boroh saab*. A big man. *He's too important for us now*, they'd say. *Rah, look how he's ignoring us.*

One day, Amin turned up in a gray hoodie and jeans.

"Ey yo, what's going on, man?" asked Zain.

"You won't believe it, mate. They fired me."

"Wait, what?"

"They said I stole from the petty cash."

Zain narrowed his gaze on him. "And did you?"

"Nah, course I didn't."

"Then they can't do that!" Zain got so riled up but mid-rant he registered Amin's nonchalance. He was hit with a cold suspicion that Amin had done it on purpose; had got himself fired because he was tired of being othered, not by his colleagues at his fancy office but by his friends right here at home. Selborne Estate was a safety net but one with a ceiling you couldn't escape.

It's partly why when Zain's parents suggested the move, beneath his initial resistance, he felt a seed of relief. He hadn't known then that they'd end up in this wasteland of a street.

"Seriously though, I can't wait to leave," Jamie cut in.

"Where would you go? Uni?"

Jamie shrugged. "Start my own company maybe."

Zain laughed but then caught his look of hurt. "Sorry, I just—it's not that easy, is it?"

Jamie ducked a little, embarrassed. "No, you're right. It's stupid."

"Nah, man," Zain backtracked guiltily. "It's not stupid. It's better than working for someone else."

"I've applied for some funding from Google's startup fund."

This piqued Zain's interest. "Oh yeah? So you have an idea?"

"Kind of." Jamie hesitated. "Well, yeah."

Zain raised his brows to show the younger boy that he was impressed. "What is it?"

Jamie withdrew, suddenly shy. "Well . . . Hang on." He retreated into his room and returned a few seconds later. He handed Zain a stack of designs with mock-ups of an iPhone screen. "It's an app," he said, "to help deaf people communicate with hearing people."

Zain looked through the designs. "How does it work?"

Jamie explained the app's purpose—a real-time sign-to-speech translator—and talked him through the designs.

"How come you're interested in this?" Zain asked.

Jamie set down the stack on the wall. "Well, I don't know if you can tell, but I'm partially deaf. I was born three months premature but they didn't realize there was anything different until I was about four. By then, certain sounds had escaped me. I've seen a speech therapist, but even now, I sometimes miss letters. It's kind of like talking in a different accent, you know? You always have to be concentrating, so eventually I decided, so what? What's normal anyway?"

"Good on you, man," said Zain.

Jamie flushed. "Thanks. I just need to find someone who can build the damn thing now."

Zain fixed his gaze on him. "You know I code, right?"

Jamie did a double take. "Really? Would you be interested?"

Zain considered this. "I mean, *maybe*." He studied the designs again and quizzed Jamie in more depth. "Okay," he said finally. "Why the hell not?"

"Seriously?"

"Yeah, seriously."

Jamie beamed. "Fuck, man. That would be fantastic." He reached out his hand again.

Zain shook it and something warm pitched inside him: a sense of purpose and comradeship.

There was a call from inside Jamie's house. "Shit, that's Mum. I better go. Here, take my number."

Zain keyed it into his phone and listened to Jamie scurrying inside. He looked out over the inky grass and felt a new thrill of hope. Maybe he *would* be all right here. Maybe, retrospectively, he hadn't lied to his dad after all.

SALMA TURNED SIDEWAYS IN THE sunlit mirror. She groaned, noting the paunch around her midriff.

"No one tells you that after forty, you basically can't eat bread," she said.

Bil leaned in and nuzzled her neck. "You don't look a day over twenty-five."

"Get orf," she said, mimicking the boys from the eighties Accrington Stanley milk advert.

"Oh my god, are you trying to do a Scouse accent?"

She frowned. "Were they Scouse? I thought they were Geordie."

"God, you Londoners." He threw up his hands in surrender. "You're all hopeless."

She laughed, warmed by the playful push and pull of their marriage.

Bil threw on a T-shirt. "Will you have time for breakfast?" he asked.

"Sorry. Not today." She felt a thread of guilt as she kissed him good-bye. When his restaurant shut down, Bil went straight back into work, taking a job beneath his skill level at a curry house in Newbury Park. He was on grueling split shifts, but still woke up every morning to make her breakfast. It was through sheer luck that she had married into kindness. It had never appeared on her wish list for a husband. Hardworking, yes. Ambitious, confident, and successful—but kindness felt somehow twee, old-fashioned like grandfather clocks and shoe polish. It didn't quite say "sexy." The first time she saw Bil, he was fully in work mode: charming but in the studied, patient manner of someone with pressing things to do. A diner at the next table had insisted on meeting the chef and Salma had been surprised by his age: late twenties at the oldest. As the diner droned on, intent on impressing his date, Bil caught Salma's eye with just enough of an eyebrow raise to signal his amusement. Salma had laughed out loud and watched Bil struggle to keep a straight face. For months afterward, she had repeatedly visited that same restaurant until Bil finally got the hint and asked her out. She had a picture of what he would be—a young, brash culinary prodigy—but the man she got to know was fun, playful, and, most of all, kind. Nearly two decades on, he was still cooking her breakfast in the mornings.

The thought made her smile even as she grabbed an apple from the kitchen and hurried out the door.

Outside, she noticed that Zain's banner was on the ground again. She picked it up and traced the flimsy fabric. **BLACK LIVES MATTER**, it said, printed black on pink. She had demurred when Zain first displayed it.

"I think we should meet the neighbors first before we put up something like that," she'd said.

Zain had looked at her scornfully. "Because *that* will inform whether Black lives matter?" he'd asked.

She'd sighed. "Just put it somewhere not too in-your-face." Now she stuck it back in the plant pot. As she headed to the bus stop, she heard a beep to her left. Her neighbor Tom was in his car and she raised a hand to wave. He rolled down his window and beckoned her closer.

"Morning, Salma."

"Hi, Tom. How are you?"

"Good, good." He took off his sunglasses. "Listen, can I ask you a favor?"

"Of course."

He grimaced as if this pained him. "Can you guys try to park in front of your house?"

Salma looked at her car, which overshot her house by a foot. "Oh, sorry! I didn't realize there was designated parking."

"No, no. There isn't. It's just we have two cars, so if you over-shoot, we can't get both of ours in."

"Oh, right." Salma frowned. "Well, sometimes people park outside ours, so we roll forward a bit so our car will fit."

"Ah. Maybe you could find out who's doing it and have a word?"

"Um, I mean, sometimes it's different cars."

"Okay, well . . ." He tapped the steering wheel as if trying to find a solution. "If you can't figure out who it is, then that's fine obviously, but it *is* a bit of a pain for us to park around the corner."

"Of course," said Salma evenly. "I'm sure it is. We'll try our best."

"Thank you," he said apologetically.

Salma readied to go, but Tom stopped her.

"Sorry. While I'm being annoying, I should say that the fence between our gardens has a loose board. We fixed it last time, and then again when the house was empty, so maybe you guys could have a look at it?"

Salma smiled. "Of course."

"Great." He beamed. "Thank you for understanding. Have a good morning."

"You too," she said, her cheeks burning hot. Surely, it wasn't reasonable to claim a section of the road just because it passed your home? She wished she hadn't agreed so easily. Or that she'd at least made a pointed joke to show him this wasn't okay. She found herself preoccupied all the way to work. Next time, she would speak her mind.

She approached her school, a flat gray building in a godless corner of Ilford. She passed through the security gates and headed up to her classroom. There, she felt at ease. Unlike some teachers she knew, Salma loved her job. She enjoyed the constant hum and activity, and thrived on being busy. It didn't even bother her when people made snarky comments about *all that time off.* Very few people could do what she did effectively and that fact made her proud. She settled into the room, a small rectangular space dripping with maps and trinkets. Salma took comfort in crowded places. Perhaps that's why she struggled with Blenheim: all clean lines and large, wide spaces. She stowed her bag and prepared for her tutor group, but a knock on the door interrupted her.

"Miss, can you help me?" It was Haroon, a shy, rake-thin boy in her class. He hovered at the threshold.

"Yes."

He came in and sat by her desk. "Miss, I've been trying to fill this in, but I can't work it out." He held out an A4 form.

She glanced over the first page and saw that it was a housing benefit application. "Can it wait until clinic tomorrow?" she asked.

"If I don't send it today, there'll be a gap in our payments."

Salma nodded. "Right, okay, well, the class is coming in, but can you drop by here at break? We can go through it then."

"Can we finish it in twenty minutes though?" he fretted.

"Should do. If not, I'll call them and ask for an extension."

This relaxed him a little. "Thanks, miss." He headed to his desk at the back of the classroom.

The "clinic" Salma referred to was her labor of love. She had pitched it as "a Citizens Advice Bureau for pupils," but met resistance from the head.

"It plays into stereotypes," George had said, "that people of color can't help themselves."

"But what if they *can't*?" Salma had asked, frustrated.

"Then it's not our place to help them."

Salma couldn't bite her tongue. "This is where your leftie sensibilities actually interfere, George," she'd told her.

After a protracted battle, George had acquiesced. "Fine. But if the press get wind of this, they'll make a meal of it."

"It's volunteer-run!"

"On school premises."

"Are you in or out?"

"Fine," she'd relented. "I'm in."

And of course there *was* a need for it because despite what George had said, there were plenty of pupils who needed help. Children like Haroon, with parents who couldn't speak English, had to navigate labyrinthine systems like HMRC, the NHS, and DWP. Last week, a pupil came by the clinic and asked her to explain a bowel cancer home test kit so that he could translate it for his mother. Salma watched the young boy redden as she explained it step by step. Eventually, she asked if he would prefer to have one of the Urdu-speaking female teachers call his mum and explain. The boy had agreed with great relief.

Haroon took his seat and the rest of the pupils filtered in. They were a lively group, but after four years in Salma's class, easy to control. She had enjoyed watching them mature: Patrick, who had started off a nightmare but was now a fine young man; Ritesh, who was far too serious but had bloomed into a comedian. Some kids, like Haroon, stayed the same and others went the opposite way. Tara, a studious, gawky kid, had discovered boys and makeup, and let her grades plummet.

Salma hoped that she had the balance right. When she first became a teacher, to her, "making a difference" meant creating doctors and lawyers, fulfilling parents' dreams and funneling pupils to top-tier universities. She slowly accepted that this wasn't possible—not with the budget and restrictions they had. Then she realized that "making a difference" didn't have to be so grand. It could be as simple as helping Haroon with paperwork so that he could rest easy today, or telling Faisal that he needn't explain to his mum an embarrassing medical test. It was taking the web of a million worries that made up adolescence and unpicking a little corner of it.

The bell rang to signal the start of teaching hours. "All right, settle down, please," she called. She opened the class register and started a new school day.

WILLA BEEPED THE CAR HORN once, then again, this time more prolonged to make sure that Jamie heard. He came hurtling out the door and hurried into the car.

"I haven't got all day, mate," she said.

"Oh, really? Women's bake sale pressing, is it?"

She tapped his arm in a light rebuke. "Hey, remember what I told you?" she asked.

"I won't tell Dad," he promised.

"Good." She gestured toward their new neighbors' house. "You should have come yesterday. You could have met their son, Zain."

"What were they like?"

Willa scrunched her nose. "Hard to say. They kind of seemed to be putting on an act."

"Yeah, but everyone does that at first."

"*I* don't," said Willa.

Jamie made a face.

"Do I?"

"No, but you go the opposite way."

"How so?"

He shrugged. "I don't know, Mum." He reached for his phone, but she stopped him.

"How so?" she pressed.

"You're overly honest. It's like you *enjoy* making people uncomfortable."

Willa felt embarrassed by the implication. If her sixteen-year-old son could see through her, could others do the same? She resisted the urge to grill him further. God forbid she become *that* sort of mother.

She maneuvered out of the cul-de-sac and drove three miles to South Woodford. She parked outside what looked like a large house. She led Jamie inside and through to the waiting room, all hushed tones and plush upholstery.

Jamie's audiologist, Tania, greeted them and led them to an oblong room. At the end stood an audiometric booth—a small enclosure almost like a photo booth—which was used to test his hearing. Willa had noticed lately that more and more sounds were evading him. His condition wasn't degenerative, but she worried that the amount of time he spent indoors was making him less fluent.

Tania took him through his standard raft of tests, usually done once a year. This session was additional. Jamie sat inside the booth and Tania ran through the usual spiel: *If you feel anxious, then just say and we'll let you out.* Jamie was asked to press a button every time he heard a sound. In another test, he was asked to repeat what he heard in his ear. Willa hated this test. It was always the one that made him lose heart.

Tania would tell him, "Even if it's a fraction of a word, try to say it. Even if it's an approximation, say it. Just say whatever you think you heard," and Jamie would always start by trying— *oof, lek, sen*—but then dwindle into silence, embarrassed by how hard he found it. Willa tried to catch his gaze, but he studiously ignored her.

Eventually, Tania released him from the booth. "Are you keeping up with your verbal exercises?"

He gave her a guilty look. "When I can."

"Jamie." She angled her head in disapproval. "It's really

important that you keep up with this. I promise you'll see an improvement."

Willa stepped forward hesitantly. "Tania, could we try the Opn hearing aids again? I know we said we'd leave them, but I want to give them another try."

Jamie frowned. "Why?" he asked her.

"Because they help you."

"But I don't need them." Last time, he had said the same, but she'd seen the way his eyes had lit up when he put them in. He was only saying no because he knew they couldn't afford them.

"Just try them, Jamie."

Tania rolled over to her desk and took out a pair of the premium aids. She helped Jamie try them and encouraged him to take a walk around the building. As he stepped out, Willa's voice dropped low.

"We'll take them, Tania, but can I change our billing address?"

"Of course."

Willa read out the new details and hurried to explain why the name and address were different from hers. "They're my dad's details," she said. "Do you need to speak to him?"

Tania waved away the question. "I'm sure you're not out there stealing credit card details," she said with a laugh.

Jamie re-appeared in the doorway.

"They're yours," said Willa.

He looked from her to Tania. "How?"

"Grandad," she answered. "But don't tell your dad, okay?"

Jamie exhaled, clearly ill at ease. For a second, it seemed he would refuse but then he nodded hesitantly. "Okay," he agreed. They settled up with Tania and returned to Willa's car. Jamie braced himself against the dashboard.

"Are you okay?" asked Willa.

He nodded. "It's . . . weird. I can hear you breathing."

Willa grew still, quieted by emotion. She turned her gaze to the road so that Jamie wouldn't notice. She felt angry with herself for heeding Tom for so many years. He was a proud man and refused to take money from Willa's family, so Jamie had suffered substandard care. After seeing his reaction to the Opn aids, she'd secretly asked her father for help.

"I'm proud of you," she said.

He shifted awkwardly. "Whatevs."

"No, hey, I *am*."

"Thanks," he said, looking sheepish. She and Jamie had always been more like friends and these bouts of earnestness often embarrassed him.

She reached out and ruffled his hair. "Come on, let's go." She drove him to school and then headed home alone.

There, she flopped on the sofa, a seaweed-colored Chesterfield gifted by her mother. It wasn't *leisure* that Willa had a problem with—working did not appeal to her—but that *this* wasn't leisure at all. She had imagined floating from room to room in a Central London townhouse, working on her art perhaps—but then she'd met Tom.

At first, she was charmed by his insistence that he pay their way. She was thrilled by his old-fashioned gallantry, but equally, she assumed he would change his mind after they were married. They would need a nice house, good furniture, a quality education for Jamie, but Tom refused to take her family's money. He clashed with Willa's father and did not want to owe him a thing. Initially, Willa didn't care. When you'd never worried about money, you assumed you never *would*. In fact, her new low status felt desirable: a contrarian "fuck you."

Money issues, she would say with a tinkle of a laugh as if it were a rare piece of furniture, but then she realized that most people lived on forty thousand pounds a year, and really, that was nothing at all. When her friends realized that her money issues weren't of the *crumbling estate, old money* variety, some began to distance themselves as if poverty might be catching. Tom remained adamant that he wouldn't take her father's money and Willa had relented, but damn him for letting it affect their son.

She sat cross-legged on the sofa and rubbed her belly with a palm. It would be different this time, she decided. This child would get everything that Jamie had lacked; everything that she, at twenty-two, hadn't been equipped to give.

For years, she and Tom had tried for a second child. Eventually, they accepted that it wasn't in the cards, so when she realized she might be pregnant, she wanted to be certain before telling Tom. Things would be better this time. Willa would be the mother she had failed to be at twenty-two.

SALMA LOVED THIS TIME OF day when the students had left the building and the heat of recent bodies cooled, the hum in the air now quiet. When Zain was younger, she would rush from her school to his, pedaling furiously on the relentless circuit that made up working parenthood. Now she basked in this time: the lull between her professional and personal lives.

If pushed, she might even admit that this was her favorite room in the world. Her antique compass and the Mercator map on the far wall were more powerful than art to her. She taught geography, but her subject was irrevocably twined with history: the straight lines of Africa, Britain's place in the center, the international date line, Greenwich Mean Time. Was there any other image that spoke of so much?

When Salma was eleven, she made a list of four places she wanted to visit: Easter Island off the west coast of South America, Tristan da Cunha off the west coast of Africa, Baffin Island in Canada, and continental Antarctica. These, to her, were the four corners of the earth and it saddened her now to realize that she hadn't got anywhere near them. Maybe next year if their finances were in better shape and Zain had sorted himself out, she and Bil could make some plans. *If.* A tiny word that puts entire lives on hold.

She sighed, wistful, and packed up for the day. On her way home, she popped into her local Tesco, adding up what she needed to make it to the weekend. In the end, she bought more than she intended and, on leaving the supermarket, felt her left knee grind—an old cycling injury. Annoyed, she ordered an Uber. She hated to waste the money but knew that she shouldn't strain it. The car arrived within minutes and she bundled inside with her shopping. It was a short drive along Horns Road and they soon turned onto Blenheim. The driver parked across from Salma's house and she got out and thanked him. As she dragged the first bag toward her, a tin of beans spilled out and rolled beyond her reach.

"Sorry!" she called to the driver. "Can you give me a minute?"

"Of course, love." He cut the engine. "Take your time."

Salma bent down to retrieve the tin. Across the street, a flicker of movement caught her eye. Tom Hutton was in his front garden, throwing a yellow tennis ball from one hand to the other. Casually, he approached the fence that divided his garden from hers. He paused there and glanced up and down the street, his gaze skimming right past the Uber. He whistled nonchalantly, then raised the ball and threw it into her garden. It knocked the banner from her plant pot and went skittering across the lawn. The whole thing was so quick that Salma nearly missed it. She blinked, not quite able to decode what she'd seen. Tom glanced up and down the street again. He tugged the hem of his blazer, then turned and disappeared into his house.

"You all right, love?" called the driver. "Need some help?"

"No," said Salma quickly. She snatched up the tin and stuffed it in her bag. "No, thank you." She retrieved her second bag, stalling until Tom's door was closed. Finally, she stepped back and the car moved off. There, alone in the open street, she felt acutely exposed.

Almost immediately, she started to doubt what she'd seen. She had been crouched in an awkward position and flustered by the delay. Could she have misread his actions? But no. There had been something very deliberate in the way he glanced around and carefully taken aim. A singe of fear arrived with a question. *Where the hell have we moved?*

CHAPTER 2

S alma sat on the sofa, her knees drawn neatly together. She felt rattled and couldn't put her thoughts in order. She had briefly considered lobbing the ball back into Tom's garden. Instead, she'd brought it inside along with the crumpled banner. She glared at the items now as if *they* had committed the crime. She heard the front door open and Bil walked in with their dog, Molly, who bounded over to Salma. She petted her absentmindedly.

"Hi, honey." Bil lined his shoes in the corridor, ready for his second shift at the curry house. "Good day?"

"Something weird just happened."

Bil set down Molly's collar. "What?"

"I don't know exactly." Salma explained that she'd taken an Uber on her way home from Tesco. "I looked across and saw Tom next door looking shifty in the front garden. He walked to our fence, then knocked down that banner." She gestured at the pink fabric.

Bil frowned at it. "Why would you think that?"

"I saw him."

"You saw him pull up the banner?"

"Yes. Well, no. He threw the ball at it and knocked it out."

The tension left his shoulders. "Well, hon, obviously it was an accident."

Salma recalled Tom's vigilance and the precision of his aim. "It wasn't an accident. He looked up and down the street to make sure no one was watching, then he literally took aim and threw it."

Bil looked bemused. "Come on, Salma. It was clearly an accident."

"Then why didn't he walk round and collect his ball or set the banner right? I've found it on the ground twice before, so it must have been him."

Bil studied her. "Are you being serious?"

"Yes!"

"Are you sure it wasn't their son, Jamie? He's a kid. He was probably just playing around."

"I know the difference between a kid and a grown man."

Bil picked up the tennis ball. "I don't think we should jump to conclusions."

"I think we should say something."

Bil looked at her sideways. "Come on, hon, let's just think for a sec."

"That's how you deal with bullies, Bil. You stand up to them."

"Is that what you teach at school?" he teased.

"Come on, you know what I mean." She looked at him expectantly. "It wasn't an accident, Bil."

"Okay." He set the ball down carefully. "Let's say it was intentional. Maybe it was just a lark. You know how men are."

"A lark?"

"Men see things and they want to take aim at them. Look at urinals. They paint a dot on them to make us aim for it."

Salma stared at him. "Why are we talking about urinals?"

"I'm just saying, maybe it wasn't malicious."

"Then what was it?"

"I don't know, but . . ." He shrugged a shoulder. "Look, we're new here. Let's not rock the boat, eh?"

"Fine," Salma huffed. "I hope you're right." She picked up the banner and walked to the window. She stuck it to the glass facing outward. It was more conspicuous than before—now at the front of the house instead of the side of the garden.

Bil looked on dubiously. "Are you sure that's a good idea?"

"Why wouldn't it be?"

"Well . . ." He ran a hand through his hair. "We don't want to provoke them."

"They destroy our property and you don't want to 'provoke them'?"

"Come on, hon. They didn't 'destroy our property.' Tom seems like a decent bloke. I'm sure he wouldn't do something like that maliciously."

"That's your problem, Bil. You always give people the benefit of the doubt."

"Well, what's the alternative? Live in a constant state of war?"

"Maybe," she said petulantly. She motioned to the banner. "Either way, that's staying there."

Bil tipped his head in assent. "Okay, fine, but let's not say anything to Zain. I don't want him to create a stink."

"Fine," she agreed.

"Okay, well, I need to get ready for my shift. Will you feed Molly?"

"Yeah. Course."

Bil gave her a quick kiss, then went upstairs to change. Salma smoothed a crease in the banner, ignoring her unease. It was strange how childhood hang-ups stayed with you. When Salma was eleven years old, she got caught up in the excitement of a World Cup match—1990 she thought it was—and mocked up a St. George's Cross, which she taped to their living room window. When her dad came home from work, he ripped it down with an urgency she had never seen before.

"Don't ever do that again," he said. "We'll get a brick through our window."

Salma was frightened by his ferocity and though she didn't understand it, she obeyed straightaway. Even now as an adult, she didn't know if he thought that the danger lay in her claiming the flag as her own, or because he simply associated it with violence. It broke her heart that her father, who couldn't read English words, recognized danger in that single image.

Salma hoped that Bil was right. Sometimes we all did silly, inexplicable things like killing an ant as a child or kicking an empty bottle instead of putting it in the bin. Perhaps it *was* a momentary lapse. Perhaps Tom would be mortified if he realized she had seen him. Perhaps he *did* deserve the benefit of her doubt.

ZAIN LEANED AROUND THE BRICK and reached for the piece of paper. A neat list of names was printed in a column: *Heard.it, Synco.phy, Sign.ly.*

Zain read them skeptically, then handed back the sheet. "I'm not sure, man."

"Really? I thought they were good."

"They're difficult to communicate. We need something simpler."

Jamie was crestfallen. "Oh, man. I worked on those for ages."

"Well, why don't we brainstorm some better names?"

Jamie brightened. "That would be amazing." The two of them planned to apply to a startup fund aimed at diverse founders, but had to choose a name beforehand.

Zain stubbed out his cigarette and gestured over his shoulder. "Why don't you come over?"

Jamie jumped up on his wall, then carefully sidestepped the protruding column between the two balconies. Zain led him inside and felt a little embarrassed by the neatness of his room. His technical guides—Swift, Python, JavaScript—were stacked on his desk, their white spines all aligned. His shoes were in a neat row and even the smell—a faint lemongrass from the oil his mum liked—seemed overtly girlish. It didn't quite fit the image of a technical genius. He watched Jamie from the corner of his eye but he didn't seem to notice or care. They sat side by side at the desk and began to brainstorm names.

> InSync?
> - Like the boyband?
> Ah, maybe not.
> - Hear Hear?
> Too generic. What about ListenIn?
> - Who are we? The NSA?
> Grapevine? As in "I heard it though the"?
> - Oh, that's actually good.

As they shaped a short list, Zain looked across at Jamie. "What's it like for you? Your hearing loss?"

Jamie set down his pen. "What's it like for you *not* having hearing loss? It's just a different way of being in the world."

Zain grimaced. "Sorry. I should have asked if you mind talking about it."

Jamie shrugged. "I don't mind."

"Is it hard? Like being out and about?"

Jamie considered this. "I mean, yeah, I guess so but you have to get over it. I used to try and hide it when I was like twelve or thirteen, but I met this tutor who said it's easier if you're up-front about it. Sometimes it's not nice when waiters and people get impatient with me but if I point out my hearing aids, then usually they're nicer."

Zain leaned forward and studied Jamie's aids. "You can barely see them."

He adjusted one self-consciously. "They're new. At primary school, I used to have these humongous ones. It was so embarrassing."

"And now?"

"I mean, sometimes I'm embarrassed, but not as much. I'm okay in restaurants and cinemas and ordering stuff, but I still don't really . . ." He lifted a shoulder. "Talk to girls and stuff."

Zain laughed but with kindness. He drew back and squinted at Jamie. "Is there one in particular we're talking about?"

Jamie's gaze shifted shyly. "I mean, yeah." He blushed. "Her name's Camilla. I knew her in primary and she was always nice to me, but in secondary she's been a bit . . . . off."

"In what way?"

Jamie tensed. "Well, like if I mishear something in school, she used to be nice but now she laughs along with the rest of them."

"What do you mean?"

"You know, like if the teacher asks, 'Is this A or B?' and I answer, 'Yes' because I haven't understood her. Sometimes, I have to fill in sentences; guess at the bit I missed, hoping that I'm right. When I get it wrong, they laugh."

Zain felt angry on Jamie's behalf. "Mate, you're better than this Camilla."

Jamie puckered his lips in doubt. "Yeah, but you haven't seen her."

Zain felt a protective instinct. Jamie was missing an edge and if he wasn't careful, life would cut him open. He wanted to reach out and touch him somehow—an arm around his shoulders, a squeeze of solidarity—but their relationship did not have that fluency. Instead, he punched him lightly on the arm. "Well, let's see how Camilla likes you when Grapevine earns us millions."

Jamie pretended to pop his collar, and the awkward, self-conscious way that he did it filled Zain with affection.

"Hey, do you want to make it official? Like sign a contract and be proper business partners?"

Jamie lit up. "That would be amazing."

Zain extended his hand. "This isn't exactly Menlo Park, but maybe we can work with it."

Jamie shook it firmly. "What's Menlo Park?"

Zain laughed. "Mate, we have a *lot* of work to do." He stood. "But first: snacks. Wait here. I'll be back in a minute." He left Jamie in his room and headed downstairs to the kitchen. As he walked past the living room, he saw his mum pull away from the window. Tacked onto the lower left square was his *BLACK LIVES MATTER* banner.

Zain frowned. "What's going on?"

She smiled. "Oh, nothing." She rubbed the nape of her neck, a nervous tic he recognized.

"Oh-kay," he said suspiciously. He nodded at the banner. "So I won you over then?"

She laughed, jittery. "Yeah. You did."

"Mum, is everything all right?"

"It's fine."

"Okay, well, is it all right that Jamie's upstairs?"

"Jamie?"

"From next door?"

She stiffened. "From next door?" She glanced at the stairs. "When did he come over?"

"Just now. I met him yesterday. Is that all right?"

"I'd like to meet him."

Zain sighed. "Mum, don't be weird about this."

"I'm not being weird. I just want to know who my son is consorting with. Is that too much to ask after—"

"This isn't the estate, Mum. Isn't that why we moved here?"

"Zain, please don't talk back to me."

He sighed dramatically. "Okay, but can we have some food then, so he doesn't feel like he's being interrogated?"

"Of course. What do you want? Nachos? Chips? I have some samosas in the freezer and some of that amazing Bonbibi sauce."

Zain couldn't help but laugh then. She could be a bit of a tiger mother but when it came to food, she was a hostess through and through. "I'll do the nachos, Mum. Please just don't be weird."

He headed upstairs and fetched Jamie. "Hey, man, my mum said we can pop downstairs and eat. That cool?"

Jamie stood and smoothed his T-shirt. "Yeah, sure."

Zain led him downstairs. In the kitchen, his mum was waiting with an eerie grin. He gave her a look of warning and she relaxed a little, rolling her shoulders with the effort.

"Mum, Jamie. Jamie, Mum."

"It's nice to meet you, Mrs. . . . ."

"Khatun," she said and shook his hand. "But you can call me Salma."

"Oh. Thank you."

"You're in your final year, aren't you, Jamie? You must be busy with your GCSE exams?"

"Yes, that's right."

"Have you chosen your A level subjects yet?"

Zain prepared the nachos and listened to his mother quiz Jamie. He could tell she wasn't impressed with his choice of A levels: art, graphics, and IT. With her encouragement, Zain had chosen math, physics, and chemistry—but it all amounted to nothing.

"I believe your father leads a big team at Sartre & Sartre," she was saying. "He must be quite the disciplinarian?"

Jamie nodded. "Yeah, it can be hard."

"Is he quite conservative?"

Jamie shifted uneasily. "Um, I guess so."

Zain threw his mother a look. "We'll be in the living room, Mum." He ushered Jamie toward it, then turned back and gestured at her. *What's going on?*

She forced a smile. *Nothing.*

He shook his head, then turned back around and wondered why she was lying.

WILLA LEANED AGAINST THE DOORFRAME and tweaked her pose here and there for maximum effect. She didn't usually try this hard—full makeup, big hair, and heels—but the pregnancy was already making her unwieldy and she thought she needed the help.

Her patience began to dwindle as Tom continued to rummage

in the shed. Waiting for him was spoiling the mood. Jamie had texted earlier to say he was at a friend's, so Willa had taken this opportunity to put on her favorite dress. She ran her palms down the fabric and wondered if she would ever fit back into it. When she had Jamie, she was young enough to regain her shape, but now, at thirty-eight, she wondered if motherhood would destroy her body for good.

She heard a clatter in the shed, and finally, he emerged. When he saw her, he froze mid-step on the path. A wide grin spread on his face.

"Well, look at you." He came over and circled his arms around her waist.

She pushed his hands away. "You're dirty."

He raised a brow. "And *you're* not?"

She smiled, doe-eyed, and led him inside. At the dinner table, she sipped from her glass coyly.

"What's going on?" he asked, glancing around the room.

She raised the glass a little. "I'm drinking lime and soda," she said pointedly. "Instead of wine." She leaned an elbow on the table. "Because I can't drink wine."

He looked at the glass and it took him a moment to catch her meaning. "No . . ." he said in shock.

"Yes."

"Are you serious?"

"Yes."

"But . . . are you *sure*?"

Willa nodded, her eyes shining. "A hundred percent."

Tom dropped to his knees beside her. He drew his arms around her and pressed his face to her torso. "How long have you known?"

She shifted guiltily. "A week."

"A week!"

"I wanted to be sure before I said anything." She looked at him shyly. "Are you happy?"

He didn't speak, only nodded, and Willa knew that he didn't trust his voice. She leaned into the heat of his body and softly kissed his hair. At first, he relaxed against her, but then she felt him tense. He pulled away a little.

"Wait, you've known for a week?"

"Yes."

"But . . ." He released her. "You were drinking at the barbecue."

Willa gestured at her lime and soda. "This was just for show. I can drink for the first few weeks."

"What? No, you can't."

Willa rolled her eyes. "Tom, who knows more about pregnancy? You or me?"

"Come on, Willa. Don't be glib. You were smoking as well."

"Only one."

"Sweetheart, I've seen you smoke every day."

Willa sighed, loud and theatrical. "Fine. I'll give it up."

He took her hand in his. "I know it's not fair but we've got to do this. We've got to keep our baby safe."

"I *know* that," she said sourly.

"Tell you what. I'll give up drinking too. For the whole nine months."

She shuddered. "Oh god, don't do that. We don't *both* have to be bores."

He smiled lopsidedly. "Okay, but you promise?"

"I promise."

He twisted round and plucked her cigarettes from the mantelpiece. "So these are gone?"

She waved nonchalantly. "Gone."

He aimed them at the wastepaper bin and landed the shot easily. "Gone!" He poured her more lime and soda and opened a bottle of beer. "Things will be so much better this time. We have a garden. A car. A spare bedroom!"

Willa felt something knot in her stomach. Jamie's early years weren't easy with the three of them crowded in her Camden flat, but the thought of raising a child here, in Blenheim, felt like a sort of surrender. "Don't you miss those days though?"

He scoffed. "What? Hitting my head on the ceiling every time I went downstairs? And your dad lording it over me that he was paying your rent? No, thank you."

Willa sighed. "But don't you miss being part of that life?"

"We're parents now. We have different priorities."

"But it might be good for our child. To be part of something that isn't so . . . stationary." She pictured herself pushing her baby along Primrose Hill, stopping at a café to meet Sato, Sophia, and Amelia. She imagined strolling the streets, pausing to photograph an interesting door to upload to her Instagram.

Tom laughed. "I don't even know what that means, but I think you're being romantic." He sipped his beer. "Things are so much better here."

Willa's picture changed: Now she was standing on the lawn watching Tom push a little pink bicycle that carried a pigtailed blonde girl.

Willa pushed away from the table and tugged at her neckline, feeling claustrophobic.

"Why don't you head upstairs?" said Tom. "I can do the dishes."

Willa nodded and stood. On her way out of the kitchen, she paused by the wastepaper bin. She hovered there for a second and then, with a backward glance at Tom, plucked her pack from the bin. She tucked it at the very back of a drawer that no one ever went through. She didn't plan to smoke them, of course, but why should Tom tell her what to do? It was a purely symbolic act of defiance. She covered it with old batteries and coolly left the room.

SALMA WOKE UP BEFORE HER alarm, roused by the bed-spring that dug into her side. She curled like a fetus to try to avoid it but could still feel its knotty claw. She and Bil had talked about replacing the mattress but moving homes had cleaned out their savings. Right now, they had two mortgages: on Blenheim *and* Jakoni's. They had tried to rent out the retail space while they looked for a buyer but couldn't find a taker. It was a terrible time to start a business. They had taken a mortgage holiday but that was just a Band-Aid. Maybe they should have cut their losses with this house, but what was the alternative? To stay in Selborne Estate and watch Zain veer off course? Salma wanted better for her child.

When she was younger, she believed that progress would happen naturally; that their children, by dint of being third generation, would do better than they did. But then she saw her neighbors' children fall into the same jobs: grueling schedules for minimum wage. She wanted Zain to have a choice. Staying in Selborne Estate would have culled his chances.

People often asked her why she had never had another child. Perhaps she *would* have in a place like Blenheim, but raising one child in Selborne Estate was challenging enough. There, they slipped away alarmingly fast. She had seen it with Zain's peers and wanted something different for him, even if it stretched them financially. She and Bil would get through this. They always did.

She closed her eyes and willed her mind to quieten, but soon gave up on sleep. She crept out of bed, careful not to wake Bil, and went downstairs to the living room. Sunlight streamed through the window, bathing the room in butter. She set the coffee to brew and tidied up a few bits and pieces: the throw that Zain always left in a heap, the magazine he used as a base for his laptop so the pouf wouldn't get too hot. She plumped the cushions and listened to the gentle putter of the coffee. She neatened the curtains, and then she froze.

At first, she thought she was mistaken; that the light was just hitting it strangely. She reached forward and pulled the banner from the window. A hot poker of shock sunk into her skin. The bottom-left frame of her window was daubed with white paint—not haphazardly but in neat, deliberate strokes, filling the entire pane. Her mind filed through the possibilities—an innocent prank, a coincidence, an accident—but landed on a dreadful truth: This was Tom's work. For a moment, she stood there at a loss, her mouth moving silently as if working loose her thoughts. Finally, she set down the banner and went upstairs to wake Bil.

He rubbed his eyes like a child and followed her down to the living room, snapping awake when he saw it. He rubbed two fingers across the pane.

"Surely not." He met her gaze, and before he could smooth it away, she caught the flash of dread. He shook his head to chase it away, then put on his slippers and went outside, Salma trailing behind. They stood side by side and stared at the neat square of white. She touched it and felt her anger mount.

"It's dry." She turned to Bil. "What should we do?"

He chewed the inside of his cheek. "There's some white spirit in the shed."

Salma balked. "No, Bil. We shouldn't just clean it."

"Well, we can't leave it like it is."

"But we can't not say anything."

"We don't know who did it."

Salma exhaled sharply. "I think I have a good idea."

"Come on, Salma, it could have just been some kids."

"It wasn't just kids."

Bil angled his head in doubt. "We can't just go accusing someone without any proof."

"I do have proof. I saw him."

"You saw him do one thing. This is another thing."

"So what do we do? Just calmly live next door to a racist?"

Bil flinched. "Shh," he said urgently. "Be careful, Salma. You can't just say that word."

"Why not?" she asked hotly.

"You know how people get."

Salma clenched her jaw, then spun and headed inside.

Bil followed. "What are you doing?"

She marched up to their bedroom and changed into a bra, T-shirt, and pair of jeans. "I'm going to say something."

"Oh, hon, just calm down a sec."

"No, Bil. He fucking *vandalized* our home."

"Come on, Salma. We need to think logically. We're new here and—"

"We don't want to 'rock the boat.' I get it, but this is *not* acceptable, Bil."

"He's a grown man, Salma. A father. Do you really think he'd do this? Maybe it *was* just kids."

"I don't think so."

Bil gripped her shoulders. "I think we should let it go. The banner was obviously not welcome, and, hon, this isn't even our fight."

She shrugged out of his grip. "No, Bil, because guess what? If you don't stand up to bullies, you get bullied." She didn't let him speak; just turned and marched back down. He tried to calm her, but Salma was determined. Outside, she stepped over the low fence into Tom's front garden and strode across the lawn. She rapped on the door, then rang the bell. Stepping back, she crossed her arms, ready for confrontation. Bil stood next to her and pressed his palm downward to tell her to stay calm. Salma felt the race of her heart, her adrenaline feigning courage. She waited, then knocked again, louder yet. After a minute, she heard the turn of a lock.

Tom opened the door, wearing gray joggers and a loose white T-shirt. When he saw Salma and Bil, his scowl smoothed to a polite smile.

"Hi!" he said with a note of surprise. He glanced at his watch, ostensibly casual but designed to signal that this wasn't normal. "Everything all right?"

Salma glared at him. "Can I have a word?"

"Um . . . Yes?" He didn't invite them in.

Salma pointed across the lawn. "Our house has been vandalized."

His lips parted in a show of shock. He followed the direction of Salma's finger, but then frowned, confused. "How so?"

"Bottom-right window," she said curtly.

He squinted. "Oh, I see." He seemed unimpressed. "Sorry to hear that. It's probably kids from down the estate."

"It's not though, is it?" she said. Bil touched her arm, but she shrugged him off, making no attempt at discretion.

"What do you mean?" asked Tom.

"I saw you," said Salma. She saw a flicker of hostility before he wiped it clean.

"Excuse me?" he asked in that self-righteous tone that Salma hated so much.

"I saw what you did with our banner."

He feigned confusion. "What banner?"

"Tom, I saw you," she said firmly. "You knocked it into our garden."

His face changed, revealing irritation. "Have you read the neighborhood guidelines?" he asked.

"What?"

"It specifically says that banners aren't allowed on the street itself."

Salma was stumped. "Are you having a laugh, Tom? What is this? North Korea?"

He looked at her defiantly.

"You're serious? We can't put any banners in our front garden?"

"Read the guidelines."

She faltered, for she had always followed rules. She had thought that she had the high ground and this slight misstep unsettled her. She felt the heat of his glare and worked to gather her thoughts. "Okay, but why not tell me that like an adult? Why knock down my banner and leave it on the lawn?"

"Because I'm tired of people like you ruining our neighborhood."

Salma flinched. "People like me?"

His eyes grew wide. "I didn't mean it like *that*." A flush of red crept up his neck. "I meant people who come here and don't read the regulations." He exhaled sharply, realizing how he sounded. "You know what I meant."

Salma's voice was ice. "Oh yes, Tom. I know *exactly* what you meant."

He held out his palms in a mea culpa. "Look, can we start again? I'm a pedant, okay? I live by the rules and so when people move here and they don't even bother to read the guidelines, it gets my goat. Yes, I should have knocked on your door and told you so, but you should have read the rules."

She stared at him. "And you thought the best way to communicate that to me was to vandalize my property?"

He looked over at the square of paint. "That wasn't me."

"Sure it wasn't."

"I'm telling you: It wasn't me."

"Right. Well, I'll be reporting this."

He watched her carefully. "To who?"

"To the police."

He scoffed. "Oh, come on."

"Come on what?"

"The police have more important things to do."

"Someone vandalized my property, so obviously I'm going to report it to the police."

For a moment, they stood at an impasse. Then he stepped closer to her. "Go ahead. I can point the way. In fact, I've got some friends there. I can tell you who's on duty if that helps."

Salma stepped back, catching the subtext. "Right," she said softly. Then she turned and walked away, Bil still mute by her side.

WILLA HOVERED AT THE TOP of the stairs and listened to the voice in the doorway. She took a step down, careful to avoid the creaky one. It was the woman from next door: Saima?

Sama? *Salma.* Willa wrinkled her nose at the harsh tone of her voice. It was funny: Willa could—and often did—deal with angry men, but angry women made her uncomfortable. Perhaps it was because she knew that a man couldn't or shouldn't strike her, but a woman, boiled to just the right heat, *could* and possibly would. She had never been in a physical fight and was certain she would struggle. Of course, there had been plenty of disagreements, some of which had rattled her.

There was that time at the supermarket with that awful aggressive woman. Her child was blowing a shrill whistle and Willa turned in the queue to throw her a pointed look. A few minutes later, the woman dropped a coin and Willa didn't pick it up for her. Instead, she stepped aside to let the woman reach it more easily. The child wasn't in her arms and she was perfectly capable of getting it herself.

"You have a problem?" she asked rudely.

"Excuse me?" said Willa.

"I said, 'Do you have a problem?'"

"Why would I have a problem?" Willa asked, her voice cool above her panic.

"The way you're looking at me."

Willa scrunched up her face in confusion. "I'm not allowed to look at you? I'm sorry. I didn't realize." She turned back around and the woman continued talking to her.

You think you're all that. Hoity-toity. Stuck-up.

The checkout woman did not intervene and Willa packed up quickly. When she finished, she met the woman's eye. "Have a nice day," she said airily.

"Fuck off," the woman called back.

Willa was so indignant. Some people *enjoyed* playing the victim. Willa had merely *looked* at her. Some people just didn't help themselves—like this Salma. Why barrel over here and accost Tom on his doorstep? Why not discuss this calmly? She waited until after Tom closed the door to join him in the hallway.

"What's happening?" she asked.

Tom laughed derisively. "It looks like our new neighbors are barmy."

"But what was she talking about?"

He fanned his T-shirt to cool his body. "Okay, so maybe it was partly my fault. Yesterday, I knocked her ridiculous banner to the ground and apparently she saw me, which is why she's throwing a hissy fit."

Willa narrowed her gaze on him. "You knocked over their banner? Why?"

"Because it's not allowed."

"But what about the flags Ben next door had up?"

Tom scowled. "That was different. It was for VE Day and it was only up for a couple of days."

"So was theirs."

"Yeah, but it was a political thing. That's not allowed."

She arched a brow. "The union flag isn't political?"

"Umm, no," he said slowly as if speaking to a stupid child.

Willa decided to let it go. "Well, what did she want?"

"A fight, I guess."

"But she said something about vandalism?"

He rolled his eyes. "Someone painted a bit of her window and she thinks that it was me."

Willa smirked at this. Tom was overzealous, but he would never break the law. "God, even if it *were* you, she didn't have to make a scene at seven in the morning."

Tom flexed his fingers and cracked his bones—a habit she despised. She noticed a film of sweat on his skin, pinkish in the heat. "You didn't paint it, Tom. Did you?"

He looked at her reproachfully. "Of course not. It was just a coincidence. I have to say though: Maybe they were asking for it. Not everyone is as tolerant as we are."

Willa listened to her husband and wondered if her new neighbors would give him that awful label: gammon. These days, it seemed to be flung at every middle-aged white man. Tom was more progressive than she! Willa had been raised with a stiff upper lip and a suspicion of the "other." Tom, meanwhile, was far more accepting. Yes, he voted Tory but that was for the sake of his family. He was a good man and it annoyed Willa deeply that Salma had implied otherwise. She could tell that Tom was bothered too. She went to him and rubbed the back of his neck, easing the tension there. "Come on, let's have some coffee and forget about her."

He nodded, but his focus was elsewhere.

"Come on." She pulled him toward the kitchen, away from his mood. When something got under his skin, he found it impossible to let it go. He approached it from different angles, pressing and poking to work it out. Only then would he set it down. It was the pragmatist in him: something always whirring in the back of his mind, trying to make the pieces fit. She touched his arm to try to bring him back to her. "Let it go, okay?"

He nodded absently.

"Okay?" she pressed.

"Yes," he said. "Okay." He leaned back in his chair, but Willa could see the cogs still turning in his brain.

SALMA STALKED THE LENGTH OF the living room, her blood still hot in her veins. If Tom thought he could bully her into submission, then he needed to think again. She recalled his smarmy look. *I can tell you who's on duty if that helps.* She understood the message. *There's nothing you can do.* It didn't matter though. Salma still planned to report it. She had to prove to him that she would stand up for herself.

Years ago, in her first year of teaching, Salma broke up with a cheating boyfriend, an accountant named Jay. After she moved out, he took two thousand pounds from her bank account to pay the next month's rent. When she called to confront him, he was unduly combative.

"Your name's still on the lease, so you have to pay half the rent," he said.

"But I've moved out!"

"So?" he said coldly.

"You can't just take money from my account!"

"Well, you shouldn't have left your documents here. I haven't actually done anything wrong."

Salma called her bank, which said they could act only if she filed an official police complaint, given that she and Jay had been in a relationship. Salma marched straight to her nearest station. It took an hour but she got a crime reference number and called the bank again. Jay's own account was promptly frozen. He phoned her almost immediately and begged her to drop the complaint. If he was found guilty of fraud, his career would be over, he said. Salma instantly recouped the money he stole and learned an important lesson: When someone bullies you, you strike back with more force than expected. A man like Tom didn't believe that Salma could stand up to him—but she could and she *would*.

She took pictures of the window from inside and outside the house, then transferred them to her laptop.

Bil watched in dismay. "What are you doing?"

"I'm logging evidence."

"Why?"

"To go to the police."

He sighed. "Honey, listen, what do you think the police will do? It's a petty crime and they're not going to bother. If you report it and nothing happens, he'll only be emboldened."

"I'm not leaving it, Bil. I'm not letting him do this."

"So then what? We start a war with our new neighbors?"

"*He* started the war."

"Come on, Salma. Don't be melodramatic."

"He had the temerity, Bil, to sneak up to our house after dark and white out our window. Think about that."

Bil sat down next to her. "Look, we can't afford to move again. We need to make a go of this." He waited. "If we go to the police, everyone on the street hears about it and we become the troublemakers. Are you comfortable with that?"

Salma shoved her laptop. "Fine," she said like a petulant child.

Bil traced the soft ridge of her knuckles. "I know how much this bothers you but we need to make a go of this."

"I *know*," she said.

Bil stood wearily. "I'll go and get the white spirit."

Salma waited for him to leave, then pulled back her laptop. She browsed to Twitter, uploaded two pictures, and drafted a caption.

> *Yesterday, I saw our neighbor knock out this banner and leave it on our lawn. I brought it inside and put it in our window. This morning, we woke up to this. Three cheers for tolerant Britain.*

She added three icons of the St. George's Cross and pressed SEND. She sat back, feeling a little giddy. Immediately, she began to accrue likes, retweets, and messages of sympathy. She hovered over the DELETE button, knowing if her school caught wind of this, she could end up in trouble. But, no—people needed to see what women like her had to deal with. Systems were built to keep her silent and silence never changed things. She snapped the laptop shut as Bil came back with the white spirit. He gave her a resigned smile and went out to clean Tom's mess.

CHAPTER 3

For the first time in months, Zain woke up feeling hopeful. Lately, weekdays had taken on a cast of censure as his parents readied for work while he still lay in bed, the long stretch of day ahead of him. His life had no direction and he had no idea how to find it. He'd always hoped to work for the European Space Agency, to have a piece of his code literally aim for the moon. He'd known it was unlikely, but to have this dream snuffed so early had left him careening.

Now, with Grapevine, he had a second chance. It was too late for space, but tech was a good alternative. Zain liked the idea of renting out a garage in Menlo Park or Mountain View, on the doorstep of Facebook and Google. He enjoyed the origin stories of big companies even when they were mostly myth: Steve Jobs and Steve Wozniak creating Lisa in their garage, or Larry Page and Sergey Brin vowing to do no evil. Now that Zain had found Jamie—and a cause that mattered to him—he felt freshly energized. It was true: Blenheim wasn't exactly a thriving hub, but a great innovator once said, *I don't know of any place or any time where there aren't great possibilities*. Maybe he and Jamie could really do something worthy.

Zain switched on his laptop and drummed his fingers on the

desk as it slowly ground into gear. If they were to start a company, he would need a faster machine. He opened Xcode and waited for it to load. After a full minute, he decided to try the downstairs laptop.

In the kitchen, his mum was dressed in what he joked was her "school uniform": a loose black blazer rolled to her elbows, jersey top, and skirt. In some ways, he had to respect the consistency. It reminded him of Facebook's Mark Zuckerberg, who wore the same thing every day so he wouldn't waste time deciding. Unlike Mark, his mother was crouched by the washing machine, separating whites from colors.

"Hey, Zain, I've got to get to work. When this is done, can you take it out please? If something's not dry, can you just put it through again?"

"Yep," he said, taking a seat at the desk. He opened up her laptop and saw that it was already on. He entered her password—"zain2004" would you believe—and saw that it was logged in to Twitter. He moved to switch profiles but then froze. His hand gripped tight on the mouse. "Mum?" he said unsurely.

She was busying around the kitchen, rushing through her routine.

"Mum," he said more forcefully.

"Yeah?"

"Can you come over for a sec?" He felt her stiffen next to him as he circled a spot with the cursor. "What's this?"

7,623

She grabbed the mouse from him and clicked the notifications. The screen filled with tweets. Zain saw that they were all replies to something and clicked the original message.

*Yesterday, I saw our neighbor knock out this
banner and leave it on our lawn. I brought it
inside and put it in our window. This morning,
we woke up to this. Three cheers for tolerant
Britain.*

Zain exhaled. "Mum, when did this happen? Why didn't you
say anything?"

She looked at the tide of replies. "Oh my god." She scrolled
down and initially it looked like it might be fine—***What an
awful thing; I'm so sorry; Have you reported this?; Sending
you love and strength***—but then came a deluge of others.

*Why use the St. George's Cross? What are
    you trying to imply?*
*Divisive drivel. Try doing something
    productive.*
*Why are you co-opting #BlackLivesMatter?
    #NotYourFight*
Virtue signaling of the highest order.

She reached out to delete the original tweet but Zain grabbed
her hand. "What are you doing?"

"Getting rid of it."

"Why?"

She waved at the screen, panic in her eyes. "Because of
this."

"So?"

"Zain, I can't have this on my feed."

"Why not? People need to know what happened."

She reached for the mouse again. "Not if it puts us at risk."

Zain pushed the mouse away. "Then when?" He pointed at the screen. "Mum, you did a brave thing. Don't undo it."

"But all those people."

"What about them?"

"I'm a teacher. I can't have this on my feed."

"So teachers aren't allowed to speak about abuse?"

"Come on, Zain. It's not as simple as that."

"Why not?"

"Listen." A tremor rose in her voice. "I'm going to be late. Please can you just delete it?"

"Mum, let me deal with it. I'll go through your old tweets and delete anything that identifies you, but I think we should leave this one up there."

She winced with indecision, then finally said, "Okay, but please be thorough."

Zain felt a swell of pride. "I will. Don't look at Twitter. I'll deal with it—promise."

"Okay." She shook out the nerves from her hands. "And don't tell your dad. He'll only worry."

"I won't. Now go!"

"Okay." She dithered for a moment, but then picked up her handbag. "Look after Molly," she said.

"Drive safe," he called after her, noticing her jitteriness. He scrolled through more replies and he himself felt a creeping unease. He blocked dozens of requests from journalists, thankful that none of his mother's tweets revealed her identity. The thought brought on a twinge of shame. It occurred to him that while he had attended a BLM march and posted a square on his Instagram, he hadn't put his body in peril. He had always had the option of sidestepping danger. If he put up a banner only when it was safe to do so, then it was true: He *was* virtue signaling. He pushed back from the desk, away from the spew of vitriol. He picked up the banner and ran a finger over the letters, now speckled with dirt. He took it to the sink and washed it. Then he went to the front garden and planted the banner back outside.

SALMA TRIED NOT TO SWEAR as she fiddled with the cable on the school laptop. A fault in the equipment meant that she had to pull out the HDMI cable, wait a moment, put it back in, and then press PLAY at the exact right moment to get the projector to pick up her screen. It had become something of a game in her class: a group cheer when she managed it and jeering when she didn't. Today, she snapped at them to be quiet.

"Gosh. Miss didn't have her Weetabix this morning," said Ritesh, the class clown.

"She got out the wrong side of bed," added Patrick.

"She's bent out of shape," said Tara.

"She's flying off the handle," chimed in another. They were learning about clichés in English class and this was another of their games.

Salma felt her temper flare and tutted loudly in warning. The projector finally picked up and she started her lesson on tectonic hazards. As she moved through the material, her mind churned with what she had seen that morning. She wanted desperately to look at the latest responses, but she had a full timetable today, which meant she barely had time for a toilet break, let alone browsing Twitter.

"Miss." Naina, one of her more challenging students, raised her hand. "I was watching *The Chase* last night and how come only six people died in the Great Fire of London?"

Salma paused. "That's not the lesson, Naina."

"I know, miss, but I was wondering why that was. Everyone said the fire was this massive thing, so how come not many people died?"

Salma was caught in the balancing act between teaching the curriculum and feeding organic curiosity. "Well, we don't know for sure. Some historians say that the deaths of poorer citizens weren't recorded."

"So how many poor people died then?" asked Patrick.

"It's hard to say. The heat may have cremated some bodies. Archeologists found a piece of melted pottery in Pudding Lane that shows that the temperature reached 1,250 degrees Celsius."

"For real?" said Ritesh. "But wouldn't they have found teeth and stuff?"

Salma sighed and lowered her laser pointer. "Okay, I guess we're going off-plan today." She searched the school's intranet for resources on the Great Fire of London. It wasn't on her syllabus but the pupils were uncommonly engaged.

When the bell rang an hour later, it took Salma by surprise. That was both the best and worst thing about the classroom: You never had time to watch the clock. Her lunch hour was the first moment she managed to catch her breath. She pulled out her phone and opened Twitter. The notifications were still coming and the deluge left her coiled with tension. She texted Zain: DID YOU LOOK THROUGH MY TWEETS? CAN PEOPLE WORK OUT WHO I AM?

His reply came quickly. RELAX. NOTHING THERE IDENTIFIES YOU.

The tension eased a little. Some of her colleagues followed her on Twitter and would surely see what was happening, but she didn't want to be known publicly. If that happened, then Tom might also be identified and she dreaded to think how he would react. On reflection, Salma wondered if she should have listened to Bil: *Just clean the glass and carry on. No use rocking the boat.* Now they had made an enemy, and if he found out what she did, things would only get worse.

WILLA PARKED HER CAR, A silver Dacia that had embarrassed her at first but that she had grown to love. She lifted her groceries from the crowded boot and cursed when a bag split open. A lemon dropped to the ground, rolling off the curb. She bent to pick it up and saw a pair of sneakers pause.

"Do you need help, Mrs. Hutton?"

Willa straightened. "It's Zain, right?"

"Yes, we met at the barbecue."

She was amused by his formality. "Call me Willa, for Christ's sake. Mrs. Hutton is Tom's mother, and Jesus, I don't want to be likened to *that* witch."

He shrugged in an offhand manner. "Willa," he said, trying it out. He locked eyes with her and repeated it more decisively. "Willa."

She handed him the torn bag. "Help me take this in?" She led him inside and through to the kitchen. She could smell him: sweat mingled with aftershave—something cheap and masculine. As she unpacked, she felt his eyes on her and pushed her hair into a messy tousle. She didn't speak, knowing that men always worked to fill her silences.

"Where's Mr. Hutton?"

"At work." Her gaze flicked to his and she tried to decide what to use on him: negging (*adults have a thing called jobs*) or flattery (*like every boring adult on this street*). Willa didn't even realize she did this; manipulation was a basic instinct. She could hardly be blamed though. Men made it so easy.

"He works in advertising, is that right?"

"Yes, but god, I don't want to talk about my husband. Can't we find something else to do?"

Zain studied her and something dawned in his eyes. "Um." He stepped back from the counter. "I should let you get on with it."

"Should you?" she asked.

He hesitated and she saw the clench, unclench of his fist. "Uh, I've got stuff to do." He raised a hand in parting, then turned and hurried out.

"Zain," she called.

He turned again. When she didn't speak, he asked, "Yes?"

She smiled coyly. "Thank you for helping me."

"No problem," he said, his tone clipped. "I've got to go."

"Okay," she said, stretching the word petulantly as she watched him leave. The sound of the door closing left her feeling strangely rejected. She sighed and dropped into a dining chair. God, she was so *bored*.

She flicked through Jamie's schoolbooks, then drifted to the living room. She had tried her best with the bare white walls. It would have genuinely hurt her to fill them with cheap prints, so she opted for local artists instead and a few inexpensive but tasteful pieces. She had considered putting up one of her own— a charcoal portrait of her younger self caught in a moment of pain—but thought it might be tacky. Willa had always carefully curated her image. In photos, she would angle the lens strategically to catch the best parts of her home. She would hate for her friends to realize that she lived in a house with plastic windows. They had thought her impossibly cool when she went from her degree at St. Andrews straight into a coveted residency at the Jermyn Gallery. She hadn't known that she would be pregnant five months later, essentially ending her career. She had vowed to continue, but when Jamie came along, he swallowed all of her time. And now? She had nothing to show.

She took out her phone and idly browsed Instagram, pausing on a post from Sophia. She was Willa's best friend from St. Andrews and, in some ways, lived the sort of life that Willa had imagined: a published author with a column in British *Vogue* and a backlist of modern romances that critics called "biting" and "incisive." *Incisive romance? As if.*

Willa read Sophia's latest update. **Some personal news**, it announced in that smug parlance of authors and journalists. **I'll be adapting my own novel for Working Title, owned by Universal Pictures!** Below, a long list of comments congratulated her. Willa sighed and added her own. **Congratulations! This calls for #champagneandcaviar. I'll text you!** She reread her message, added and deleted a champagne emoji, then deleted the final exclamation mark. She pressed SEND and saw that Sophia liked it but didn't reply. She set down her phone, frustrated. Soon, she would be able to make her own announcement—but congratulations for a pregnancy were never quite the same as a film deal.

Willa thought of the endless stretch of day ahead and felt a sense of lethargy. She glanced at her watch, then stole into the kitchen. She poured herself a small glass of wine, knowing that Tom wouldn't notice the shortfall. She drank it by the sink in case she needed to tip it out. On her phone, she opened Twitter and scrolled through her feed. There was Sophia again announcing her film deal on another platform. Below that, she had retweeted something with a comment of her own: *I'm so sorry this happened to you. What awful people they must be.* Willa read the original tweet.

> *Yesterday, I saw our neighbor knock out this banner and leave it on our lawn. I brought it inside and put it in our window. This morning, we woke up to this. Three cheers for tolerant Britain.*

For a moment, she was confused but then she looked at the pictures and realization hit: This was Willa's street. That was Salma's house. The "neighbor" in question was Tom. What the *hell* was this woman implying? Willa was furious and fought the urge to march over there, but screaming wasn't her style— unlike Salma's, it seemed.

Willa scrolled through the replies and felt a juddering dread. People were calling them all manner of things: *vile, bully, fascist, Nazi.* She read on and felt her anxiety thicken. It was one thing to criticize the act; it was another to threaten the culprit with murder, rape, dismemberment. How could Salma have exposed them to this? How could she have been so petty and thoughtless? Willa felt a destructive flare and tried to snuff it out. This needed delicacy, a gentle reengineering.

Perhaps she could invite them over for dinner and talk in a civilized manner. Would Salma be willing, she wondered, or did she enjoy the drama? Either way, Willa would remain calm and courteous. She would show Salma how *adults* dealt with conflict.

———

ZAIN LEFT WILLA'S HOUSE FEELING strangely agitated. Had she been *flirting* with him? The thought prickled his skin with warning. He glanced back at her house, then hurried into his own. He found his dad in the kitchen, wolfing down a sandwich.

He pushed the plate across the granite counter. "Want half?"

Zain eyed the plain cheese dubiously. "For a chef, you have some pretty awful taste."

His dad laughed. "This is straight from the Wensleydale Creamery I'll have you know." He took another bite and frowned as he chewed. "Is everything okay?" Could he tell that something was wrong or was he just asking by rote?

"I'm fine." By Zain's calculation, his dad asked this question three times a day: morning, afternoon, and evening. He knew he was trying to help but the staged, scheduled nature of it had the opposite effect. There was no lightness in the question, and every time he asked it, it sounded not like *How are you* but *Who are you? Are you the son I raised? Do I really know you?*

"I saw your friends yesterday," his dad continued. "Out by the high street."

Zain stiffened. *What friends?* he thought dourly.

"Have you been in touch with them?"

Zain shrugged. "They're busy with exams and stuff."

His dad was quiet for a moment. Gently, he said, "I wish you'd talk to me, kid."

"I'm fine."

"Are you really?"

Zain was silent, loath to revisit that time. He remembered the day as a series of sounds: the initial trill of shock when they found the knife in his locker, the glue-like noise in his throat, the rapid click of panic. *It's not mine*, he told them but wouldn't say whose it was. He thought that when it came to it, Imran would do the decent thing and confess that it was his, that Zain had merely stored his gym kit to save him a trip across campus. Instead, his friend said nothing and Zain was expelled from school under their zero tolerance policy. Later, when he confronted Imran and told him to do the honorable thing, it ended in a fistfight, but somehow *Zain* was ostracized. His parents overreacted and now here they were at Blenheim. Zain knew that his dad had found it harder than his mum. *She* had always accepted that there would be secrets between mother and son. His dad, however, had always been his confidant and saw the episode as a personal failure.

"I'm fine," he repeated. Before his dad could speak, Molly padded in, granting Zain an exit. He dropped to his knees to pet her but also to hide his face, stippled red with memories. "I'll take her on her walk," he said.

With resignation, his dad agreed. "Your mum and I are at the restaurant tonight, so you'll have to fend for yourself."

"No problem," said Zain, keeping his eyes on Molly, making sure not to look up until they were alone.

SALMA WALKED OUT OF SEVEN Kings station and felt herself relax. The stretch near the station was far from attractive but the area felt like home. She headed to Jakoni's but took a longer route, passing through Ilford Cemetery. This small patch of green was her sanctuary, the one place she came when life got noisy. Growing up, she would sometimes make up errands and sit here with a book: Jules Verne, H. G. Wells, Edgar Rice

Burroughs, anything with an adventure. A neighbor once told her that Muslim women weren't allowed in graveyards alone, but it never put her off.

She walked into the churchyard now and took a seat by the clock tower, overcome by homesickness. She loved this corner of the city for its noise and color and edge. Blenheim felt like a different planet: a bland sci-fi utopia that was prim and perfect. The thing about edge, of course, was that sometimes you fell off it and she couldn't let that happen to Zain.

Her phone cut into her thoughts with a message. SHALL I ORDER SOME PIZZA? IT'S GONNA BE A LONG ONE. She felt guilty that Bil had booked off Friday evening only to spend it redecorating. She texted him back, then headed to the restaurant, walking past peeling billboards, clotheslines bowing with weight, and shopfronts flanked by graffitied bins. It looked impossibly grotty and she felt a pang of shame for being able to recognize this. When you lived here, you became immune to it. It was only in leaving that you came to see its reality.

She stepped through an unmarked door and climbed a flight of stairs to Jakoni's. The restaurant had been known for its Bangladeshi street food: bhortas, shingaras, daler bora, and aubergine fritters—the cuisine of their ancestral home. It had earned critical acclaim and a healthy cult following, but two years under a pandemic had fatally dented the business. Now it lay empty, cold seeping from every wall. She heard the low tone of the radio and followed it to the kitchen.

"Hi."

Bil startled a little. "Oh, hi."

She noticed a box on the counter. "God, how are you still finding things?"

He tapped the box. "It's the knives I lost. I don't know whether to leave them for the next guy or try to flog them separately. They're worth a fair bit."

Salma peeked inside and saw two dozen knives. "We could see if Suli wants them? Maybe at a discount?"

"That's a good idea." Bil taped up the box. "I'll text him tonight."

Salma changed into an old T-shirt and picked up a roller. Bil always painted the edges, for he never veered into the skirting and ceiling given his chef's precision. They worked in silence and she noticed that Bil was unusually quiet.

"Everything okay?" she asked.

"Yeah," he said absently.

"Something on your mind?"

"No."

"Bil," she said sternly.

He lowered his brush. "I thought this place would sell by now." He puckered his lips in thought. "Sometimes I wonder if we made the right decision."

Salma felt a lance of fear. A marriage was a balancing act: When one of you had doubts, the other would allay them—high and low, yin and yang—but if both of you crashed at the same time, then there was a problem.

"I know why we had to move," said Bil, "but sometimes I think we panicked."

"We didn't panic, Bil. We had to take care of our son."

"I know. I just . . ." He pushed a hand through his hair. "If we don't sell this place soon, we'll go into overdraft."

Salma felt a snap of denial. She had never known true poverty. Her mother was extraordinarily skilled at recipe planning, so even though her family had very little money, they always stretched it far. Salma and her brother, Samir, had grown up on just the right side of the line: poor enough so that Friday sherbets and Crunchies would fill them with sheer delight, but not so poor that they ever went hungry. She couldn't truly believe that this was a possibility.

"Did you call the estate agent?" she asked.

"Yes. He said the market's slow at the moment. They haven't had much interest." Bil gestured vaguely. "We're okay for now. As long as one of us doesn't lose our job and we tighten our belt for the next few months, we'll be all right."

Salma felt uneasy. Her job was secure. Bil's, on the other hand, was precarious. Even a reduction in hours could prove catastrophic. She motioned at the wall. "Let's get this thing finished and see how we go."

They worked solidly until the pizza arrived, then sat shoulder to shoulder on the plastic-covered floor. Salma ate her first piece and regarded Bil guiltily. "I've got something to tell you," she said.

He narrowed his eyes, familiar with this tone. "Go on."

"When you went to get the white spirit yesterday, I posted the photo of our window online."

Bil's hand paused in the air, his slice of pizza wilting. "On Facebook?"

"No. On Twitter."

Bil placed his slice back in the box. "Why would you do that? That's just asking for trouble." He wasn't on Twitter but knew it was a place of debate and disaster. "Did anyone say anything?"

She hesitated. "Quite a few people, but I made sure I wasn't identifiable, so it's okay."

"What if Tom and Willa see it?"

Salma shrugged with false nonchalance. "Then they see. It's not like I named them."

Bil frowned. "You're going to get us into trouble, hon."

Salma remembered Zain's words. *You did a brave thing. Don't undo it.* "Maybe," she admitted. "But maybe it's worth it."

WILLA HATED THEIR LOCAL "CHIPPIE." Everything about it made her cringe: the wipeable menus dotted with grease, the stale smell that clung to her clothes, the yellowed posters on the peeling wall. Usually, she would wait outside but it was cold for May, so she huddled in a corner instead. She looked at the two Formica tables and wondered who on earth dined in. Willa didn't even *like* fish and chips but Tom's parents were visiting and Friday fish was a holy tradition.

Tom was picking them up from the station and Jamie was on his way home from tutoring, so it was up to Willa to collect the food. She reminded herself that it was a small price to pay. The alternative was to cook and she hated that even more than this seedy chip shop. She picked up the bags of food and asked to pay with contactless. It was the twenty-first century for god's sake. Why did they always look so gormless when she asked to pay by card? She hurried out and huddled against the cold, biting down her preemptive anger. Tom's family always set her on edge. His father, Harry, had owned a string of estate agencies, but went bankrupt in the 2008 financial crash. He had a boisterous manner and was clearly of the mind that volume could stand in for dignity.

Tom's mother, Donna, was a slim and flighty woman who coddled him excessively, leaping up for a tissue as soon as he sniffled. Willa knew that Donna didn't like her because she didn't pander to Tom. In the early days, she had tried to ingratiate herself, buying trinkets that Donna would like—a small amulet, a piece of jade—but these were received with such lukewarm thanks that eventually Willa stopped.

She turned into Blenheim and sighed when she saw Tom's car already parked outside. She had hoped for a few more minutes. In the hallway, she paused by the mirror to smooth her hair and fix on her warmest smile. She walked into the living room and handed the bags to Tom. She kissed Donna, who didn't get up to greet her, and then Harry, who gave her a Cheshire grin.

"There she is!" he said. "Looking as ravishing as ever."

She gave him a coy smile, then offered them drinks and joined Tom in the kitchen.

"Shall we tell them our news?" he asked.

Willa scowled. "It's too early. You *know* that, Tom."

"But not for family."

"It *is*," she said tetchily. "Besides, I'm not in the mood for a big thing."

"Fine," he said and left in a sulk.

Willa wished for the umpteenth time that Tom's family weren't so close. Why couldn't they be like hers and see one another twice a year? She shook out the chips on the heated plates and wrinkled her nose at the sharp tang of vinegar. She peeled a slice of lemon off a sweaty piece of fish and spooned out the mushy peas. Two by two, she took in the plates, glancing at the clock. Jamie was unusually late.

"So the bint comes and knocks on our door at seven in the morning!" Tom was saying.

Donna's face crumpled in distaste. "Some people have no manners. What did you say her name was?"

"Salma Khatun."

"Cartoon? What country are they from?"

Willa placed a jug of water on the table. "They're British, Donna," she said smoothly.

The older woman rolled her eyes. "I know that. I wasn't suggesting they're not. I just haven't heard that name before."

"I think they're Pakistani," said Tom. "Or maybe Bangladeshi."

"It's all the same," said Willa but the irony didn't land. She cut into a soggy bit of fish and chewed it slowly as she listened to them debate. Harry was of the mind that Tom shouldn't have damaged the banner, but Donna, of course, defended him.

"You give them an inch, they'll take a mile," she said, pointing at Tom in warning, as if she had met the Khatuns.

Tom waved dismissively. "Anyway, it'll blow over. I haven't seen them but if I do, I'll say hello and good-bye just as with anyone else."

Willa felt uneasy. Tom hadn't seen the tweet yet. She hadn't wanted to show him before his parents' visit.

"Make an effort to be friendly, son," said Harry. "They're new here. You should try to put them at ease."

"Why should *he* have to put them at ease?" said Donna. "They're the new ones. They're the ones who should be making an effort."

"They might be intimidated."

"Well, that's their choice," said Donna.

Willa swallowed her soggy mouthful and no one spoke for a while. Harry cleared his throat and turned his gaze on Willa.

"So, tell me, darling, how are your Russian classes going?"

Willa shifted uneasily. "Oh, they're on a break right now. The teacher had to go back to Russia." She avoided looking at Tom. She didn't know why she had told the lie. Harry asked her all the time what she was up to and she hated saying *shopping, cooking, cleaning, dreaming,* so one day, off the cuff, she said she'd enrolled in a language class when, in reality, she had only downloaded an app. Harry had beamed and asked her twenty questions. Willa answered each one on the fly: *at UCL, in the evenings, two hours, eight students, thirty weeks, three hundred pounds.* Afterward, she had taken Tom aside and told him to uphold the lie.

"That's a shame," said Harry. "What else have you been up to?"

What have you? she wanted to snap. The same things anyone does. "Oh, the usual," she said vaguely. God, she hated these evenings. The front door opened and Willa sprang up, grateful for the distraction. Harry and Donna doted on Jamie and he always made these dinners easier.

His footsteps pelted down the hall, followed closely by Lola. "Mum, have you seen this?" he called. He skidded to a stop in the doorway when he saw Harry and Donna. He flushed. "I'm sorry. I forgot." He walked in sheepishly and greeted them in turn.

"Have we seen what?" asked Tom.

Jamie placed his phone on the table. "Did you tell Grandma and Grandad about next door?" he asked.

"Yes. Why?"

Willa pushed a plate at Jamie. "Yes, we've talked all about that. Now, let's eat, please."

"But look!" Jamie handed his phone to Tom.

"No phones at the dining table." Willa tried to reach for it but Tom moved it away. As he scrolled, his skin turned pink.

"What is it?" asked Donna.

"It's nothing," Tom said curtly, returning the phone to Jamie.

"It doesn't look like nothing."

"It's just a stupid meme on the internet."

"What's a meme?"

Tom grit his teeth as he tried to answer his mother civilly. "It doesn't matter, Mum. It's just a silly joke."

Willa wished that Jamie had waited and could see from his expression that he was thinking the same. The rest of the meal passed as it often did: with stilted conversation and low-level conflict. By the time they were ready to leave, Donna was a little tipsy and turned her attention to Willa.

"You're too skinny," she said. "I understand why women need to diet but my Tom's losing weight as well. I know you don't like to cook, Willa, but you have two grown men in the house. You can't feed them what you eat."

Willa held on to her smile. "I'll try harder," she said.

"*Mum,*" Tom said impatiently. It annoyed both him and Willa just how long it took his family to get out through the door. First, there were final bathroom breaks, then a hunt for a shoe-horn, then words of advice to Jamie, followed by plans for their next meeting, and, finally, good-bye. By the time they left, Tom was coiled with anger. He asked Jamie for his phone, testily waggling his fingers. He read the words out loud: "'Yesterday, I saw our neighbor knock out this banner and leave it on our lawn. I brought it inside and put it in our window. This morning, we woke up to this. Three cheers for tolerant Britain.'" Tom shook his head. "This is unbelievable. How dare she call me intolerant?" The pink in his skin deepened. "I'm not having this."

Willa knew she had missed the window to calm him. She raced for a way to appease him, but the whir of her thoughts was slow and Tom had already marched out the door.

YEARS AGO, SALMA HAD READ about the concept of "winter counts," pictorial calendars used by the Lakota people and other Native American tribes. Instead of charting days, winter counts recorded the biggest event of each year. In this way, they would chart entire lives. Salma often thought of this in times of upheaval. It was comforting to know that difficult months would pass, a mere blip in the vastness of a person's life span. On the other hand, it reminded her of the quickness of life: how an entire year could slip by unmarked. She thought of Zain and how he had come to a standstill. They had given him everything—private tutoring, after-school clubs, and mentoring—but when he was thrown out of school, he lost all motivation. In recent days, however, she had seen a spark return. He was working on an app, he said, and though Salma would prefer that he get a real job, she was pleased that he was occupied. She watched him now—hunched over her laptop, fingers flying over the keyboard—and felt a small shoot of hope. She was proud of him and was about to tell him so when she heard their doorbell ring, followed by an aggressive thumping.

Zain turned and looked at her. "What's that?"

Salma felt a pulse of dread. She stood gingerly and walked into the hallway. At the front door, she peeped through the spyhole and saw that it was Tom. She started to back away when the postal flap opened and he peered straight in.

"Can you open the door?" he said.

Salma didn't feel she had a choice. She steeled herself and opened the door. "How may I help you, Tom?" she asked evenly.

"Who the fuck do you think you are?" There was spittle on his lips.

Zain appeared behind Salma and she held out a hand to steer him back. "Can you calm down?" she said to Tom.

He shoved his phone at Salma. "What the fuck is this?"

She saw her tweet on the screen and felt a surge of dread.

"'Three cheers for tolerant Britain'? You don't think I'm tolerant? You're having a laugh if you think that's true."

"You couldn't tolerate a harmless banner," said Salma.

"Because you're not allowed!" he shouted.

Zain moved forward now and out onto the lawn, forcing Tom back. "Can you not shout at my mum like that?"

"Step back, little man," he snarled.

"Excuse me?"

"If you think you can take me, then come on. Otherwise, go back and hide behind your mother."

Salma intervened. "Tom, you're an adult. Please don't threaten my son."

Tom turned his glare on her. "I'm not threatening your son. Jesus Christ. You really do love playing the victim, don't you?"

Zain, now behind Tom, started to film on his phone.

"And you call *me* intolerant?" Tom carried on. "If I were intolerant, I'd tell your husband not to park in our bay and I'd tell you to shut up that fucking dog of yours." He pointed a finger in her face, his temper now smoking. "I'd tell you to fix that fucking fence. And I'd tell you to keep your windows closed so you don't stink up our clothes with your cooking!"

The words landed like a gunshot. For a second, they stared at each other, locked in mutual shock. A breeze gusted across the lawn, chilling Salma's skin. There was panic in Tom's expression. At first, it seemed he would apologize but then his features hardened.

"I'm not being funny," he said. "I'm just telling you the truth." He squared his jaw. "If you can't tell the objective truth anymore, then this country really has gone to the dogs."

"I think you should leave," said Salma.

"What's this all about, eh? You want to prove how big you are?" He gestured in surrender. "It was just a fucking banner."

"I said: I think you should leave."

"Oh, don't worry. I'm leaving but I'll tell you this: Don't get involved with my family. That means no talking to us, looking at us, or fucking *posting* about us online. Nothing. You stay away from us or you'll see what I can do."

Salma held her poise. "I am perfectly happy to do that," she said.

Tom sneered at her, then turned and marched away.

Salma felt the adrenaline leave her body, coating it in sweat. Her heart was palpitating and she felt unduly giddy. She spotted the phone in Zain's hands, still filming. "Switch that off," she snapped. She pulled him inside and closed the door. "Were you recording the whole time?"

"I caught the part about our smelly cooking if that's what you're asking."

Salma felt drained—by the confrontation but also from the burden of having it on film. She navigated to the clip but paused when she heard Bil's footsteps on the stairs.

"Do I still have paint on me?" he asked, rubbing at his scalp. "That primer stuff is lethal." He stopped, catching the stress on her face. "What's wrong?"

Salma felt an illogical clutch of anger that Bil had missed the entire thing. She handed him the phone and watched his features tighten as he played the recording. "Jesus." He blew air into his cheeks. "Has anyone else seen this?"

"Not yet," said Zain.

"I think we should keep it that way."

"Why?"

"Because it'll only make things worse," said Bil.

"But didn't you hear what he said?"

"I did, kid, but come on." Bil gestured wearily.

"Come on what?"

"We do the same thing, no?" He turned to Salma. "We pack up the washing when you're cooking curry."

She stared at him. "Bil, that is *not* the same thing."

"Come on, Salma. Don't be one of those people who reads oppression into everything."

"You know, Bil, sometimes it's okay to play devil's advocate but this is not the time."

He grimaced. "Look, I appreciate all this rabble-rousing that the new generation are doing, but honestly, it's like the boy who cried wolf. If we moan about every small thing, what happens when big things happen? We can't get people's attention." He motioned at the phone. "I think we should delete it."

Zain refused. "I think we should back it up, Dad, and put it somewhere safe. We might need to prove what he's like."

"He has a point," said Salma. "That man is aggressive. What if it escalates? We might need to document things."

"This is getting out of hand," said Bil, "but if you think that's best, then fine." He handed back the phone. "But can we try to stay out of their way for a while? Life won't be bearable with nightmare neighbors."

"Fine," Salma agreed. The kicker was that Tom probably thought *them* the nightmare.

Bil squeezed her hand. "Go and finish grading your papers," he said. "I'll make you some tea."

She returned to her place at the table but couldn't focus at all. This, she supposed, was the price you paid for standing up for yourself. She picked up her red pen and tried to disguise the shake in her hand before she set to work.

TOM STEAMED IN AND SLAMMED the door so hard, the rattle reached the ceiling. Willa turned from her vantage at the window.

"What the fuck were you thinking?"

He blinked as if surprised to see her there. "I couldn't let her get away with it."

"You could lose your job!"

Tom scoffed. "What are they gonna say? That I *raised my voice* at them?"

"You were so aggressive, Tom. It won't look good on film."

He stared at her. "What film?"

"Tom, please tell me you saw that the boy was filming?" He flinched so hard that she knew the answer was no. "Oh god, Tom. What did you say?" Sweat slicked his upper lip. "Tom, what did you *say*?"

He made a low groan. "Fuck." He thumped a fist against his own thigh. "Fuck. Fuck. Fuck!"

Willa hated when he got like this: so consumed by self-pity that he forgot to think of her. "Tom," she snapped. "What did you say?"

He covered his face. "I said that we have to close our windows when they cook because they stink up all our clothes."

Willa broke into a garish smile as if bested by a joke. "You're not serious?" When he didn't answer, she grabbed his shirt. "Tom, tell me you're joking."

He pulled out of her grip. "I'm not."

Willa's face soured with blame. "Tom, if you lose your job, then what the fuck are we going to do?" She pressed a palm to her belly. "We need to fix this. Right now."

He wiped the sheen off his upper lip. "I didn't know he was filming." The gravity of this dawned on him.

Willa waited for him to say more, then sighed pointedly, knowing that *she* would have to fix this. She gave him a snide look. "I'm going to invite them to dinner so we can smooth this out."

"No. I'm not having that."

"Then what, Tom? They put the film on the internet and your colleagues see what you said?"

"They know I'm not like that."

"Okay, but does everyone else? Your boss? The mob on social media? *Journalists?* Have you forgotten your racist car ad?"

"It wasn't *my* ad."

"It was your agency!" cried Willa. She remembered the furor over the clip, which showed a giant white hand flicking a Black man away from a car. "These things escalate, Tom. We need to call a truce."

"I doubt that that woman wants that."

Willa heard the snap in his voice and foresaw disaster. "Maybe I should talk to her by myself—woman to woman."

"Whatever you want," he said glibly. He saw the look on her face and the one on his own softened. "I'm sorry," he said, stooping with guilt. "I'm being a prick."

"You are," said Willa. She pulled away from his touch. "You're such a big oaf, you know that?"

He nodded. "I do know that." He reached for her again.

"Not now. I need to talk to Salma before this gets out of hand." She headed out, knowing this would take every ounce of her charm.

CHAPTER 4

Salma was agitated. She had spent all of Saturday on errands and was now stuck at Westfield. The Central Line had made her late—something that always stressed her. She had wanted to arrive first to have a chance to go to the bathroom, brush her hair, and powder her skin, which often turned shiny on the tube. When she entered the café, however, Willa was already waiting. She wore minimal makeup but her dark eyeshadow gave her eyes a sunken supermodel look. Salma instinctively smoothed her hair, feeling like an ugly duckling. As she walked, she noticed the clop of her sensible shoes. She bet that Willa's heels didn't sound like this.

Willa stood up to greet her. "Salma, I'm so glad you came."

It was strangely reassuring to hear Willa say her name—a fact that made Salma embarrassed. The bar was so low for beautiful women.

Willa fussed over her: ordered her a coffee and hand delivered it, then slid back into the chair opposite. "Can I be honest with you?" she said.

Salma nodded.

"Tom can be an arsehole." She grimaced prettily. "After our first date, he nearly didn't call me because I turned up three minutes late. He said it was a 'show of disrespect.'" Willa took out a pack of cigarettes and laid them on the table. "I thought he was a controlling prick but here's the thing about Tom: His father was a disciplinarian." She preempted Salma's reaction. "I know, I know, it sounds pathetic. *Daddy didn't love me enough,* but honestly. Listen to this. When Tom was twelve, he snuck out of the house one night, so his dad locked him out. All night. In December."

Salma stopped mid-sip.

"That isn't even the half of it. Basically, if Tom broke a rule, he'd pay for it, so he grew up with the belief that rules keep you safe. Following them, upholding them, honoring them, is sacred, which is why he's the way he is. He *always* complains when people don't follow the rules, so when you came along and stuck up that banner inches from our fence, he kind of lost it a little. Of *course* it was excessive but if you knew the context, you'd understand that it really wasn't an act of aggression."

Salma considered this. She knew from her pupils just how much damage a bad parent could do, but this didn't absolve Tom completely. "Painting my window white wasn't an act of aggression?"

Willa laid her hands on the table. "Salma, I swear that wasn't him. I *swear* to you. I know my husband. He wouldn't dare trespass on your property. He'd be too worried about breaking the rules. That's how he operates."

"You're saying that there happened to be *two* separate people that objected to the banner?"

Willa sighed. "Look, do you know Abbey Estate nearby?"

Salma nodded. She and Bil had viewed a house there—a pebble-dashed monstrosity.

"There are lots of young dickheads there who come here to

cause trouble—stealing Amazon deliveries, letting air out of tires, generally being shitty. More than likely, it was one of them. I promise you: Tom did not paint your window."

Salma studied her carefully. "Are you sure, Willa?"

Willa reached out and placed her hand on top of Salma's. "I'm positive. And I'm *so* sorry for the crappy welcome you've had. I'm sorry about his behavior. I'm sorry about all of it. Please can we start again?"

Salma tried to gauge if she was being fooled. Was this a genuine call for a truce or a cynical ploy to protect Tom? "I don't think you're the one who needs to apologize," she said.

Willa withdrew her hand and Salma caught a flash of irritation. Had her mask slipped a little? "Look, he's stubborn," she said, "but I will get him to apologize. It might just take some time."

At this, Salma felt a ping of relief. If Tom was willing to apologize, perhaps they could all move on. She had been worried that this would turn into a full-scale war. "Okay, but until he does, I'm not sure things can be normal."

Willa flushed with gratitude. "I know and I appreciate that." Her voice took on a sisterly tone. "Can I ask one more thing of you? Please can you not post that video anywhere? We can't afford for Tom to lose his job." Then she dealt her coup de grâce: "I'm pregnant, you see."

This had the intended effect on Salma, stirring a primal empathy. She was about to agree when Willa reached for her bag—a powder-blue Mulberry.

"We can pay you," she said.

Salma blinked. "Excuse me?"

Willa's hand froze midair. "We can—" She caught the look on Salma's face and realized she had offended her. "Not like a payoff," she stammered. "I mean, like, for the window and the damage."

"Why would you feel the need to pay me?"

"I just thought . . ." Willa faltered.

Salma's voice grew brittle. "I'm not going to share that video, Willa, and you don't need to *pay* me hush money."

"That's not how I meant it."

Salma drained her cup and sensed that Willa was about to touch her, so she scraped her chair back. "Thanks for the coffee," she said, then snatched up her bag and stalked out.

JAMIE PLACED THE TEXTBOOK ON his desk next to a bowl of popcorn. On the cover was a close crop of *The Creation of Adam*: God's hand reaching out. *Cheesy*, thought Zain as he opened the book. The graphics were dated and the pages were tatty but the information was still useful.

"Okay, so the very basic thing when talking to a deaf person is that you face them head-on. Don't cover your mouth or your face. Enunciate but don't, you know, treat us like we're thick." Jamie spoke in a slow drawl. "Heh-lo, my name is Jaaay-meee."

Zain frowned. "Listen, man, is it cool to use that word?"

"What word?"

"'Deaf.' Like is it politically correct and stuff?"

Jamie shrugged. "If someone says they're deaf, then call them deaf. If they say they have hearing loss, then say they have hearing loss."

Zain angled his head in doubt. "I don't want to offend anyone, not if we're building this app."

"Look, man, I'll be honest. I'm not an expert. I'm proud of

who I am but I'm not, like, Deaf with a capital *D* and I can't speak for everybody."

Zain considered this. "Okay, but are there things that I should avoid?"

"I suppose, for me, the number one thing I hate is when I ask someone to repeat something and they say 'Never mind' or 'Don't worry' or 'I'll tell you later.' That makes me feel like shit."

Zain felt a painful twinge of empathy. Mentally, he vowed to never treat Jamie like this. He flipped the page and started to work through the first chapter. Midway, he looked across at Jamie. "Hey, man, can I ask you something?"

"Sure."

"Your old man. Does he know I'm here?"

Jamie leafed to the next page. "I don't know. I haven't mentioned it."

"Do you think he'd have a problem with it?" Zain wasn't comfortable there but Jamie's powerful iMac was much faster than Zain's laptop and so it made sense to base themselves there. It wasn't a garage but worked well as a makeshift office.

"Why would he have a problem?" said Jamie.

"Were you around yesterday? When he talked to my mum?"

"Kind of, but I didn't hear anything."

Zain explained what happened, leaving out the comment about stinking up their clothes. "Look, you don't have to tell me, but is he a bit funny with people like us?"

"'Like us'?"

Zain rolled his eyes. "Like me and my mum and dad." He waited. "*Brown* people," he said impatiently.

Jamie gave him a comical look. "Mate, my dad doesn't discriminate, all right? He hates everyone equally."

Zain didn't laugh. "I just don't understand why a person gets so worked up over a banner. Or a tweet that didn't even identify him."

"Mate, my dad gets worked up when people don't put things back on the right shelf at Tesco, or if they park their car an inch over their bay, or if they don't throw out an empty box of tea from a cupboard at work. He's a complainer. It's got nothing to do with you being brown. Trust me."

Zain wanted to probe to see if there were off-color comments made behind closed doors. Ultimately, he decided not to. "You know what, if we're going to do business together, let's agree that whatever happens with them stays there. It doesn't affect us."

"I'm good with that," said Jamie.

Zain pushed away the textbook. "All right, enough of that. Teach me some chat-up lines innit."

"What are you going to do? Hit up a girl at deafPLUS?" Jamie tutored a small group at the center each Friday.

Zain gave a cheeky shrug. "Why not? I'm an equal opportunity Casanova." He ducked and weaved like a boxer.

"Please don't do that in front of her."

Zain elbowed him. "C'mon. I can be your wingman."

"I have Lola for that. All the girls there love her."

Zain shook his head in mock despair. "Upstaged by a fucking dog." They both broke into laughter, warm in the glow of a friendship that hadn't yet been tested.

SALMA STORMED INTO THE HOUSE and hurried to the utility room to hang up her dripping coat. The surprise downpour had further stoked her temper, already boiling with all the things she hadn't said to Willa. How little that woman must think of her, assuming that she could *buy* her. If Willa had appealed to Salma's decency, then it would have been fine, but to assume that she would kowtow to cash was thoroughly offensive. Salma paced the kitchen and ran through fragments of sentences that she had left unsaid.

Zain's footsteps sounded on the stairs. "Hey, Mum. Is there food?" He glanced at the oven.

"There's a frozen pizza in the fridge," she said. Zain wrinkled his nose and she glared at him, daring him to complain.

"Is everything okay?"

"It's fine," she snapped.

"Mum?" he asked unsurely.

"They're unbelievable!" She couldn't hold back her rant. "Those people." She pointed at Willa's house. "Do you know she offered me money?"

"Money?"

"To keep quiet. To not show that video to anyone."

"Why would she do that?"

"You know why. If anyone saw it, her husband would lose his job."

Zain was quiet, the cogs in his head turning. "Maybe we should post it."

"If she had just treated me with dignity instead of as a *serf*, then maybe I'd be inclined to listen."

"So you think we *should*?" said Zain.

Salma heard the surprise in his voice. "No, Zain, I don't think we should. I'm just angry. Seriously. What do these people think of us?" She exhaled sharply. "I just wish that Tom had come and talked to me. If he had a problem with the banner, then he should have come and explained that I can't put one up. Why do what he did?" She saw the uncertainty in her son's face and felt guilty for burdening him. She had planned to save her rant for Bil but couldn't help herself. "Do me a favor, Zain. I know you and Jamie are friends, but I don't want you going round there."

Zain grimaced. "But, Mum, his computer is way faster than my laptop. I need it for our app."

"There'll be other apps."

He began to protest but saw the look on her face. "What are you going to do with the video?"

Salma had pondered this on the train home. She had always stood up to bullies but knew from experience that it could backfire. In her first real job as a teacher, she had worked at a selective grammar school with a woman named Helen Antwi. They were in competition for a permanent role and when Salma began to shine, Helen—who had been at the school for longer—began to undermine her. She would exclude Salma from the BCC field when sending important emails, or highlight harmless errors to give them outsize weight. Once, she changed the location of a meeting and updated everyone but Salma, who sat in an empty room, wondering where everyone was. She had combed the halls in a panic, finally hearing the drift of voices. When she hurried into the correct room, she saw Helen turn theatrically, brows raised in rebuke. When Salma reported her behavior, *she* was the one who was branded petty and frozen out by colleagues. Helen got the job and Salma had to leave.

She looked at Zain. "Let's not do anything drastic. I don't want to provoke them." She spoke firmly in an effort to convince herself that this was an act of peacekeeping and not straightforward cowardice.

MOLLY BOUNDED AWAY AS SOON as her lead was off. She was a gentle, curious dog and still behaved like a puppy despite approaching her eleventh birthday. Salma and Bil had adopted her when she was six months old: a skinny, underfed thing that cowered when you tried to pet her. These days, she was more confident, lolloping here and there to paw a thing of interest. She ran ahead as they approached Fairlop Waters but skidded to a stop by a figure.

"Molly! Come here, girl," called Salma. As the figure drew closer, Salma realized that she recognized her: Linda, the hostess of the barbecue.

The older woman shooed Molly away. "Ah, there you are!" she called.

Salma felt a pinch of guilt. She hadn't yet sent her a note to say thank you.

"I've been by your house once or twice but no one ever seems to be home." Linda cast a look at Molly as if it might be her fault. "You've been busy, I take it?"

"Yes, sorry. I've been meaning to drop by but we've barely had a moment to breathe." For some inexplicable reason, she wanted Linda to like her. She could sense that she held a form of unofficial power and wanted her as an ally. They chatted idly as Salma tried to decide if she should mention the problem with Tom. In the end, Linda brought it up herself. She leaned in close and lowered her voice.

"I heard you've had some trouble with Tom."

"Yes, it was . . . unfortunate."

"I'm sorry to hear that. Can I ask what set the whole thing off?"

Salma weighed this up. It was clear that Linda was after

gossip but she didn't want to rebuff her. She leaned in close as well. "Well, it started on the night of the barbecue," she said, matching Linda's conspiratorial tone. She relayed the story of the banner.

"Unbelievable," said Linda. "What do you plan to do?"

"Nothing, just hope it blows over."

Linda nodded in approval. "Sometimes it's best to let these things lie."

"Yes. I don't want things to escalate."

Linda gestured airily. "Oh, you don't have to worry about that. Tom's not one to retaliate."

"Is that so?" said Salma.

Linda smiled. "Listen, you don't have any reason to worry. I've known Tom a long time, which is why I genuinely find this unbelievable. He's a gentle giant though—honestly. And you and your husband—Bil, was it?—have absolutely no reason to worry. You're completely welcome in this neighborhood. I assure you."

"That's nice," said Salma politely. She needed this woman onside. Molly paced impatiently and nudged at Salma's calf. "All right," she chided her gently. "I should get on," she said to Linda, "but it was so nice to see you." She thanked her for the barbecue and hurried away with Molly. After they rounded a corner, she leaned down and scratched her ear. "Thank you, Mol," she whispered. Together, they ventured farther, keen to continue exploring.

TOM STRODE INTO THE ROOM and took a seat at the conference table. He propped one knee on the other and adjusted a cuff link in what he hoped was a Don Draper–like gesture. He knew he looked good even if he did have to suck in his stomach. As an executive, he had to look the part, and good suits were his one expense. He didn't mind driving a sensible Volkswagen or wearing a secondhand Seiko, but he didn't scrimp on clothes. An ill-fitting suit was career suicide as far as he was concerned. He wanted to be regarded seriously, maybe even with envy.

He still remembered the day he first came to these offices, fifteen years ago. He was on a delivery and was told to leave the boxes in the office of Scott Makinson, who, he didn't know then, was a legendary adman. Tom walked into the empty office and stacked the boxes by a giant desk. An advert was spread across one side of it: an A4 poster for Marmite. Tom looked at it and scoffed. When he turned, Makinson was watching him.

"Something funny?"

"Sorry, no." Tom moved to scuttle out but Makinson held up a hand.

"Go on, spit it out," he said impatiently.

Tom looked back at the advert. "Well . . . unless that's aimed at pirates, it should say 'mate.' No one says 'matey.'"

Makinson stared at him, then barreled toward the desk. Tom flinched, thinking that he was coming for him, but instead he snatched up the phone. "Isabella, has the Marmite ad gone to print?" He listened, then barked, "Hold it! We're changing it." He clicked his fingers at Tom. "You, come with me." By that afternoon, Tom was officially employed by Sartre & Sartre International. It took him a while to fit in but now he too had a glass-walled office and interns at his beck and call. He particularly enjoyed it when Willa joined him at office parties. He knew what his colleagues were thinking. He could see them practically salivate. On those occasions, he would feel himself swell with pride. He would take Willa home those nights and fuck her like they were strangers.

But she was pregnant now. Willa had always wanted a second child and he did too, of course. But he remembered how she had ballooned when she fell pregnant with Jamie. She wasn't like other fine-boned women whose weight dropped off instantly. Hers stuck to her thighs for years, and though she was glowing and luminous, his libido genuinely struggled. Tom had never been unfaithful though, despite the opportunities. In advertising, there was a steady stream of pretty young things. Unlike some of his colleagues, Tom firmly resisted. He was tempted only once, by a girl who looked like a poor man's Willa: blonde but from a bottle, a little bit chunky but with gorgeous lips. *Such* gorgeous lips. They had flirted but it never went beyond that. The last he heard, she was shacked up with a divorced ex-colleague of his. *Lucky bastard.*

There was a knock on the door and Susie, his fellow interviewer, led in a young woman: petite, Chinese-looking with straight black hair cut into a bob. Her calm manner and tailored suit immediately won his respect. *Case in point,* he thought. Tom's colleagues hated recruiting but he thoroughly enjoyed it. He liked probing interviewees beyond their practiced answers to uncover the person beneath. The company had a rule in place imposed by Susie, their diversity leader. For every role, they had to interview at least one non-white person. *Person of color,* he corrected himself. They were underrepresented in advertising and this, they were told, would deliver an uptick. She had faced some pushback but so far it had worked. Tom, for one, didn't care as long as they hired the best person for the job. It didn't matter if they were white or Black or purple. As long as they pulled their weight, he was okay with it.

He nodded at a chair. "Please sit."

The woman unbuttoned her blazer and sat, her feet neatly perched together.

"Ms. Chou?" he said. "Can you tell me a bit about yourself?"

"Please call me Jennifer," she said, revealing a row of shiny white teeth. "I grew up in Greenwich," she said. She stopped and grinned. "Actually, I grew up in Deptford but I say Greenwich because it sounds better."

Tom instantly warmed to her. "I'm from Barking, so I know the feeling," he told her.

She smiled, cheered by their comradeship. "I studied philosophy, politics, and economics at Oxford and did an internship at D&AD."

Tom stiffened. It was to be expected in the context but he always did hate it when people wielded their university as if it were a medal. It reminded him of Willa's friends. He *hated* Willa's friends. "What do you do for fun?" he asked, straying from education.

"I play piano. I ski and I'm currently learning Russian."

It took all his might not to roll his eyes. Deptford or not, Jennifer had hit the grand slam of privilege: elite university, instrument, sport, language. "That's impressive," he said flatly. For the rest of the hour, he listened to her polished answers, not bothering to probe as he might usually do. Women like Jennifer Chou had ready-made answers for everything. He took a final look at her CV, then thanked her and bade her good luck.

The next candidate was a scrawny young man in an ill-fitting suit that put Tom's teeth on edge. He introduced himself as Pete and told them about his graphic design degree from London Metropolitan University. Tom weighed up the two candidates. He strongly believed that merit should be measured by the distance traveled. Most people focused on who finished farther, but if you measured distance instead, you could uncover true gems. A girl like Jennifer, albeit a person of color, was privately educated and had had a far better start than Pete.

Tom put a tick next to his name and a question mark next to Jennifer's. The third candidate was their final one: an older woman who wore a fusty tweed suit. She was nice enough but lacked the spark she needed to thrive. Halfway through the interview, there was a knock on the door and Isabella, Makinson's PA, looked in.

"We're in the middle of an interview," said Tom.

"I'm afraid Mr. Makinson wants to see you now."

Tom felt a skittering unease. Makinson rarely summoned staff to his office—and only if it was urgent. He excused himself and followed Isabella. "Everything okay?" he ventured. She nodded diplomatically, never one to be indiscreet. Tom knocked on Makinson's door and waited nervously. The man was known to be gruff and abrasive. When he was angry at someone, he would send them an email with a single character: ? If you received the dreaded question mark, you had to shield your jugular.

"Come in," said a voice that Tom didn't recognize. Makinson would have barked, *Enter!* The old man had taught Tom a few of his tricks: "When leading a meeting, stand up so that you're physically looming above your subordinates," "Stand with your legs apart but not so much that you look like that Tory twat," "Those who report to you are not your friends. Treat them like they're lower than you."

Tom entered and was surprised to find that Makinson wasn't

there. In his place was Vanessa, an executive at the agency who also happened to be Makinson's daughter. Her elbows were spread on the walnut desk and her lipstick cracked when she smiled, mean and brief as it was.

"Tom," she said curtly.

"Vanessa," he said with a nod. Then, "Where's your dad?" He couldn't help but highlight the nepotism every chance he got, which was no doubt why Vanessa disliked him.

"Please take a seat."

He rested a hand on the chair wing. "Did *you* and I have a meeting booked?"

"No," she said airily.

So he had been summoned here to see Vanessa? He felt the heat in his cheeks but shrugged nonchalantly as if accepting an impromptu coffee date. He sat, annoyed that he couldn't spread his legs in the narrow seat—another of Makinson's gambits. He waited in silence, refusing to speak first and yield his power to Vanessa.

She laced her fingers on the desk. "Do you know why you're here?"

"I have no idea, Vanessa, but I'm sure you will enlighten me."

She studied him coolly. "Tom, are you friendly with your neighbors?"

He froze. "Friendly enough." He was dismayed by the give in his voice. "Are *you*?"

"Tom, can we stop the bullshit for a second please?"

He swallowed his unease. The animosity between them was always unspoken, swapped mainly through passive aggression. That Vanessa had voiced it now filled him with alarm. "Okay," he said.

"Have you ever made a racist remark to your neighbors?"

Tom felt a slingshot of panic.

"Specifically, that your Asian neighbors 'stink up' your clothes with their cooking?"

Blood rushed in his ears. Desperately, he riffled through his options: denial, dismissal, anger, apology. "It wasn't like that," he managed.

"It wasn't like that," Vanessa mimicked. She stood and looked out at the horizon. "Do you know how my dad came to accrue this? He's not the smartest, the strongest, the most inventive or nimble. What he *can* do is read the room. He can look at the current climate and"—she clicked her fingers—"adapt to it. Some call him a populist, but what's wrong with being popular?" She turned. "You're a fucking idiot, Tom."

He couldn't think how to respond.

"You should have read the room. It's all bleeding hearts and wokerati out there and you—big lumbering idiot that you are—tell your Indian neighbor that she *stinks up your clothes* and have the fucking stupidity to have it caught on film?"

So, it was true. The video was out. "It wasn't like that," he insisted.

"No?" She was seething now. She whipped her laptop toward him. There, on-screen, was Tom's hulking figure looming above his petite neighbor, her shoulders tensed defensively. He was shouting at her: "I'd tell you to shut up that fucking dog of yours. I'd tell you to fix that fucking fence. And I'd tell you to keep your windows closed so you don't stink up our clothes with your cooking!"

And then, just as bad: "I'm not being funny. I'm just telling you the truth." The squaring of his jaw. "If you can't tell the objective truth anymore, then this country really has gone to the dogs."

Tom was shocked that it was him up there, spitting those

words at her. His father had taught him better than that. "It's not what it looks like," he said feebly.

"How the *fuck* is it not what it looks like?" Vanessa jabbed the screen. "This is a fucking publicity nightmare. It's the last thing we need after that fucking car ad. It looks like we *actively* employ bigots."

"That's not fair."

"What's not fair, Tom, is you marching over to your tiny little neighbor's house and telling her that she stinks."

Tom fell quiet. He looked at the image on-screen, at the way Salma stood her ground with every ounce of her courage. The sight made his cheeks sting.

"Do you know what they're saying?" said Vanessa. "I'll tell you." She spun the laptop back round. "'Another vile racist at Sartre & Sartre. No surprise it's the same agency that made that disgusting car ad.' 'Racism? In advertising? Sounds about white.' 'No doubt Sartre & Sartre are "horrified" and will do much "soul searching" before it's trebles all round at The Wolseley.'" Vanessa watched him icily.

"I'll take the blame," said Tom. "I'll apologize and—"

"Actually, you won't," said Vanessa. "You're fired."

Tom stared at her. "You can't do that," he said in a choke.

Vanessa crossed her arms.

"I've worked for your dad for fifteen years. You can't just fire me."

"You did this to yourself."

He rose to his feet. "Vanessa, please. Willa is pregnant. We've got a baby coming."

"You should have thought about that before you behaved in that way."

"I wasn't thinking. I was angry."

"Maybe our true colors are shown in anger."

Tom felt his frustration grow. "Oh, come on, Vanessa. You've never left an Indian restaurant and worried about the smell on your coat?"

"I've not been filmed on camera yelling it at the waiter."

He clasped his hands together. "You can't do this. I want to speak to your father."

"He's aware of my decision."

"Can I at least talk to him?"

"Think about it from his perspective. You've got to go."

Tom clenched his jaw, his panic ticking over like a stove top. He and Willa were already in so much debt. One month without his salary and they could easily sink. He refused to go begging to her father. "This is ridiculous, Vanessa. It's just so fucking spineless." On seeing her indifference, his panic caught flame. "At least I had the balls to say what I said to that woman's face. As if you fucking weasels don't pick and choose who you're renting your flats to. Didn't Daniel say *just the other day* that his tenants had turned the walls yellow?" He raised his finger at her. "You say you stand for freedom of speech, but you're a fucking coward."

"You need to learn when to stop, Tom."

"Fuck you, Vanessa."

"Oh, that's really mature. Well done for handling this like an adult, Tom." She buzzed her intercom. "David, Tom is ready to go. Please escort him to his desk."

Tom was numb with disbelief. "So that's it? After fifteen years, it's just"—he brushed his hands as if wiping off dirt—"it's 'fuck off' without even the dignity of Scott telling me personally?"

David, the security guard, opened the door and loomed at the threshold.

Tom glared at Vanessa. "This is really how we're doing it?"

"I'm afraid so." She nodded toward the door. "Good-bye, Tom."

He burned with humiliation as he followed David out of the room and packed up his desk in full view of his colleagues. His thoughts turned to Salma. That woman had blown up his life at the touch of a button—after promising Willa that she wouldn't. Tom saw now that he had underestimated her. Salma was underhanded in ways he hadn't predicted. The realization left him smarting. Something dark and grubby twisted in his gut, knowing she had outplayed him.

THE LUNCHTIME BELL SOUNDED AND Salma's students sprang to life, rushing to gather their books and bags. A knock on the door cut into their chatter. Fareena, the head teacher's assistant, hovered at the threshold as students streamed out around her.

"I'm sorry to disturb you, Ms. Khatun," she said in that official tone that teachers used in front of students. "Can you pop over and see Ms. Newton?"

On hearing the head teacher's name, the remaining students raised a chorus of *oohs*. Salma waved to shush them. "Yes, of course," she told Fareena. "Do you know what it's about?"

"Um, I'm not sure." Fareena's gaze shifted to the students and Salma knew that she was lying.

"I'll be there in five minutes."

Fareena thanked her and left.

"What's going on, miss?" said Ritesh.

"Can we hurry up please?" she said tartly, waving at his desk. She waited for the room to empty and wondered why the head had summoned her. Salma had recently requested more funding for the clinic, but that was standard practice and wouldn't call for a personal meeting. She locked her classroom and headed over.

Georgina "George" Newton was a lean woman, a marathon runner with gray hair that she always wore in a bun. She had an efficient manner that Salma had tried to emulate when she first joined the school. Alas, Salma was just too soft. A give-away smile would curl on her lips when a student cracked a good joke. There was no such weakness in George.

Inside the office, George pushed her phone across the desk. "Salma, is that you?" She fiddled with the PLAY button, press-ing it three times before it obeyed.

There, on-screen, were Salma and Tom. He was shouting and she was standing impassively. It was odd to see herself as a stranger might. In the moment itself, she had thought she was standing firm, but here, she looked small and scared.

"Who sent you this?"

"A colleague who saw it on Twitter."

Salma wilted. *Oh, Zain.*

George watched her. "So, it *is* you."

The question was a formality. Salma's face was clear in the video. She waited, expecting a rebuke, although she wasn't sure why. The public nature of this seemed like a trespass, a breach of their professional code. "Am I in trouble?" she asked.

George looked confused. "No, of course not." Her features softened. "I wanted to check that you were okay."

Salma leaned away from the phone. "I'm a bit taken aback, to be honest. *I* didn't put it on social media." She felt it was impor-tant that George understood that.

"We've had several phone calls from media outlets wanting to talk to you."

Salma covered her mouth. "Oh my god, I'm sorry."

"Will you be addressing it publicly?"

"No," she said. "Why? Do you think I should?"

George grimaced. "From my point of view, I'd prefer to keep all coverage mentioning the school positive and this is clearly . . . not positive."

Salma understood but it felt like a reprimand. She didn't *want* to address the video but wished that George had given her the right to do so. "In that case, I won't say anything." She motioned to the door. "Should I say something to the pupils?"

"I suspect they'll say something to you."

Salma nodded grimly. The thought of her students seeing her like this, stripped of authority—a precious commodity in her job—made her feel ill. A more dreadful thought followed on its heels: *Tom*. Salma had told Willa that she wouldn't share the video. How would they retaliate?

"I think the best thing to do is to let it blow over—but you *are* okay, aren't you?"

"Yes, I am."

"This man. Is he . . . dangerous?"

"No," said Salma instinctively. It seemed melodramatic to assert otherwise, but as she said it, she realized that she didn't really believe it. There was something in his tone and the way he spoke to her that teetered on the edge of violence. But would he really act on it? Tom had a good job. Surely, he wouldn't put that in jeopardy.

CHAPTER 5

The call came through precisely eight minutes after Salma left school. Her battery was about to die when Zain's name flashed on-screen. She prepared to lay into him for sharing the video but stopped when she heard his voice. He sounded strange: hollow, like he was standing in an empty stairwell.

"Mum, I think you need to come to the restaurant."

She heard him swallow—a thick, sickly sound. "Why? What's wrong?"

"Please come now."

"Zain—" The battery died.

Salma clung to a rope of calm, coiled it tight around her hands to stave off thoughts of trauma. Zain was okay. Of *course* he was, or he wouldn't have been able to call her—but what was he doing at the restaurant? She turned and bolted in the direction of Jakoni's, which was half a mile from her school. Cars zoomed by on High Road, spitting up water from the rain. She huddled into her coat, then broke into a run when she saw the open shutter of the restaurant.

"Zain?" She climbed the stairs and waited at the threshold. She heard a bark she recognized. "Molly?" She stepped inside and it took her a moment to understand. The fresh white walls were daubed with graffiti in garish reds and pinks, colors that were made to scream. The carpet squelched with moisture and the booths were ripped apart, foam spilling out like pus. There was a mess of empty beer cans, cigarette butts, and tobacco dust dotted across the room—and the kitchen was even worse. When she smelled the stench of ammonia, she burst into tears. Molly whined and padded over, but Salma was disconsolate. She couldn't make sense of any of this. She and Bil were on a financial precipice and this had snatched their safety net. She looked across at Zain and a question occurred to her.

"Zain, why are you here?"

He hesitated for just a split second but it was enough to stir her suspicion. "I was walking Molly and I thought I'd swing by and check on the restaurant."

"Zain," she said, stern through her tears. "What were you doing here?"

He shifted uncomfortably. "I come here sometimes to chill."

"To 'chill'?" Anger rose in her voice. She pointed at the beer cans. "Is that stuff yours?"

"No, I promise. We come here to work."

"We?"

He swallowed. "I brought Jamie here last week."

Salma stared at him. "Jamie from next door?"

"Yes." He watched her face and grew defensive. "Mum, don't even say it. This wasn't Jamie."

"You don't know that."

"I *do* know that. He would never do something like this."

"You've barely known him a week."

"Mum, don't blame this on me. It's not my fault."

A chilling thought occurred to her. "Has Jamie told his dad about the restaurant?"

Zain grew sober. "Last week, he mentioned his dad was surprised that we owned a second property. He said we must be rolling in it."

Salma felt the dredge of anxiety. Could Tom be their culprit? She glared at Zain. "When did you put up that video?"

He hunched guiltily. "Last night."

Was a single day long enough for Tom to do this damage? Surely, he was at the office all day. "Are you *sure* Jamie didn't do this?" she asked.

"I'm positive, Mum. There's no way."

She exhaled, letting her breath out slowly. This was Ilford. It *could* just be random vandalism. She surveyed the damage and felt her heart rate slow as the initial shock wore off. She took off her jacket and hung it on a door handle. She went to the kitchen and retrieved a roll of rubbish bags.

"What are you doing?"

"I'm cleaning, Zain."

He shifted on his feet. "Sh-shouldn't we call the police?"

"Should we?" she said. "What are they going to do?"

"For insurance and stuff?"

"Our insurance ran out, Zain. We couldn't afford to renew it." Immediately, she felt guilty for telling him this. She and Bil had made the decision to move and Zain wasn't to blame. It was her responsibility to keep this stress from him. "Look, find a locksmith, will you? And a carpet cleaner. We can't leave it like this." She pulled out the bucket of cleaning products that she stored beneath the sink.

Molly lay down in the corner where her dog bed used to be. The sight of her golden coat against the bare floor filled Salma with unbearable sorrow. She kneeled down and placed her arms around her, but Molly wriggled out. Salma remained there for a moment, shifting the weight of her burdens so she could stand again. Over the next two hours, they scrubbed and scoured the restaurant. To her relief, the graffiti sanded off and the smoother patches of paint weren't noticeable unless you were really looking.

It was only after the locksmith left that Salma relaxed again. She sat in one of the damaged booths and patted the space next to her. Zain reluctantly took it. She weaved an arm around him. The new toughness of his body stirred a sense of nostalgia. She missed her soft, squidgy son with his fat cheeks and joyful laugh. This older, somber version sometimes felt like a stranger.

"Can we talk about the video?" she said.

He nodded wordlessly.

"I asked you to back it up, not share it."

He pulled away to face her properly. "I did, Mum, but then that woman offered you money like you were her *kamla beti*. Who does she think she is? People like her think they can buy anything."

"But I told her we wouldn't share it. She's going to think I lied."

"So? Why do you care what she thinks?"

"I don't like to go back on my word."

"Your word only matters to people who listen. Everyone else can screw themselves."

Salma couldn't be angry at Zain for doing something she had wanted to do herself. "Zain, please don't bring Jamie here again. In fact, I'd rather you stay away from him."

"I know," said Zain. He stood and reached for her hand, and she let him pull her up.

WILLA WAS INCENSED. SHE HAD a baby on the way and without Tom's salary, they would have to . . . what? Go on *universal credit*? Absolutely not. She paced the length of the dining room, her woolen top now damp with sweat. She imagined her friends finding out that she was claiming benefits. The shame would be unbearable. She knew that her dad would give her money but would ask for one thing in return: that Tom acknowledge the gift and thank him for it personally. She had had to beg him to fund Jamie's hearing aids without crowing about it to Tom. There was simply no possibility that he would give her more money and *not* let it be known. She looked across at Tom, maddened by his vacancy. He stared at the far wall, his spine as rigid as the backrest he leaned on.

"She promised me." Willa grit her teeth. "That sneaky bitch *promised* she wouldn't upload that video and as soon as she gets home, she does it. What sort of snake *is* she?" She glared at Tom. "Believe me. She's going to regret making an enemy of me." She waited for him to respond. "For fuck's sake, Tom, snap out of it."

His own temper flared. "Shut up, Willa," he spat at her.

"Oh, that's wonderful, Tom. Go ahead and blame me. In fact, blame *everyone* but yourself. You didn't have a hand in *any* of this, did you?"

A thick rope of muscle tensed in his neck. "Fifteen years I gave to that company and they throw me out like garbage."

Oh, great, thought Willa. *Here comes the self-pity.* She was many things but not one for tea and sympathy. She preferred to set out practical steps: a plan, solution, and execution. She fixed her gaze on him. "Tom, let's be sensible about this," she said more calmly. "I'll call Dad and—"

Tom cut in derisively. "That's your solution to everything, isn't it? Every tiny fucking problem, Miss Spoiled Little Rich Girl wants to run off to her daddy. Not everyone has that option, Willa."

She sneered. "God, I'm so sick of you saying that. Your parents live in Kent now for fuck's sake! Your dad's an estate agent. It's hardly the coal mines of Burnley."

He snapped back: "So why do you pretend that it *is*? Why do you joke to your friends that you're 'slumming it'?"

Willa faltered. When she and Tom first started dating, she and her friends did joke about it. *Willa's bit of rough,* they called him—and she rather enjoyed it. Tom wasn't a banker or barrister like her friends' partners, so instead of settling for something banal like an estate agent's son, she muddied some details to exoticize him. Clearly, she hadn't been subtle. Knowing this was true, Willa changed tack smoothly. "I'm sorry," she said tearily. She touched her belly. "I'm just worried how we'll cope with this little one coming."

Tom pushed a hand through his hair, splitting it into furrows. "I'll find something."

"But how? Everyone knows everyone in advertising."

"I'll find something," he insisted.

"But where, Tom? Didn't two thousand people apply for a job at fucking Costa Coffee?"

"I'll go and work in a warehouse if I have to."

She almost scoffed at this but knew not to wound him further. "Okay," she said, blinking back her tears before her skin got blotchy.

"But first," said Tom, "I'm going to deal with Salma Khatun."

"You'll get her to take down the video?"

"No," Tom said mildly. "The damage has already been done."

"Then what?"

He walked to the window and looked out, a faraway look in his eyes. "I'm going to teach her to respect this neighborhood."

ZAIN HEARD THE SOFT CLINK of knuckles on glass. He looked up and saw Jamie waiting outside. He would have seen the clip by now. Had he come for a showdown? Zain opened the balcony door and let him step inside. Jamie was wearing a thin T-shirt and shivering from the evening breeze. Neither of them spoke for a second, then Jamie gestured glumly.

"Dad lost his job today."

Zain hid his shock. "Does he get a payout or something?" he asked glibly.

"He wasn't made redundant, man. He was fired. Because of that video."

Zain tried to think of something appropriate. He hadn't known Jamie long enough to gauge what the boy was feeling. "I *had* to put it up, man," he said eventually.

Jamie studied his nails and carefully pressed down his cuticles. "Dad shouldn't've said what he said, but you didn't have to put it up, Zain. You know what can happen these days."

Zain was fazed and resented being made to feel that way. "What was I supposed to do?"

"Think about me?"

Zain blinked, surprised by Jamie's honesty. Back in Selborne Estate, no boy would ever have said this. The unexpected candor made him sting with guilt. "I'm sorry. I didn't want you to get caught up in this but I had to do it."

"Mum's completely stressed out. The vibe at home is . . . weird."

"Then you can come and hang here."

"My parents won't like it."

"Neither will mine but . . . " Zain shrugged. "We don't have to tell them, do we?"

"But what if they find out?"

"Then fuck 'em." Zain leaned toward him. "Listen, your parents don't own you, okay? I'm telling you: There's gonna be a day when you realize that your dad can do fuck all to you. He's got no power. He dreads the day you'll learn this, so I'm telling you: If you want to hang out here, he can't stop you. What's he gonna do? Lock you in?"

Jamie smiled weakly. "I wouldn't put it past him."

Zain couldn't detect whether he was serious. The possibility scared him, leading too quickly to somewhere too dark. "Then you kick down the door," he said, filled with bravado.

Jamie shifted unsurely.

"Come on, man. Sit down. We said they wouldn't mess with us." He motioned at his desk. "I'll get us some nachos and that shitty guacamole you like so much."

Jamie hesitated.

"Come on! We've got to get ready for our call with the fund!"

Jamie relented. He sat at the desk gingerly and spun the chair to face Zain. "Fuck 'em," he said and broke into a grin.

"Fuck 'em!" Zain repeated. He slapped his palm against Jamie's and smiled all the way to the kitchen.

BIL STUFFED THE SANDWICH INTO his bag, careful not to nick the foil. He added a flask of water and an overripe banana. He always ate the brownest ones so Salma wouldn't have to.

"Are you sure you don't want me to stay?" he said.

"Come on, Bil. You can't pull out now." There was an edge in Salma's voice, for she knew his offer was empty. Bil had been booked to cater a wedding on the Isle of Skye—a word-of-mouth referral from an old customer who used to frequent Jakoni's. Bil's fee was equivalent to three months of his new salary, and he'd had to beg for the leave. He couldn't back out now.

"Okay," he said glumly. "The upholsterers will be at Jakoni's this evening, so don't forget to let them in. Also, can you collect the box I taped up? Suli's nephew will pick it up next week." Bil reeled off a list of duties, pausing midway. "You will be okay, won't you?"

"Of course." She tried and failed to reassure him.

"Please don't worry, honey. What happened at Jakoni's was unrelated. I'm sure of it."

In a way, she hoped that it *had* been Tom, for it surely meant his anger was spent. If it really was unrelated, then Tom's revenge might still be waiting and she was sure it would be swift and strong. "Do you think I should speak to him?" she asked.

"No," said Bil vehemently. "I think you should stay away." He watched her closely. "Salma, *promise me*. I'll be back in two days. Please stay out of their way until then."

"I will," she promised. "Now go. You'll miss your train."

He kissed her firmly, then rushed out through the door, leaving her alone with Molly. The dog whined and Salma kneeled down to pet her.

"I know, sweetheart," she said softly. "But we'll be okay. I promise." She pressed her cheek against Molly's coat. "I've got to go but Zain will look after you."

Outside, she spotted it immediately. She walked closer, her breath thick in her lungs. Her car had a deep, silver key mark all the way down the left side. She circled the car and felt a hot rush of disbelief. It was all the way round: an intentional act of vandalism. She looked up and saw a curtain fall back into place on the first floor of Tom's house. Instinctively, she raised her middle finger.

"Salma?" The voice behind her made her jump.

She turned around, forming a fist to hide what she'd just done.

Linda looked at her with befuddlement, then glanced at Tom's window. "Is everything okay?" There was an edge in her tone, making it clear that she had seen the gesture.

Salma didn't have the energy to be friendly. Instead, she just pointed at her car.

Linda gasped and clutched the zipper of her jacket, scrunching it in her fist. "Oh dear," she said. Slowly, she too circled the car, muttering with sympathy. But then she paused abruptly. "Wait, you can't possibly think that . . ." She looked up at Tom's window, her brows knit in doubt.

"Honestly? I don't know what to think."

Linda studied Tom's house for a moment. "No," she said officiously, as if she had divined the truth. "This isn't Tom. I know he's angry about his job, but he just wouldn't do this."

Salma tensed. "His job?"

Linda feigned distress, but her face betrayed her pleasure at being the one to reveal the news. "Haven't you heard? Tom lost his job yesterday."

Fresh dread dawned on Salma. If Tom had been angered by a simple banner, how livid would he be now?

"I saw him yesterday," said Linda. "And he said that he'd been sacked over the video." There was unmistakable blame in her tone.

"Yesterday?" Salma's thoughts wheeled in her head. "What time?"

"Around noon. Why?"

Noon. Which meant that Tom *could* have gone to the restaurant. "Did you see him come and go at any point?"

"Why?" Linda wouldn't reveal any more unless she got an answer.

Salma knew not to say too much. "I just wondered when this happened." She gestured at the car.

Linda tutted. "Honestly, Salma, I really don't think this was him. I've known Tom for a long time and there's never been any trouble of this sort. It might be those thugs from Abbey Estate. They're the only ones who cause issues around here."

"Okay, thank you, Linda." Salma was done with this conversation. She looked at her car, thoroughly dispirited. She couldn't afford to fix the scratch, which meant she would drive around marked like a scarlet woman.

"If you'd like, I could host a mediation session? I'm a trained counselor," said Linda.

Salma smiled politely. "Thank you, but I think we're all right for now." She glanced at her watch and used it to excuse herself, leaving Linda midflow. As she walked off, she saw Tom's curtain move again. This time, it was obvious, as if *designed* to signal that Salma was being watched.

CHAPTER 6

S alma drummed the handle of her cart and tried hard to relax. The supermarket was neutral ground, a safe distance from Blenheim. Over the last two days, she had been on high alert around anyone who looked like Tom: the man leaving Timpson on the high street wearing an orange cap, the broad-shouldered jogger by Fairlop Waters who ran past her and Molly, the muscular commuter on the 169 who took her favorite seat. She was grateful that Bil would be back today.

She skirted up and down the aisles, collecting the favorite things of the two men in her life: Pop-Tarts for Bil, who hadn't yet outgrown them; honeyed cashews for Zain, who ate them all day, and a large bag of nachos, which seemed to disappear at an alarming rate. She paused in the coffee aisle and dithered over a deal, eventually choosing the cheaper product. Bil used to laugh at her for doing this—a habit from her childhood—but lately it had become a necessity. His pay packet from the wedding had bought them some time but it wouldn't last for long. They *had* to sell Jakoni's.

Outside, as she loaded her bags in the boot, she heard her phone vibrate. She answered and listened as pressure rose in her chest. She dove into the car and zoomed off, letting the ice cream melt. Nearing Jakoni's, she parked on a side street, barely remembering to lock her car before rushing to the restaurant. Bil was already outside and though he pulled her into his arms, they were both too preoccupied for a proper reunion.

"Have you been upstairs?" she asked.

"I'm waiting for Stu."

At that moment, Stu, their twenty-something estate agent, exited the building. A sheen of sweat slicked his forehead and a lock of hair had escaped the gel that sculpted it in place. He cracked his knuckles in a nervous tic. Seeing his distress, Salma felt her own panic swell.

"Are they leaving?" she asked.

Stu shook his head, a pinkish color rising in his cheeks.

"Did you speak to them? What did they say?"

He rubbed his sparse stubble, inexperience turning him mute.

"Stu!" she cried.

"They're not leaving. They say they have a right to be there."

"And do they?"

He pulled out his phone and began to search on Google. Salma watched, mortified. They had chosen Stu because of his cut-price fees compared with the nearby Keatons. She could see now that they had made a mistake. He squinted at his screen. "It says here that squatting in a nonresidential building is legal."

"So what do we do?"

"I guess you could call the police."

"You 'guess'?" Salma wanted to shake him. "But what do you advise?"

Bil stepped in. "Should I go up and talk to them?"

Stu lifted a shoulder. "I mean, you could try."

Salma could see that Stu would not be helpful. Perhaps she

and Bil would do a better job of talking to them, whoever *they* were.

Stu shifted from one foot to the other. "I've got another appointment. I've already stayed here longer than I should have."

Salma exhaled. "Okay, fine, Stu. You go ahead and get on with your day."

If he caught her sarcasm, he did not show it. "Good luck," he told them and hurried away.

Bil and Salma looked at each other. "I'm going to go up. You stay here," he told her.

"No," she said firmly. "I'm coming."

"Okay, but stay back, would you? Stu seemed pretty rattled up there." He stepped into the building and Salma followed gingerly. They moved quietly up the stairs and paused at the sound of voices shouting over music. They advanced slowly and stopped at the landing. Salma could feel the beat of her heart as Bil reached out and turned the doorknob.

Almost immediately, the door flew open and a boy, or young man, confronted them. He was gaunt with bony features stippled with acne and was talking on the phone. Salma noticed that it was an old Nokia with two stickers on the back: a marijuana leaf above a glittery skull and crossbones. The boy hung up and glared at them.

"What do you want?"

Bil cleared his throat. "You're in my property," he said.

The boy grinned, revealing bad teeth. "Says who?"

"Says me."

He scoffed. "This is *my* property now." He tried to close the door but Bil held it open. "Man, get the fuck out of here!" said the boy. He threw his weight behind the door but Bil forced it open. Salma hung back but could see that the walls were covered with graffiti in the same garish colors she had blamed on Tom. She realized that he might have been right all along; these boys were the ones targeting her home. *You love playing the victim,* Tom had told her. What if she'd misread it all?

"Oi, Rich, what's going on?" called a voice from the kitchen.

"Get in here!" the gaunt boy, Rich, called back. Two others filed in and spotted Bil at the door, Salma waiting behind him.

"Can you get out of my restaurant?" said Bil. To the casual observer, it wasn't visible but Salma could see that he was nervous. It was in the way he smoothed his shirt and how his lips tensed and relaxed repeatedly. She wanted desperately to protect him, to step between him and the men.

Emboldened by his friends, Rich squared up to Bil. "What're you gonna do, old man?"

"I'll call the police."

Rich laughed. "What if I break your fingers? What will you call them with?"

Salma held her breath. She had seen plenty of young male bravado in her job but this was something else. This young man was spoiling for a fight. She reached for Bil but Rich got there first. He grabbed his lapels and pushed him against the doorframe. Bil was caught by surprise, and when Rich raised a fist, Bil instinctively flinched.

Rich aborted the punch inches away from Bil's nose and burst into laughter. His friends joined in behind him. "Look at this pussy," he said. "Walking in here acting like the big man." He spat and the glob landed next to Bil's ear. "Get the fuck out of my house, man." He shoved him out.

Bil stumbled and Salma grabbed him to stop him from falling. She pulled him down the stairs, trembling with fear and rage. Bil was shaking too and it broke her heart to see the look in his eyes: shame.

"It's okay," she said and cupped his chin. "It's okay. We'll go to the police. Let's just get out for now." She pulled him outside, back toward their car, but Bil shook her off. He leaned on a wall to catch his breath.

"We shouldn't have moved, Salma."

She nodded, but underneath, she felt a pulse of hostility. She was the one who had pushed for the move and Bil's overt regret felt like a rebuke. She wanted to defend herself but she and Bil were a team, and right now, they needed unity. "Are you okay?" she asked instead.

He smoothed his rumpled collar. "I'm fine."

"Are you hurt?"

"No. They were just kids." He shook his head, blasé, but then why couldn't he meet her gaze?

"They weren't 'just kids,' Bil. That was horrific."

"Look, it's nothing I haven't dealt with before."

Salma fell quiet. Sometimes she forgot what life had been like for Bil. People often assumed that Salma had the tougher childhood, growing up in Ilford. In truth, she had grown up among her own people, which lent her a sense of security. Bil, on the other hand, had grown up in a town in Hampshire—a far tougher experience. He liked to tell a story, which Salma knew was half a lie.

When they first moved to Hampshire, it went, their neighbor gave them a bottle of wine. Bil's dad, Hussain, reciprocated with a box of chocolates. For the next few years, they exchanged those same gifts at Christmas and thanked each other warmly. A decade later, the neighbor discovered that Hussain didn't drink, and Hussain learned that the neighbor was vegan! Here,

Bil's audience would invariably break into laughter. He would slap his thigh and declare it *the most British thing I've ever seen!* That was the story Bil liked to tell his liberal middle-class white friends. The truth, Salma knew, was somewhat different.

Soon after they moved, Hussain came home one day armed with six boxes of chocolates. He recruited his young son, Bil, and off they went to say hello to their neighbors. The first, a middle-aged woman who lived opposite, looked at the proffered box and politely said *no thank you.* She shut the door, leaving Hussain on the doorstep, awkwardly clutching the chocolates. The other neighbors accepted the gift, but a week later, Hussain saw the chocolates in the communal bin, each box left unopened. Bil's family essentially lived in isolation until, years later, Hussain had a stroke and they moved back to London for better support. It wasn't quite the tale that Bil shared with his friends. Salma knew that he even hid details from her: verbal abuse retold as jokes, threats recast as harmless. She never could tell if he downplayed the gravity for his own sake or for others'.

She watched him now, picturing how hard he had flinched when that boy feinted a punch. "We have options," she told him. "The police. The courts. Bailiffs." She pulled him into a fierce hug. "Please don't worry."

"I'm not worried," he said and his voice was so assured that Salma almost believed it.

WILLA LOVED TELLING THE STORY of how she and Tom met, partly because it was funny but mostly because it made her look good without overtly bragging. She was one month into her residency and finding her way as an artist. She would sit in the gallery for hours and observe people engaging with the art. She imagined herself recalling this to journalists later, at the height of her fame. *Oh, my early stuff was so derivative,* she would say. *No, no, it is true. I used to go to museums and galleries and literally watch what people enjoyed.*

It was on one such occasion that a group of men walked into the room. At first, she thought they were rugby players—all of them strong and stocky—but inferred from their banter that they worked in a warehouse. As they talked, Willa grew annoyed that none of them had noticed her. She was used to being the most beautiful thing in the room. The hubris of that thought never occurred to her as she sat there in a gallery. She was satisfied when, slowly, a hush crept through the group as, one by one, they noticed the girl perched in the corner with a sketch pad on her knees. The hush broke into jeers and teasing, the men splaying their feathers. She noticed that they suffered somewhat from the "cheerleader effect," each appearing attractive in a group, but not individually. One, however, did stand out: Tom.

They locked eyes briefly and she haughtily looked away but that was all the encouragement he needed. He contrived a debate with his colleagues and then called her over to adjudicate.

"Excuse me," he said. "You look like a cultured woman."

She smiled tightly.

"Do you mind settling a debate for us?"

She sighed, set down her pad, and walked over, tipping her chin up just a little to present her best angle to them. She felt their eyes slide over her and enjoyed the feeling of power. She put one hand on her hip. "What can I help you boys with?" she asked, playing along.

"Okay, settle this for us . . ." He tilted his head by way of asking her name.

"Willa."

"Willa!" he repeated, clicking his fingers as if it had been on the tip of his tongue. "Hi, Willa. I'm Tom." He pointed at a canvas. "Tell me: Is this worth six thousand pounds?"

She puckered her lips and studied it. It was a large unframed oil painting on a rectangular canvas. The base color was a bubblegum pink, overlaid with a square in baby blue—a Barbie-doll version of Rothko. "Well, it depends on what you value in life."

Tom narrowed his eyes. "Okay, based on what *you* value in life, is this worth six thousand pounds?"

She looked at it again. "Based on what *I* value, yes, that is worth six thousand pounds."

Tom's friends jeered at him, loud and cheerful after winning the bet.

"But it's so . . . pedestrian," he said. "And yet it qualifies as high art because some fusty curator says so. You wouldn't see a James Gillray or Herblock here, despite their art taking so much more thought."

If Willa had known that these were cartoonists, she might have scoffed at Tom. Instead, she said nothing, fearful of revealing her ignorance.

"This in comparison is just . . ." Tom made a jabbing motion. "But the guy who did it is laughing because he's six thousand quid up. This guy, this"—he paused to read the artist's name—"Willa Calthorpe." He froze. "Oh god, it's not you, is it?"

Her lips curled regretfully. "I'm afraid so."

A roar of laughter went up in the room. Someone slapped Tom's back, making him judder a little. He covered his face and groaned.

Willa melted into a smile and then laughter. "It's my first painting in the gallery and it went up ten minutes ago."

"Oh god." Tom squeezed his eyes shut. "I was only trying to impress you. I actually like the fucking thing!"

"You don't have to say that."

He looked at her imploringly. "Can I make it up to you with a drink?" Jeers went up behind him.

Willa shrugged, carried away on the mood. "Okay," she said lightly, inciting cries of disbelief.

"Willa, if I tell you it's shit, will you have a drink with me too?" said one of Tom's friends. He dropped to his knees and pressed his palms together in prayer—or at least that's what Willa told her friends. There was indeed some jeering but Tom extracted her quickly and whisked her away to a nearby bar. She told him about her piece in the gallery, but left out the fact that her father knew the curator. It's not like he'd engineer her entire career. This was her foot in the door. Everything else she would do herself.

She enjoyed Tom's awe of her. Being near him stirred something inside her and she thought, *Why not? I'll play with you for a while.* They went home together that night to her flat in Camden. She disliked the boho vibe of the area, but it suited her image as an artist. Tom was a little unsure at first, fumbling with her expensive bra as the clips eluded his fingers. He maneuvered her gently, as if she were a delicate thing. When he realized, however, that she preferred aggression, he touched her with more confidence. It's true that she gave him plenty of cues but that first time with Tom lit something inside her. This man—this strong, confident, earnest brute—was so different from the men she knew who were always braying insincerely about one thing or another. If anything, Tom was *too* sincere—unable to shake off a slight or sarcasm with the same ease as she.

There were teething problems. Tom hated her friends and she looked down on his, but the two of them had something key: They enjoyed spending time together. Whether it was physical, or listening to stories about his childhood, Willa liked being with him. She and her friends often spoke about the "holy trinity": looks, charm, and money. They all agreed that two out of three were essential in a future mate. Willa, who had never worried about money, put looks and charm first, so when Tom came along with his meager savings, she didn't have cause to worry. Naturally, her parents disapproved, but in the end, the decision was sealed. Five months after meeting Tom, Willa found out she was pregnant.

She was surprised by her own reaction. Usually so cool and rational, she found herself gorged with emotion. The pregnancy unlocked a chamber inside her, a place of dewy tenderness. It changed Willa's sense of herself so profoundly that she cast about for a new one. For months, she played the *artistic earth mother*, but didn't have the patience. She bagged up those ugly flowing things and threw them in the bin, keen to destroy the evidence. Then Jamie came early and those first few months of motherhood changed the weight of gravity: each step, each act, each *breath*, taking twice the effort. But, slowly, she regained balance and her love for Jamie grew fierce, just as the propaganda had said. Now she had to prepare to do it all again. She stubbed her cigarette on the garden fence and headed back inside.

Jamie was in the kitchen and Willa asked if he wanted some cookies. He rolled his eyes but his smile betrayed him. When he was younger, they would curl up on the sofa together with misshapen cookies and warm milk, and just spend time together.

Willa knew that she wasn't a perfect mother, but that her teenage son still enjoyed spending time with her surely earned her credit.

She set out the milk and cookies and beckoned Jamie to the sofa. "How are you feeling about having a little brother or sister?"

He mulled the question over. "I mean, it's going to be weird."

"And?"

"And nothing. It'll be nice, I guess. Kind of like when we got Lola."

Willa laughed. "Oh, believe me. It's nothing like having a dog. You were a little terror."

Jamie looked at her ruefully. "Did you ever wish I was . . . normal?"

Willa slid an arm around his waist. "I wouldn't change a thing about you." She kissed his head. "Would *you*?"

He shrugged. "I mean, yeah."

Willa stilled. "You would?"

"Yeah, of course." He noted her surprise. "Why? Is that weird?"

"No, I just thought you were happy with the way things are."

"I am but I was telling someone about this the other day. I don't see my deafness as an identity. It's just a thing about me. If I could click my fingers and have perfect hearing, of course I would. Wouldn't you want that for me?"

Willa considered this. "No," she said, realizing the answer was true. She really wouldn't change a thing about Jamie. He was a sweet, soulful boy and she was certain that this was thanks to his hearing.

"That's weird," he said.

"It's not weird. I love *you. You're* my son. If you were fully hearing, you'd be someone else."

A corner of his lips lifted. "Don't be soppy, Mum."

She didn't respond, just wrapped him in her arms and fiercely kissed his cheek. He let her hold him for a moment before pulling away. With a socked toe, Willa moved her glass of milk closer. Laughing, Jamie handed it over to her. When their fingers touched, Willa realized that despite everything—her thwarted ambitions and enviable friends—she was actually happy, here with Jamie and Tom.

"MISS, IS IT TRUE?" RITESH'S voice rose above the din.

"Is what true?" asked Salma.

Ritesh jabbed his pencil against his textbook. "The saber-toothed tiger. Is it true it's called a Smilodon?"

"Yes. And guess what? The scimitar-toothed cat, which is very similar, used to live in Essex."

"No way." Ritesh turned to a girl called Bina. "Oi, Beens, do you get them down your ways?"

The class erupted in laughter, but Salma's mood hung low. She had been distracted all day, her thoughts pulling back to the squatters. She and Bil had gone to the police straightaway yesterday. She could pinpoint the very moment that she lost the officer's sympathy. *Your second property?* he said, freighted with distaste. Salma babbled in an effort to win his solidarity. *Yes, but we're being forced to sell it. We can't afford to keep it.* She explained that she was a teacher and that they had been forced to move after their son got in trouble, but it did little to shift his sympathies. When he told her that they would visit the site "in time," she knew she was a low priority. Of course, squatting wasn't violent, but it was still an intimate crime. Strangers had taken root in a space that belonged to her, a space that Bil had cherished for years. To be dismissed with a vague promise of an update filled her with unease. She could feel the screw turning. If they couldn't get the squatters out, they couldn't sell the property and would surely plunge into bankruptcy. They had twenty-eight days to resolve this.

Can't you borrow some money off your parents? her colleague Rebecca had asked earlier. *No*, she'd replied simply, not explaining that even if they were still around, it didn't work like that in her culture. In fact, grown-up children gave money to their parents, not the other way round. In her circle of friends, one had paid for his mother's stove; another gave his parents two hundred pounds ahead of a visit to Bangladesh; a third paid her father's utility bills. That was the way it worked. If she and Bil got into serious trouble, no one could bail them out.

The bell signaled the end of the day and a gloom settled on Salma. Debt was an awful thing. It was always there like a noose, heavy on your neck. Sometimes, when you grew distracted, it would cruelly tighten to never let you forget. She waited for the last of her pupils to leave, then gathered her things and headed to Blenheim.

When she turned in to their street, she was surprised to find Zain out on their lawn. Her heartbeat snared when she saw his face. "Zain?"

He looked up and burst into tears. "Mum, she's gone."

She followed his gaze instinctively. "Who?"

"Molly. I can't find her."

Panic strummed inside her. For a sick moment, she pictured Molly bleeding on a deserted byway. Their sweet and skittish dog was out there alone. "When did you last see her?" She clamped his shoulders when he didn't speak and gave him a little shake. "Zain, look at me. Listen to me. When did you last see her?"

He batted at his tears. "I took her for a walk and then she

came upstairs. I was due to stream on Twitch and she was getting under the rollers of my chair, so I sent her downstairs."

"And then?"

"And then I came down and couldn't find her."

"What time?"

"I don't know, about an hour ago."

Salma strode into the house. "Molly?" she called. "Molly!"

"Mum, don't you think I've tried that?" His voice trembled and it broke her heart to hear it.

"Have you checked all the corners? The laundry bin? Under the sink? The washing machine?"

"I've looked everywhere."

Salma proceeded to search the house, Zain closely in tow. "Have you called your dad? Maybe he has her?"

"No, why would he randomly come home and just take her?"

Salma tested the garden door and found that it was open. "Was this ajar?"

Zain waved a hand helplessly. "I don't know. I think I opened it when I was looking for her."

"Are you sure?"

"No, Mum, I'm not sure!"

Salma walked out to the garden and peeked under trees and bushes. "Molly!" she called, hearing her own voice tremble. "Do you think she was stolen?"

He gripped a tuft of his hair. "She's an old mutt. She wouldn't be worth anything."

"Was the front door open? Could she have wandered off?" Salma walked back through the house to check the front garden.

"No," cried Zain. "I shouldn't have sent her downstairs."

"She must be somewhere."

"But where? How could she just disappear?" Panic changed his features, pinched them sharp and mean.

"Everything okay?" a voice asked behind them. Linda stood on the curb and Zain turned away from her, embarrassed by his tears.

"Our dog, Molly, is missing," Salma told her.

Linda clucked with sympathy. "Oh dear. I'm so sorry to hear that. When did it happen?"

"In the last hour. Did you happen to see anything?"

"I'm afraid not." Linda took out her phone. "But I can ask the neighborhood WhatsApp group."

Salma blinked. She didn't know there was a neighborhood group. "Please could you?" She sent her a picture of Molly and watched her send it on. From the corner of her eye, she thought she saw movement at Tom's window. A thought struck her. "Could she have got into next door's garden?"

"I can't see how that would happen," said Linda.

Salma began to fret. "There's a loose board in the fence. We've been meaning to fix it. I didn't think Molly could fit through." She looked at Linda imploringly. "Do you think you could ask him?"

"He's in the WhatsApp group," said Linda.

"No, I mean knock on his door and ask him for me. Things are still tense between us."

A crease of irritation lined Linda's forehead. "Well, that's just childish, Salma. If you have a question to ask him, you need to ask him yourself. Tom is a perfectly nice man. You just got off on the wrong foot." She nodded at his house. "Honestly, just go and talk to him."

Salma drew back. She hadn't seen Tom since he'd lost his job and though she now knew that he wasn't responsible for the damage to the restaurant, she still feared his mood. "If he has seen Molly, he will say so in the WhatsApp, won't he?"

Linda sighed. She had clearly decided that Salma was being dramatic. "Of course he will." She tutted. "Look, if I see him, I'll ask him directly. How about that?"

Salma flushed with gratitude. "Thank you, Linda. I'd appreciate that so much." Back in the house, she found Zain pacing the living room. He was scrolling through social media, searching different hashtags for recovering lost pets and puppies.

"I'm sorry," he said, still pacing. "I should have taken care of her."

"It's okay. We'll find her."

"What if she's dead?"

"Don't say that."

"What if she got run over? What if she's lying injured somewhere?" His voice was frayed with anxiety.

Salma put an around him. "We'll find her," she promised, stamping down her own panic.

ZAIN'S MUSCLES ACHED AS HE eased into his chair. He had spent the whole evening searching for Molly, combing lanes and byways. Technically, Molly was his mother's dog but it was Zain whom she truly loved. She sidled up to him at every opportunity and nestled by his desk for hours. Zain was an only child and Molly was a stand-in sibling, the two of them navigating highs and lows. In a way, they were of a similar temperament: social and outgoing but frequently needing space. At family gatherings, they would escape to a cool corner of the house to sit and take a minute. It killed him to know that he had sent her away and snapped when she hadn't listened. Where could she have gone?

A clink on the glass distracted him. He looked up to find Jamie waiting and hurried over to let him in. The younger boy puffed out his chest triumphantly, hands on his hips like Superman.

"Guess what?" he said, excited.

"You found her?" said Zain, breathless with hope.

"Found who?"

"Molly!" Zain saw his confusion and felt his hopes deflate. "She's gone missing," he explained. He recounted the events of the evening and was touched to see that Jamie was teary. In the mere weeks they had known each other, he too had built a bond with Molly.

"We'll find her, mate. Don't worry." Jamie looked conflicted. "I do have some news to tell you." He shifted unsurely. "We won the funding."

Zain stared at him. "We what?"

Jamie couldn't hold back and broke into a grin. "We won."

"We won?" Zain shot to his feet. "We fucking won?"

"We won!"

"Oh my god." Zain covered his mouth. "You're not fucking with me?"

"No."

"Oh my god!" They embraced instinctively, overwhelmed with shock. They had just won thirty thousand pounds of funding.

Jamie gave him a shy smile. "Thanks, man. I couldn't have done it without you." He exhaled sharply. "The first half hits my account tomorrow. We'll get the second half once we up-load a working demo. The deadline's in three weeks."

"I can finally buy a new laptop," yelled Zain. An idea oc-curred to him. "Hey, maybe we could offer a reward for Molly? Like a thousand quid or something? If someone has her or has seen her, that would encourage them."

Jamie's face fell. "Um, we can't do that, can we?"

"Why not?"

"Well . . ." Jamie hesitated. "Because we submitted a budget. It all has to be accounted for."

Zain frowned. "Yeah, but it's our money now. We can spend it where we need to."

"But not on personal things."

"Who's gonna know?"

"Come on, man," Jamie said with a little laugh.

The air left the room. "Come on what?"

"We can't do that."

"Can't or won't?" said Zain.

"Can't."

Zain stared at him. "Okay, maybe just five hundred then."

"It's not the amount." Jamie fiddled with the button on his cuff. "You've read the terms and conditions. We have to account for how the money is spent."

"Yeah, but they give us some leeway."

"Not for spending on a dog!"

"She's not just a dog. She's . . ." Zain stopped, embarrassed by the sudden high pitch of his voice. "It's just five hundred quid, man."

"Maybe it could be a loan and you could pay it back?"

"A *loan* That's my money too."

"It's Grapevine's money."

Zain realized that they hadn't made things official. All their agreements were verbal and Jamie had all the money. They had named him as the principal founder because he was the deaf one. "It's a bit weird that all of it's in your account," said Zain. "Shouldn't we split it?"

Jamie was uncomfortable now. "I mean, we can leave it in my account and then we agree on all the expenses and stuff."

"Why are you being like this?"

"Like what?"

"This whole application was my idea and now you're acting like you're in charge."

"I'm not. I just want us to be careful with it. We can't just spend it on dogs and shit."

Dogs and shit? Zain felt his blood heat. "Why are you being a cunt about this?" He bared his teeth meanly. "Just fuck off, Jamie."

The boy stood there, not saying anything.

Zain was unable to deal with his anger and shoved Jamie's shoulder. "I said: Fuck off." When Jamie still didn't speak, Zain snarled at him: "What? Are you dumb as well as deaf?"

Jamie's face cracked with hurt. For a beat, neither of them moved or spoke. Then Jamie nodded and mutely turned and left. Zain clung to his temper, knowing if he let it waver, it would cave right into shame.

Zain had heard it said that the bullied became bullies, but this wasn't always true. You could have a perfectly lovely childhood and still behave disgracefully. He had learned this from experience, at the end of primary school when he was ten years old. Zain's friend Raj had invited him to his home: a flat with his mum, dad, and three siblings crammed into a tiny space. The living area had been fashioned into a makeshift bedroom and Zain remembered that Raj's mother placed them in the "machine room," a store cupboard with a giant Brother sewing machine. He and Raj squeezed onto folding chairs and ate their rice off the sewing machine, using it as a table. At school, for a reason he couldn't remember, Zain had taunted his friend. *Oh yeah, and when I went to his house, his mum made us eat off their sewing machine!* The kids in the class were equal parts scandalized and amused. They built upon the taunt, guffawing at Raj's trousers for being an inch too short. When Zain saw the look in his eye—humiliation and betrayal—shame turned over in his gut, but he knew it was too far gone, a genie out of its bottle. For the rest of the year, Raj was teased mercilessly: in PE for his threadbare socks, the heels near translucent; at the track on sports day for running in his school shoes.

It was a relief when, at secondary, they went to separate schools. It was a chance for both of them to reinvent themselves. Years later, Zain ran into Raj at Westfield. They locked eyes on the top-floor concourse and Zain wasn't sure if he should say anything but Raj approached him first. His old friend had got into a grammar school and Zain was relieved, but also surprised, to see his newfound confidence. They spoke for a while, swapping stories about their studies, and throughout it all, Zain groped for the courage to say the words *Hey, man, I'm sorry about what happened back in the day.* Or *I'm sorry about what I did.* Or *I don't know if you remember Year 5? I know I was a little shit.* But the words got stuck in his throat.

Raj lingered for a moment, knowing he was owed an apology, but Zain simply held out his hand, smacked it into Raj's, and shook it firmly. *It was good to see you, man.* Raj nodded stiffly and said, *Yeah, you too.* They parted ways and Zain's burning shame never again let him stand by and watch a peer be bullied. The impulse drew him into scrapes and fistfights and through this specific violence, Zain paid his repentance. He had thought himself reformed, but the fact that this old instinct—to harm someone weaker than him—had come back so naturally made him pulse with shame. *Are you dumb as well as deaf?* What rotten thing inside had made him ask such a thing?

SALMA STOOD ON HER LAWN and watched the potbellied man on the ladder. Fred had a mustache like a Texan cowboy and wore suspiciously clean overalls. He dabbed his brow with a handkerchief and carefully climbed back down. He drained his glass of lemonade and propped it on the window ledge.

"Thank you. That was lovely," he said, wiping his mouth with the back of his hand. "Make sure you keep that booklet over there. Any problems, just call the number on the back."

"Thank you." She gestured toward the house. "If you need the bathroom before you go, it's on the second floor."

"I'm all right, but thank you," said Fred as he finished loading the van.

Bil often teased Salma for offering their bathroom to tradespeople *with all the zeal of a pervert*, but she did it regardless. A plumber cousin had told her once how hard it was to find a commode, so she always made a point to ask. Whenever they said yes, she would glance at Bil and smugly raise a brow.

She waved her thanks to Fred, then picked up his glass and walked inside. Next to the sink was a pile of dishes that Zain had used at breakfast. Normally, she would call him down, but he was in a state about Molly.

She was just about to run the water when she heard a rap on the door. She spotted the orange cap through the window and felt her stomach drop. Tom was waiting outside. She braced herself and opened the door.

"What the hell do you think you're doing?" he said, pointing at the security camera that Fred had just installed. "You can't do that."

"Of course I can," she said, laughing a little to show he was being ridiculous.

"Will you be filming beyond the bounds of your property?"

It occurred to Salma that she hadn't checked this.

Tom caught her hesitance. "You can't do that, so point that fucking thing elsewhere."

"Can you not swear at me, Tom?"

"What the fuck are you trying to do? Film my every move so you can put it up on Twitter? Don't you dare point that thing at my house."

"I'm not pointing it *at* your house. I'm pointing it at my lawn."

"And recording parts of my house."

Salma spoke calmly. "My family have been targeted. I have every right to protect my home."

"Targeted?" He sniggered. "It was one measly banner, you bint, and you shell out a thousand pounds as if you're under siege?"

"It's not just a banner though, is it, Tom? It's the paint on my window, my scratched-up car, my stolen dog."

He looked at her with venom. "So wait, I've stolen your dog now? Is that the story you're peddling?"

"Look, I understand you're frustrated and I'm sorry that you lost your job, but—"

"Sorry!" he cut in, loud and bitter. "Is that right?"

"I didn't plan to upload that video. It was a misunderstanding."

"You knew exactly what you were doing," he said. "You *knew* the wokerati would come for me."

"That's not true."

"I've worked at Sartre for fifteen years and I say *one* thing wrong and I'm"—he clicked his fingers—"gone." Anger leaked from his breath. "I shouldn't have removed your banner—I admit that—but everything that came after? That's on you." He pointed at her face. "You don't know me. You don't know who I am. You just made presumptions based on what you see."

Salma was about to speak but another voice cut in.

"Everything all right here?"

For once, she was relieved to see Linda.

"Linda, I'm glad you're here," said Tom, sweeping up to her side and drawing her closer by the arm. "Salma here and I are having a bit of a debate." He nodded at the security camera, which, now that Salma looked at it, did look somewhat obtrusive. "She's installed a camera that films part of our lawn and I'm asking her to repoint it so it's off my property. That's reasonable, isn't it?"

Linda frowned at the camera, then looked over to Salma. "Do you really think it's necessary? This is a nice street."

"A nice street?" echoed Salma. "You saw what happened to my car this week."

Linda tilted her head. "Yes, that's true, but this seems excessive. It signals something about the street, doesn't it? I wouldn't want it to say the wrong thing. It's a bit like having bars on your windows. It degrades the neighborhood." She smiled at Salma kindly. "You really don't have to feel unsafe here."

Salma looked from one to the other, as if stuck in a farcical comedy: the straight man to two absurdists. "I would just feel safer with it here."

Linda held out her palms. "Well, who am I to argue? Was there a white one by any chance? This one seems so"—she wrinkled her nose—"noticeable."

Salma was at a genuine loss. "I . . . They were out of stock."

Linda gave a rueful flourish. "I do wish you had waited. It's a shame to do that to a pretty street, but if it makes you feel safer, then who am I to argue?" She gave Tom a meaningful look.

He saw that Salma caught it and smiled at her smugly. She looked from one to the other, not knowing what to say. The silence became uncomfortable until, finally, she compromised. "I'll speak to the supplier and ask them to narrow the field of vision."

Linda's face grew pinched, clearly displeased that Salma hadn't yielded fully. "Well, I can see I'm not making a difference," she said. "I might as well get on with my day." She nodded at Tom and headed off.

Salma locked eyes with him, maddened by his arrogance. She was tired of being bullied and wanted to strike back at him. "Maybe Linda's right," she said. "Maybe I *don't* need the camera. You and Willa will keep an eye on the street, won't you, now that you're unemployed?" Before he could respond, Salma coolly closed the door, quite unable to believe how delicious it felt to be cruel.

CHAPTER 7

Willa had dithered over what to wear ahead of her lunch with friends. She had settled on a pair of jeans and a loose white shirt from Eudon Choi that she had preserved immaculately. Her baby bump wasn't yet showing, but something light and floaty suited the occasion. Her friends had two kids each and Willa was aggrieved that she was the one who was out of sync. She had had Jamie far too early and this one far too late. One bonus, she supposed, was that her children would not compete with her friends' children, which wasn't true for the others.

Sophia was the first to arrive and Willa tipped up her cheek to greet her. Sato and Amelia followed soon after. Willa was pleased to see that they looked well, but not *too* well. This way, she could pretend that she was keeping pace with them. In some ways, not being able to afford Botox and fillers worked to Willa's advantage. Her friends had started to look a little "stretched" and she wasn't sure if she should tell them. She insisted that she preferred to age naturally, but if she had the funds, she knew she wouldn't resist.

Sato clipped her Aspinal handbag hook onto the edge of the table and used it to hang her Kate Spade. Willa and Sophia exchanged a look. Sato was always over the top. Others found her overbearing but she played an important role in their group. An implant from New York, she was the most direct of them. Without her, they might have tiptoed around their next subject for weeks.

"I heard about Tom," she said to Willa. "What happened?" She stressed the second word, leaning on it for empathy.

Willa gestured outward. "He said something idiotic and our neighbor's kid, the little brat, filmed it and put it online."

"What did he *say*?"

Willa rolled her eyes. "Come on, Sato, as if you haven't seen it."

Sato gave her a sporting smile. "Okay, yeah, I've seen it." She lifted a shoulder. "It really was idiotic of him."

"I don't know what the big deal is," said Amelia. She pulled a nail along the tablecloth, her ropy veins flexing with the motion. "Why do we clutch our pearls over this? We all have an opinion on who we *do* and *do not* want to live next door to, but god forbid we ever acknowledge this."

"Not all of us," said Sophia.

Amelia scoffed. "Yeah, right. You seriously don't have an opinion on who you'd like to live next door to?"

"I mean, I don't want to live next to criminals or twenty-four-hour party people, but beyond that, no."

"Sure you don't."

Sato cut in. "So what's Tom doing now then?"

Willa sighed theatrically. "Moping about at home."

"He's getting paid though, right?"

"No." Willa noticed her friends tense and moved quickly to appease them. "But we're fine obviously. In fact"—she paused dramatically—"we're having another baby."

Sato's face lit up. "Seriously?"

"Positive. The doctor has confirmed it."

Her friends erupted with joy and Willa ducked, embarrassed by the noise. "All right, let's not get so worked up about it. All I did was spread my legs."

Amelia wrinkled her pert nose. "Don't be so crass, Willa."

Sato laughed. "Don't be such a prude, Amelia." The two of them swapped a sour look, but their sparring was good-natured, a basic component of their enduring friendship.

Sophia kissed Willa's cheek. "I'm so happy for you. Darling Jamie must be delighted."

Willa flushed with pleasure. Her friends were sometimes judgmental but they absolutely adored Jamie. "I'm a bit scared, to be honest."

"Scared? Why?"

"It's just been so long and we went through so much when Jamie was premature. I'm too old to do that all again."

"It'll come back to you. Trust me."

Willa nodded unsurely. "I hope so."

"So—names!" declared Sato, bored of Willa's worries.

"It's much too early for names."

"You must have some ideas."

Willa hesitated. "Well, I do love the name Gaia if it's a girl."

Sato grimaced. "It's so . . . uncommon."

"You're called Sato!"

"Wanky parents. What can I say? Do you want your kid to say the same about you?"

Sophia cut in. "I think it's a beautiful name."

"Thank you," said Willa, aiming it tartly at Sato.

"If she's anything like you, she'll be stunning," said Sophia.

Willa felt unexpectedly emotional at the thought of her friends meeting Gaia.

Sato sighed when she noticed. "It's one of life's most vicious cruelties," she said, "that you can't drink when you need it most." She beckoned the waiter over. "Your largest slice of chocolate cake for this young lady over here, please, sir."

Willa was grateful to have these women in her life. She hoped that her daughter would grow up to be as fierce, intelligent, and successful as them. There would be barriers but she and Tom would manage it. He would get another job soon and they would cobble together the money to send her to a good school. She would be fed, warm, happy, and safe, and together they would flourish: *Tom, Willa, Jamie, and Gaia.*

SALMA SAT IN THE KITCHEN, still wearing her work clothes. Usually, she showered and changed as soon as she got home, but today she had struggled to find the energy. It had been a tough, long week. She, Bil, and Zain had searched for Molly every evening to no avail. They had shared a notice on social media and put up posters around the area. Yesterday, Salma had logged on to the Nextdoor app in case someone had seen her. She'd nearly cried with relief when she saw the thread titled

> **Does anyone know the owner of Molly the dog?**

She clicked into it, but the rest of the thread was a punch in the throat:

> *Could you have a word in their ear about the posters? Flyposting isn't allowed here and leaves awful sticky marks on the lampposts. It's very sad obviously that they've lost their dog but let's not mar our streets over it.*

Salma couldn't fathom how people could be so callous. Several times she had typed, deleted, and retyped a response before finally deciding not to say anything at all. She reloaded the post now, unable to resist. Before she could load the comments, however, her phone began to ring. She answered quickly, hoping there was news about Molly.

"Hello, is this Ms. Khatun?"

"It is."

"I'm calling from HSBC about your mortgage holiday."

The rope tightened around her neck. "Yes?"

"I'm calling to see if your circumstances have changed. As I'm sure you are aware, your mortgage holiday is due to end this month."

"Yes, I'm aware." Salma's accent shifted, as if cut glass could shield her from the sting of judgment.

"We're here to help," said the woman, following a pre-written script. "Would you like to speak to our debt recovery helpline?"

"We just need a bit more time," said Salma. She heard the woman sigh and that tiny lapse in empathy made her bristle with shame.

"Ms. Khatun, I'm very sorry but we can't extend a mortgage holiday beyond six months. There are some things we can do, such as increasing the length of your mortgage term, but this may affect your credit rating."

"I see," said Salma with a meekness that was new to her. "Okay. We'll try to find the money," she promised. Then, fearing that her voice would break, she swiftly ended the call. Despair hung in the air and she so nearly succumbed to it, but inertia was a luxury. She and Bil had run out of options. They *had* to sell Jakoni's.

Salma had filed for an interim possession order to get the

squatters out but was told there were delays. Locking them out was illegal, violence wasn't acceptable, and legal action required capital. If the squatters stayed in place for another two weeks, they would gain more legal protection. She and Bil *had* to try again—this time with diplomacy.

They set out in the early evening, in between Bil's split shift. As they drove in silence, Salma realized how much of a toll this had taken on him. It had sapped all the playfulness out of him. Friends often joked that the two of them were still "like new": escaping to the balcony at gatherings to flirt and chat animatedly. Salma was grateful that they had never turned into one of those couples that stayed together from habit. You could spot them easily at dinner parties, trading barbs disguised as jokes, their contempt refashioned as banter. Bil in comparison was happy-go-lucky and always saw the best in things. Watching him drive morosely made Salma yearn to comfort him. She placed a hand on his knee and Bil covered it briefly before returning it to the wheel.

They drove on in silence, both of them growing tense as they approached Jakoni's. Bil reached for his key, but Salma promptly stopped him. Instead, she rang the bell like a stranger. She wanted to believe that these young men could be reasoned with.

They heard footsteps shuffle closer and the dead bolt unlatch. Rich, the boy with the bad teeth, peeked out and then grinned.

"Ah, what's this? What's this?" he said, fast like an auctioneer.

Salma tried for a smile. "Can we talk?"

"About what?"

She felt Bil stiffen next to her and subtly placed a hand on his back. "Can we come in for a moment?"

"'Fraid not."

Sweat pooled in her underarms. "Listen, Rich, is it?" She

gingerly stepped forward. "Are there problems at home? Is that why you're here?"

Rich narrowed his gaze on her. "What are you on about?"

"You must have a home. I'm trying to understand why you needed to leave it."

"This is my holiday home," he said, lips curling with the cleverness of his joke. He turned. "Oi, fellas, hear that? This is our holiday home!"

Bil cut in. "Listen, the joke's over now. We need you to leave, please."

"That ain't gonna happen."

"For you, this is a jolly, but we stand to lose our home."

Salma was about to speak when they heard a sound they recognized. She froze. "Molly?" The dog barked again and Salma cried out in disbelief. She rushed forward, but Rich blocked her from entering. She pushed at him but he didn't move. "Molly!" The dog barked again and this time Bil jostled forward. Rich tried to slam the door shut but Bil threw his weight against it so that it flew back on its hinges. Molly came bounding up to them but Rich grabbed her by her bright blue collar. She yelped in surprise.

"Molly!" cried Salma.

"Get the fuck out of here." Rich pulled her back. His friends heard the commotion and joined him by the doorway.

"That's our dog," said Salma. "Give her back!"

Molly barked, distressed, and strained at her collar.

"That ain't no Molly. This here is Yoda."

Bil tried to grab her but Rich yanked her away.

"Please," Salma cried. "Why are you doing this? Stay here if you have to but please give us our dog."

"I told you. She ain't your dog. She's ours."

"Liar! That's her collar. That's Molly. Why are you doing this?" She lunged for the boy but he pushed her back with ease. "Get the fuck out of here."

"Please! You can't do this."

"Watch me." He tugged Molly cruelly, making her whimper. Salma thought she saw her limping and felt a neon panic. Bil broke free and charged forward, but the two boys wrestled him back. One pulled out a knife and there was something in the way he handled it that made them both fall still.

Bil's voice took on an eerie calm. "Okay, fellas, things have clearly got out of hand here."

"Get the fuck out," said Rich.

Beads of sweat collected on Bil's upper lip. Slowly, he spread his arms obediently. "Please just give us the dog and we'll get out of here."

"That ain't happening."

Bil exhaled. "Rich, come on, just give us Molly and we'll go."

Salma touched Bil's shoulder, granting him permission to leave. She knew he wouldn't, *couldn't* leave Molly here, so made the decision for him. She felt him tense beneath her palm and in that breathless moment knew he would go for the knife. "No!" She yanked his shirt just as he began to charge. The imbalance of forces made them both stumble just far enough so that the thugs were able to slam the door. Bil rammed his shoulder against it, but Salma pulled him away.

"We need to call the police," she said, biting back her tears as she heard Molly cry.

Bil bent over, hands on his knees, and drew in long, slow breaths.

Salma dialed 101, the nonemergency police number. The officers arrived an hour later: one white man in his mid-forties and another a little younger. Salma was surprised to see a tattoo of a blue crucifix on the younger one's earlobe. She hated to admit that it made her trust him less.

The older officer rapped on the door. "Hello. Police! Open up please."

There was an audible scramble inside. A minute passed before Rich opened the door.

"Good evening, sir," said the older officer. "I'm PC Lismore and this is my colleague, PC Howland. Do you mind telling me if you have any weapons on you?"

Rich scowled, offended by the question. "No. Course not."

Lismore looked into the property. "Do you have a dog in there?"

"Might do."

"Can we see it, please?"

"Why?"

"We have reason to believe that the dog belongs to this lady."

Rich tutted and instructed one of his friends to bring out the dog. "That ain't her dog. It's mine. It's called Yoda. Mum got it from Battersea last year."

"Do you have proof of that?"

"You can call my mum and ask if you want." He shoved his phone at Lismore, the gold sticker on the back glinting in the light.

Lismore looked over at Salma. "Are you sure it's your dog they've got in there?"

"Yes! That's Molly!" She took out her own phone and scrolled through pictures: Zain and Molly smiling, Molly playing with a rope.

Lismore squinted at the pictures, then down at the dog. "The collar's different."

"Forget the collar. Look at the patch beneath her eye."

Lismore tried again. "It's not definitive."

"That's crazy. Of course it's her." She called out but Molly only barked feebly, held back by her collar. "Please. She's limping. God knows what they're doing to her."

Lismore grimaced. "I'm afraid I can't just take their dog."

"It's not their dog!"

Lismore held up a hand to calm her. "In that case, you have to prove it." He advised her to visit her local police station with Molly's microchip details and documents.

"So we just have to leave her here?"

"For now, yes."

It seemed absurd that Molly was a few feet away but they couldn't bring her home. "Please," she implored Rich one more time but he coolly shut the door.

SALMA AND BIL SAT IN the car outside Blenheim. Darkness hadn't yet fallen but the street felt eerily blank without any streetlights. There was so much talk of safety here, yet Molly had been snatched in daylight. Had those thugs *stalked* them and lain in wait outside? Salma was secretly angry at Zain. She had told him numerous times never to leave the door unlocked, even when he was home. It was a distinctly male habit, she had discovered years ago. When she first moved in with Bil, he would leave their flat unlocked if one of them was home. The first time it happened, she thought he'd done it by accident, but when she brought it up, Bil was confused.

"But *you're* home," he said. It occurred to her that men locked doors to shield their belongings while women locked doors to protect their bodies. She had tried to explain this to Zain, but would often come home to find it unlocked. Clearly, that's how Molly was taken.

Bil looked across her. "We know where she is now. We can get her back."

Salma leaned on her knees. "How did we get to this point, Bil? We were mostly happy on the estate, weren't we?"

"We were."

"Are you unhappy now?" she asked.

He took a moment to answer. "I'm the unhappiest I've been in a long time."

Here they were again: a mutual low, each unable to buoy the other. For years, they had used the same low as a reference point. *At least it's not as bad as 2005.* Bil had been through some especially tough years. In his early thirties, he put his father, Hussain, in care after his second stroke. In their community, this was an unspeakable taboo. You simply did not put your parents to pasture; you kept them close and cared for them in their dotage—but this was a full-time job and his mother couldn't handle it. She was frail and couldn't speak English, so was unable to navigate the system. Bil's only sibling, a younger brother, lived miles away in Scotland. Bil agonized for months and finally made a decision when his mother fell down a flight of stairs while trying to guide his father to the bathroom. After that, Bil made the call. Within two weeks of being put in care, his father passed away and his mother never forgave him. He couldn't bear the heartbreak, she said, of being left to rot. They reconciled before she died, but Bil never got over the blame.

For more than a decade, that year was their litmus test: *At least it's not as bad as 2005. We got through 2005, we can do this.* But now, a new low: first, the trouble with Zain last year, then the end of Jakoni's, the debt, the squatters, now Molly. Salma couldn't see a way out of it.

"Do we tell Zain?" asked Bil.

Salma thought it over. Was it better to think that Molly was missing, or stolen by the squatters? She didn't want Zain to do something stupid but surely he deserved to know. "I'll talk to him," she said. "I'll tell him the police are on the case."

Bil gave her a sour look. "Hardly."

"So what do we do?"

"I don't think we'll solve anything this evening." He looked at his watch wearily. "You go ahead. I'm already late for my shift."

Salma kissed him and headed inside. She went upstairs and knocked lightly on Zain's door. There was no answer and she pushed it open a little. She saw that he had his headphones on.

"Zain?"

He startled and quickly closed his laptop but not before she saw the figure on the screen: £15,000.

"What are you doing?"

"Oh. Just playing a game."

"Your screen said fifteen thousand pounds."

"Oh. That." He picked up a paper clip. "It's a game. You invest things for fun. I've made fifteen grand on Ethereum—not real obviously." He smiled and the paper clip snapped in his hand.

Salma stepped inside. "Listen, can I talk to you for a minute?" She sat on his bed and patted the space next to her. She slung an arm around him and gently explained what had happened with Molly. As she spoke, she was surprised by Zain's reaction. He didn't shout and rage but folded into her body, his teenage indifference sloughing off him.

"Why are they doing this?" he asked, the words half lost in her shoulder.

She kissed the crown of his head. "I don't know, sweetheart." She could take a good guess but didn't want to voice it. Maybe it was far too late, but she realized now that she wanted Zain to be more like Bil. She wanted her son to see the best in everyone, to live carefree and happy, unworried by the blight of prejudice.

CHAPTER 8

S alma sat in her car outside the squat brown building. The window was streaked with drops of water and the space inside looked empty. She had felt embarrassed walking in, across the worn gray carpet to a flimsy desk the color of wheat. She had always thought of Citizens Advice as a place for the helpless and vulnerable, labels she didn't want for herself. Over the weekend, she had called the police multiple times, but was punted from place to place. *What if it were my child who was missing?* she'd asked at one desperate point, cringing at her own hysteria. Citizens Advice was her last resort but the adviser, a kindly woman named Ellie, told her there was nothing she could do but wait. So now she sat in her car, doing nothing and waiting.

She had meant to beat rush hour, but by the time she headed home, it was well past five o'clock. She crawled along Ley Street, cursing when she caught yet another red light, this time on the junction with Benton Road, where it stayed green for only seconds. She switched on the radio and scissored through the stations, settling for one playing stadium rock. As she waited for the traffic to move, a flash of orange caught her eye. She looked up, and sure enough, there was Tom on the corner of Benton

Road. He was with his son, Jamie, and they were both laughing. The picture was oddly comforting. Caught in a moment of mirth, or even tenderness, Tom didn't seem so scary. *This* was a man that Salma could reason with.

The light turned green and Salma inched forward but was promptly caught again. Now she was closer to them. Jamie leaned close to Tom, who held out a lighter. Salma frowned. She didn't know that Jamie smoked. He tucked his phone into his back pocket so he could cup the flame from the wind. Salma felt a jolt of fright when she saw the sticker on the phone: a golden skull and crossbones. She realized that the boy with Tom wasn't Jamie at all. He shifted into profile and when he grinned, Salma saw his row of crooked teeth. The boy with Tom was Rich. Rich, the squatter who had taken over their property. Rich, who had taken Molly. Things began to click into place. The light turned green and a horn sounded behind her. Tom looked up and the two of them locked eyes. The driver behind her leaned on his horn and Salma was spurred into action, pressing the gas and lurching forward. She tried to find a place to stop—for what reason she wasn't sure—but the flow of traffic carried her forward a mile down the road. When she was finally able to U-turn, both Tom and Rich were gone.

Dread lined her stomach. The garden door might have been ajar and Molly could have wandered out. Could it be true? Could it really be Tom who had taken Molly? Could he really be so vindictive? In her gut, she knew that it was possible. Tom knew about their empty restaurant. Was all of this his engineering? A neon anger crackled in her skull. She was going to kill him. If he didn't fix this, she was *actually* going to kill him. She U-turned again, each mile further stoking her anger. She parked directly in front of Tom's house, then stormed into her own and out into the garden. Even in her state of fury, she knew to avoid spectators. She unlocked the gate in their shared fence and walked through uninvited. She rapped on his kitchen window and then his French doors.

"Tom!" she called. "Can you open up, please?"

Zain looked down from his balcony. "Mum?" he called, confused. "What's going on?"

"Stay there," she barked at him. She rapped the glass again. "Tom, open up! Now!"

She saw a shadow emerge and Willa opened the door. Salma felt an irrational spike of anger that she looked so composed.

Willa's features wrinkled as if she'd caught a bad smell. "May I help you?"

"Where's your husband?"

"He's not home," she replied tartly.

"Tom!" Salma yelled.

Willa drew back as if she'd been slapped. "Excuse me, can you not shout in my face, please?"

Just then, the front door opened and Salma caught a flash of orange. Tom saw her too and strode along the corridor, something panicked in his movement as if Salma had threatened Willa. He pulled her back to shield her. "What the hell are you doing?"

"What the hell are *you* doing?" she cried. "You took our dog."

He narrowed his gaze on her. "What are you on about?"

"You took Molly and you gave her to Rich. I saw you."

He laughed now but there was something false in it. Salma had been a teacher long enough to know when someone was masking the truth.

"This is harassment," he said.

"*You're* harassing us!" she cried.

"And yet you're on my doorstep."

"Tom, please." Salma changed tack, biting back tears now. "We've had her for eleven years. She's on her last legs. She needs to be at home with us."

Tom shrugged. "I don't know what you're talking about."

"I saw you with Rich. I know you know him!"

"The lad with the bad teeth?" Tom smirked. "You really have no clue, do you?"

"I saw you with him literally a minute ago!"

He threw up his arms, exasperated. "I was buying weed, okay?"

Salma faltered. "You're lying." Just then, Tom's dog, Lola, padded into the hall. Salma leaned forward and called the dog over. "Lola!" She patted her thighs. "Lola, come here!"

Tom scowled. "What are you doing?"

"Lola! Come on!" Salma's voice grew shrill and Lola began to approach.

"Tom, what is she doing?" cried Willa.

Zain appeared at the open gate. "Mum? What's happening?"

Salma ignored them all. Instead, she took ahold of Lola's collar. "You've taken my dog. I'm taking yours."

"Don't be ridiculous." Tom teetered between humor and anger, not sure which way to go. His face changed when Salma led Lola out. "What the fuck are you doing?"

"Mum, what are you doing?" Zain's voice was tense with warning.

"Tom! Do something!" said Willa.

Tom tried to grab Lola's collar but Salma swiftly eluded him. He swiped again but she blocked him with her body. "Give me back Molly!" she cried. Tom grabbed her shoulders and pulled her backward to get at Lola. His nails dug into flesh and Salma cried out in pain. Zain barreled forward and pushed Tom off her. Caught off guard by the sudden force, Tom fell backward and knocked into Willa. She stumbled, and for a second, her features crowded with horror. Then she fell, landing on one elbow. She shrieked and Tom rushed to her aid.

Salma felt the air drop around her. Willa screamed—so loud and consistent, it sounded more like anger than pain. She locked eyes with Salma.

"You fucking maniacs! Get them away from me!" she screamed. "Tom! Get them away!" She writhed on the floor and cried in loud, long bleats. Dread shot through Salma, for she knew that a woman's tears—especially from one like Willa—could be gravely dangerous.

"It's okay," said Tom, trying to calm her. "She'll be okay. I promise. She'll be okay."

She? With a jolt, Salma remembered that Willa was pregnant. *Oh god. No.*

Tom looked up and growled at her. "Get the fuck off my property!"

Salma fumbled with her phone. "I'm calling an ambulance." She bundled Zain away and hovered by the gate.

"Mum?" Zain was ghostly pale. "Was it my fault?"

"No," she told him urgently. "It wasn't your fault. Tom knocked into her."

But Zain pushed him. While we were on his property. Forcibly taking his dog.

Pressure rose in her chest, swelling and swelling, ready to burst. A siren blared in the distance, rousing her into action. Not knowing if Tom would allow her into his house, she ran through her own to meet the paramedics. She knew that a crowd would gather to watch this rare drama at Blenheim and guided them quickly inside. When they filtered into the garden, Willa's cries grew shrill. She pressed her palms around her belly and told them she was pregnant.

The paramedics set to work calmly and methodically. They checked for signs of trauma and bleeding, and questioned her about the pregnancy. When they finished, the older paramedic, a soft-spoken man with bony hands, leaned on his knees next to Willa. "You seem okay, but just to be sure, we'd like to take you in to have you checked out."

Willa nodded, teary-eyed. "When will the police get here?"

The paramedic instinctively looked up at Tom.

"No." Willa pointed at Zain. "It was him. He pushed me."

The man twisted round to look at Zain. "We were told it was a fall. We can inform the police but we should take you in now just in case. Can you walk?"

Willa winced in pain. "I don't think so," she said weakly.

The paramedics lifted her gently onto a stretcher and maneuvered her along the corridor.

Tom followed, pausing only long enough to raise a finger at Zain. "Get the fuck away from here."

Salma flinched when he slammed the door, leaving her and Zain in the garden, the air ringing with trauma. She collapsed against him, knowing from the press of his weight that he was leaning on her too. Her first instinct was to call Bil, but he would be starting his second shift and what could he realistically do?

The doorbell rang, raising a dart of panic. Salma thought they would have more time. She looked at Zain. "Whatever happens, tell them the truth, but *don't* say it was your fault. It wasn't. It was an accident. You were protecting me, okay?" She noted the haunted cast in his eyes and felt vastly under-equipped. Should she instruct him to say no comment or would that make him seem guilty? Should she call a lawyer or was that overreacting?

The bell rang again, more insistently. Salma hurried to answer it, pausing by the mirror to feign composure. She opened the door but tensed when she saw who it was.

"Linda?" said Salma with a hostile emphasis.

"Oh, hello. I saw the lights and was concerned. Is everything okay next door? I knocked but all I heard was the dog."

Salma smiled tersely. "I'm sure it is."

Linda looked in over her shoulder, sensing information. "Do you know what happened?"

"Not really," she lied.

"You didn't see anything?"

Salma was dangerously close to telling the woman to mind her own business, but that's not how things worked at Blenheim. "I'm sorry, but I'm in the middle of something right now."

Linda's interest grew. "Anything I can help with?"

"I appreciate it, but no." Salma waited and when Linda still didn't leave, she used the lull in the conversation to close the door in her startled face. The last thing she wanted was for the police to arrive with Linda still on her doorstep.

She led Zain to the living room. "Just tell the truth," she said when the knock finally came. Then, more urgently, "But remember what I told you."

THE MAN SEEMED TOO YOUNG to be a doctor, but when he spoke, his voice had a gentle authority. He was handsome, and Willa focused hard on this fact so she wouldn't have to listen to his words. He was mixed race in some way—almost white but not. It was a pleasing mix, she thought: light skin but dark hair and lips with a hint of red that was actually their natural hue.

"Mrs. Hutton?"

Willa blinked to attention. "Yes?"

He nodded at her chart. "Any drinking or smoking through-out the pregnancy?" His pen preemptively hovered over "no."

"No," she said. "None." Tom next to her crossed his arms, impatient with the question.

"Any strenuous exercise?"

"No. Just walking."

"Any stress?"

"Yes," Tom cut in. "We've had ongoing issues with our next-door neighbors."

The doctor wrote down a few more details, then set down the chart. "Okay, I'm going to send you for a scan. There's no reason to be alarmed. It's standard procedure to check that mum and baby are okay." He smiled, sleek and competent. "A nurse will be with you soon." He slipped away with an ease that made Willa wonder if he was once a dancer, forced into ballet by an overeager mother.

"Don't worry," said Tom, misreading the thought on her brows. "She'll be okay."

"Gaia. That's her name."

He smiled. "I love it, but we don't know for sure that we're having a girl."

"*I* know."

He brushed aside a strand of her hair. "Okay," he said gently. "Gaia it is."

Willa collected her hands in her lap. She hated hospitals, but not for the reason others did: death, illness, and pain. To her, they were a place of tenderness where doctors and nurses treated you with warmth and patience, and every time she was on the receiving, infantilizing end of it, she realized how much she had missed in childhood. She had yearned for kindness and whenever she witnessed its salving ability, it left her feeling raw.

Tom saw her tears and pulled her into his arms. "She'll be okay," he soothed.

Willa willed herself to believe this, as if the sheer force of conviction might dissuade death from her door. But, like an actor breaking character, she couldn't keep up the illusion. "What if she's not?" she asked.

Tom stroked her hair. "Then we'll try again."

Willa stiffened. Tom must have felt it because he pulled back to look at her and she gave him a hostile smile. "As easy as that, is it? Replace one child with another?"

Tom held in a sigh. "That's not what I was saying."

She turned away from him and focused on the mute TV. Part of her wanted him to leave her alone, to give her space to think. The other wanted to fight.

"Come on, Willa. Don't do this."

She ignored him.

"Can we talk like adults?"

"Adults?" she snapped. "If you'd acted like an *adult*, I wouldn't be here right now."

He stared at her. "You're blaming *me*?"

"It was you, wasn't it, Tom, who knocked that woman's banner to the ground? Who set this whole thing in motion?"

His lips pressed in a thin, tense line.

"That's the reason she and that fucking brute of hers stormed into my house."

"Come on, Willa," he chided, thinking her dramatic.

"Come on *what*?" She challenged him to argue.

He started to speak but then stopped and raised his palms in agreement.

Willa wasn't done lashing out. "If you'd swallowed your ego and just said sorry to her, none of this would have happened." She saw his focus drift and she raised her voice to bait him. "Did you take their fucking dog?"

He stared at her. "Of course I didn't."

"You're a liar."

"I can't believe you're asking me this."

Willa felt a pulse of satisfaction, her blows finally landing. In truth, she knew that Tom wouldn't do this. He had a temper and could be overzealous, but he was never cruel. She goaded him only because she was stressed. More than that, she was angry—at Salma and Zain for attacking her, at Tom for not protecting her, and at her parents for not being here, then or now. It never occurred to her to be angry at herself.

THE MAN ON THE DOORSTEP introduced himself as PC Norton. He was small and mustached and his mouth protruded from the rest of his face, giving him a murine look. Next to him was PC Byrne, a taller man with pockmarked skin and impossibly bright blue eyes. Salma invited them in and offered them tea, which they both declined.

PC Norton explained that they needed to ask Zain some questions but that he didn't have to answer them.

Salma gestured magnanimously. "Of course. He'd be happy to help." As she spoke, it occurred to her that she had inherited her father's approach to authority: obliging and subdued. It had always made her wistful to see her loud and gregarious father cowed by men in uniform.

Zain sat on the sofa and faced the two officers. Salma wished that they had accepted the tea—anything to ease the strained, formal tone of this.

"All right, Zain," said PC Norton, adopting a matey tone. "We've had a report of assault against your neighbor. Do you mind telling me what happened?"

Zain shifted and the leather creaked beneath him. He relayed the events of the evening, just as Salma had instructed. He kept his tone neutral, tamped down his teenage bravado, and leaned heavily on euphemism: "discuss" instead of "confront," "visit" instead of "trespass," "jostle" instead of "push." Throughout, PC Byrne made notes on a tablet.

"Were you told to get off the property?" asked Norton.

Zain squinted. "I don't think so."

"You don't think so, so you're not certain?"

Zain considered this. "I'm fairly sure but not one hundred percent certain."

Salma ran through her own reel of memory. It had happened so fast, it was hard to pinpoint specifics.

"When you pushed your neighbor, was it intentional?" asked Norton.

"No. It was self-defense."

"Was he attacking you?"

"No, but as I said, he was attacking my mum. I was defending her."

"Did you intend to injure his wife?"

"No. She was just in the wrong place at the wrong time."

Norton and Byrne spent the next half hour probing and testing Zain, drawing out the details.

"What happens now?" asked Salma.

Norton answered. "Your son may be charged with common

assault or, depending on the victim's injuries, actual bodily harm."

Salma grew rigid. "Injuries? But she was barely hurt."

"That's for the evidence to say," said Norton, not unkindly but with an edge.

Zain cut in. "Could I really get done for this?"

"As I said, it depends on the victim's injuries." Norton stood. "We'll be in touch."

Salma stopped them at the door. "How serious a charge is ABH?"

Norton gave her a rueful look. "It carries up to five years in prison." He glanced at Zain, almost jolly. "But it's your first offense, so that would be extreme." With that, they turned and left.

Salma broke out in a sweat as she recalled a dreadful statistic that she'd read in a paper last year: Of all the young men in UK prisons, over half were men of color. It was why she had left Selborne Estate in the first place—but here they were anyway and all it took was a single pointed finger.

Zain watched her with nervous attention. "Mum, what's going to happen?"

Salma tried to conjure what he needed: an easy smile, a crystal ball. "Don't worry, sweetheart. I'll talk to Willa. We'll smooth this out."

"Forget Willa. What about *Tom*?"

Salma looked at him sadly. "You don't understand, sweetheart. Women like Willa wield power and if they choose to, they can wound far deeper."

"Women like Willa?"

"Pretty. Educated." After a beat, she added, "White." She hated to infect him with this poisonous thought but had seen it all her life: tears used as a weapon against people like her. It was in actions large and small. Sometimes they were atrocious, like that woman in Central Park who accused a Black man of threatening her simply because he'd asked that she put her dog on a leash. Sometimes they were subtle, like the time Salma accidentally toed a classmate's mat in their weekend yoga class. The look of revulsion made her feel like an ogre: larger, darker, hairier. Salma had apologized but received a scowl in return. From that day, she arrived to class ten minutes early to make sure she was in the back corner, far away from her classmates. People like Salma made a thousand adjustments for the sake of others' comfort. Zain might have learned this in his own time, but he needed to know it now.

"You're not still working with Jamie, are you?" she asked.

"Not really, but Jamie and I are—"

"No. Jamie and you are nothing. Your father and I do not want you seeing that boy."

"But our—"

"No, Zain. Promise me. This isn't a joke anymore."

A muscle worked in his jaw. Finally, he nodded.

"I'm sorry, but it's just the way it has to be," she said. And with that, as all mothers must do, she cut away another piece of his meager innocence.

CHAPTER 9

Salma hovered in the space between sleep and wakefulness. She had slept erratically, for everything in her room felt tight and oppressive: the coarse texture of the sheet that they only used as emergency bedding, the window that wouldn't open which left the bedroom stuffy, their bedside cabinets that loomed higher than head height. At six A.M., she gave up on sleep and padded downstairs in her ratty gown to make herself some tea. Bil had come home exhausted last night, smelling of stale onion, desperate for a shower before they could talk. She had told him everything, speaking quickly to get the words out, repeating certain sections to convince herself they had actually happened.

"Oh, honey." He'd looked at her, disappointed. "You should have called the police and told them you saw Tom with Rich."

Salma had grown frustrated. She had wanted a bigger reaction—anger, outrage, or at least disbelief—but Bil's natural equanimity kicked in. He insisted that they needn't worry and though Salma wanted to believe him, she resented the casual flick of his wrist. She could tell that he was lagging, but she still needed to talk and she needed her husband to listen. She watched him struggle to focus and eventually gave in. "There's nothing we can do tonight," she said, noting his relief. "Let's just go to bed."

Bil had fallen asleep instantly but Salma had lain awake, lingering on the junctions that could have made a difference: if she'd knocked at the front door instead of the back; if Lola hadn't come out of the house; if Tom had been standing an inch to the right; if Willa had been farther inside. When she finally did sleep, she had a chain of clamorous dreams, all of which eluded her now.

She drained her tea and lay back on the sofa. She must have drifted off because when she heard the knock on the door, her watch said nine o'clock. She hurried to answer it, wondering if there was news, but found Linda waiting outside. Could she *ever* get rid of that woman?

"Linda! What a surprise," she said through gritted teeth.

"May I come in?" she asked, overly polite.

Salma was acutely aware of her dressing gown and the fact that she hadn't showered or even brushed her teeth. "Yes, of course," she said regardless. "You'll have to excuse me. We're having a bit of a late start this morning." She trilled in that way she hated when trying to put others at ease. "Tea?"

"No, thank you." Linda sat opposite Salma at the kitchen table. "I thought you should know that there's some trouble brewing on Nextdoor."

"Trouble?" She thought of the complaint about her posters of Molly.

"I don't know if you use the app, so I thought I should warn you. There's a thread about you and your family. About what you did to Willa."

Salma exhaled. "For the love of god, do people have nothing better to do?"

"I'll be honest with you, Salma. You've got to expect people to talk."

"But it was an *accident*. She barely had a graze on her."

Linda studied her. "Salma, haven't you heard?"

"What?"

"Willa lost her baby."

Salma flinched. "How do you know?" she stammered.

"I bumped into Tom on my walk this morning. He said the baby died, so . . ." Linda pleated the hem of her skirt. "People are saying they feel unsafe."

"Unsafe?" Salma was at a loss. "Are they serious?"

Linda bobbed her head from side to side. "It's just a few vocal people. It's not the consensus."

"What are they saying?"

"They want you to go," she said apologetically.

"Go? Where?"

Linda colored. "I don't know, Salma, but I thought I should warn you. Maybe you should keep your head down for a while. Stay out of the way."

"Stay out of the way?"

"Listen, I know how you feel about this street, but honestly, it's really nice once you get to know it. People will come round eventually. You just have to show that you're willing to get along."

"I . . ." Salma faltered.

"I hope I'm not being presumptuous."

"No." Salma stood. "Thank you for dropping by to warn me."

Linda seemed offended. Clearly, she had more to say. "Well, I should get on." At the front door, she paused. "You will be okay, won't you, Salma?"

Salma was caught off guard by the tenderness in the question.

"I will. Thank you, Linda," she said and this time she meant it. She shut the door and slumped against it. Willa had lost her baby. Separate to everything else, Willa's baby was gone. Salma felt a complex knot of emotion: grief for Willa's loss, guilt for thinking her melodramatic, and, at core, a clanging fear of the coming onslaught.

IT WAS AN HOUR LATER that Bil came down to the kitchen, by which time Salma was showered and dressed. She prepared a breakfast of poached eggs, toast, and avocado with lashings of salt and chili flakes.

Bil sat down, rumpled from sleep, warmth still in his clothes. "How are you feeling?" he asked.

She didn't speak for a beat. She was bothered not just by his reaction last night but his broader absence. There was a quiet battle raging at Blenheim and Bil had not been present. She knew he was tired from work, but she needed some support.

"Fine," she said, unable to keep the edge from her voice.

"Have you heard anything?" He smoothly poked an egg so the yolk ran in rivulets toward the edge of the plate.

"Willa lost her baby."

"Oh god." Bil set down his fork.

Salma filled the silence. "I shouldn't have gone over there. Now she's lost her baby and it's my fault. I—"

"Don't say that," Bil cut in. He scraped back his chair and stepped swiftly to her side. "Don't say that in front of *anybody*."

"I just wasn't thinking."

"It was an accident, Salma."

"But if I hadn't gone over there, it wouldn't have happened."

"You don't know that." His voice was low and urgent. "We

both know how much she smokes and that she hides it from her husband."

"Come on, Bil. Don't blame her."

"It's true though." He grimaced as if the truth pained him. "You've seen the way she jumps to high hell when her husband walks into the garden."

Salma *had* seen Willa sneak a cigarette—but people already judged mothers harshly and damn Salma if she were to join them. "I think I should talk to her."

"No. *Absolutely* not."

"But, Bil—"

"I'm a five on that."

Salma sighed. Early in their relationship, they had devised a system to express how strongly they felt in the midst of a disagreement. If Salma was a four and Bil was a two, then they went with Salma's choice. Bil *never* invoked a five, and the fact that he did so now made Salma concede. "So what do we do? We can't just ignore them."

"Yes, we can. They started this, Salma, but we can finish it. We just don't rise to it."

"They still have Molly."

"I'll get her back."

"How?"

"Somehow. I'll buy her if I have to."

"But we can't afford that."

"Then what do you want me to do, Salma?"

She saw the strain in his face and realized how much pressure he was under—not just now but for months. Bil had always dreamed of running a Michelin restaurant. Jakoni's had been his first step—but it had failed, and though he cheerily assured her it was a bump in the road, she could see how much it pained him.

"I'm sorry." She fit her hand over his. "We'll be okay. I promise."

"Promise me something else. You'll stay away from those people."

"But, Bil, how can we live next door to them and not sort this out?"

"We ignore them, Salma. We keep our heads down and we get on with it."

But will they do the same? She didn't ask the question, for Bil was under enough stress. Instead, she nodded weakly. "Fine. I'll stay out of the way."

He laced his fingers with hers. "Promise?"

"Promise."

ZAIN DIDN'T USUALLY SMOKE IN the morning, but he needed something to settle him. His muscles were knotted as if he'd slept all night in a stress position. He exhaled and the breeze snatched the smoke away—a pity because watching it curl and dissipate was part of the therapy for him.

His mother had told him the news about Willa and he felt strangely adrift. He couldn't imagine what she was going through, and not in the way of hollow platitudes but in a literal inability to conjure what she was thinking. To him, pregnancy, birth, and child-rearing were abstract shapes in a distant future. He knew she must be devastated, but his sympathy had a formal, contained quality, like what you might feel for a classmate who had recently lost a parent.

Neither his mum nor his dad had voiced the question they were all thinking: What did this mean for Zain? Would he be blamed? But it wasn't his fault—was it? Anxiety curled in his stomach and he sucked his cigarette, cheeks concave with the effort. He heard a clatter in the house next door and flattened himself against the wall. Willa marched into her garden, and Zain quickly stubbed out his cigarette.

"No. I will *not* keep my voice down," she was saying.

There was a murmur and Zain craned his neck toward the source. Tom was standing with his hands outstretched.

"They acted like cunts, so I'll call them cunts."

"Willa." Tom's voice was pleading.

"It's all right for your dad to lecture us on how they built this country, but *he* doesn't live next door to them, does he? You won't see *him* moving to Ilford or fucking Southall."

Zain's skin prickled with heat.

"It's all well and fine to spout stats at me, but let's see *him* move here and live like this."

"Willa, come on."

"Come on what?" she spat. "What do you want me to do?"

"Just keep your voice down."

"No! I won't keep my voice down. I'm going to stay here and if I have to scream at the top of my lungs, then I'll do it." She tipped her head back and shouted, "Get the fuck out." Tom reached for her but she pushed him away. "Get the fuck OUT," she repeated and turned in Zain's direction.

He ducked with fright though he knew she couldn't see him. In that moment, he felt impossibly young and it made him sing with embarrassment. He backed away, gently to avoid attention. Downstairs, he found his parents by the kitchen window. They were holding hands and that small act of solidarity filled him with secondhand courage.

"Mum?" He caught the strain on her face before she had a chance to hide it. The sight raised an odd, sickly feeling inside.

"Sweetheart."

"Did you hear the things she said?" Zain asked.

She smiled, stiff and robotic. "It's okay, sweetheart. She's just lashing out."

Snatches of Willa's voice rose above their own. "All over a fucking *dog . . . kill* that fucking thing."

His mum bundled him into the living room. "Don't listen," she said. "She's just acting up. She needs to rage for a while."

Zain tried to latch on to this, but his alarm was too intense. "Molly," he said. "They're going to hurt Molly."

"No, no," she assured him. "They won't go that far, Zain. The police will get her soon."

"Maybe I could talk to Jamie? See if he knows anything?"

His dad cut in. "That's not a good idea, Zain. Their family is grieving."

"But, Dad—"

"Listen, kid." He propped his hands on his shoulders and though Zain was now taller than him, he felt like a child in comparison. "I know there's a lot on your mind right now, but we're your parents and we're going to handle this, all right? The whole point of us is that we worry about things so you don't have to, so do me a favor and stay away from them. We're going to get Molly back and we're going to sort out this mess and your mum and I are going to take care of you, all right?"

Zain felt a rush of emotion. His dad must have sensed his tears because he pulled him into a rough hug. It lasted only a moment before he released him with a fortifying slap on the shoulder. Zain nodded once, firm and blunt, in his best guess at stoicism.

Just then, his mobile rang, startling them all. Straightaway, he recognized PC Norton's voice.

"Hello, am I speaking to Zain Khatun?"

"Yes," he croaked, then cleared his throat and tried again. "We have some news."

Dread corkscrewed inside him. "Yes?"

"The police will be taking no further action on your case."

Zain remained cautious. "But . . . you've spoken to Mrs. Hutton?" he asked, wanting to make sure that they had factored in the miscarriage.

"The complainant? Yes. I spoke to her a few moments ago. We've reviewed the evidence and don't feel there is enough to support a charge."

Zain remained cautious. "What happens now?"

"The incident will stay on your file, but other than that, we consider the matter closed."

He let his breath out. "Thank you," he said, embarrassed by the quiver in his voice. He hung up and nodded in answer to the question in the air. His parents crowded around him, aggressive in their relief, pressing him to the point of pain. When they parted, however, he saw something darker shift in their features. He realized what they were thinking: Willa wasn't just grieving but choking with a sense of thwarted justice. Now Willa was *truly* angry.

CHAPTER 1O

It happened three days later, on a Tuesday morning—at precisely five A.M. Salma knew because she read the red digits
on her alarm clock as soon as she jerked awake. It came again:
a battering sound downstairs. Her senses heightened, an awak-
ening of primal instinct.

She shook Bil. "There's someone downstairs." She felt the heat
roll off him as he sat up in bed, groggy at first but then instantly
alert when he heard it himself.

"Stay here." He was out of the room before she could protest.

It happened all at once: a stampede of footsteps and the voices
of angry men. Three burst into her room.

"Police! Get out of bed. Now!"

Salma's legs didn't move and one of the men, a hulk clad in
protective gear, pulled the duvet off her. "Get up and against the
wall!" When she didn't—couldn't—comply, he moved to her
side quick as a dart and yanked her out himself. She spilled onto
her knees, unable to maneuver her feet in time. He tugged her
roughly upward, as if she were a rag doll, and pressed her
against the wall. "If you don't listen, we'll put you in cuffs," he
shouted in her face.

In the periphery, she saw two, three, four men file up the

stairs. She couldn't find the breath to shout up to Zain, and somewhere in the midst of her panic, she also understood that she was failing. She was a mother and was meant to breathe fire to protect her son but instead she had fallen mute.

"Move," the man instructed her. When she didn't comply, he pushed her a little. "Move!"

Salma stumbled onto the landing. Downstairs, she found Bil facedown against the floor. The baseball bat he kept for security was a few meters away along the corridor. She realized that he must have opened the door with the bat poised in his hands.

"Do you have a garage?" said the man standing above him. He was taller than the hulk who had pulled her out of bed. "A basement?" he asked. "Storage of any kind?"

Bil raised his head but then instinctively pulled it low again. "No. Just a shed. In the garden. It's usually locked. The key is on the kitchen rack."

In seeing her husband like this, Salma felt the urge to charge at the men, to release a banshee scream, to warn them off with death.

"Get up," the man was saying.

Bil and Salma were corralled together. Goosebumps rose beneath her nightgown and she realized she was shaking, her body in survival mode. She flinched at the sound of a bang upstairs and instinctively moved toward it.

The hulk reached for his yellow Taser. "Don't move!" he shouted. "Don't you move!"

Tears leaked from her eyes and she tamped down the howl in her throat. "Why are you doing this?" she cried.

The taller man looked in her direction, featureless behind his visor. "We have reason to believe that your son has been supplying knives to under-eighteens."

"Knives?" Bil was incredulous. "You must have the wrong

house. My son would never—" He stopped and a strange look dawned on his face. His voice changed: low and more controlled. "Officer, please tell your men to stay calm. My wife and I and my son will cooperate, but please tell them to be calm."

Salma remembered the raid in Forest Gate when the police shot a young man in his home. Were the same ghouls in her house right now? The possibility forced her to her senses. "Sir, please listen. I'm a teacher." She pulled on her profession like a protective cloak. "I work at Ilford Academy. We've lost a student to knife crime. It's absurd to think that my own son would be involved in something like this."

"Please be quiet," said the taller officer.

"Please," said Salma.

"Quiet!" the hulk shouted.

There was a thud upstairs and Salma strained for the sound of Zain's voice. She knew he wouldn't be quiet in this situation and the fact that she hadn't heard him raised a white alarm in her brain. "Where is he?" she asked. "Where is my son?" She called out to him, "Zain!" There was no reply. She waited. "Zain!" She felt a lick of hysteria. "Bring me my son," she shouted at the hulk. "Bring him to me!"

"Salma." Bil's voice was hard with warning. "It's okay. He's okay."

Salma wanted to throw herself against him, to punch through his composure. Why was she the only one reacting with any logic? For a moment, she believed that this was all a grotesque dream, but the clarity of dawn, the familiar creak of a floorboard, the nightgown pasted to her skin, told her it was real.

The taller officer, who she now knew was called Wilson, ushered them outside. Salma was distressed to find that the street was quiet. It felt like a bad omen, a sign of something unspeakable. Her nerves fired, shooting through her body like sentient beings, stirring full-blown panic. She was so close to losing control, but then she heard a glorious sound.

"Mum, I'm okay!" Zain was led from the house.

Salma folded in relief. She was anchored once again, saved from something bottomless. She tried to go to him but Bil held her back and weirdly tried to shield her from him. That's when she saw it: a dark patch in Zain's gray joggers, in between his legs. The sight filled her with a keening sorrow. What had they done to Zain—her brave, cavalier boy—to cow him in this way? She moved toward him as they loaded him in the car, but the hulk forced her back.

"What are you looking for?" She turned to Bil. "What are they looking for?"

He pumped a hand, telling her to stay calm.

She watched the shapes of men in her living room, upending her life and home. She thought again of the Forest Gate raid. If these men had had guns, Zain could have been shot—and for what? Supplying *knives*? Where had they got this information? It was true that Zain spent hours on Reddit and had a teenage distaste for the "system," but he would never do something as reprehensible as supplying knives illegally. Even as she thought this, a cool and professional voice inside her asked if she was sure. If her years as a teacher had taught her anything, it was that parents were naive.

Salma mentally scanned her home, layer by layer like a laser. Zain had a large closet in his room and the last time she had looked, it was filled to the brim with old boxes, bits of paper, shoes, sports bags, and vinyl from his music phase. Was there anything that she had missed, or that could be misconstrued? With a start, she remembered that Zain had gone through a rocket phase at the age of twelve. She remembered the paraphernalia: innocent vinegar and baking soda but also an advanced chemistry set and a handbook on explosives. Was there a chance he still had those things? Would the police uncover them? She agonized until an officer emerged from the house and shook his head at Wilson. She watched them talk and tried to read meaning into each of their gestures: a broad sweep of an arm, a frustrated flick of a wrist, a petulant shrug. Finally, Wilson approached her.

"What's happening?" she asked.

"You're free to return to your home."

"Where's my son?"

"We're bringing him to the station."

"Why? Which station?"

He sighed impatiently and gave her the details.

Salma saw the tension in his features. "You didn't find anything, did you?"

"We'll be in touch," he said.

"You'll be in touch?" She scoffed with disbelief. "That's it? You drag us out of bed at five A.M. and you tell me you'll be in *touch*? What reason did you have to do this?"

"Please, madam, return to your house."

"No. Tell me!"

Bil touched her elbow gently. "Salma, come on. We need to go to the station."

"This is fucking outrageous," she said, emboldened by their cheerlessness. Surely, if they had found something, they wouldn't be downbeat.

Wilson began to walk away and Salma moved to follow him, but Bil tightened his grip on her arm. "Someone told them," he said, a brittleness in his tone.

She looked across at him. "What?"

"I didn't want to say anything until they were gone, but some-one must have told them." He let his breath out slowly. "The box of knives from Jakoni's. Suli's nephew picked them up. Zain gave them to him."

Salma paled. Suli's nephew was only seventeen. "So they might have a case?"

Bil didn't answer as he watched the last car leave. His features were sharp and drawn, cheekbones gaunt beneath his stubble. Salma's head was buzzing. It was daylight now and signs of life blinked on around them: the metal clang of a distant gate, the ignition of a car. The sweep of a curtain caught her eye and she turned to see Willa at her window, a strange, beatific look on her face.

Salma was hit with a poisonous realization. "Bil, it was her." She knew with impossible certainty that Willa was the cause of this. She pelted over and struck the window. "Was this you?"

Willa stared at her impassively.

"Open the door." Salma fought another urge to smack the window. "Open the door."

Willa appeared to consider this, then shrugged as if to say *Why not?* A moment later, she opened the door.

"Was this you?"

Willa folded her arms. "What is it *now*?"

"Was this you? What just happened to my son?"

"I have no idea what's happened to your son."

"The police raided our house! At five A.M. Willa, do you not understand what happens to boys like mine? He could have been killed."

A shadow fell over Willa's face, quelling her initial petulance.

Salma waited, unable to articulate what she was feeling. "Was it you?" she repeated, not knowing why she expected the truth.

Willa shook her head and there was such honesty in her sorrow, the air went out of Salma's fury. She covered her face with her hands. What was she *doing*? This woman had lost her baby and Salma hadn't even said she was sorry. When had she lost her common decency? She looked across at her now. "I'm sorry about what happened, Willa, I really am. I hope you know it was an accident." She waited, and for a moment, she thought that Willa would reciprocate, but instead she shut the door. A clean, cutting sound that severed a fragile link, once and for all.

WILLA CLOSED THE DOOR AND returned to the window. The problem with anonymous tips was that they were easy to submit and, by extension, easy to ignore. It must happen all the time: a spurned lover taking revenge, a troll targeting a public figure, a teen playing a practical joke. The police were well versed no doubt, so Willa knew that she had to hide in plain sight.

The idea came to her after she was told that her baby was dead. No, not *dead* but *lost*, as if that feeble euphemism might ease the weight of the news. Willa had received it blankly, the words like a foreign language. Tom folded in half and Willa waited for the impact to hit. Instead of falling apart, however, she only felt herself harden: an ugly thing calcifying with hate, rage, and vengeance.

The doctor explained that the pregnancy would pass naturally and that she could take painkillers if needed. He placed a set of leaflets on her bedside table, paper-thin comfort in a colorless void. She picked one up, her sweat staining the gloss, and looked at it like a diligent student.

"There are avenues of support," said the doctor. "If you feel you need them." His words were kind but clipped, the tone of someone under pressure to move on to the next patient.

"Thank you," she said. "I'll take a look at them."

"A nurse will help you get your things together." He left in a blur of professional sympathy.

Willa was quiet and felt herself coil like a spring, brimming with a sort of madness.

Tom must have seen the eerie look on her face, for he stuttered when he spoke. "Are you okay?"

"I'm fine." She folded her hands in her lap. "Or maybe I'm not, but I will be," she said—and that's when she started to plot. She might have not acted at all had the police not called her the very next day to say they were taking no action. The decision was so swift, so perfunctory, that Willa seethed with a sense of injustice.

The day after the call, as Tom was heading out on a marathon run, Willa lied and said that she needed to see her friends. She pulled on a preppy white sweater and a pale gray skirt that skimmed her figure. She patted her hair with coconut oil to smooth the flyaway strands, careful not to lay it on thick. She exaggerated her Cupid's bow with a carefully chosen color, not red but a pale and pleasing pink. Sweet, innocent, subtle. Her heels were sleek, stopping short of sexy. Everything about her screamed *credible*. When she walked into the station, she looked around unsurely, wide-eyed and lost. The thick-necked man on the front desk sprang to his feet when he saw her.

"May I help you?" He blinked rapidly as if caught in the glare of something blinding.

Willa smiled nervously. "Um, I—I'm not sure if it's anything really," she said, "but I thought I should come in just in case."

"Yes, of course," he said. There was something childish in his tone: a boy asserting authority, an imaginary gun by his side. *Hands up, you punk.*

"It has to be confidential," she said—haltingly, as if undecided.

"Of course." He led her to another officer, this one thin and girlish, who introduced himself as PC Buckley.

In the interview room, Willa spoke carefully. She had to give herself enough leeway so that when it all turned out to be bunk, she could claim innocent ignorance. As she dithered, however, she saw impatience cross Buckley's face and subtly changed tack. This man would need some maneuvering.

"I'll be honest," she said. "At first, I thought it was drugs. The family moved from Selborne Estate and I hear there's a bit of a problem there, but the boys dropping by seemed far too young— fifteen or sixteen, sometimes younger—and I just couldn't see them mixing with drugs. Then . . ." She rolled her eyes, embarrassed at her naivete. "I wondered if they were lads' mags or something along those lines, but with the internet and all, I knew that that was silly. Then, last week, I saw it." Willa let out her breath. "It looked like something out of a horror movie: a curved serrated knife with this bright green handle. I honestly would have thought it was a toy if I didn't already know that something strange was happening."

Buckley watched her and she tried not to squirm beneath his scrutiny. She itched to draw out her ace, but knew she needed to bide her time.

"Ms. Hutton, how did you see the serrated knife with the green handle? Did the buyer just brandish it on the front lawn?"

"No. It wasn't like that. He got into a car and showed the knife to the driver. They were laughing and joking over it." Willa grimaced. "I saw that *Panorama* about knife crime and, honestly, seeing their glee just turned my stomach."

"Did you see the knife being handed to him by your neighbor, this Zain Khatun?"

Willa paused as if thinking. "No. Not directly."

"So he could have been collecting something else?"

"Yes, but I'm certain it was the knife."

Buckley sighed. "Okay, well, thank you for reporting it."

Willa nodded. "I did the right thing?"

"Yes."

"So that's it? I can go?"

"Yes."

Willa exhaled, relieved to have done her civic duty. "Thank you." She stood and adjusted the strap of her bag. "I almost let it be, but if something had happened with one of those knives, then . . ." She swatted the thought away. "Well, thank you, Officer." She headed toward the door. "Oh, I almost forgot." She turned back around. Time to play her ace. "I recorded him one time." Buckley looked up with renewed interest and Willa suppressed a smile.

"You recorded him?"

Willa fumbled in her bag and placed her phone on the table. "Yes, on my iPhone." She took a moment to locate the clip and turned the screen to Buckley.

"What are you doing?" Zain's voice was loud enough to hear.

"I'm checking them out, bruv," said a younger boy. He ripped into a taped-up box, separated the cardboard lid, and pushed through loose polystyrene, sifting it like rice. Then he pulled out a large silver cleaver. He inspected it as sunlight glinted off it just as it might in a movie. He pulled out a second weapon, this one a large knife, and took a step back from Zain. He swung the weapons in a crisscross shape and whooped like a ninja. From the camera's vantage, it was clear that Zain was panicked.

"What the fuck, Krish? Put that shit away."

"Ain't no one's gonna fuck with me with these beauties in my boot."

"Jesus, put them away, will you? People will see." Zain surveyed the street and that's where the clip ended. In hindsight, it was serendipitous that Willa had recorded it. She had actually been filming the younger boy's parking, which encroached on her property. Capturing the knives was a bonus.

"Can we keep a copy of this?" asked Buckley.

"Of course." Willa kept her voice light. "I should mention: He received a delivery yesterday. Three boxes like the one in the video."

Buckley stood up, a new urgency in his body language. "Can you give me a moment, please?"

"Of course." She held the frown on her face until Buckley left the room.

At best, she had hoped for intimidation. Maybe they'd drag Zain to the station and question him for an hour. She hadn't dreamed of a raid at dawn, six or seven officers combing through Salma's home. She thought of Salma's question. *Do you not understand what happens to boys like mine?* Clearly, it was hyperbole but it still raised an uncomfortable feeling. Willa didn't want violence nor did she seek vengeance—how could one pay for the loss of her child?—but she *did* want them humbled. She wanted them to understand that they couldn't behave the way they had and not face any consequences.

ZAIN WAITED IN THE AIRLESS interview room. There were no windows and he had no idea how long he had been there. His mind was spinning, a zoetrope of this nightmare morning: men folded over his bed, screaming in his face. The terror he'd felt was profound and primal. He had cowered from them and to his great shame wet himself like a five-year-old. The men didn't seem to notice, but he knew that his mum had seen it. At the station, they gave him a change of clothes and though the officer acted neutral, Zain saw his smirk reflected in the windowpane.

The questions had been endless: How did you buy the knives? Do you use Tor? Do you own any cryptocurrency? What type? How much? How many knives have you sold? Zain had tried to explain that the clip was entirely innocent. "The knives are from my dad's restaurant," he'd said. "His friend Suli said he'd buy them. He sent his nephew to pick them up. I was just handing them over because Dad was at work that day."

But then the questions had got stranger: Have you ever been to Pakistan? Why do you have a copy of *The Anarchist Cookbook*? What did you mean when you tweeted "End the Monarchy"? What about "Free Palestine"?

Zain had always thought that people could see him for what he was: a coder and a nerd. His room was the archetype for fuck's sake: a *Blade Runner* poster on his wall, *Ready Player One* on his shelf, *Ready Player Two* on his desk—but these questions eroded everything about him except the way he looked. Zain had been tempted by sarcasm—*yes, I love making bombs in my spare time*—but swallowed it back from the tip of his tongue. This was no time for jokes.

Zain tensed as the door to the room clanged open. His interviewer, a wiry man called Officer Buckley, tossed a file on the table. "You're free to go," he said.

Zain was confused. "Go?"

"We spoke to your dad's friend and your story checks out."

"So . . . that's it?"

"Yes."

Zain tried to decipher if this was a cruel trick. He pictured pulling at the door handle, only to find it locked. Buckley would burst out laughing. *Gotcha!*

He stood up gingerly and waited, expecting more—a parting word or apology—but Buckley just sighed impatiently. There was so much that Zain wanted to say, but he didn't want to risk his release.

Outside, his parents crowded him, fretting like worried butterflies. He swatted them off, mortified by the look in their eyes. In the car, he ignored every one of their questions. At home, he escaped upstairs as soon as he could. He felt a charge of shame when he saw that his sheets had been changed, now a bright white instead of blue. In a way, it worsened the incursion, made it hard to pretend that nothing at all had changed. He couldn't bring himself to touch the bed, so slumped in his chair instead. He closed his eyes, expecting sleep, but the anger in his chest roused him repeatedly. He punched his armrest, hoping to shift the violence inside him, but it left him more frustrated. When sleep finally came, it was strangely cyclical, taking him through the same lurid dream over and over again. It was hours later that he jerked awake. His mouth was cottony and his sinuses felt hot and bloated. His head throbbed and he wondered why his parents hadn't woken him.

That's when he heard it: an undeniably familiar sound. He froze, worried that he had imagined it, but then it came again. He sprang up from the chair and pelted downstairs. He hadn't imagined it: There was Molly in the corridor, vigorously wagging her tail. Zain cried out and leaped over the final few stairs, falling to his knees in front of her. He put his arms around her, but Molly squirmed away.

"Molly, come here. Come here, sweetheart." He pressed one arm around her and she finally came to rest against him, tail still wagging. "How?" he asked.

His dad stepped closer. "I stopped there after my shift and saw that the top window was smashed. I thought it didn't make sense—why would they want to sleep in the cold?—so I looked in and they were gone. All their stuff as well. I went inside and there was Molly." He swallowed. "They left her behind."

Zain broke into tears. "Oh, Molly." He ran a hand over her coat, checking for injuries or signs that she'd been mistreated. "How long was she there alone?"

"I don't know."

"Oh, Molly, how long were you there?" His tears landed softly in her coat. "I will never send you away again. Never." He looked up at his dad. "Should we feed her?"

"Yes, but we have to be careful. They've had her for nearly two weeks. Who knows what they've been feeding her. We need to take her to the vet as well."

"I'll do it," said Zain, brimming with relief. He couldn't believe that she was back. "I'll call them now," he added, getting to his feet. "Dad," he croaked. "Thank you."

"You're welcome, kid," he replied, his voice gummy with emotion. Instinctively, they hugged and Zain felt like a child again. When they parted, his dad ruffled his hair and then hurried away. Perhaps he, like Zain, needed a moment alone to wash off his distress.

■■

CHAPTER 11

T om ran until he felt sick, and then he ran some more, pushing his body further and further until he was too tired to
think. Two weeks had passed since Willa's miscarriage and the
fact that she had bounced back so quickly made him feel uneasy. She had lunched with friends one day, gone shopping another day, then swimming and the gym. He thought she was in
denial, but as the days went on, he realized he was wrong. Tom
had brought it up last night and she had replied acidly: *What am
I meant to do? Mourn forever?* Tom had fallen quiet. He had always felt outpaced by her—outgunned, outclassed. She was the
holy grail and while he was proud to have won her, he didn't
know how to wield her, even after all these years. He would bel-
low loudly at parties and hold her arm possessively, but privately he suspected that she regretted being with him, that
maybe she wished she had chosen more wisely. He felt like he
was always running to catch up with her, so when she spat
those words—*Mourn forever?*—he hadn't felt able to say, *Maybe,
yes, because I will be.*

It had hit him harder than he'd expected. The fact that she
had a name—Gaia—had made it all too real. Stupidly, soppily,
as he passed the clothes aisle in the supermarket, he had

imagined buying her first booties, her first sneakers. Arguing over her first pair of heels. He even looked forward to those teenage years. Unlike other fathers, he wouldn't become the enemy. Tom and Gaia would be comrades. He'd even pictured giving her away on her wedding day. He couldn't remember her face in his dream—just a blank prettiness—but he knew that she would be beautiful. He couldn't say any of this to Willa because she would only look at him with that cold amusement. He loved his wife fiercely, but he was also a little afraid of her, of the hurt she might inflict at a moment's notice. And so he had headed to the track instead, forcing out his sadness, trying to shape it into something else: acceptance, peace, or even rage, for that was easier to bear. *That* he knew how to deal with.

He ran onward and thought of the other ways his life had changed because of Salma Khatun. His reputation was ruined; his friends refused to return his calls; and his career lay in tatters, replaced by a job in a warehouse that paid minimum wage. Salma Khatun acted so haughty because she was protected. Would she be so bold in Pakistan, where they stoned women for impertinence? It was an ugly thought, but it was true. Women like Salma were so confident, so outspoken, because they knew this country—and men like Tom—would protect her. He remembered the insouciant look on her face, the defiant lift of her chin, and felt his anger stir. What would she do if he reached out and slapped her? He *wouldn't* of course—he wasn't that sort of man—but sometimes women just didn't know when to stop. If he gripped that delicate neck of hers, she wouldn't be so loud or bold. The thought raised a curious feeling in his belly and he quickened his pace to try to outrun it. He couldn't think like that. He wasn't that sort of man. He wouldn't hurt Salma. He just wanted her to believe that he could. He hated that cool way that she ignored him, sleekly folding into her car and staring straight ahead. Earlier this week, he had paused on the curb and glared at her but she had seemed oblivious. He'd held the position until she was gone, then finally relaxed, feeling foolish on the corner by himself.

He was tired of feeling foolish, sad, and weak. It was why he went out on these marathon runs. Perhaps if he pushed his body far enough, struck the pavement hard enough, he could churn it all into rage.

SALMA SHIFTED UNEASILY IN HER plastic chair. For the last two weeks, she and Bil had avoided the garden, never fully relaxed in clear view of their neighbors. Today, they had ventured out, reassured by a macabre logic. Willa had lost her pregnancy and retaliated harshly, so surely the balance was clear—vengeance at a standstill. With this in mind, she and Bil had settled on the patio, Molly yapping happily.

Salma reached over and touched Bil's fingertips, drawing his attention to her. "Do you think he'll be okay?" She gestured at Zain's balcony.

"I think so," said Bil, but his smile was strangely bloated, his cheeks pulled into chipmunk circles.

"Be honest," she snapped impatiently.

Bil rubbed his stubble—a rough, matchbox sound. "He was so happy when Molly came back but I've seen moments where he's been so . . . *angry.*"

Salma felt a dart of anxiety. She had seen this too but had hoped she was being paranoid. Zain had always found it easy to talk to her, but something had passed between them that morning when she saw the patch in his joggers. Now he could barely look at her.

Bil continued. "Yesterday, when I walked into the kitchen, he couldn't open a jar and smacked it against the counter. I've never seen him do something like that."

Salma had witnessed similar bouts of anger. "Do you think we should book a therapist?"

"I wish we could, but . . ." He didn't have to finish the sentence. They were both aware that good therapy cost money.

"Maybe once we sell the restaurant?" said Salma.

Bil nodded.

"Do you think we should sell this house?"

He looked across at her. "No. Why would we?"

"Because of everything that's happened—Tom losing his job, the miscarriage, the raid."

"Honestly?" Bil cut in. "I think if we'd just let the paint thing go, we'd be barbecuing with them right now."

"Really? Would you want that?"

He thought it over. "Not knowing what I know, but none of that would have happened if we'd just ignored the paint."

"But what's the point of friends that want to keep you in your place?"

Bil gestured philosophically. "Look, either way, we have to live next to them now, so I think we just—"

"Keep our heads down and get on with it, I know."

Bil grimaced. "You think I'm an Uncle Tom."

"I don't think that," she said, but her voice took on an edge that wasn't there before.

If Bil picked up on it, he didn't show it. "I don't know, Salma. These young kids today. I'm kind of awed by them, but I also think they'll burn themselves out. That Yale thing a few years ago when that professor got in trouble because he didn't know his students' names? I just found it baffling. Maybe I'm out of touch. Maybe I'm an idiot for feeling grateful, but I *do* feel grateful to be here."

"My husband, the good immigrant," she said mildly. She sensed him tense and could tell he was insulted, but made no move to reassure him. The last few weeks had exhausted her kindness.

"God, maybe I *am* delusional." Bil closed his eyes and pinched the bridge of his nose. "When I think of what could have happened to Zain . . ."

Salma didn't respond. She watched Molly play at the foot of the garden. "Thank you for getting her back," she said. In that moment, it was the only honest thing she could say that wouldn't make him feel worse.

ZAIN FELT THE PENCIL STRAIN, then snap in two in his hands. It was something of a compulsion now. For a time, Molly had helped. Being near her calmed him, but when she wasn't in the immediate vicinity, he found himself raging over the simplest things: a wire that wouldn't untangle or his phone charger that wouldn't dislodge from its socket. The rage would build and make him want to scream. He had done so once when his parents were out but felt guilty for scaring Molly. He didn't know what she had been through and blamed himself for her strange ducking motion when he reached to stroke her head. He had known boys like Rich, boys who had been treated cruelly and so would treat Molly the same.

He set down the broken pencil and prowled the length of his room. He felt restless, like a fly tapping and tapping a window, not accepting its fate. He stepped onto the balcony with his last cigarette. He thumbed his lighter but the flame refused to catch, stirring a familiar rage.

"Zain?" Jamie's voice was next to him.

Zain leaned out and saw him on his balcony like the first time they'd met. The two of them hadn't spoken since their clash three weeks ago. *Are you dumb as well as deaf?* So much had happened since then.

"What the hell, man? I've been texting you."

Zain ignored him.

Jamie looked at his watch. "We've got to upload our demo today."

Zain leisurely lit his cigarette and leaned on the balcony wall.

Jamie grew agitated. "Look, I've got to get to tutoring. If we don't do this now, we'll lose the rest of our funding."

"You wanna talk? Let's talk," said Zain. He stubbed out his cigarette, then climbed onto the ledge and stepped around the central column onto Jamie's balcony.

Jamie spoke quietly. "You can't just ignore me, man."

"No? Oh, okay. What shall we talk about then? How your dad stole my dog? How your mum had me arrested for assault?"

"You pushed her!"

"I didn't fucking push her. I pushed your *dad* off my mum. What story did *you* hear?" He scoffed at Jamie's confusion. "Your mum's a liar, mate. She had coppers raid my house, for fuck's sake."

"She didn't do that."

"She *did*."

"I know my parents, Zain. You're blaming them for something they didn't do. You're treating *me* like shit when I haven't done anything to you."

"The fuck you haven't."

"What's that meant to mean?"

"I asked you for five hundred quid for Molly and you pulled rank on me."

"So you act like *this*?"

Zain smiled unkindly. "What are you going to do about it?"

Nervously, Jamie blinked.

Zain normally found this tic endearing, but today it enraged him. He blinked in a pantomime manner, cruelly aping Jamie. "Well, what is lil old Jamie gonna do about it?" The stress of the past few weeks coursed through his body. He shoved Jamie's shoulder, feeling his heart rate soar.

"Zain, don't do this."

He pushed him again. "Do what?"

Jamie took a step back. He held out a hand to defend himself. "Come on, man." He tried for nonchalance, but his voice was too high and tight. "I've got to get to my tutoring."

The pathetic note in Jamie's voice made him want to lash out more. "Jesus Christ, mate. Stop being such a fucking pussy. Stand up to me." Zain pushed him again. "Stand up to me."

This time, Jamie pushed back.

"That's it!" Emboldened now, Zain swiped at Jamie's ear. He barely touched him but made him flinch. "Come on," Zain goaded, pushing at his chest. "Come on."

Jamie put his fists up and Zain laughed in cruel approval, even as he felt something precious slipping away from him.

CHAPTER 12

Salma had spent most of her life wishing she had more money, but strangely, she was also thankful for the lack of it. *Nothing makes you less appreciative than having too much money*, her father would tell her in youth—and it was true. It's why she and Bil had been so happy with Jakoni's. They had worked hard, strived, and earned enough for a comfortable living but not enough to waste. She had never imagined that when it fell apart, it would almost undo them. She looked around the empty space, now freshly painted, and felt a new lightness in her bones. The estate agent had told them that tomorrow a keen buyer was coming for a viewing.

Salma indicated the bare walls, stripped of all their history. "Are you feeling okay?" she asked Bil.

He nodded.

"Really?"

"Not *really* really, but I'll get there." He gestured toward the empty kitchen. "I did everything right, you know? The menu, the produce, the team, the marketing, the money—but who could have predicted a global pandemic?"

"I know," Salma sympathized.

"But it's more than that," said Bil. "It was *such* hard work and a part of me felt relieved, like this was an excuse to fail, you know? That I could say, 'Well, it wasn't me; it was the circumstances,' and I don't know if I surrendered too quickly."

Salma blinked in surprise. "Bil, I saw how hard you worked. There is no way that's true."

"I don't know, Salma. There'll always be a part of me that wonders." He jangled the keys in his palm but lingered at the window, not yet ready to leave. Salma joined him and looked outside. There was no romance on this street but the fact that this could be their last time here stirred a dense nostalgia. Her phone broke the spell with a short, sharp trill.

"Salma?" said the caller. "It's Linda."

"Oh, hi," said Salma, surprised. "Is everything—"

"You have to come home." Linda spoke in small gasps as if she were treading water.

"Why? What's wrong?"

"I can't hear you, Salma, but please come home. *Now*."

Salma tuned out her panic. "Why?" she repeated.

"Something's happened."

"Is it Zain?" She heard Linda swallow and then the three short beeps of a lost signal. "We have to go," she told Bil.

"What's happened?"

"I don't know. Linda said we need to go home."

They bolted from the building, down the street to their car. Bil drove uncharacteristically fast, changing lanes with an agility that Salma had never seen. When they reached Blenheim, she felt her stomach drop. Three police cars and an ambulance were parked outside her home. When she got out, however, she saw that they were clustered around next door. Had Linda been mistaken? She searched for her, then tried to stop an officer who just barked at her to get back.

She followed Bil into their house. "Zain?" she called. She searched the kitchen and living room while Bil rushed upstairs.

She checked the garden door, then hurried upstairs as well. Zain's door was ajar but the room was empty. There were voices outside and Bil was on the balcony. When he looked at her, it was with a strange and glassy vacancy. Salma dashed out to join him. It took her a moment to see through the thicket of police and paramedics. Then they cleared, and Salma screamed.

WILLA LISTENED TO THE TINKLE of music in the Mayfair brasserie. She tried to decide how to play it: light and breezy and *c'est la vie*, or thoroughly distraught. She had to choose one or the other because she couldn't reveal her true feelings: a destructive flare that wanted to level *everything*. She had told herself not to be so absurd. Gaia wasn't real—not *really*—and it was this sort of mawkishness that undermined pro-choice. It was barely anything, to make a great show was melodramatic . . . and yet.

Willa spotted Sophia, who paused by the maître d' and swung back her glossy brown hair—an act she had practiced in youth until it came off as natural. She cut across the room and kissed Willa's cheek. She saw the large glass of wine in her hand and looked at her curiously. A thousand words passed between them and Willa waved to clear them away.

"C'est la vie," she said but her voice cracked in the middle.

"Oh, honey." Sophia sat down with urgency. "When?"

"Two weeks ago."

"Why didn't you say?" She rubbed Willa's forearm, pressing a thumb in the crook of her elbow.

Willa was conscious of nearby diners. "It's fine," she said, smoothing her top. "I don't want to make a big deal of it." She said the same to Sato and Amelia, who joined them minutes later. She told them what happened that day: Salma storming over, Zain attacking her, and the police doing nothing at all.

Sato was outraged. "They can't behave that way. Let me call Matthew. He'll know what to do." She reached for her phone, making a show of calling her husband, who worked in corporate law.

"No, stop it." Willa was aware that she had embellished her story somewhat, making Salma and Zain more aggressive and intentional than they actually were. "I just want to move on."

Sato rapped the table. "But you can't just let this go!"

"I don't think it's worth pursuing," said Willa. "The healthiest thing is to move on." She did not tell them that she had already retaliated. Her friends were cynical and even a little spiteful, but even they would think her extreme.

Amelia cut in. "Hon, you process this how you need to, okay? Don't let anyone tell you what is and isn't right." She threw a look at Sato.

"And how are you feeling now?" asked Sophia.

Willa traced the tines of her fork. "I'm fine. It was a shock obviously, but at least I have Jamie." She smiled ruefully. "And I can fucking drink again!"

Her friends tittered, but their laughter was shallow and hesitant, clearly designed to humor her. Sato beckoned a waiter and ordered a bottle of Dom Pérignon. Willa tried to stop her to no avail. With Tom's job gone, it seemed obscene to spend so much on drink—but Willa couldn't admit this, so she smiled instead and said, "What the hell."

They were dithering over dessert when Willa got the phone call. Her friends fell quiet, but she waved them on and took her call to the corner of the restaurant. Tom's voice shook as he ordered her to Barkingside Police Station, then paused, and directed her to the hospital instead.

"Go to Accident & Emergency at King George," he said. "Ask for Zain Khatun at the desk."

THE FIGURE ON THE GRASS was clear now: Zain, inanimate, his skull braced by large red blocks. The purple of his hoodie against the dark green formed the colors of Wimbledon, a fact that Salma registered even as her mind unhinged itself. The sound she made wasn't shrill like a scream queen's but a guttural wail—low and ferocious. Bil pelted out of the room. Seconds later, he appeared in their garden and moved through the gate into Tom's. In her daze, Salma was awed by her husband: by his quickness and decisiveness as he fought his way to their son. He moved to different vantage points to give the medics space, then shouted up to Salma.

"He's breathing!"

Salma moved to join him, but her limbs were slow and unwieldy. She stumbled downstairs and into the garden. She felt queasy when she saw him. His skin was pallid as if death had already begun to claim him.

The paramedics worked with a quiet efficiency. They spoke in muted tones, but Salma caught an appalling pair of words: *spinal injury.* She backed away and Bil caught her in his arms. She tried to pull free, squirming back and forth to throw him off, but he held on firmly. Salma didn't want a harness on her madness; she wanted to rage and roar, to stamp violence into the soil.

Bil tightened his grip as the paramedics lifted Zain onto a yellow stretcher and maneuvered him into the house. Salma spotted Tom in his kitchen window, surrounded by four officers. He looked at her with glazed exhaustion. He seemed on the verge of calling to her but the officers drew him away. Questions fired in her head: *Why is Zain in Tom's garden? Did he fall? Did he lose his footing or . . . ?*

Bil bundled her through their own house to meet the paramedics on the other side. The ambulance was leaving already and they followed in their car. Salma snapped at Bil for lagging too far behind and he skated past the speed limit to try to keep up. This small infraction made Salma quail with shame. How cruel that in a crisis, her instinct was to turn on him. Bil touched her knee, a brief brush, granting her forgiveness before she had even apologized.

In the hospital, they sat for hours in Accident & Emergency as sounds and shapes moved around them. In this place of decay, motion was a life force: the pump and hiss of a ventilator, the steady green beats on the screen of a monitor. Stasis was a killer—so what did that mean for Zain?

When the news came, she received it with a strange civility, as if collapsing in the corridor might inconvenience the doctor. Zain was in a coma, he said. The trauma to his brain was severe and while most patients recovered within a few weeks, they couldn't say more at this stage.

"Do you have any questions?" asked the doctor.

Salma just stared at him, her horror so profound that sound could not escape her. The doctor understood, told her gently that she would have other chances. It was only after he left that her legs buckled beneath her. The tears came in low, pathetic sobs—her grief leaking slowly lest it drown them all. For a long time she wept but Bil made no effort to comfort her and when she reached for him, his embrace was stiff and mechanical. That small disloyalty felt like an unmooring. In all their time together, Bil had been her constant: strong, cheerful, generous. And kind when she couldn't be. Now he just stood there, pallid and bare. Salma dug her nails into his body in a bid to rouse him, but he didn't seem to feel it, or her, or anything.

CHAPTER 13

Tom sat in the muggy interview room and listened to the drone of a generator. His underarms felt sticky and he raised his elbows at an odd angle to try to avoid the moisture. The room smelled of McDonald's and he wondered if some coppers had sneaked their lunch in here.

The door opened and two officers walked in. The man was white, gray-haired, gym-toned but with a slight paunch, on the short side with a meaty nose. When he sat down, Tom caught the reek of smoke. The woman was Black, younger but frumpy with shoulder-length hair and a fringe she kept blinking off. She wore an ill-fitting suit that sagged around her chest and smelled of cheap detergent.

"Are you comfortable?" she asked. "Need anything? Tea? Coffee? Water?"

"No," said Tom.

"I'm DC Martin," said the man, "and this is DC Rayner."

Tom wished that the woman wasn't here. He knew how to bond with men like Martin. Unlike his colleagues at Sartre who would drop their *t*'s around tradesmen and awkwardly call them "mate," Tom was comfortable around working-class men. Rayner, however, threw him off with her sloppy manner but critical gaze. She ran through some formalities and Tom tried hard not to fidget in case it signaled guilt.

Rayner smiled at him kindly. "Can you tell us in your own words what took place today?"

Tom tried to order the pieces in his head. It had happened in a matter of minutes.

"Tom, we're not trying to catch you out, okay? We're trying to put together a picture of what happened and we very much need your help." She planted her elbows on the table. "Let's start simply: You told officers on the scene that you found Zain Khatun unconscious on your lawn. When was the last time you spoke to him?"

Tom told himself to deal with this one answer at a time. "He lives next door, so I see him a few times a week."

"Okay, and when was the last time you had a conversation with him?"

"A couple of weeks ago."

"Can you tell us what that was about?"

Tom urged himself to be calm. "We had a bit of a tiff. We've lived in that street for seven years and never had any problems, but since the Khatuns moved in, it's been constant."

"What do you mean by 'constant'?" asked Rayner.

"Normal neighbor stuff, but . . ." He sighed to signal exhaustion. "They started getting aggressive, posting about me and my family on social media. They even filmed me once and put it up on Twitter."

"How did that make you feel?"

Tom realized that no one had asked him this before—not his colleagues, his friends, or even Willa. "It felt like a violation," he said.

"You felt violated?"

He squirmed at the phrasing but said, "In a way, yes."

"Were you angry?"

"Yes."

"Did you confront them about it?"

He paused, weary of a trap. "No. I wanted to stay out of their way."

"So how did you come to have a tiff with Zain?"

Tom explained what had happened that Friday when Salma came to take Lola. He tried to stick to the facts, knowing that showing his anger would not serve him well. Rayner was clearly sniffing for a motive and he was damned if he would hand her one.

"Did you report any of this?" she asked.

"Yes, but the police didn't do anything."

Rayner blew out her cheeks. "That must have been hard on you."

"Yes, but I understood."

"Oh?"

"A thing like that is hard to prove."

She eyed him curiously. "So you still thought Zain was at fault?"

"Wouldn't you? If it weren't for him, we'd still have our baby."

"I sense some anger," said Rayner.

Is that a question? he wanted to say. "You would be right," he said instead.

"Do you want to tell us about that?"

Not really. "My wife and I were trying for a baby for a very long time. I know what happened was an accident, but it's hard not to feel bitter. My anger isn't aimed at Zain but the situation."

"I see. And in the intervening weeks, did you see Zain in passing?"

"Yes."

"And were these encounters civil?"

"We didn't talk to each other, so they were neither civil nor uncivil."

"Okay." Rayner glanced at a sheet of paper. "You told the arresting officer that you came home to find Zain in your garden at around five fifty P.M. Where were you when you spotted him?"

"I was in the kitchen washing my hands and that's when I saw him. I ran out because at first I thought it was Jamie but then I saw the black hair. I saw that he was still breathing, so I called an ambulance straightaway."

"Did you go upstairs at any point?"

"No."

"Are you sure?"

"Absolutely."

Rayner laced her fingers. "Tom, it's really important that we get this bit right, okay, so I want you to think about it carefully. You walked into the house and straight into the kitchen. You didn't go upstairs at any point before the police arrived?"

"That's right." He looked from Rayner to Martin. "Why?"

"What if I told you that a witness saw you on your top-floor balcony minutes before you called an ambulance?"

Tom's face twisted in seeming amusement—a nervous tic that he hated. "What witness?"

"Come on, Tom. Tell us the truth. Did you go upstairs?"

"Is there really a witness?"

"There is, Tom, and they're certain that they saw you."

He searched for a way to explain this. "They must be mistaken."

Rayner was disappointed. "Okay, fine, Tom." She waved at Martin as if to say *I can't be bothered with this.*

Martin took over and as the interview drew on, Tom grew in

confidence. There seemed to be no strategy in their line of questioning. It zigzagged from the day of the accident to the weeks before it, bouncing from *Did you check Zain's pulse?* to *How long were you trying to have a baby?* Tom settled into a rhythm, certain that he could outwit them.

As the hours drew on, however, he noticed that Martin was repeating certain questions but posing them differently, subtly testing the consistency of what Tom was saying. The realization perturbed him and he became distracted as he scanned back through his answers, searching for discrepancies. Damn him for getting complacent.

"I'd like to speak to a lawyer please," he said, cutting into Martin's question. He saw the two coppers exchange a look.

"Very well," said Martin. He stopped the tape and shrugged his blazer back on.

Tom cringed when he saw that he had left the label on the sleeve. "You're meant to take that off," he said, unable to help himself.

Martin looked at the offending patch of material with a stricken look on his face.

Tom smiled kindly. "I thought it would be helpful to know."

Martin nodded bluntly. As he guided Tom from the room, he subtly pulled off the label and secreted it in a pocket.

Tom tried to mask his satisfaction. He didn't enjoy making people feel small, but he *did* want them to understand the extent of their faux pas. Martin led him into a cell and Tom looked around, feigning nonchalance. The last thing he wanted was for this two-bit cop to know that he was rattled. "Not quite the Four Seasons," he quipped, but his voice was too loud and jovial, clearly rigged with artifice. He waited for a comeback, hoping they might spar awhile, but Martin just shrugged and walked out, leaving him alone in the airless box.

Even then, he didn't quite believe that he would not be walking out of this, which was why when his solicitor appeared hours later, he greeted the woman brightly. She was white, gauntly thin, with mousy brown hair in a middle parting. She barely wore any makeup, which gave her a harsh mien—not a bad trait in a lawyer.

Tom folded his arms across his chest, then unfolded them straightaway. He wanted to appear neutral, unassuming, inoffensive. *Not guilty.*

"Tom," said the woman. "I have some bad news."

He grew rigid.

"The Crown Prosecution Service are charging you. They think you pushed Zain."

He blinked dumbly, unable to absorb the news.

"They're charging you with attempted murder."

And just like that, the illusion shattered.

PART II

S alma sat outside the head teacher's office, waiting to be summoned. The clock overhead seemed to tick too fast, willfully intrusive. The door snatched open and George stuck her head out.

"Come in, Salma. Sorry to take up your lunch. I wanted to catch you before you left." She attempted a look of sympathy. "How *are* you?" she asked, the emphasis on the middle word, a tip no doubt from her leadership training.

"I'm okay." Salma didn't know what else to say because the truth was that, even after all these months, she still felt short of breath, the slam-bulk of tragedy still pressing on her chest.

"Zain's still the same?"

Salma hated this question. It had been five months since his fall and though there were few outward signs of improvement, it didn't mean he was "the same." He had moved out of a coma into what doctors called a "continuing vegetative state." She didn't say this to colleagues, however, because they assumed that "vegetative" was worse when in fact it showed progress. "More or less," she answered.

"I know the trial starts on Monday and I just wanted to check if there's anything else we can do."

Salma searched for something to ask for just so she could leave. George had already allowed her to switch to a part-time schedule and take time off for the trial. She was unceremonious, but also big on mental health. Her own father suffered from bi-polar disorder—a fact that she had confided at last year's Christmas party. Salma gave her a weak smile. "The extra leave is more than enough."

George folded her birdlike hands. "I'm sorry we couldn't offer you more."

"Not at all." Salma knew how hard it was to give teachers term-time leave and hoped that the trial would be finished in the allotted two weeks.

George glanced at her watch. "Well, I better let you get to your class. Please know that my door's always open."

"I appreciate that." Salma shook George's hand, feeling a little emotional. Outside, the halls were busy, the students heading to their post-lunch lesson, drunk on sugar and sun. Unlike other teachers, this was Salma's favorite period. The children were fed and watered and feeling a little weary, but not so much that they lagged. She walked to her classroom and the pupils filed in noisily.

"Pop quiz, hotshot," said Ritesh.

Salma looked over at him, feeling her mood lift a little. "Go on."

"There are two doubly landlocked countries in the world. What are they?"

A smile played on her lips. "At least challenge me."

"Well then?" he asked tartly.

She shrugged as if it should be the most obvious thing in the world. "Liechtenstein."

Ritesh smiled. "Okay, correct. And?"

"And the other one's easy," she said.

"Ah, she's stalling!" cried Tara.

"We got her. We finally got her!" Ritesh stood and did a little two-step.

"You did not get me."

"Well?" he said, still dancing. He caught her glance at the map on the far wall of the classroom and moved into her line of sight, even though it was much too far to see.

She leaned back in her chair and laced her hands behind her head. "Uzbekistan."

"You cheated, miss!" said Tara.

"We saw you looking!" cried Patrick.

Ritesh shushed the class. "Okay then, what are those two countries surrounded by?"

Salma swatted the question away. "Enough of this. I've got a class to teach." They roared with indignation but she swiftly quieted them. "Come on. Take out your textbooks, please."

This class, these kids, were a glimmer in the murk of her grief, crowding her with their persistent cheer. *They* had calmed her rage when Tom was granted bail. And *they* had soothed her nerves when the trial loomed like a specter: a woman in white at the foot of her bed or a babadook creeping across her ceiling. When she couldn't move, it was her work that pulled her onward. And now she was finally here: at the cusp of a trial in which "guilty" was meant to be a panacea. But would any of that matter if Zain never woke up? In that case, no sentence given to Tom would ever be enough.

WILLA CHEWED THE SOGGY PELLET of fish beyond any taste or texture and forced herself to swallow it. She gulped from her glass and winced at the taste in her mouth: greasy fish and vinegar mixed with cheap red wine. She dreaded these evenings. She resented dressing down for Donna lest she comment on Willa's "fancy habits" despite their struggles with money. She resented eating this food and drinking this gritty wine they brought every week and insisted she open for the meal. She thought she would get a respite in the weeks before the trial but the schedule grew more rigid, as if Tom might crumble if he went one week without his mother.

Donna speared a piece of fish and waved her fork in the air. "Are the police sure he didn't just do it himself?"

Willa bristled. "Donna, we've been through this."

The older woman sighed. "But how do they *know*? There were no signs of a struggle, so how do they know he didn't jump? Lots of young men do it, you know."

"He didn't do it himself," said Jamie.

Willa looked across at him, surprised by the edge in his tone.

Donna swallowed her piece of fish. "Well, you don't know that, Jamie. There's so much pressure on young men." She slid her eyes toward next door. "Especially in their culture. Perhaps he *meant* to jump but didn't want his parents to know, so made it look like an accident."

"I think you've been listening to too many true-crime podcasts," Willa cut in to defuse the tension.

"You don't need to patronize me," Donna said tartly. "I'm just saying that it's a possibility."

"He didn't do it himself," said Jamie, fixing his eyes on her.

"Son, you don't know what people are going through. Lorraine said—"

"I don't give a *fuck* what Lorraine said."

Donna gaped at him, blank with shock. Jamie had never

raised his voice at her, let alone sworn. Harry and Tom looked on, similarly speechless.

"Jamie," Willa started, but he sprang from his chair and stormed out.

Willa excused herself and hurried after him. She knocked on his door, but he didn't answer. She knocked again more loudly. "I'm coming in," she called. Jamie was sitting on the bed, holding his hair in fists. "Hey," said Willa gently. "What's going on with you?"

He pointed at the door. "She knows fuck all about Zain, so why the fuck is she saying this?"

His anger disturbed her. She had never seen him like this. "Honey, you know what your grandma's like. She'd insist the sky was green before saying a bad word about your father."

"But she doesn't know the truth." Jamie gazed out at the balcony. "I shouldn't have left him. None of this would have happened."

"It's not your fault."

"You don't know that, Mum."

Willa felt regret. She could have eased the tension between them all, used her charms to loosen the knot. Instead, she chose to pull.

"What if he never wakes up?" Jamie's voice was small and wounded.

Willa didn't have a good answer to this. She sat next to him and held his head to hers, giving him somewhere to lean. "I need you to keep it together," she whispered. "I can't do this alone." She neatened a strand of his hair. "Your dad needs us." It wasn't an empty platitude. Lately, Tom would disappear for hours at a time, turning up from marathon runs wide-eyed like a madman. She and Jamie *had* to unite behind him. "I know that Zain meant a lot to you," she told him, "but right now, your dad needs you more." She fixed her gaze on him. "They're going to go after him, Jamie; and it's our job to protect him." She waited, watching him try for composure. "This is your dad's last weekend before the trial. Can we try to be there for him?"

Jamie nodded.

"Okay, come on. You owe your grandma an apology." She pulled him up and felt her anxiety churn. She wished she could carry him forward in time, past this nightmare trial. Or perhaps backward—before the point of Zain's fall to catch him just in time.

CHAPTER 15

Tom sat in the dock, behind a pane of bulletproof Perspex. He avoided looking at the judge even though he was sitting directly in front. He imagined judges to be toffee-nosed, lily-livered waifs, but Judge Braithwaite was nothing of the sort. Broad shouldered and heavy jawed, he sat like a king in his crimson gown. Tom tried to glean if he was half something else—Black, maybe? Surely not Asian with a name like Braithwaite.

His own barrister, Julian Hughes, fit the mold more closely. He was in his mid-forties, sharply dressed and with a haughty accent that filled Tom with confidence. He turned his attention to Salma's lawyer. She wasn't *Salma's* lawyer per se, as she represented the Crown Prosecution Service, but he also knew that this fight was between him and her.

Charlotte Ashman was in her late fifties, he suspected, and though her face was aged by fine lines, she had a delicate, refined air that made her if not alluring then certainly striking. Her light gray eyes were piercing and part of him wished he had a better vantage. The dock was behind the benches, which meant that she mostly had her back to him. Above him, the public gallery was hidden from his view. He knew that neither

Willa nor Jamie was there. They weren't allowed to watch the trial until they had given evidence.

To his left was the jury box with twelve men and women. Tom scanned them subtly. There were two Asian jurors, he noticed, two Black, and eight white. This lent him little comfort. Often, white people were the most staunchly anti-white, keen to show off their bleeding hearts. Might that fate await him?

Judge Braithwaite ran through his instructions for the jury. Tom listened impassively. His barrister had given him pointers on how to behave in the dock: Don't slouch or fidget, don't look aggressive, always assume that the jury is watching. Tom's instinct was to defy this but he was no longer a child in a classroom, smarmily faking obedience. Today, he had to mean it. He steeled himself as Charlotte Ashman stood to set out the case for the prosecution.

"Members of the jury. I appear for the prosecution in this trial and my learned friend Mr. Hughes appears for the defendant." She smoothed her black gown. "We've all heard the phrase 'appearances can be deceiving.' It's a cliché but like many clichés, it holds a kernel of truth. On the face of it, the defendant, Tom Hutton, seems perfectly respectable. Until recently, he held down a job at Sartre & Sartre, a well-known advertising agency. He is a husband and father and he takes an active role in the community. In May of this year, however, Mr. Hutton mounted a campaign of intimidation against his neighbors, culminating in the attempted murder of their son, Zain Khatun.

"Zain was only eighteen years old when he was found in Tom Hutton's garden on Friday the third of June of this year with grave injuries caused by a fall from height. Zain was taken to hospital but fell into a coma. Five months later, he remains in a vegetative state. So—what happened that day?

"According to Tom Hutton, he came home at five fifty that evening. He claims that he found Zain lying in the garden. He claims that he has no idea how Zain got there and that he immediately called the emergency services. It is our case that Tom Hutton knows exactly what happened, that he in fact *pushed* Zain from a third-story balcony, in the full knowledge that this could result in death. Here are four facts of the case.

"One: A neighbor saw a man matching Tom's description on the balcony at five fifty P.M., five minutes before he called the emergency services.

"Two: By his own account, Tom arrived home at five fifty P.M. This means that either the unknown man on the balcony and Tom were in the house at the same time and that man escaped without anyone else noticing—or the unknown man and Tom *are* the same man.

"Three: Leading up to the attack, Tom mounted a racially charged campaign of intimidation against the Khatun family. You will hear evidence that his own son, Jamie, hid his friendship with Zain for fear of reproach from Tom.

"Four: Tom had, on a prior occasion, threatened to hurt Zain. So, when he came home one day to find him in his house—at Jamie's invitation—he reacted violently."

Charlotte pointed at the dock. "Now, if Tom claimed self-defense, or said that he mistook Zain for an intruder, we might have understood, but he denies that he was there at all. He offers no alternative explanation, only that *he doesn't know*. According to Tom, it must have been a stranger that snuck into his home, pushed Zain from the balcony, then escaped just in time for Tom to arrive and discover Zain on his lawn. He offers no evidence to support this and so we have to rely on the facts. We know that Tom Hutton repeatedly clashed with his neighbors.

This is a central part of the puzzle, so this is where I'll start—with Zain's mother because it's Tom's relationship with her that led to his campaign: verbal abuse that became physical and ultimately verged on lethal. If you are convinced of these facts, members of the jury, then we ask that you find Tom Hutton guilty." She turned to the judge.

"If it may please my lord, I would like to call the first witness for the prosecution."

SALMA WALKED INTO THE COURTROOM, using long strides to signal confidence, false as it might be. She wished she hadn't worn a trouser suit, which so easily made short women look dumpy. She stepped into the witness box and resisted the urge to clear her throat in case it revealed her nerves. Years ago, she had watched a TED Talk by a famous voice coach who advised the audience to eliminate "uptalk," to lower the pitch of their voice, and to practice using pauses. Afterward, Salma had walked into the kitchen and fixed her gaze on Bil.

"What?" he'd asked, chopping a pepper, a preemptive smile on his lips.

"I watched a talk on speaking with authority and I'm learning how to use the . . . pause."

Bil had laughed and chucked a pepper at her. "Nicely done. Now help me with dinner."

She wondered now if Tom had ever had a need to worry about his credibility. He looked completely at ease in the dock: upright but with a looseness in his shoulders and no outward sign of stress. How strange it must be to never have to adjust yourself.

Salma turned her gaze to the jury and was pleased to see a

diverse mix. She didn't try for a smile in case it looked contrived, designed to curry sympathy. She spoke in a clear, measured tone as she took the oath, swearing to tell the truth, the whole truth, and nothing but the truth. She wouldn't dare do otherwise, almost expected an alarm to ring as soon as she told a lie.

Charlotte Ashman began with some basic questions. The prosecutor was on Salma's "side," but her clipped, efficient manner came across combative. With Salma's evidence, she sought to do two things: to prove that Tom acted aggressively and to sow the seed that this was racially motivated.

Piece by piece, she moved through the early incidents: the banner, the spray paint, Salma's tweet about "tolerant Britain," and the ensuing confrontation.

"Did Tom and Zain argue that day?" asked Charlotte.

"Yes. Tom was extremely aggressive."

"Did it get physical?"

"Almost. He got in Zain's face and was baiting him."

"In what way?"

"Saying things like 'little man' and 'if you think you can take me, then come on' or 'go and hide behind your mother.'"

"Did Tom threaten to hurt Zain?"

Salma had turned this over in her mind, trying to fashion what Tom had said into an explicit threat. "He said, 'Don't get involved with my family or you'll see what I can do.'"

"What was his tone of voice when he said this?"

"Aggressive. Angry. He was red in the face, baring his teeth. Just really, really . . . scary." Salma realized that this was true. For all her foot-stamping feminism, she was genuinely scared of Tom.

Charlotte angled her head. "If Tom had a problem with *your* tweet, why would he hurt Zain?"

Salma explained that Zain had recorded the confrontation about the tweet. "Tom's employer saw it. He blamed Zain for getting him fired."

"And he wished to make him pay?"

Julian whispered at Charlotte aggressively. "How can the witness possibly know that?"

Charlotte moved on smoothly. "What happened after the confrontation?"

Salma recounted the following days. The vandalized restaurant, the scratches on her car, the squatters, and then the day that Molly was taken. To Salma's dismay, Charlotte glossed over her suspicion that Tom had taken Molly. They had no real evidence but Salma knew, she *knew*, that Tom was responsible.

They moved on to Willa's miscarriage and Charlotte took pains to point out that this gave Tom another motive. Throughout the morning's evidence, Salma struggled to find momentum. She second-guessed every detail in case it came back to haunt her. She couldn't bear to be the reason that Zain was robbed of justice. By the afternoon, Salma was coiled with tension, ill-equipped to face the defense.

Julian Hughes pulled on a pair of glasses and adjusted them on his nose. His skin was so smooth and one-toned that Salma wondered if he used Botox. When he spoke, she found herself briefly disoriented. He couldn't be older than forty-five but had a voice from a different era, an era of wartime dispatches and black-and-white reels from British Pathé.

"Ms. Khatun, all of this seems to have started with the video clip, so I'd like to begin there, please."

Salma wanted to correct him but didn't want to seem combative. Really, it had started with the banner.

"Did you and Tom's wife have a coffee to discuss the video?"

"Yes."

"What was said during that meeting?"

"Willa asked me not to share the video."

"Did you agree?"

"Yes."

"And yet you shared it regardless?"

Salma tensed defensively. "No. My son uploaded it."

"Did he know at the time that you had promised not to share it?"

"I didn't 'promise.' I agreed."

Julian waved his pen. "Yes, yes. Fine. Did he know you *agreed* not to share it?"

"Yes."

"But he did it anyway. Why?"

"He . . . I was upset that Willa had offered me money not to share the video. I had already agreed not to and then she offered to pay me and it felt . . ."

Julian was flicking through his notes and looked up impatiently. "Felt what?"

"It felt demeaning."

"Ah! You felt like she was trying to buy you?"

"Yes."

"And you didn't like that?"

"No."

"Why?"

"Why?" Salma frowned. "No one likes to feel like they can be bought."

"No?" Julian feigned confusion. "But we all sell ourselves all the time. At least those of us who are employed. Did you have a specific issue with being offered money by a white person?"

Salma drew back in surprise. "No. Not specifically."

"Do you have an issue with white people?" He glanced down at his notes. "With white women in particular?"

"No, I don't."

He frowned. "I know it's a distasteful thing to admit, Ms. Khatun, but please tell the truth."

"That is the truth."

He winced as if his next act pained him. "Mr. Usher Gentleman, please."

The TV screens clicked on. A tweet was circled in red.

WW genuinely think they rule the world and that we're all just here to serve them.

"The username @eastlondonteacher—is that you?"

Heat rose in her cheeks. "Yes."

"Are you on Twitter very often?"

"Not often."

"But this *is* you? Dated last year?"

"Yes."

"Can I ask: What does WW mean?"

Salma squirmed. "White women," she said quietly.

Julian squinted at her. "White women?" He raised his brows in a stagey manner. "So that sentence in full reads: 'White women genuinely think they rule the world and that we're all just here to serve them.' Is that correct?"

Salma could feel the sharp focus of the jury. "Yes," she admitted.

Another tweet was shown on-screen.

WW are unbelievable.

This one was attached to a video and Salma wished that they would play it for much-needed context. It showed a middle-aged white woman preventing a Latino man from entering his own building because she did not believe he lived there. Julian gestured at the usher and another tweet came up.

WW's tears are lethal.

This was attached to a video that, again, was not played for the jury. This one was filmed by a bird-watcher who was verbally abused in Central Park after asking a woman to put her dog on a leash. Well aware that she was being filmed, the woman called the police and flagrantly feigned panic as she claimed she was under attack by an *African American* man. Salma had listened to the sickening tremble of the woman's voice and dashed off the tweet without thinking.

There were yet more.

Someone just told me not to park my car there because she wants the spot. The entitlement is strong with WW.

Salma dared not look at the jury.

"Do you know if your neighbor—a white woman—is on Twitter?"

"I don't," said Salma.

Julian pushed up his glasses. "I can tell you that she is. Would you like to see a sample of her tweets?"

Charlotte sprang up. "My lord, if I may, is there a point to this?"

Judge Braithwaite was busy reading the screen. "I'm interested to see where this goes, Ms. Ashman."

Now a sample of Willa's tweets were shown.

> *Just had the most amazing time with my*
> *bestie.*

This was attached to a picture of Willa and a pretty Asian woman holding cocktails up to the camera. Salma exhaled—a sharp, cynical sound that was louder than she'd intended.

> *Women of color need our support.*
> *Let's keep our feminism intersectional please.*
>   *#translivesmatter*
> *Representation matters. #OscarsSoWhite*
> *As a woman, I see the chasm between how I*
> *and my husband are treated. Now, imagine if*
> *I was also contending with race, class,*
> *disability, sexual orientation, gender identity.*
> *The UK establishment is NOT a meritocracy.*

Julian turned to Salma. "Does this look like someone who is racist?"

She tried to think how to answer this. "It's not Willa that hurt my son. It's her husband."

"And you think a woman like that would stay married to a racist?"

"I think, Mr. Hughes, that you would be surprised what people are willing to condone when not on a public platform."

"If that's true"—he pointed at the screen—"and you're already comfortable publicly disparaging white women, what do you say behind closed doors?"

She returned his glare. "I'm not the one on trial."

"No, but we do need to interrogate your reasons for accusing Tom Hutton, don't we, Ms. Khatun?" He waited, letting the rhetoric settle. "Tell me: Have your neighbors ever called you a racist slur?"

Salma considered this. "Not outwardly."

"What do you mean?"

"They've said things like 'these people.' Like 'These people don't know how lucky they are.'"

"'These people'? How do you know they weren't talking about teachers or chefs or neighbors or any number of things? Why assume the worst?"

Salma shook her head. "You're gaslighting me."

Julian scoffed. "No, Ms. Khatun, I am interrogating the facts. You cannot simply claim gaslighting to protect yourself from scrutiny. We are in a court of law, so I'll ask you again: Why did you assume the worst?"

"It wasn't an assumption. It was obvious."

"If they didn't use a racist slur, then it *is* an assumption, Ms. Khatun. You claim that they painted your window. Did you find a threat or slur edged into the paint?"

"No." Salma felt exhausted.

"Could it be that in your crusade against white women, you saw things that simply weren't there?"

"No."

"Well, what proof do you have?"

Salma tried to form a cogent answer, but Julian barreled on.

"According to you, when you and your son trespassed on Tom's property, he said, 'You'll see what I can do.' Why did you take this as a threat?"

Salma was choked with frustration. "Because it *was* a threat." She looked at the jury helplessly. "Are we really saying that it wasn't?" The jurors stared back impassively. "What else could he have meant?"

"I don't know, Ms. Khatun. Perhaps he meant the fandango. What I do know is that we simply cannot conclude that this was a threat of violence."

"I *can* conclude that and I am," said Salma.

"Well!" he said derisively. "You think all white women are out to get you, so . . ."

Charlotte aimed something vicious at him.

"Oh, not *you*, I'm sure," he said to Charlotte theatrically. "You're probably all right in her book."

"Mr. Hughes," the judge admonished.

Julian cracked a grin with a swift apology, then turned back to Salma. "Ms. Khatun, you moved to Blenheim in May, is that right?"

"Yes." Sweat lined the seams of her clothes and she prayed that it wasn't showing.

"Why?"

"We wanted more space."

"Where were you living before?"

"Seven Kings."

"Specifically Selborne Estate, is that right?"

"Yes."

"Your husband used to run Jakoni's, is that correct?"

"Yes."

"My wife and I dined there. It was very good."

Salma didn't know how to react to that. "Thank you," she replied, her manners kicking in.

"I was sad to see that it closed—around January time, wasn't it?"

"Yes."

"Why did it close?"

"It's the nature of the business. Most of hospitality struggled last year."

"So your restaurant closed in January and you moved to Blenheim in May. Presumably, selling the restaurant helped?"

Salma wasn't sure where this was headed. "We hadn't yet sold the restaurant."

Julian frowned. "You had to shut down your restaurant and yet you moved to a nicer house. That must have stretched you financially?"

"It did."

"So why didn't you wait awhile?"

"The sale was agreed and we didn't want to back out."

"No other reason?"

"That's the main reason," she told him.

"What other reasons did you have?"

"We wanted to move to a better area for the sake of our son."

Julian flicked a page of his notebook. "Why? Was he in trouble?" he asked casually.

Salma sensed a trap. "In a way."

"What kind of trouble?"

Salma tried to stay neutral. "Zain was involved in an incident at school. A weapon was found in his locker and he was expelled because of it."

"A weapon? What sort of weapon?"

"A knife." She felt the jury tense.

"Why did he need a knife?"

"It wasn't his."

"Whose was it?"

Salma shifted. "He wouldn't tell us."

Julian scoffed. "Well, isn't that convenient." He continued. "Were there any other signs that he was in trouble?"

"He came home one day with a bloody nose. It looked like he'd been in a fight but he wouldn't say what happened."

"So it's clear that someone wanted to hurt your son?"

So *this* was what Julian was trying to do: shift the blame from Tom.

"Ms. Khatun?" he pressed. "Did someone want to hurt your son? Is that why you left the area?"

"We wanted to give him a better life. Good kids can turn bad in a place like that."

Julian pounced on this. "Good kids can turn bad," he said with relish. "And that's what happened to your son, is it? He turned bad?"

"No," said Salma. "But he may have if we hadn't left."

"Ms. Khatun, just so we're clear: Your son is found with a knife. Soon after, he is attacked but you don't know by whom. You move a mere two miles away with the express goal of keeping him safe, and not long after, someone attacks Zain again. Is that the long and short of it?"

"This wasn't the same people."

"How do you know?"

"Because . . . they don't know where we live."

"You still work at the same school, no? Could they have followed you home?"

"That's not what happened. Why would he be in—"

"The fact is," Julian cut in, "there are people who wanted to hurt your son and you thought the threat was so real that you moved home even though you couldn't afford to, is that not correct?"

"No," she snapped.

"Which part?"

Salma faltered.

"Which part, Ms. Khatun?"

"We moved for several reasons. Because we wanted a better life."

"Because 'good kids can turn bad'! Well, Ms. Khatun, yours got mixed up in some very nasty business and you, in full flush of victimhood, automatically blamed your white neighbor. Isn't that true?"

"No."

"It is true, isn't it, Ms. Khatun?"

"No."

"I think it is."

"No, they . . . You're twisting things."

"That's not true, is it, Ms. Khatun?"

She couldn't unpick the question to answer the right way. *No, it's not true* that I'm blaming my neighbor, but *yes, it is true* that you're twisting things.

Julian looked at her pityingly. "I think we'll leave it there," he said.

Salma left the witness box, feeling marathon weak. Outside, she crumpled into Bil's arms and cried exhausted tears. She had thought that this day would bring relief, but instead she felt depleted, rendered mute and clumsy, and robbed of her chance at justice.

THE HOSPITAL LIGHTS WERE ON full blast—one of many things that Salma hated here. There was no slow advance to nighttime, no dusky evenings or soft lamplight. It was full beam, then sudden darkness: a harsh click of a switch. Funny because so many patients here were stuck in the gray between: light and dark, life and death, a murk from which they might never escape.

She took Zain's hand, which was cold to the touch, and saw

that his nails were blue. She held them to her mouth and gently blew to warm them. In that moment, with her own icy hand around his, she felt so endlessly ill-equipped. More than ever, she wished that her parents were alive. She needed people near who shared the same blood as Zain, as if they might revive him by sheer dint of volume. Samir, her brother, visited when he could, but he was based in Leeds and the trip down wasn't easy with three kids of his own. Most days, like today, it was just Salma and Bil.

She watched him maneuver a chair inside and squeeze in beside her. He looked tired, aged by this trauma. In the run-up to the trial, they had finally sold Jakoni's, but their finances had barely improved with Salma reducing her hours.

"How do people live like this?" he asked softly. He picked up a magazine and flipped it absentmindedly. On the back was an advert for Cartier: an elegant woman in a diamond bracelet. Salma found it hard to believe that such beauty remained in the world. Somewhere, this woman with her razor cheekbones was gliding through the same space and time. The thought seemed absurd.

Bil massaged his temple. "How can we go on like this?"

Salma didn't answer and realized that they were doing it again. Lately, she had noticed that they would loop into silence, one not answering the other's question, letting it stretch in the air, another distance between them. Yesterday, Bil had offered her a cup of tea and she hadn't responded, too weak and tired and emotionally exhausted to churn out a mere three words— *no, thank you*—so she hadn't said anything at all.

A nurse walked in and both she and Bil sprang to their feet as if she were bringing news when they knew full well it was just routine: blood pressure, temperature, feeds, a cursory nod at the parents, paired with a smile that turned down at the corners. In the early days, Salma had bought doughnuts and gift baskets for the nurses, convinced that if she bribed them hard enough, they could magic Zain into waking—that they would give him extra care, extra drugs, extra attention—but as the months wore on, she realized that they could only care so much. They would fluff his pillow, check his sores, and wash his pallid skin, but could only give so much of themselves. Salma wanted him treated with special care, but of course he wasn't special to them, which was why *she* was here, making sure that he knew he was loved.

Bil gestured toward the door, not quite meeting Salma's eye. "I'll wait downstairs," he said. He didn't like saying good-bye to their son, so left that duty to Salma. She didn't mind. She needed those minutes alone with Zain. Even in a long marriage, it was embarrassing to fully reveal yourself. She and Bil had been through so much, but she didn't want him to see her pray, to desperately beseech the universe to bring her son back to her.

She bent and rested her forehead on the soft blue blanket. She did what she always did: bargain with a higher power. If Zain woke up, she would never ask for anything again. If he regained his health, she would surrender hers. If he would only speak, she would give all her money to charity. If he did not, however, then she would sneak into Tom's house one night and pick up his biggest knife and sink it into his son. *You took my child, so I'll take yours.* It chilled her to realize that Tom had already lost one. Had he had the very same thought? *You took my child, so I'll take yours.*

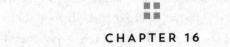

CHAPTER 16

Salma watched Bil in the witness box and was thankful for all those subtle markers by which others judged him: the preppy way that he dressed, the accent forged in Hampshire, his calm, unshowy manner.

Charlotte stood to question him. "Bil, why did you and your family move to Blenheim?"

"We wanted a better quality of life," he said. "Fairlop is nicer than Seven Kings, which is why we moved."

"Any other reason?"

He glanced at the jury. "Well, I was lucky in that I grew up in Hampshire. I saw that there was life beyond London, beyond tower-block living, and I wanted to give that to my son."

"Give your son what exactly?"

"An insight into what this country really is. Green and pleasant, yes, but also kind and tolerant, civil and generous. When you live in the thick of a city, it's easy to forget these things. I wanted him to see what I've seen."

Salma yearned for the country of Bil's description. She looked over at the jury and could see that they were taken by him.

"What was Blenheim like?"

Bil smiled. "It was lovely. Green, quiet, no litter, no graffiti, no godforsaken mattress on the corner of the street."

At this, a few of the jurors smiled.

"It was everything we wanted." Bil visibly tensed. "Until it wasn't."

"Why?"

"Our neighbors made our lives very difficult."

Salma listened as Bil ran through the same litany of issues, starting with the banner and ending with the police raiding their house at dawn. In his mouth, each took on a deeper gravity. Here was a man who believed in Great Britain and Great British Values, so if *he* said there were problems, then maybe it was true.

Julian Hughes was clearly keen to test this and stood with a sharklike relish to cross-examine Bil. "Mr. Khatun, I believe that you met the defendant, Tom Hutton, at a neighborhood barbecue. Is that correct?"

"Yes."

"Was there any animosity between you at that barbecue?"

"No."

"No insults traded? No slurs exchanged?"

"No."

"Do you think that your neighbors are racist?"

Bil hesitated and Salma squirmed with impatience. He always gave people the benefit of the doubt but this was no time to hedge. *Come on, Bil, for fuck's sake.*

"I think they exhibited racist behavior," he said.

Julian made an outraged sound. "That's a very serious accusation, Mr. Khatun."

"More serious than actually being racist?"

Salma was startled by this. Bil was rarely this spiky.

"If it's a false accusation, then yes," said Julian.

"My son is lying in hospital, so please don't talk to me about why name-calling is worse than actual violence."

"I must contest that, Mr. Khatun. It's not mere 'name-calling' to label someone a racist. It is life-destroying behavior and we should not condone it."

"Neither should we condone people attacking others because of the color of their skin."

Salma felt a loping sorrow. Her stoic, pragmatic husband was being driven to say things on which he normally demurred. When they had debates at home, he would play devil's advocate but here he was, being "that type of Asian."

Julian moved on smoothly. "Mr. Khatun, you mentioned that the police raided your home on the morning of Tuesday the twenty-fourth of May. Can you remind me of the reason?"

Bil shifted uneasily. "They received a false tip that my son was dealing knives."

Julian frowned. "Dealing knives. As in selling them illegally?"

"Yes."

"And was he?"

"No." Bil explained the real reason Zain had had those knives.

"Who do you think reported it to the police?"

Bil glanced at the dock. "I believe it was Tom Hutton."

"And did you want to retaliate? Is that why you claim that Tom Hutton hurt your son?"

"My son was found in his garden. I don't think that's a coincidence."

Julian tapped his pen against his palm. "But isn't it true that your son had issues while you were in Selborne Estate? Tell me: Does moving two miles across the A12 suddenly make Zain a good boy?"

Bil looked at the floor. "You won't understand," he said.

"Well, explain it to me, Mr. Khatun."

A muscle tensed in his jaw. Salma knew from the look on his

face that he was trying to make a decision. Was this worth the hassle, or was it easier to nod and carry on?

"Where do you live, Mr. Hughes?" asked Bil.

Julian smirked. "I'm not the one in the witness box, sir."

"I know, and I will answer your question but will you first indulge me?"

Julian clearly sensed the jurors' interest, for he tilted his head graciously. "I live in Kensington."

"I see. Do you think there's a difference between, say, Grenfell Tower and Kensington Park Gardens?"

Julian sighed. "I see what you're trying to do, Mr. Khatun, but—"

"There's less than a mile between," said Bil with a small, bitter smile. "But it might as well be a thousand, so you can stand there and patronize me, sir, but I'll still tell you the truth: Yes, I *did* believe that moving two miles would make a difference to our son." His voice held a hairline crack. "But maybe I was wrong. Maybe I was a fool because my son still ended up in hospital."

Julian righted his robe and Salma could see that he was stalling. He had given Bil too much leeway. "So you agree then?" he said, maneuvering him to where he wanted. "There were people who wanted to hurt your son despite the fact that you had moved?"

"Yes," Bil said quietly. "I suppose there were."

It broke Salma's heart to see the give in his eyes.

Julian shifted gears. "Did Zain take drugs?"

Bil didn't answer straightaway. "He occasionally smoked marijuana."

Salma bristled. She wasn't aware of this.

"I caught him once in the shed—but what kids *don't*?"

"Did he ever deal it?"

Bil drew back. "No, of course not."

Julian gestured at the usher and the courtroom screens blinked on. A square picture was shown, taken from Zain's Instagram feed. It showed a stack of fifty-pound notes next to a dusting of what could have been marijuana. The caption read: *high on life & getting coin*.

Bil made a face as if to say, *Come on, give me a break*. "He was sixteen then. Clearly, he was just posturing."

"Why clearly?"

"Because he was young. That's what boys do."

"Where did he get those fifty-pound notes?"

"His best friend's dad owns a takeaway. He helped out there sometimes. They were probably clearing out the till."

"So you're absolutely certain this isn't drug money?"

"That's ridiculous."

"Why?"

"Because it *is*. Jesus Christ, you really can't win." The judge cleared his throat and Bil muted his tone. "Mr. Hughes, my son was *not* a gang member or a drug dealer or, what's next on your bingo card—terrorist? He was none of those things. He was just a normal boy who was trying to work out what to do with his life."

"Such as 'getting coin,' you mean?"

Bil shook his head with resignation. What else could he possibly say?

Julian Hughes looked at the judge. "I have no further questions, my lord."

SALMA LET MOLLY OFF HER leash as they entered Fairlop Waters. She didn't usually venture here on their evening walk—too conscious of every distant sound and footfall—but today she needed time to walk off her mood. She was angry that Julian Hughes had recast her son as a thug. It made her feel hopeless. More than that, it made her feel *homeless*—a strange new membrane in her body that showed she didn't belong.

Behind Salma, Molly barked at something approaching. A figure emerged from the fog, setting her senses on high alert. She told herself to be logical. Clearly, the man would run on but instead he slowed to a jog. She saw the rope of muscle in his arms and with a jolt realized who it was. Their eyes met, and instinctively, Salma pulled Molly closer. Her gentle old dog offered little protection, but she felt safer next to her. Tom took a quick glance behind him and came to a stop by Salma. She realized then that she had wandered off-path by autopilot, onto a deserted trail that she and Molly walked by day. Had Tom followed her there?

"I want to talk to you," he said.

She backed away, straight into a tree trunk. "Did you follow me?" Her voice had a watery quality.

He regarded her with cool amusement.

"Did you follow me?" she repeated.

"Yes," he sneered, enjoying the look in her eyes. He stepped closer, his face inches from hers.

Salma's alarm magnified everything around her: the gust of wind pleating the water, the crackle of static in her scarf. She wanted to reach out and push him but knew that this would give him an excuse for violence.

He watched her for a few more seconds, and then he burst out laughing. "No, I didn't fucking follow you, you stupid bint."

"Then what are you doing here?" She spoke with studied

calm, like one might do to a predator. If she panicked, he would surely react to it.

"You fucking *know* I didn't hurt your son. You *know* I didn't."

"I don't know that."

"Don't fucking *lie*." He slapped the tree behind her and Salma made a sharp, involuntary sound.

"Why do you hate us?" she asked.

He smirked. "You know why I hate you? Because of this." He plucked at his vest, a thin wicking material. "Because I can't even go on a run without being accused of harassing you. If I wanted, I could hurt you." He clenched a fist and pressed it on the bark above her head. "But I won't—and yet look at you, shriveled up like a fucking louse, terrified of me."

Salma let her breath out. "Don't men like you enjoy that? Scaring women?"

He scoffed. "Give me a break. If I wanted to scare you, you wouldn't be standing in front of me."

"Would I be lying in the hospital?" She found a crumb of courage.

He bared his teeth in a grin. "Maybe. Or maybe you'd be in the ground."

She flinched and could see that he enjoyed it.

His cold laughter billowed in the air as he moved away from her, back into his run, snaking deeper into the trees. Salma began to shake, her panic tuned to the nearness of him. Her fingers kept slipping as she snapped Molly's lead back on. She broke into a jog and didn't stop running until they were home. There, Salma found that she couldn't stop shaking. Molly padded to her basket and sat there solemnly. Salma knelt in front, needing someone near to calm her. She thought about calling Bil, but he was at work after a full day in court. She imagined the strain in his voice—*do you want me to come home*—and knew that he would if she just said the word, but really what could he do? She considered calling DC Rayner to report the run-in with Tom. She thought of the hours-long interview, the probing for proof she couldn't give and, worst of all, the likely delay of the trial. She couldn't put that in jeopardy, not after so many months of waiting.

Molly whined and placed a paw on Salma's knee as if offering comfort.

"It's okay, sweet girl," said Salma. "He barely scared me anyway." She pressed her cheek into Molly's fur. "We have to carry on, sweetheart. That's the best thing for Zain." Molly made a mournful sound and Salma stroked her coat. "I know you miss him. He misses you too." She let the tears come, Molly's warm body breathing in her arms.

WELL INTO HER SEVENTIES, JOSEPHINE Steinem was a formidable woman. Her thick gray hair was in a sixties flip, lacquered into submission, and she wore royal-blue trousers and a crimson jacket with gold epaulets and buttons. She was the sort of woman you noticed: a mix of Jackie O grace and wartime grit that spoke of former glory.

Josephine was the final witness for the prosecution and the jurors watched with interest. For the last two days, they had sat through medical and forensic evidence and clearly wanted something more engaging to close out the week. Salma waited nervously as Josephine took the oath. She wondered how a woman like her had ended up living at Blenheim. She seemed more suited to country estates than their soulless stretch of the suburbs.

"Ms. Steinem," Charlotte started. "Do you remember what you were doing between five P.M. to six P.M. on Friday the third of June?"

"Yes, I do. I was watching *The Chase*, a quiz show on ITV. My husband and I watch it every evening." She smiled fondly. "I always fare better than him."

Salma warmed to the woman. She and Zain watched the same show—a tradition she had started following his injury. She found comfort in its questions, which were neither too hard nor too easy, just the right mix to make the viewer feel clever.

"Where in your house were you watching it?" asked Charlotte.

"In the living room."

"On the ground floor?"

"Yes."

"Did you at any time leave the living room?"

"Yes. I went upstairs to collect a blanket. My husband no longer does well with stairs. I struggle too but less so."

"Where did you get the blanket from?"

"The spare room on the top floor. I don't tend to use the one from our bedroom because we have to remember to take it back at the end of the evening."

"What time was this?"

"Five fifty P.M."

"That's very specific. Did you happen to look at a clock?"

"Oh no." She smiled. "The advertisements always come on at five fifty before the Final Chase, so I popped upstairs for the blanket."

"What did you see while you were there?"

"I saw something move on the balcony opposite. I pulled

the curtain to take a look and saw someone on the balcony looking into their garden. I couldn't see what they were looking at."

"Could you see who was on the balcony?"

"Oh yes."

"Who was it?"

"My neighbor Tom Hutton."

"Your neighbor Tom Hutton," Charlotte repeated. "And how do you know it was him?"

Josephine gestured as if it should be obvious. "Because I know what he looks like."

"You would have been over twenty meters from his balcony. Are you sure that it was Tom Hutton you saw?"

"I'm absolutely certain. He had the same build and the same color hair."

Salma looked on and felt a shoot of hope. If this calm and confident woman had seen Tom herself, then surely he couldn't deny it?

"How did he seem?" asked Charlotte.

"I couldn't really say. It seemed as if he had dropped something because he was looking down at the garden."

"Did he seem agitated? Stressed? Worried?"

Josephine grimaced. "Again, I couldn't really say. It wasn't remarkable enough for me to stop. I took my blanket and went downstairs."

Charlotte seemed satisfied by this. "And just to reiterate, you are absolutely certain it was Tom Hutton you saw?"

"Yes. Positive."

"Okay, thank you, Ms. Steinem. Please remain there, as I'm sure my learned friend will have some questions for you."

Julian Hughes stood now and smiled at Josephine. "You're a

wonderful speaker, Ms. Steinem," he said. "Do you have experience with public speaking?"

She beamed at this and fiddled with a button on her crimson jacket. "Oh no. Not at all."

"No teaching or maybe even acting?"

She laughed girlishly. "Heavens no. My husband was a civil servant and I brought up our children."

Julian put on a joshing tone. "But you've been to court before I bet. You're so confident up there!"

She laughed again. "Well, if you must know, I've been a witness before."

"Oh? When was this?"

"Just last year in fact."

He nodded. "Any time before that?"

"Well, in fact, the year before that too. There was a road traffic accident and I—"

Julian cut in. "And before that?"

"Well . . . there have been several occasions. I seem to always be in the wrong place at the wrong time!"

Julian didn't laugh. Instead, he pulled out a sheet of paper from the pages of his notebook. "Is it true, Ms. Steinem, that you have given evidence in a total of twelve trials over the past ten years?"

Her eyes rounded. "Well, it couldn't possibly be that many."

Julian nodded at the usher who handed her a piece of paper.

Josephine squinted at it.

"Were you a witness in all these trials, Ms. Steinem?"

She clucked with surprise. "Well, I suppose I was."

"Ms. Steinem, have you ever inserted yourself into an investigation?"

"Inserted?" She was flummoxed. "I've *helped*, if that's what you mean."

"In a total of twelve cases?"

Salma looked on with increasing dismay. Julian was trying to insinuate that Josephine was a busybody.

"Well, yes," she admitted. "According to this."

"I notice you squinting at the sheet, Ms. Steinem. Do you have problems with your eyesight?"

She scowled, affronted now. "Only when I'm reading. It's perfectly fine at a distance."

"Is that so?"

"That's so."

"In that case, would you mind pointing out Tom Hutton in the dock?"

Josephine scoffed and before Charlotte could stop her, she raised a finger at Tom in the dock.

"Why do you think that's Tom?" asked Julian.

"Because he's less than ten meters away from me," she said impatiently. "Because I know what he looks like. And because he's wearing his orange cap."

"Fair enough," Julian conceded. He turned toward the dock. "Could the gentleman in the orange cap please stand up?"

For a moment, no one moved and the sounds of the court amplified. Then Tom stood up and took off his cap. To Josephine's obvious shock, it wasn't Tom at all. This man was of a similar build but with different-colored hair—almost blond to Tom's dark brown—and completely different features.

Julian continued smoothly. "Will the defendant, Tom Hutton, please make himself known?"

This time, it was Tom who stood up. He was at the opposite end of the dock, in clear sight line of the witness box.

Julian swallowed a smile. "I have no more questions, my lord."

Charlotte re-examined Josephine but the damage was already done. Valiantly, she tried to salvage her denouement, but eventually, she stopped and turned to the judge. "That is the case for the Crown, my lord."

Even from where she was sitting, Salma could see the defeat in her shoulders.

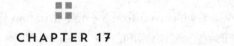

CHAPTER 17

Tom knotted his tie but then saw that the tip was two inches too short. He swore and started again, the sweat of his fingertips staining the burgundy silk. Willa came up beside him, already dressed and ready. Sometimes, in the morning, when she had no makeup on, Tom could not believe that she had chosen him. Now, in full glory, she could bring a man to his knees.

She redid his tie and Tom searched her face for traces of respect. He had heard a thousand songs about falling out of love, but no one had told him how shaming it was to lose your wife's respect. Six months had passed since he'd lost his job at Sartre & Sartre and still he worked at the warehouse. In these times, there was little use for disgraced admen, but everyone needed online shopping. Tom knew that this embarrassed Willa and had fretted that this would be the thing that drove her away. As it turned out, it wasn't taking a job at the warehouse that lost him her respect. It happened four weeks after that when Willa asked him to book dates in his diary for a friend's wedding in Italy.

"We can't afford to go," he told her, scrolling the custom website.

Willa fixed her gaze on him. "You don't have to come but I'm going."

"Hon, we can't afford a single thing on their registry."

"Everyone is going," she snapped. "I've already given up so much. I'm not giving this up as well." She stalked out, leaving him mute with shame. If Tom had stuck to his convictions, things would have been okay, but instead he did something that he vowed he never would.

He found Willa downstairs and sat her on the sofa. "Okay. I'll apologize."

She blinked, confused.

"I'll apologize to your dad and you can ask him to help with money." Tom exhaled as if a great weight had been lifted, but then he watched her face change: crease into something sour. That's the moment it happened, when Willa lost respect for him. Up to that point, Tom had been firm, principled, unyielding. Now he was . . . what? A loser whose pride had cost her so much but ultimately proved worthless.

Willa didn't ask her father after all, and somehow that made it worse. It was her coded way of telling Tom, *You may have lost your pride but I still have mine*. In the months since, things had been unsteady and Tom knew without a doubt that if he was found guilty, Willa would not wait for him. If he was convicted, he would lose her. Lose everything.

Today, it was his turn in the witness box and he was keenly aware that just one careless look could turn the jury against him. The lie told by the courts was that justice was blind—rigorous and foolproof—but there were prejudices at play: experiences and inferences that invariably filtered through. Tom would try to present himself as moral and upstanding, but if they got just a glimmer of his rage, then that would be the end for him.

Nerves fired in his limbs and he thought of that day in the garden: running to Zain, checking his pulse, calling the police in a panic. He really *had* willed him to wake, really *had* willed him to be okay. But now, fingered as the villain, he only wished ill on Salma. He wanted nothing for her but pain.

SALMA BRISTLED AS SHE WATCHED Tom walk to the witness box. In his navy suit, burgundy tie, and pocket square, he looked every inch the gentleman. Sure enough, as he took the oath, his voice dropped to a respectful key with none of his usual bravado. Gone was the man who shouted across a barbecue to call for another beer. Gone certainly was the man who cornered her last week under the cover of darkness. She recalled his vicious smile and was appalled that an expensive suit could mask who he really was.

"Mr. Hutton. Tom, if I may," said Julian. "What was your first impression of your neighbors?"

"They seemed nice. Educated. Professional. A little bit reserved but that's normal when you move into a new area. We wanted to make them feel welcome, so we made an effort to talk to them."

"Did anything happen that night to make them think you had a problem with them?"

"Not at all. We had a nice chat and they seemed to be having a good time although . . ." Tom hesitated. "I got the impression that they were humoring us."

"In what way?"

"Well, at one point, the hostess, a lovely woman named Linda, said to them that she loves spicy food, and next time, they could bring something with a bit more 'zing' I think she said. Salma and her husband didn't seem to like that."

"What makes you think that?"

"Well, I saw them exchange this look as if they were sneering at her. Maybe they thought that Linda was being, I don't know, 'offensive,' but they didn't seem to like it."

"So they came across as somewhat sensitive?"

"Yes."

Salma squirmed. They *had* been a bit judgmental that night and clearly Tom had sensed it.

"When was the first time there was friction between your families?" Julian asked.

Tom mulled over this. "I suppose it was when I asked if she and her husband minded not parking in front of our house. She got a bit passive-aggressive, said something like 'Oh, I didn't realize there was *designated* parking.'" He said the words tartly—nothing like Salma's actual tone. "I didn't want to say that this was poor etiquette, so I sort of waved it away, said that if she had to, it was fine obviously but it was a bit of a pain for us to park around the corner."

"And this was how many weeks after they moved in?"

"Oh, days. Maybe a week."

"And there were already problems?"

"Yes."

Julian nodded meditatively. Over the next hour, he took Tom through their various clashes. "Did you ever try to call a truce?"

"Yes. Willa took her out for coffee to smooth things over, but Salma stormed out. She was offended that we offered to pay for the scratches on her car as a gesture of goodwill. To be honest, it seemed like she had written a victimhood narrative for herself and refused to entertain anything else."

"Was she angry at Willa?"

Tom shifted uncomfortably. "Yes. I got the sense that it was Willa in particular that she didn't like."

"Oh?" Julian tilted his head. "Why?"

"I caught her looking at Willa sometimes with this strange scowl on her face like she annoyed her."

Salma squirmed, embarrassed by the fact that Tom had noticed this. It wasn't *Willa* in particular but the archetype of her. Beautiful, skinny white women who wore their looks with false humility, constantly insisting that *I'm just like you. Look at me make this ugly face which isn't ugly at all!* Salma knew that she should have outgrown this puerile jealousy, but women like Willa still rankled.

"Tom, did you ever get the feeling that Salma disliked Willa because she's a white woman? A 'WW,' as she puts it on Twitter?"

Tom frowned. "To be honest? No. I thought it was just feminine competition but maybe I was wrong."

Julian nodded sagely. "Much of what happened were small neighborly disputes, but just so we're clear: Did you ever key Salma Khatun's car?"

"No, sir."

"Did you steal her dog?"

"No, sir."

"Did you tell someone else to steal her dog?"

"No, sir."

"Did you report her son for selling knives?"

"No, sir."

"And did you paint her window?"

Tom exhaled slowly. "Yes, I did do that, sir."

Salma stared at him, shocked by the fact that he had admitted it. So, it *was* him after all.

"Why did you do that?" Julian asked.

"It was a stupid thing. I should have acted like an adult but I was annoyed that they put up the banner when the regulations clearly state that you're not allowed to. I wanted to discourage them and I thought they would blame the local youths and that would be that. It was a moment of stupidity, but to leap from that to some of the things they've accused me of . . . It's just madness."

"Now, Tom, you accept that you should not have touched their banner. Can I ask: Did you have a problem with its message? I believe it said . . ." Julian paused to squint at his notebook. "Black. Lives. Matter." He raised his brows. "Did you disagree with that?"

"Of course not. It could have said Blue Lives Matter for all I cared. I just wanted them to understand that it wasn't allowed."

"So why not talk to them?"

Tom grimaced. "I know now that I should have, but honestly, I thought that making it look like local kids would make them feel more comfortable. If you think your neighbors are nit-picking over everything, you'll never feel at home. If it's just local kids, it doesn't feel so intrusive. I honestly wanted them to feel safe here. I just did it in a clumsy way and for that I am genuinely sorry."

Salma was almost convinced by this display of remorse. Tom was so emphatic, so earnest, it was hard not to believe him. She watched for giveaway signs—the nervous dart of his eyes, a compulsive tap or tic—but he was calm and credible.

Julian continued. "Tom, did you have any sort of conversation with your neighbors about your wife's miscarriage? Did they give you an explanation? An apology?"

Tom faltered and the effect on the jury was palpable. Here

was a father still grieving. "No," he said softly. "We were left to mourn our child alone."

"And how did that make you feel?"

"We were . . . devastated."

"Were you angry?"

"Yes," said Tom. "A little."

"Enough to seek revenge?"

He drew back in surprise. "No, sir. I live by rules. It's partly why I reacted so strongly to the banner in the first place."

Salma felt heat in her cheeks. This thoughtful, penitent man was nothing like the one in the park, but the jury couldn't see this.

"Did you have any contact with Zain after the day of your wife's miscarriage?"

"No, sir. As far as I was concerned, we could all move on separately—but then I found Zain in our garden."

"What went through your mind when you found him?"

"I didn't think. My training as a first-aider kicked in. I checked his pulse and called an ambulance. I was scared to put him in recovery position because he . . . His body was twisted awkwardly and I didn't want to do any damage."

"Did you go with the ambulance?"

"No, the police took me to the station and the next thing I know I'm being arrested for attempted murder. All because I painted a window."

CHARLOTTE ASHMAN FIXED HER STONY gaze on Tom. "Mr. Hutton, you make a meal of the fact that you follow rules and believe in regulations. What regulation states that you can't display a banner in your window?"

He didn't miss a beat. "Section twenty-four of Blenheim's housing regulations."

"And you are the self-appointed keeper of the regulations, are you?"

He ignored the tartness in her tone. "No, but we live in the sort of place that cares about the rules."

"Is placing a banner in your window against the law?"

"No."

"Do you know what *is* against the law? Painting a neighbor's window."

Salma saw the hard knot of his Adam's apple as he worked to form an answer.

"I regret that deeply," he said. "I should have spoken to them directly, but I didn't want them to feel unwelcome."

"You see, I don't understand that logic. You wanted them to feel welcome, so instead of having a friendly word, the next time you bumped into them, you made a very clear act of aggression. Wouldn't that make them feel the opposite of welcome?"

Tom shifted uneasily. "As I said, I thought they would blame the local youths and that would help preserve the idea that *we* are a community and that those forces are outside us."

"That is some tortured logic there, I have to say, Mr. Hutton."

"And I'm sorry for that. It reflects how muddled I was at the time."

Charlotte moved on. "Have any of your other neighbors put up banners from time to time?"

Tom thought this over. "Occasionally."

"And have you ever knocked out those banners?"

"I can't recall, but I may well have."

"Interesting. We had a look at various videos uploaded to Blenheim's Facebook page. Do you know what we saw?" Charlotte gestured at the usher and the TV screens blinked on. Three separate houses were shown on-screen, all displaying the St. George's Cross—one on the front door, another in a plant pot, and a third hanging limply from a makeshift pole. A fourth house showed the union flag.

"These pictures show houses on your street, taken last year. Did you remove any of those flags or banners?"

Tom cleared his throat. "That's different. It was during the football."

"Okay, but according to—what was it?" She glanced at her notebook. "Section twenty-four of Blenheim's housing regulations, residents couldn't display any sort of banners, and you felt so strongly about this that you were willing to break the law. But these, you just left?"

"As I said, the football was on and one was for VE Day. It would be petty to force people to take them down."

"So it wasn't *all* banners with which you had an issue? Just ones that stated that *Black Lives Matter*?"

Tom grew impatient. "It seemed deliberately provocative. Look, I would understand if Salma were Black, or had a Black family, but she's not and she doesn't, so what was she trying to prove?"

"So you did have a problem with the message of the banner and not the banner itself?"

Tom colored.

"The fact is: If that banner was a St. George's Cross, you would have left it alone, yes?"

He didn't answer.

Charlotte's voice grew louder. "Mr. Hutton, isn't it true that if that banner was a St. George's Cross, you would have left it alone?"

"No," he said testily. "The people who know me know me. This isn't what you say it is."

"Is that why your employers fired you? Because they *know* you?" She waited. "Tell me, Mr. Hutton. Why did they fire you?"

He took a moment to answer. "They saw a video of me and Salma arguing and they didn't like it."

"This is the video recorded by the victim, Zain Khatun?"

"Yes."

"What happened on the video that your employers felt they had to fire you?"

Tom glanced at the public gallery. "Salma called me intolerant and that upset me. I was trying to explain that I *was* tolerant."

"How?"

"Like, I tolerate it when they park in our space or when their dog barks at night."

"What else?"

He swallowed. "I don't remember exactly."

"Really? This video got you *fired* and you 'don't remember exactly'?" Charlotte motioned at the TV. "Well, why don't we jog your memory?"

The screen showed the clip of Tom, bent aggressively over Salma. "And you call *me* intolerant?" he was saying. "If I were intolerant, I'd tell your husband not to park in our bay and I'd tell you to shut up that fucking dog of yours." He pointed a finger in her face. "I'd tell you to fix that fucking fence. And I'd tell you to keep your windows closed so you don't stink up our clothes with your cooking!"

Audible shock rose in the courtroom, a stark shift in loyalties. A juror stared open-mouthed at the screen. Another visibly squirmed. Salma understood now why Charlotte had waited to show the video. She wanted the jury to see the respectable face of Tom before she unmasked him.

"Stink," said Charlotte. The word echoed cleanly. "What did you mean by that?"

The color in his face deepened. "Cooking that smells," he said.

"Of what?"

"Of whatever they're cooking at the time."

"What are they usually cooking?"

A muscle twitched in his jaw. "Look, people think I specifically meant Indian food, which sometimes has strong flavors, but I meant *in general*." His lips screwed in frustration. "She just took everything the wrong way. When you move into a new area, you should try to get along, not make a big deal of your differences, try to fit in."

"Especially if you're not white?"

"That isn't . . . Stop making this into something it's not."

"The truth is, Mr. Hutton, that you expected your neighbors to be quiet and unobtrusive, and when Salma Khatun dared to stand up to you, you took that personally. You wanted to teach her a lesson, didn't you?"

"No. She's the one that's been spitting hate on social media. Maybe you should question *her*."

"Isn't it also true," said Charlotte, "that your son, Jamie, hid his friendship with Zain from you?"

Tom stalled.

"On the evening of Friday the third of June, Jamie gave Zain permission to work in his room while he went to his tutoring. You were not aware of this, so when you came home to find Zain in your house, you lost your temper, isn't that right?"

"No, I didn't even go upstairs."

"Why did you push him, Mr. Hutton?"

"I didn't."

"Was he giving you lip?"

"I didn't."

"Did he stand up to you? Get in your face?"

"No."

"But didn't you threaten him mere weeks earlier with 'you'll see what I can do'?"

"No."

"You didn't say that?"

"I did, but—"

"So you did threaten him?"

"It wasn't a threat. I was just posturing."

"Were you posturing when you pushed him?"

"I didn't push him!"

Charlotte scoffed. "Well then, can you explain this?"

This time, there was no video on the screens, just the blue status bar of an audio clip.

With cold horror, Salma realized that it was Tom's call to the emergency services.

Yes, he's breathing. Tom's voice was high and manic. *You've got to hurry. Please! I don't know. Okay. Okay, I'll stay on the line.*

Salma closed her eyes and the image came to her: Zain bent at an awful angle, purple against dark green.

There was a rustle on the line as if the phone had been set in the grass. Then Tom's voice came in a faint whimper, but the words were unintelligible. Charlotte paused it.

"Members of the jury, you will hear those last few seconds again but this time amplified by three hundred percent and cleaned of additional noise."

Tom's voice was still low but the words were far clearer: *I didn't mean it. Oh god, I didn't mean it.*

Charlotte paused it again. "What didn't you mean, Mr. Hutton?"

His face changed, now a mask of sorrow.

Charlotte let the silence steep then, almost gently, repeated, "What didn't you mean?"

"All of it," he said finally. "The things I said to his family. The way I acted."

Charlotte tilted her head. "That would be a very odd choice of words, Mr. Hutton, and a very odd time to apologize for something unrelated."

"I wanted to say sorry. I wanted him to know he was safe." Tom drew an uneven breath. "There was something I read about the Stephen Lawrence case years ago. The woman who found him, she cradled him and she said, 'You are loved.'" Tom stopped here and Salma was amazed to see tears in his eyes.

"I always thought that that was such a generous and thoughtful thing to say. She didn't lie and tell him, 'You're going to be okay,' because she knew that he wouldn't, but she said, 'You are loved,' and I thought that if I was in that situation, I would want someone to be kind to me. I was trying to make Zain feel safe in case . . ." Here, Tom trailed off.

"In case he died?" said Charlotte bluntly, making Salma flinch.

"Yes," said Tom.

"He didn't die, Mr. Hutton, but he cannot speak or move or tell the truth, and the least he deserves is the truth from you, so tell us: You pushed him, didn't you?"

Tom hung his head, the stance of a man who was guilty. When he blinked, tears dripped to the tip of his collar. "It wasn't me," he said.

"Then who?" Charlotte asked softly.

He brushed away his tears. Pressure built in Salma's chest. Tom was on the cusp of speaking and the entire courtroom held its breath. But then the words died on his lips and instead he said, "I don't know."

KIA ABDULLAH ■ 256

Charlotte exhaled and the courtroom exhaled with her. For a moment, they had all believed that Tom would name the culprit. Instead, he clung to ignorance and used it as a shield. After all, how could you prove him wrong when all he could say was *I don't know?*

SALMA GRIPPED BIL'S HAND AS they left the courthouse. The wind was fierce and held a cold blade to her brain. A flash of light popped nearby and she realized there were photographers. They crowded around her and pelted her with questions. A microphone grazed her cheek and she ducked away from it, stumbling into Bil. He gripped her wrist and advanced through the mass.

"Excuse me," he said, using his free arm to ward them off. "Please excuse me." His voice grew harder as one journalist jostled his way to Salma and started shouting his question at her. Bil pressed a firm hand against the man's chest. "Please don't shout at my wife," he said, his voice edging past polite. When he tried to push past to get to Salma, Bil gave him a violent shove. He stumbled and lost his footing. Others scrabbled ahead of him and pursued Bil and Salma to their car.

"Fucking leeches." Bil slammed the door shut. He disliked journalists, often called them self-important, but Salma suspected that he'd never got over a lukewarm review of Jakoni's. This was the way of outsiders. When you finally arrived at the inner sanctum and found yourself unwelcome, you pretended you didn't want it.

"You shouldn't have done that," she said after the crowd dispersed.

"Done what?"

"Shoved that guy. There were cameras. What if he sues you?"

"He's not going to sue me."

"You don't know that."

Bil's fingers tensed on the wheel. "Well, what did you want me to do?"

"Nothing."

"Nothing," he parroted meanly. "Why? So you can call me an Uncle Tom?"

Salma was taken aback by the venom in his voice. "Bil, I have *never* said that about you."

"So calling me 'a good immigrant' wasn't a jibe?"

She flushed. "I was just teasing you."

"Sure you were."

"Bil—"

He turned the ignition, cutting her off, then zoomed out of the car park, scattering a gust of pigeons.

"Bil," she appealed. She knew that he was stressed but he had never shut her out like this. She tried again and felt her frustration build. In the ensuing silence, it cooled to something solid—another brick in the wall between them. When they reached the hospital, Bil barely looked at her.

"I don't think I'll come up tonight."

Salma checked the dashboard. "You still have time before your shift."

"Barely."

"You have fifteen minutes. That's enough time to say hi."

"It's fine. I'd prefer to make a move."

"Bil—"

"Just *go*," he snapped, making her flinch.

She waited a beat to see if he would apologize. "Fine," she replied coldly. She stepped out and slammed the door. She was a car length away when the window whirred behind her.

"Salma."

She stopped but didn't face him.

"Do you think it's true?" he called.

She turned and jerked her shoulders in aggressive query. "What's true?"

"That Tom said what he said because he thought that we might lose him?"

Salma felt herself sway. She took a few steps toward him. "I don't know," she told him.

"I want it to be true," said Bil. "I want to know that Tom was kind to our son." He looked at her, desperate. "Because what if those words are the last he ever hears?"

"Bil, don't." She reached for him, but he waved her back.

"I can't, Salma. I just . . ." He exhaled. "I can't see him today."

"Okay," she said gently.

"You give my boy a kiss for me." Bil's voice cracked and he turned on the ignition, cueing her to leave. She turned and headed inside alone, giving him space to break.

Upstairs, she walked along the same pale-yellow corridor that she had paced for months, past a set of double doors, and into Zain's room in Neurology. When she entered, Jamie leaped to his feet. For a second, they stared at each other, a deer in a mirror. Jamie stuttered an apology and hurried out past Salma.

She followed him quickly. "Jamie." She quickened her pace. "Jamie!"

He turned, slow with apprehension.

"What are you doing here?" She didn't mean to sound aggressive. In truth, she was pleased that he was here. This emissary from Zain's real life might remind him what he used to have, urge him to fight his way back.

"I wanted to see how he was." Jamie shifted uneasily. "Our, uh, the app we were working on, it's going really well and I wanted to show him. Half the company belongs to him, so I thought he should stay involved."

Salma felt a well of affection. "Thank you, Jamie. I appreciate this."

"He ..." Jamie hesitated, then waved dismissively. "I should go."

"He what?" she pressed, desperate for every morsel of news.

"I know we didn't know each other very long but he was kind of like a big brother to me."

Salma felt a choke in her throat. Jamie hovered, both unsure if they should embrace, but then the moment was gone. Jamie turned and disappeared into the pale-yellow corridor.

CHAPTER 18

W illa looked uncommonly chic in a white dress and diamond studs—the consummate English rose. Salma was
ashamed of how this made her feel: hairy and ungainly in her
wide-fit teacher's shoes.

Willa raised a delicate hand and took the oath in a tremulous
voice. Salma listened wearily. This hierarchy seemed to apply
not just in the courthouse but Salma's entire life: relegated to
second place after women like Willa.

Julian Hughes smoothed his gown. "Willa," he said with a
smile. "Like the writer, I presume?"

She nodded. "That's right."

"Can you tell me about the first time you met the Khatuns?
What was your impression of them?"

"We met at a neighbor's barbecue. They seemed nice, especially the boys, but Salma seemed a little aloof."

"In what way?"

Willa lifted a shoulder. "Before she left, I asked if she wanted
to get a coffee sometime but she dismissed it. She made a point
that she had a *job* and couldn't go lunching whenever she
wanted. That's how she put it—'lunching'—as if that's what I
do all day."

Salma's mouth fell open. That wasn't the word she'd used and certainly not in the spirit she'd said it. The lie had slipped off Willa so easily. What else would she concoct?

"Things deteriorated from there," she continued.

"How so?" asked Julian.

"Salma thought we were *targeting* her. My husband, Tom, is extremely fastidious when it comes to rules. He saw a banner in the Khatuns' front garden—I can't remember what it said now, something political—and he took it out. It was meant to be a polite way of saying that this is against the rules. The Khatuns were new, so he didn't want to knock on her door and make a point of it."

"Did this work?"

"I'm afraid not. They displayed it more prominently in their front window. My husband, in all his oafish logic, decided that rather than confront them, he would cover their window with wipeable paint." Willa rolled her eyes. "It was unacceptable of course and when I found out, I . . ." She shook her head to imply unspeakable punishment.

"And did covering the window work?"

"Unfortunately, no. Salma had spotted Tom taking out the banner, so, understandably, she read this as an act of aggression instead of what it was: a bumbling attempt to avoid conflict." Willa tilted her head winsomely. "You know how we British can be."

A few of the jurors tittered and Salma felt her stomach turn.

"After that, things escalated quickly. Salma posted a picture of her window on Twitter with the words 'Three cheers for tolerant Britain'"—Willa clucked with disapproval—"as if my husband's one impulsive act was enough to indict the whole of Britain."

Salma's cheeks burned hot. Willa knew exactly what she was doing.

"She made quite an accusation there," said Julian. "Did you try to talk this over with her?"

"Yes. My husband went over, which I now know was a mistake. Some of what he said was a little bit clumsy." Willa rolled her eyes, playing the patient wife. "At some point, he mentioned that we sometimes have to bring our washing in when they're cooking oily food and Salma took offense at that." Willa waved, implying pettiness. "Her son filmed my husband and they put the clip online. The next thing you know, Tom is fired from his job all because he mentioned their cooking."

Julian tutted with sympathy. "What happened after this?"

"Things got worse. They kept complaining. They accused us of vandalizing their second property, of scratching their car, of stealing their dog. It got to a point where I woke up every morning feeling sick because I didn't know what would happen that day."

Salma watched in disbelief. Willa had taken Salma's anguish and repackaged it as her own. She craned toward the witness box and tried to catch Willa's eye, to transmit her query there. *What the hell are you doing?*

"We've never had problems with neighbors," said Willa, "and suddenly we're being painted as monsters."

Julian nodded meditatively. He probed the details of their various clashes and paused on the day of Willa's miscarriage. "Were you scared when Salma confronted you?"

Willa squared her shoulders in a show of stoicism. "I wouldn't say 'scared.' I still thought they could be reasoned with. We clearly hadn't taken their dog and I thought we could explain this, but then she grabbed Lola . . ."

Julian took her frame by frame through the ensuing moments, recasting Salma as the villain.

"I landed hard on the floor," said Willa. She gripped the edge of the witness box as if on the cusp of fainting. "I thought I was bleeding and started to panic."

Julian took pains to draw out the next hour: the arrival of the paramedics, the transfer to the hospital, the news that Willa had lost her baby.

"My son, Jamie, and I are like best friends," she said, folding her hands delicately. "I had him so young and honestly I didn't appreciate it because it happened so easily. When Jamie was ten, we started trying for another one and it didn't happen naturally. We didn't want to put ourselves through IVF, so we decided to wait and see. We waited for years and I finally fell pregnant with Gaia." She stopped as if catching herself and looked at the jury shyly. "That's what we chose to call her." Sympathy moved across the jury. "I've tried *really* hard to be practical about this." Willa looked at the women jurors. "I've told myself over and over that she wasn't real yet. That she was just tissue and muscle but . . ." Willa faltered. "There was a human life inside me. A life with myriad possibilities, a million decisions and choices, the kindnesses she'd perform and the unkindnesses she'd learn from. She was a life, and someone *external* to our family came along and snuffed her out, so I hope you'll understand why I'm still grieving."

Julian gave her a moment. Gently, he asked, "How did Tom react to the miscarriage?"

"He was devastated. He went on these long runs every day to the point where he started to look gaunt."

"Was he angry?"

Willa thought about this. "I think so, yes. Not outwardly or in a shouty way, but yes, he was angry."

"Did he blame Zain?"

Willa grimaced. "Yes."

Julian frowned, surprised by Willa's admission. "Did he want revenge?"

"No," she said sorrowfully. "He wanted justice."

"Did he ever talk about hurting Zain?"

"No. Never."

"Do you think that he *could* have hurt Zain?"

"No, sir. Never."

Julian nodded, satisfied. He turned to the judge. "I have no more questions, my lord."

CHARLOTTE ASHMAN LEAFED THROUGH HER blue notebook, but there was no urgency in the action. This was a woman perfectly comfortable taking up time and space. Salma noted her severe gray hair and her pale, piercing eyes, and felt thankful that she was the one cross-examining Willa and far less likely to be taken in by her fragile veneer.

"Ms. Hutton, may I ask: How far along was your pregnancy?"

Willa blinked, clearly expecting a softer segue. "Eight weeks."

"Ah, so still in your first trimester?"

"Yes."

"Isn't it customary not to share news of a pregnancy until you are past the first trimester?"

"Yes."

"Why is that?"

"Well . . ." Willa hesitated. "I'm not an expert but most miscarriages happen in the first trimester."

"So it's common?"

"I guess so."

"Did *you* share the news with friends and family?"

"Some."

"Did you tell neighbors?"

"No. Not yet."

"So Salma didn't know you were pregnant?"

"Um, I told her when we had coffee once."

"So *you* obviously knew?"

Willa blinked. "Knew what?"

"That you were pregnant?"

"Well, yes . . ." Willa looked at the judge. "Isn't that what we're talking about?"

"Ms. Hutton, were you following basic advice for a healthy pregnancy?"

Julian rose to his feet. "My lord, respectfully, I fail to see the relevance to the case at hand?"

Charlotte glowered at him. "My lord, if we are to rely on Ms. Hutton as a character witness, her own character is wholly relevant, as are the circumstances of the miscarriage to which she has already given evidence."

Judge Braithwaite gave the merest of nods. "You may continue, Ms. Ashman."

She shot a look at Julian, then turned back to Willa. "I'll ask again, Ms. Hutton: Did you follow basic advice for a healthy pregnancy?"

"Well, yes, of course," she answered.

"So no smoking or drinking? Plenty of rest, sleep, and exercise?"

"Well, I don't know if I was managing all of those things," she said with a little laugh.

"What do you mean?"

Her laugh died. "Well, I don't know if I was resting or sleeping enough, but I was trying to do all those things."

"And were you smoking?"

Willa tensed ever so slightly. "Not after I found out."

"And drinking?"

"Again, not after I found out."

"Is that so?"

"That's so." A hard edge crept into her voice.

Julian aimed something at Charlotte but she smoothly ignored it. Instead, she nodded at the usher. The courtroom screens blinked on, showing a picture of Willa with three other women, all of them groomed and attractive. Two of them held up glasses of prosecco as they beamed at the camera. One of them was Willa.

"When was this taken?"

The ease drained from her face. "That was just for show. The glass belonged to one of my friends. I picked it up for the sake of the picture."

"But that *is* prosecco?"

"Yes."

The screen clicked on to another picture. This one showed Willa with the glass to her lips. "And *this* is prosecco?" asked Charlotte.

"Yes. But again I was posing."

"And this?" It was another picture of Willa, taken what looked like a second later. She was hunched a little over her glass as if she had taken a swig. The glass was visibly less full.

Willa shook her head. "What is this? You're victim-shaming me."

"I'm not shaming you, Ms. Hutton. I'm asking you if you

willingly drank alcohol while you were pregnant. You said you hadn't, so I'm trying to establish whether or not that was accurate. That is, after all, what we're here for."

Willa was indignant, clearly not used to Charlotte's tone. "I may have had a tiny sip," she said.

"So you were lying earlier?"

"I wasn't lying. I was unsure."

"You were 'unsure'?" Charlotte arched her brows. "And what about smoking?"

Willa shifted uneasily. "Maybe a few here and there," she admitted, keen to avoid another trap.

"How many is 'a few here and there'?"

"Like two or three."

"A week?"

"No!" Willa was horrified. "Throughout the course of the whole pregnancy."

"I see." Charlotte made a note, then swiftly changed tack. "Ms. Hutton, you said that your husband, Tom, had been fired from his job. You were angry about this, yes?"

Willa chose her words carefully. "I was saddened."

"But also angry?"

"A little, yes. He worked for his company for fifteen years. To let him go like that because of one small incident was absurd."

"Were you angry at Salma?"

"Yes."

"Why?"

"Because I spoke to her before she posted that video. I asked her not to share it publicly because I know we live in an age where things are willfully misconstrued and entire lives destroyed because of a single moment. Salma agreed, but then, later, she did it anyway."

"So you were more angry about her posting a video of what your husband said than at your husband for saying it?"

"He was clumsy with his words. He didn't mean it that way."

"What did you make of the backlash?" asked Charlotte.

"I think it was deliberately misconstrued. I just think . . ." She sighed as if reluctant to say the next words. "Some people see problems where there are none."

Charlotte murmured in agreement. "And do you think some people *don't* see problems when there *are* some?"

Willa considered this. "I'm sure that's true."

"Fancy that," said Charlotte. She closed her blue notebook, then looked up at the judge. "I have no more questions, my lord."

SALMA HAD ONCE READ THAT living near a busy road increased your risk of heart disease. The relentless noise and movement meant that your body never fully relaxed. That's how she felt living next to Tom: constantly stressed and alert. Even when her mind was distracted, her body remembered the threat, poised to fight at a moment's notice. She had ventured to the garden with Molly to try to decompress, but every movement of shadow next door made her tense with dread. She spoke to Molly with forced ease to trick herself into relaxing. Molly whined and Salma stroked her ears.

"I know, sweet girl. I tried but they won't let you in to see him. Maybe he'll be home soon." The doctors had spoken to Salma about Zain's long-term care. He could potentially come home, they said, and Salma had feigned enthusiasm. In truth, this felt like giving up, accepting that Zain's state was permanent, and she wasn't ready to do that.

Molly snuffled in the grass and as Salma watched, a worrying thought occurred to her. Molly was eleven years old and visibly aging now. What if she died before Zain woke up? It would haunt him not to have said good-bye.

"You've got to hang on, okay, sweet girl?" Both Salma and Molly startled when they heard the screen door open. Salma recognized the familiar lope of Jamie in the garden. He looked across at her and she couldn't place the look on his face. A scowl? Or a wince of solidarity? He glanced behind him at the light in the kitchen window.

"Hi," he said tentatively.

"Hi, Jamie."

He shifted nervously. "Come here often?"

Salma smiled at this endearing attempt at humor.

He walked to the fence. "I'm sorry I rushed away yesterday. I was scared I'd get told off."

She shook her head. "Jamie, you can go and see Zain any time you like, okay? In fact, I'd like you to. He needs to see someone other than his parents."

"Thank you." Jamie glanced at the kitchen again, clearly worried about being seen. "When he wakes up, maybe he'll remember I was there."

Salma swallowed, overcome by the thought of this.

Jamie sensed the change. "Are you okay?" he stammered.

She nodded and gestured at the space between them. "We shouldn't really be talking."

"I know," he said but didn't move. "I wish we could all start over again. I wish you and Mum and Dad could have been friends. They're honestly not bad people."

Salma didn't acknowledge this. How could she explain to him that just because someone loved *you* and took care of *you*, it didn't mean they were good? She looked at him wistfully. "What happened that day, Jamie? Because we know there was a man on the balcony and your dad is *so* convincing, so who does he say it is? At home, when it's just you and your mum, what does he say?"

Faced with this call for disloyalty, Jamie clammed up.

"*Please*, Jamie."

"I've got to go." He took a step back.

"Wait." Salma hastened to the fence. "If Zain really was like a brother to you, then I ask one thing: Tell the truth in court. Whatever the question is, please, Jamie, just tell the truth."

He gave her a quick nod. "I will. I'm sorry, Ms. Khatun. For everything." With that, he turned and hurried inside, leaving her in the dark.

CHAPTER 19

Linda walked into the courtroom, and if you didn't know her, you might assume she was forced here. She wore a gray suit with pearl earrings and her expression was calm and conservative. It was tiny subtle movements that betrayed her glee: the twitch at the corner of her lips, her thumb tapping her leg. Salma watched with a waltzing unease. In the early days, she had curried favor with the woman but as the months drew on, her patience had run dry. In their most recent meeting, Salma had been more abrupt than usual. *Sorry, Linda, I don't have time for this.* She hadn't known then that she would be speaking in Tom's defense.

Linda took the oath, her voice a little too loud for the acoustics in the room.

Julian asked some basic questions and then began in earnest. "When did you first notice tension between your neighbors?"

Linda fingered the paisley scarf at her neck. "I first knew there was trouble when my son, Jack, showed me a video of Tom and Salma arguing. It was posted on social media. After that, I saw them bicker myself. One morning, Salma thought he'd scratched her car. I tried my best to comfort her. I told her that I've lived peacefully with Tom for years, that it almost certainly wasn't him."

"Did Salma seem angry?"

"More stressed than angry I would say."

Salma relaxed a little. She had been worried that Linda would paint her as prickly, but she seemed to be objective.

Linda continued. "I did offer mediation but Salma said no thank you. After that, things went from bad to worse. It was all petty, minor things until Molly went missing."

"Molly?" said Julian.

"Oh, sorry, their dog. A darling thing. Sadly, she went missing and that's when things got a bit . . . silly."

"Silly how?"

"Well, it was almost like a conspiracy theory. They thought that the Huttons had done something with their dog, but it turned out that their squatters had taken it, so it was all a much of a muchness."

"You have mentioned the scratches on the car. Did you witness any other conflict directly?"

"Oh yes." Linda relayed their argument about the CCTV.

Julian murmured here and there in encouragement. "During these heated exchanges, did Tom ever use a slur?"

Linda frowned. "No, I don't think so." She paused. "Is 'bint' a slur?"

"Not the sort I mean," he said smoothly. "What I mean is: Did he ever use the shortened form of 'Pakistani' to describe them, or anything that called attention to their race or faith?"

"Oh no, nothing like that! God, he would be ostracized."

"In all the years that you have known Tom, have you ever heard him use a slur against a person of color?"

"Not at all. I wouldn't consort with someone like that. None of us at Blenheim would."

"But what about this video where he refers to the Khatuns' cooking and says it makes his clothes smell? Wasn't that problematic?"

Linda grimaced. "It's tricky, isn't it? If they were cooking egg salad or smoked salmon, it wouldn't be problematic, so I don't understand why this would be." She nodded toward the dock. "If Tom Hutton was like *that*, believe me, I would know it. I have absolutely nothing against Salma and her family, I really like them, in fact, but you can't just upend a community based on a perceived slight."

Julian nodded, satisfied. "Thank you. Please remain there a moment. I'm sure my learned friend has some questions for you too."

Charlotte stood and looked across at Linda with something like distaste. "Ms. Turner, were you aware of the banner that Salma Khatun displayed in her front garden?"

"Oh yes, it caused a bit of a stir."

"A stir?"

Linda hesitated. "Well, not a stir, but *interest*."

"And why is that?"

"Well, we all agreed with the message of course, but I suppose we were curious as to why someone who wasn't Black wanted to make a point about it. It felt like an indictment of the rest of us."

"The rest of you?"

Linda shifted. "Well, the rest of us who live there."

"You mean the white residents of Blenheim?"

"Well, yes, I suppose so." Her shoulders rose defensively. "No one had an issue per se. It was just . . . It made the place feel different."

"Was Tom involved in this stir or 'discussion' shall we say?"

"Yes," Linda admitted.

"Where did it take place?"

"At the barbecue before they arrived."

Salma tensed. She hadn't been aware of this. They had all discussed her moments before they welcomed her?

Linda continued unbidden. "Someone joked that we should throw it in the bin and"—she glanced at Tom in apology—"I said they shouldn't be silly and Tom kind of leaned into the group and said he'd already sent them a message."

Charlotte murmured in surprise. "'Sent them a message.' What did he mean by that?"

Linda thumbed her scarf. "He was just fooling around, playing to the crowd. He said he'd taken out the banner and left it on the ground."

"Did he take out the banner because it made people uncomfortable?"

"Yes."

"Because of what it said?"

"Yes."

"I see," said Charlotte. She turned to the judge, a new heaviness in her body. "I have no further questions, my lord."

Salma flushed with disbelief. Her neighbors had put their heads together and conspired to do this? Or at least condoned it? She felt an acute humiliation—and not just because they had othered her and made her the butt of their joke. More profoundly, with the benefit of hindsight, she wished that she hadn't let Zain display the banner. It was a feeble act of allyship, clearly not worth the trouble. She wished that she had quietly slipped into life at Blenheim and proved to her neighbors that they needn't feel uncomfortable. She wished that she had followed Bil's philosophy and made up stories to prove her willingness to assimilate. Maybe then, her son would be safe and she too would be laughing over a neighborhood barbecue.

JAMIE TOOK HIS PLACE AS the final witness of the trial. He wore a navy suit that fit him flawlessly, with none of the bagginess around the shoulders like other teens in suits. As he took the oath, however, his age became obvious. He looked small and scared, his cheekbones gaunt and razor-like in the courtroom's sallow glow. Salma felt a maternal protectiveness despite the fact that he was there in Tom's defense.

Jamie smoothed his tie and glanced up at the gallery. Salma offered a smile but he showed no hint of acknowledgment. The judge explained to the jury that Jamie was partially deaf and may need some questions repeated.

Julian Hughes stood and flashed a plastic smile at Jamie. "Can you explain your relationship to the defendant?" he started.

Jamie relaxed a little, assured that he could hear clearly enough. "I'm his son," he answered.

"Do you have a good relationship?"

"Yes, we do."

Julian asked a series of basic questions to get Jamie comfortable, then moved on to the day of the incident. "What was Zain doing in your house?"

"He and I were starting an app together, Grapevine, to help deaf people communicate with the hearing population. He came over so that we could work on it."

"Were you in the house when Zain fell?"

"No. I tutor at deafPLUS on Fridays at five, so I had to go. I told Zain to work on my computer. It's faster and we were on a deadline. I said I'd be back in just over an hour."

"Was your dad home?"

"No. He'd picked up some work at a warehouse, so he was over there."

"Was anyone else home?"

"No."

"When you left, did you lock the door?"

"No. Zain was home, so I didn't think it was necessary."

"Do you have any security devices? An alarm? Motion sensors? Anything to alert you to an intruder?"

"No. Just Lola, our dog, but she comes to deafPLUS with me."

"So anyone could have walked in?"

Jamie grimaced. "Yes."

"What time did you leave for the tutoring?"

"At four fifty P.M."

Julian directed the jury to their bundles, which confirmed Jamie's attendance at tutoring. "When did you first know that something was wrong?"

"I saw the ambulance on our street. I ran up and saw them taking Zain out."

"What time was this?"

"I finished tutoring at six P.M., so it would have been around six ten."

"Where was your dad?"

"He was talking to the police in the house."

"How did he seem?"

Jamie's gaze darted to the dock. "Dad's tough and it . . . it scared me to see him like that."

"Like what?"

Jamie gestured at his face. "Just white. Shocked."

"Did he say anything to you?"

"He asked if I knew what Zain was doing in our house."

Julian moved on. "You knew Zain relatively well. Do you know if he was in any trouble?"

Jamie cleared his throat. "No. I don't know."

"Did he seem stressed or anxious about anything? Any unusual behavior?"

Jamie didn't answer the question.

Salma watched on anxiously. Before the incident, Zain had indeed seemed angry. She and Bil had even discussed therapy. Had Jamie noticed too?

Julian grew impatient. "Jamie, it's really important that you tell us everything you know, so please: Did you notice any unusual behavior?"

"Yes," Jamie admitted. "A few weeks before he fell, Zain asked me for five hundred pounds. He said it was a reward for his missing dog, but . . . I felt like it was something else."

"Why?"

"Well, the police were dealing with it, so why would he want to spend so much? Also, he seemed really desperate and turned nasty when I said no."

"Nasty? In what way?"

"He started shouting and I sort of didn't know what to say to him and he said, 'Are you dumb as well as deaf?'"

Salma stared at him. That couldn't possibly be true. The Zain she knew stood up for vulnerable people.

"But," Jamie continued, "the thing is that *that* wasn't Zain. He wasn't like that, which made me think that the money wasn't just for Molly, his dog. It made me think that there was something else going on."

"Did he give you any indication what it might be?"

Jamie fiddled with his tie. "No, but I saw him using a gambling app and wondered if it was that."

Salma felt a cold clasp around her throat. She remembered seeing £15,000 on his screen. Had he got into trouble that he couldn't find a way out of?

"Do you know if he borrowed money off someone else? Someone who might have wanted it back?"

"No."

"Okay, here are some things we do know: Zain needed money—enough to turn him nasty. We know he was anxious about not having this money. And we know that the door to your house was unlocked. Someone may have come in and harmed him. Do you think this was your father?"

"No. Dad is tough but he's fair. He would never go for someone smaller than him."

"Has he ever been violent that you've seen?"

"No."

"Has your dad ever made racist remarks that you've heard?"

"No."

"How sure are you that he didn't hurt Zain?"

"One hundred percent," said Jamie.

CHARLOTTE ASHMAN MADE NO CONCESSIONS for Jamie. Her voice, already loud and clear enough, maintained the note of scorn that she reserved for defense witnesses. It worked in her favor. A false coddling of Jamie because of his hearing would have looked like obvious point-scoring.

She eyed him coolly. "Zain asked you for money to rescue his dog. You said 'the police were dealing with it, so why would he want to spend so much,' is that right?"

"Yes."

"Could it have something to do with the fact that the app you created together was awarded fifteen thousand pounds by a diversity startup fund?"

Jamie grew still. Clearly, he was surprised that they knew about the grant.

Salma was hit with a realization: £15,000. The figure she had seen on Zain's screen that day. But why did he hide it from her? A flutter of shame reminded her that she had warned him away from Jamie, forcing them to work in secret.

Charlotte continued. "Perhaps with this amount of money in the bank, Zain didn't think that spending five hundred pounds on something he loved—a living, breathing member of his family—was very much at all?"

Jamie shifted. "But the money was for our app. We couldn't spend it on personal things."

"Yes, but it makes more sense now, doesn't it? It's not that Zain was angry at you for not conjuring money from your piggy bank. He was upset that he couldn't use some of this substantial sum—half of which was rightfully his—to ensure the safe return of his dog?"

Jamie blinked. "Yes, but that's not what the money was for."

Charlotte changed direction. "You said that Zain used a gambling app. Can you describe it to us?" She listened intently to Jamie's description, then nodded at the usher. A picture came up on-screen. "Was it this?"

"Yes. I saw him losing money on it."

"This," she said slowly, "is an app called CoinPace. Do you know what it's used for?" The scorn in her voice dialed higher. "It's an educational app that helps developers play with crypto-currency in a simulated marketplace; at their own pace, so to speak, with absolutely no risk to any real money. So," she concluded icily, "not a gambling app at all." She sighed theatrically, clearly disappointed that Zain had been smeared like this. "What we *know* is that Zain didn't *need* money; he merely wanted it to rescue his dog. He wasn't a gambling addict or in any sort of financial trouble, nothing that would cause a stranger to harm him, or for him to harm himself. So, we come back to your father, Tom Hutton, who you say has never been violent or racist." She narrowed her gaze on him. "Tell me, how did Zain come into your room?"

Jamie wiped his upper lip. "He came from his balcony to mine."

Charlotte gestured at the screen, which now showed a picture of their two balconies, separated by a protruding central wall. "In order to get to your room from his, he needs to step around this wall. Why use such a dangerous passage?"

"It was easier."

"No, Jamie. It was easier for him to use the front door."

Jamie squirmed. "We used it because Dad didn't know we were working together."

"You hid it from him?"

"Yes."

"Why?"

"He wanted me to stay away from Zain. He said he was bad news."

"Why? What gave him that idea?"

"I don't know. He was just being paranoid."

"Why? What things make him paranoid?"

Jamie faltered, not knowing how to answer.

"A person's height, weight, hair length? Do those things make him paranoid?"

"No."

"A person's age, dress, accent?"

He lifted a shoulder. "Maybe."

"A person's name, faith, or color?"

"No," he said but his expression differed.

"Then what? What made your father take a look at Zain and decide that he wouldn't be good company for you?"

"It was more to do with what happened with his parents."

"Ah yes, your father tampered with their banner and painted their window. I wonder why that was. And I wonder how he would react if he came home one evening to find the boy he had warned you off in his very own house."

"My dad didn't do this."

"Then who did, Jamie?"

"I don't know."

"I think you do know. I think you know what your father is. I think you know what he did, and I think you're protecting him."

"I'm not."

"Your father's a bully, isn't he?"

"No."

"If that's true, then you won't mind telling us what happened with your friend David Adeleye, will you?"

Jamie froze, wild-eyed as he scanned the dock for his father.

"Will you tell us about the night that David Adeleye came to your house?"

Jamie's lips moved, soundlessly at first. "It was years ago now," he said. "David came to a sleepover."

"Go on," Charlotte pressed.

Jamie spoke haltingly. "There were seven of us and we were packed into my room. We were being silly, wrestling and having a laugh, eating chocolate and crisps and getting it all over the floor. Someone suggested we arm wrestle. The bed was too soft, so we went downstairs. Mum was out at dinner, so Dad was keeping an eye on us. He saw what we were doing and had a laugh with us."

"And then?"

"Well . . . David kept winning and Dad said it wasn't fair because he was naturally stronger than the rest of us."

"Why did your dad think that?"

Jamie looked at the floor. "Because David was Black."

Noise rose in the courtroom.

"And then?" asked Charlotte.

"Dad wanted to even out the playing field, so he went to his shed and he got out these weights that he uses for running and he tied them around David's wrist to put extra pressure on him."

The jury watched in astonishment.

"David was really embarrassed and he said he didn't want to play but Dad told him he was chickening out because now things were fair. David still won and Dad got annoyed. He was looking around for something else to put on his arm and I told him to leave it but it was like he didn't want to, so then he said *he* would wrestle with him."

"How old was David?"

Jamie swallowed. "Twelve."

"What happened?"

"It was an accident."

"What happened, Jamie?"

"Dad didn't know how strong he was."

"What happened?"

"He broke David's arm."

The news stilled the courtroom and Charlotte let the silence hang. She turned to the judge. "I have no further questions, my lord."

WILLA RUMMAGED THROUGH HER CUPBOARD for something sweet. She found a packet of popcorn and warmed it in the microwave. After the day she'd had, she could allow herself this one indulgence. She couldn't *believe* that the prosecution had dredged up that awful episode. She remembered the day that David Adeleye came to stay at Blenheim. He was a sweet-looking boy who always seemed on the edge of a smile, as if an old joke or memory was running through his mind. She had heard things about him early on, that he'd got into a fight on his first day at school. Willa had defended him when the other mothers whispered, *Well, he may have passed the eleven-plus exam but he clearly needs to work on his manners.* It took time to adjust. People were so snobby about social climbers. Willa's mother liked to point out faux pas to her, and her own friends laughed at that ginger pop star who swapped to demure pastels after marrying up—but what was wrong with bettering yourself?

Willa took David under her wing and assured his mother, Joy, not to worry. She even visited their tiny flat in Walthamstow, sitting on the sofa with one leg tucked beneath the other to assure her that *yes, I'm comfortable here.* Joy was oddly cool and Willa felt a little put out by this tepid response to her effort, but she vowed to win her over. She gifted David books and one of Jamie's old laptops—with Joy's permission of course. At Christmas, she gave him a Kindle because she knew he loved to read. She even offered to share Jamie's tutor if David could

KIA ABDULLAH ■ 284

get to Blenheim twice a week. Joy had declined, just as she'd declined the sleepover, but Willa had convinced her.

When she came home from dinner that night to find David wailing in their living room, she was sure he was being dramatic, but then they took him to the hospital and were told there was a fracture. After the accident—and it *was* an accident—Joy gave Willa the cold shoulder, as if it had been intentional. Willa did everything she could to win back her favor. Tom had called Joy personally, but she was terse and unresponsive, neither accepting nor rejecting his apology—just leaving it there to hang. Willa was deeply sorry, of course, but also a little irritated. Yes, Tom was an idiot—keen to show off to Jamie's friends—but there was no malice in his actions. It was an accident and the prosecution using it now to paint him a certain way was inexcusably cynical.

The microwave pinged and Willa sent a text to Jamie. NEW SEASON OF FARGO? This could be their last weekend as a normal family and she was determined to enjoy it. 1 MIN, came the reply, followed by his tread on the stairs. She emptied the popcorn into a glass bowl and together they settled on the sofa.

"How are you?" she asked, tousling his hair.

He pulled away from her touch. "Fine." He wasn't fine but Willa knew from experience that he had to speak up in his own time. He picked out a hard kernel of popcorn and rolled it between his finger and thumb. "If Dad goes to prison, it'll be my fault."

Willa swallowed the bite in her voice. After months of shepherding her family through this, she had simply run dry of sympathy. "It's not your fault," she said, although she did wish he hadn't said quite so much about David Adeleye.

Jamie squeezed the kernel in his fist. "He could get thirty

years, Mum. He'll be seventy-four when he comes out. I've been looking at the prisons in London. The stories are unbelievable."

Willa tutted. "For god's sake, Jamie. Why would you do that?"

"To be prepared."

"Your dad is not going to prison."

"How do you know?"

Willa fixed her gaze on him. "Because he didn't do it."

"But, Mum, are the jury really going to believe that I left the house, then some random person came in to hurt Zain, and Dad turned up at the exact same time?"

She sighed. "Jamie, houses like ours get targeted all the time by the junkies from Abbey Estate. They could have seen you leave without locking up and thought it was their lucky day." She raised a finger to punctuate her point. "Your father is *not* going to prison."

Jamie studied her. "You're really not worried?"

"No," she said firmly. This time when she touched him, he didn't shrink way. "Okay?" she checked.

Jamie exhaled. "Okay."

She handed him the bowl. "Come on, let's forget about the trial for one evening."

Jamie took a handful of popcorn and turned to watch the screen. He leaned into the cushion, slack with relief.

SALMA WATCHED THE YOUNG LOVERS ahead and felt a spike of hostility. Everything about them seemed to provoke her: the way the girl skipped at the climax of her joke, how the boy plucked the hat off her head and held it out of reach, as if their bodies were too full of energy to stick to something as prosaic as walking. Even the weather betrayed her with its postcard version of deep November: the sun slanting through trees, the blue voltage of the sky, the dewy scent of earth. How could they be so brazenly beautiful? Even Molly found joy in the morning, loping from one trunk to the other, briefly freed from thoughts of Zain.

They approached Fairlop Waters and Salma tensed when she saw a jogger who looked like Tom from a distance. Civility was a powerful force. Whenever she saw him at Blenheim, she diligently ignored him instead of doing the things she wanted to: hurl abuse at him, or pick up a palm-size rock and smash it through his window. No insult seemed potent enough. There was the p-word for people like her, the n-word that young David Adeleye had no doubt heard, the k-word for her Jewish friends—but what was there for Tom? What was the very worst thing that he could be called? *Gammon?* Even vocabulary failed her.

Molly darted for something in the water and Salma shouted at her to be careful. On hearing her own words, she realized that she hadn't spoken at all that morning. Bil had been asleep when she'd left and her voice was unworn and croaky. She watched Molly frolic in the water and took a seat on a nearby bench. She picked up a discarded paper and idly leafed through it. On page eight, she paused. She frowned and took a closer look at the grainy black-and-white photo. Sure enough, she recognized the boy: thin hair, narrow nose, bad teeth. It was their squatter Rich.

Teen Found Dead in Ilford Stairwell

Salma felt a pang of shock and quickly scanned the article.

The body of an 18-year-old male was found in the stairwell of a disused building in Ilford on Tuesday

*morning. The building, part of Abbey Estate, was
evacuated for demolition in March 2019 but has stood
abandoned in the years since, becoming a magnet for
drug users and crime, with two reported stabbings. The
deceased male, identified as Richard Fremont, was found
in the early hours by an outreach team from St. Mungo's,
a homelessness charity. Fremont was pronounced dead at
the scene, reportedly caused by a drug overdose.*

Salma had once despised this boy, but now she only felt sad
about his pathetic legacy. If Zain died, he would be remembered
in a certain way: smiling, suited, happy. Salma would be devastated if he were pictured like this, in grainy black and white,
sneering at some unseen thing. What had gone wrong in this
boy's life to make him end up like this? Wearily, she replaced
the paper on the bench. As a teacher of nearly twenty years, she
knew the answers were legion.

Molly bounded up to her, finally tiring. Salma knelt to fix on
her leash and flinched when a jogger passed by too closely.
These past few months had changed the contours of her home-
town, mapped no-go areas in her mind. This was not entirely
new. Growing up, they had avoided places like Millwall and
Barking, but now new areas had formed—seemingly genteel
places that harbored insidious voices. *You can't just upend a
community based on a perceived slight.* As if Salma wasn't aware
of this. She teased Bil for trying too hard to fit in, but in truth,
she was just as keen. She remembered how her cousin had pejo-
ratively referred to an Asian politician as "Pick me Patel." Salma
had squirmed, for she too yearned for acceptance. In truth,
whenever Bil told his story about his father swapping gifts with
his neighbor, Salma would take his arm sweetly and laugh on
cue at the punch line. Now she felt ashamed of every smile,

every dismissive wave when someone mangled her name, or told her she was "eloquent" with the tiniest hint of surprise. But worst of all, she would do it again if it meant living safely and getting ahead. *Pick me Khatun.*

THE REST OF THE WEEKEND passed quietly. In the before times, their days had been varied. Bil would play cricket with friends while Salma caught up with grading papers. There were differing beats to their days. Now there was only monotone: breakfast, walk, hospital, read, walk, home. Rinse and repeat. She could sense it killing their marriage—a slow desiccation. She didn't know how to stop it. Bil had always been the stoic one, but he had slipped into a sort of paralysis, a liminal state between grief and healing. Without him, Salma was left anchorless.

As with other Sunday evenings, they settled in front of the TV, the house too quiet without it. Molly huddled on the floor as if she could sense the malaise and was scared of drawing attention to herself. Zain's injury had changed the gravity of their home, drawing them in so that all their living was done in this room, the air too heavy elsewhere.

Salma looked across at Bil. "I'd like to bring him home," she said.

He watched the screen and for a moment Salma thought he hadn't heard her, but then he nodded morosely. "Okay."

Previously, she had insisted that the hospital was best for him, but it was nearing six months and they had to start thinking long term. "What do you think will happen tomorrow?" she asked. The closing arguments were scheduled and they would likely have a verdict soon after.

"I think the jury will let him go."

Salma bristled. "If he's freed, I don't want him living next to Zain."

Bil nodded but without conviction. The truth was that they couldn't afford to move again. The sale of the restaurant had only just covered the mortgage and the debt that they'd accrued. Salma was on a part-time salary and Bil's was thousands lower than what he'd earned at Jakoni's—but how could they possibly stay here?

"Promise me," she urged him.

"We'll work something out."

"No, *promise* me."

"We can't afford it, Salma," he said tensely.

"So then what? He just carries on living next door? Meters away from Zain?" She vehemently shook her head. "I won't do it."

"Then what?" Bil sprang to his feet, agitated. "We'll what, Salma? We can barely pay our bills anymore. How do you think we can afford to move?"

She stood up to talk to him at eye level. "We can't stay here."

"Well, we can't move."

"You're not even trying."

"I'm not even trying? Jesus Christ, Salma. That is *all* I've done since we moved here. I've been breaking my back working split shifts so we can afford your switch to part-time."

"Would you have our son be left alone at the hospital?"

"I'd have you be my *partner*. I can't take care of everything."

"I asked you about switching and you said yes!"

"I didn't know it would last six months."

"Then what did you think? That after a month I'd leave our son to rot? Did you think he would *die* so you wouldn't have to bear the load?"

Bil blanched at this. A pop of a sound left his mouth as if he'd been slugged by a bullet.

Salma's guilt was instant. "Bil, I didn't mean that." She reached for him but he jerked away. "Bil, please."

"How can you say that to me?" He stared at her. "You think you love him more than me? He's my baby too, Salma." He cleared the choke in his voice. "You remember when we first brought him home? He wouldn't latch and I had to wake up each time and put the crook of my finger in his mouth. He's my baby too, so how dare you say that to me?"

Salma's cheeks were hot with guilt. "Bil, I'm sorry."

"I'm trying, Salma, and maybe it's not good enough, but then tell me what I'm supposed to do. Tell me and I'll do it, but don't *ever* say that I'm not trying."

"I didn't mean it, Bil. I was angry."

"Maybe I'm angry too, Salma. Maybe I'm livid, but I refuse to be so fucking cruel."

Salma flinched. That word—"cruel"—was so hostile and yet so startlingly accurate.

"I'm trying to keep our family together," said Bil. "I'm trying to keep us going, to give you space to break, but I'm going to need some help because I can't keep going like this."

Salma saw for the first time the sacs of blue-gray beneath his eyes, a new thinness in his hair, a sag in his jowls. The past months had aged him years. "You're right," she said. "I'm sorry." She touched his arm, but it was rigid and unyielding. "Come on, Bil. We're a team."

"Are we?"

Salma could tell from his tone that the question wasn't rhetorical. "Yes, we are."

He held her gaze. "Then I need to tag you in."

"Okay. I'm here." This time when she reached for him, he didn't jerk away. He exhaled and she felt the release against her own chest. She vowed that whatever happened in the next few days, she and Bil would face it together. They had come too far to let this case destroy them.

CHAPTER 20

Salma slid into the front row of the public gallery with Bil close behind. She had chosen this row on her first visit here because it had the best vantage, but in hindsight she wished she had chosen the back, where Willa now sat with Jamie. Their presence behind her made her hackles rise and she had to fight the urge to turn around and look at them.

On the main stage below, Charlotte Ashman stood to make her closing arguments. "Members of the jury, the defendant, Tom Hutton, has been charged with attempted murder, a crime that was in part racially motivated. There is quite a lot to unpack here, so I want you to think of it in two parts: the crime and the hate. The defendant denies both of these trespasses, but let us examine the facts in turn. First, the crime. Then, the hate.

"It's Friday the third of June of this year. Tom Hutton arrives home at around five fifty P.M. He—or a man fitting his description—is seen on the top-floor balcony of his home, the one from which Zain was pushed. Five minutes later, Tom Hutton calls the emergency services.

"So—who did the witness see on the balcony? I ask you, members of the jury, to disregard the theatrics you saw earlier in this trial. There was no doppelgänger or interloper in Tom Hutton's house that day. *He* was the man on the balcony. He arrived home and found Zain Khatun—the person he holds responsible for his wife's miscarriage—upstairs in his home. As far as he knew, there was no reasonable explanation for why Zain was there.

"It is our case that an altercation followed, and in the midst of that altercation, Tom Hutton physically pushed Zain over the balcony. Like any adult of a sound mind, he was fully aware that this could result in death. Today, Zain Khatun remains in a vegetative state as a direct result of what happened that day.

"This was not a random act carried out by a stranger. There was no stranger. There was no random act. There was *meaning* and *motive* behind the attack, which leads me to the second part of the charge." Charlotte paused. "The hate."

Here, she ran through the familiar litany of crimes. "Consider this," she said. "As a result of this sustained campaign against his neighbors, Tom Hutton was fired from his job. His employers were rightfully worried that he would bring their corporation into disrepute. When you consider that he broke twelve-year-old David Adeleye's arm because *Black boys are stronger than white*, you can understand why his employers were worried. What else might he do given carte blanche?

"So at the end of this series of events, Tom Hutton blames his neighbors for the loss of his job of fifteen years, the loss of his public reputation, and the loss of his wife's pregnancy. What's striking is that he was targeting his neighbors before *any* of those things had happened. Consider, members of the jury, what it would take for *you* to wait for the cover of dark one day, to retrieve a can of spray paint from your shed, to steal into your neighbor's front garden, to creep up to their window and blank out a pane with paint. Tom was already at that stage *be-fore* he lost his job and reputation. Imagine what he was capable of *afterward*." Charlotte let the rhetoric settle.

"In truth, we don't have to imagine because we already know. A young man ended up in hospital and he may never leave it." She closed her notebook. "This case has covered violence and conflict and retribution but I ask you, members of the jury, to put all this aside for the one thing, the *only* thing, that matters here today: justice. Does Zain Khatun deserve justice? Does his family, who moved to Blenheim for a better life, deserve justice? If your answer is yes, then I ask you, members of the jury, to find Tom Hutton guilty." Charlotte bowed her head in a show of humility. She smoothed the pleats of her gown, then handed the floor to Julian Hughes for the final word of the trial.

JULIAN STOOD SLOWLY, HIS EVERY act imbued with gravity: the careful removal of his glasses, the slight tensing of his jaw, the pause before he addressed the jury.

"I agree with my learned friend on one thing," he started. "This case is complicated. It's complicated because it's not as easy as Johnny No-Good touched my girlfriend's bum so I punched him outside the pub, or Johnny cut me off so I rammed him with my car. It is far more complex. The Crown claims that Tom Hutton deliberately pushed a young man from a balcony because he was consumed with hate. Thankfully, my learned friend has laid much of the groundwork for me and broken it into two elements: the crime and the hate. So let's talk about each in turn."

Here, Salma did look over her shoulder. Willa's gaze was fixed on Julian and didn't even flicker toward her. Salma was strangely irked by this. It felt like yet another insult. Bil gently touched her knee, drawing her back round.

Julian pointed at the dock. "Tom Hutton arrived home at five fifty P.M. on the day in question. Five minutes later, he placed a call to the emergency services. If the Crown is right, then in those mere five minutes, Tom went upstairs, fought with the victim, pushed him from the balcony *with the intention of killing him*, then immediately had a change of heart, ran downstairs to administer care and call the emergency services." Julian cocked his head. "That's quite the change of heart," he said archly.

"There is no forensic evidence to support this narrative: no skin beneath the fingernails, no blood splatter, no defensive wounds, nothing to suggest that Tom was involved in an altercation. He called the emergency services straightaway and he fully cooperated.

"Now we come to the stranger on the balcony. Ask yourself this, members of the jury: Has the Crown proven beyond a reasonable doubt that that man was Tom Hutton? You have seen firsthand how easily the witness mistook a completely different man for Tom. How can we possibly be certain?

"My learned friend has made much of the fact that it couldn't have been a random stranger. But what if it was? What if it *was*? The front door was unlocked. There were troublesome youth in the area. Can we be one hundred percent certain that the stranger was Tom? If not, then this case has not been proven beyond a reasonable doubt. It simply has not."

Julian let the jury absorb this. "You have been told over and over that Tom Hutton intimidated his neighbors. He has admitted that he did indeed paint their window. He tells us he did it this way in an effort to keep things friendly between them.

This may seem illogical at first, but consider this. If a neighbor kept leaving their bin in front of your house on collection day instead of their own, would you knock on his door and tell him to stop it, or would you subtly push it back across the boundary? Some brave souls would knock on the door but many more of us would timidly push it back. The same goes for an overhanging branch in our garden. We may not confront them about this, but we may discreetly snip it. Tom's actions were clumsy but they were born of this same instinct: to avoid conflict with his neighbors; to gently nudge them and say, *By the way, this is problematic.*"

Julian's tone grew indignant now. "Much has been made of the cooking comment. The fact is, when Tom was talking to Salma Khatun, it wasn't the color of her skin that was on his mind. If it *was*, I daresay he wouldn't have made that comment in a million years. Rather, he was talking to her as an individual and an equal. He wasn't thinking, 'Oh, I mustn't say that because they're brown.' He was thinking, 'I'm not intolerant! Look at all the concessions I make!' To attach outsize significance to this comment does us *all* a disservice. It says that we must never forget the color of the person to whom we're speaking—and this is surely the opposite of what we want as a society."

Julian folded his hands together. "We have heard about an accident that happened with one of Jamie Hutton's friends. This wasn't a case of white against Black; it was adult against boy. Tom Hutton should have known better but he has a boyish heart and he wanted to get involved. He did not *hate* this boy. He simply wanted to showboat. It was silly and foolish—but innocent. Tom is a good-hearted man who got off on the wrong foot with his new neighbors. That is all."

Julian aimed a cheerless smile at the jury. "You have a difficult job and I sympathize with that, so I want to leave you with one simple question. What if Tom is innocent? What if he is innocent and is sent to prison for something he did not do? The fact is: We can't be sure. And if we can't be sure, then there is only one just verdict in this case and that is of not guilty. Members of the jury, I ask that you find the defendant, Tom Hutton, not guilty."

Bil reached for Salma's hand but she pulled away. "I need to get out," she said. A cold sweat beaded her brow. "I think I'm going to be sick." She didn't wait for him to respond, just darted out of the courtroom, an acid bile in her throat.

SALMA DIPPED HER HAND IN and out of the stream of water, waiting for it to heat. It was always cold in the courthouse bathroom and made her skin feel rough and starchy. Behind her, a door to a cubicle opened and Salma froze when she saw who it was. Willa's eyes were rimmed with red as they met hers in the mirror. For a second, neither woman spoke.

"Hi," said Willa hesitantly.

Salma ignored her and reached for a paper towel.

"How is Zain?"

"That's none of your business."

Willa grimaced. "You don't need to be so rude all the time."

"Rude?" Salma laughed bitterly. She turned around to face her. "Willa, you have no idea about life, do you? You just float around in that cloudy blonde head of yours thinking the world is peachy."

Willa made a face. "Do you hate me because I'm blonde?"

Salma scoffed dismissively.

"I'm serious," said Willa.

"You're ridiculous."

"Am I?" she snapped. "You don't think I see all the digs on Twitter made by women like you? Everyone thinks it's okay to have a go at blonde white women. Well, you know what? I was born like this just as you were born like that, but only one of us is allowed to attack the other."

"Why do you stay with him?" Salma cut in. "Women like you think it's okay to stay with men like him. You roll your eyes and say, *Isn't he outrageous?* Well, guess what, Willa? You're as complicit as he is."

Willa gave her a brittle smile. "That's right. Blame the woman."

"This isn't about you being a woman. This is about you tolerating what your husband has done to my family. Did he tell you that he cornered me in the park after dark?"

A look moved across Willa's face. "When?" she asked sharply.

"The week before last. He said he was out on a run, but just so happened to take the exact same side path that I did."

"What did he say?"

"He threatened me."

Willa drew back in disbelief. "He would have told me if he saw you."

"Maybe you don't know your husband that well."

Willa looked at her, reaching for something to say.

Salma tossed her paper towel in the bin and headed to the door. "Or worse," she said, pausing in the doorway. "Maybe you do." She stepped out and let the door slam behind her.

CHAPTER 21

Willa ripped off her gloves and threw them on the sideboard. One tipped over the edge and landed on the floor. She turned to Tom savagely, finally able to voice her anger now that they were home.

"What the *fuck* were you doing?"

Tom stopped wrestling with his coat, an arm still caught in a sleeve.

"Were you following Salma Khatun in the park?"

Tom freed his arm and moved to hang up the coat.

Willa snatched it from him. "Tom, what the fuck were you doing?"

He looked at her defiantly. "I wasn't 'following' her."

"Jesus. So you *did* see her?"

"Look, I was out on a run and I saw her. I just wanted to talk to her."

"The same way you talked to Zain?"

"Come on, Willa."

"Come on what? Jesus Christ, Tom. You don't seem to understand how serious this is. You can't be seen talking to her, let alone following her in the dark. What did you say to her?"

He shrugged petulantly.

Willa aped the shrug. "Tom, *what* did you say to her?"

He sighed. "I said that if I wanted to scare her, she wouldn't be standing in front of me."

Willa waited. "And?"

"She asked me, 'Would I be lying in the hospital?' and I said, 'Maybe you'd be in the ground.'"

Willa groaned. "You're a fucking idiot, Tom. What if someone had heard you?"

"They didn't."

"We can't afford any slipups. You could go to jail. You think you're tough enough to cope with that? You're lucky he didn't die, or you'd be on trial for murder."

Tom instinctively rejected this. "You heard Julian today. We've got a strong case."

"So you decided to make it harder for yourself and stalk Salma in the park?"

He gripped her shoulders. "Come on, Willa. Just loosen up."

She shoved his coat at him and pulled out of his grip. "I need to think," she said. She marched upstairs and ran herself a bath. In the near-scalding water, she watched her skin turn pink. The small swell of her belly was gone, all sign of life depleted. She and Tom had talked about trying again, but how could they when there was a chance he would go to prison?

Willa thought about what Salma had said. *You're complicit.* But just because she was married to Tom, it didn't mean they were the same. Willa couldn't be blamed for his actions. It was true that he said off-color things sometimes, but who *didn't* in the privacy of their inner circle? He didn't mean the things he said—certainly not his threat to Zain.

She thought about the boy lying in hospital. He had taken something from her, but this was a fate he didn't deserve. He and Jamie had been friends but Willa had never really got to know him. She thought back to the day that he'd helped her with her groceries. He seemed strangely self-possessed for a boy his age although, when she thought about it, this wasn't especially unusual. Men acted one of three ways around her: nervous, flirty, or studiously aloof. Sometimes the last was designed to pique her interest, but occasionally, it was born of vigilance, as if their mothers had sat them down and warned them off women like her. She wouldn't put this past Salma, a woman who truly seemed to despise her. Willa wondered if they could have been friends. It was disturbing how small dials could change the course of your life. A minute earlier or later and Salma would never have known about the banner. We all said and did awful things, didn't we? If the wrong thing reached the wrong person one day—an overheard comment, a slip-away text—how many friendships would be wrecked? To assess someone on a small crosshatch of comments was cruel and illogical. Willa knew the real Tom and she would not apologize for marrying him. He protected her and the very least she owed him was loyalty.

THE STRIPLIGHT OF THE HOSPITAL leached Zain's skin of color, tinging it with blue. Salma thought of the day he was born and how her relatives had crowded around him to coo over his coloring. *He's so fair*, they had said adoringly. *Even fairer than Bil, can you believe?* It shamed her now that this had been a point of pride, not just for them but for her. She hadn't pointed out their colorism. Instead, she had basked in the compliments and said, *If I weren't the one carrying him, I'd think his mother was white!* The memory made her cringe.

She reached out and traced the curve of his adult jaw. His shave was uneven and she wondered if the nurse had been in a hurry that day, forgetting the patch beneath his chin.

"Pop quiz, hotshot," she said softly. "Which country has the highest low point in the world?" She waited and watched for movement—a tensing of his eyelids, a twitch of his lips—but there was nothing. "Okay, I'll give you a clue. It's *not* in the Himalayas." She tucked a curl of hair behind his ear. "Come on, Zain. You know this one." She swallowed. "Okay, another clue. It's in Africa." She missed the way his forehead would bunch whenever he searched for answers. Now it lay smooth and vacant. "It's entirely landlocked by another country," she said, watching the clock, counting sixty seconds.

"Okay," she said, a sag in her tone. "It's Lesotho." She pictured his face creasing with regret that he couldn't find the answer in time and then the laser concentration as he tried to pull out a fact to impress her. *It's the only country in the world that sits entirely above one thousand meters of elevation,* he might have said and she would have laughed in approval.

Bil's footsteps brought her out of her thoughts as he came back with supplies. He placed a bottle of orange juice, a pack of Jaffa Cakes, and the day's paper on the overbed table. Salma poured two cups of juice and handed one to Bil. She took a long swig of her own and leafed through the paper. Her gaze snagged on a picture of Rich—the same one she'd seen in the park: lips parted in a grin, revealing crooked teeth, high cheekbones, and small, beady eyes. She remembered the glint of gold on his phone: a marijuana leaf above a skull and crossbones—an omen of sorts.

"What a waste of a life," she said, tossing the paper aside.

Bil folded it over and traced its bulky crease. "Do you remember that show *Quantum Leap*?" he asked.

Salma looked across at him. "Yeah," she said curiously. She remembered it well. A time traveler, Sam Beckett, was sent back and forth to different times to try to correct historical wrongs.

Bil tapped the paper. "I always wondered if you really could change the course of someone's life by making one small change in one moment in time. Could someone—a parent, a teacher, a Sam Beckett—have turned up at a pivotal moment in this kid's life and made a different decision for him? Would things have turned out differently or would he always have ended up on a filthy floor in"—he glanced at the report—"Abbey Estate, coked out of his head?"

Salma's phone cut in and she answered quickly, turning pale as she listened.

"What is it?" asked Bil.

She locked eyes with him. "The verdict is in." There was no flurry of activity, no leaping to one's feet. Instead, they looked at Zain as if he might react to the news. Salma bent low and kissed his cheek. "I love you, kid," she said, her throat working to keep her tears in.

Bil cupped her elbow. "We have to go."

She took his hand and together they headed out, leaving Zain alone underneath the striplights.

SALMA EMPTIED HER POCKETS ONTO a circular metal plate: a dusty hairband, a crumpled receipt, and a mint that had escaped its wrapper. She passed through the metal detectors and collected her bag from the scanner. In the public gallery, she spotted Willa in the back row, perched next to her son. Jamie glanced up but made no sign of acknowledgment. Salma and Bil took their usual spot at the front. Humans were creatures of habit even in the direst circumstances.

It's going to be not guilty, she told herself. *It's going to be not guilty and that's okay. We can get on with our lives. We can have closure. We can move away.*

"I believe we have a verdict, jury, please," said Judge Braithwaite.

Salma rubbed her left kneecap in a compulsive motion, much too wired to sit still.

"Will the defendant please stand?" asked the clerk.

Tom stood and fastened the button of his suit jacket.

"Mr. Foreman, have the jury reached a verdict upon which you are all agreed?"

A middle-aged man stood up, sweating despite the chill. "Yes," he answered nervously.

Salma tried to read meaning into his glance at Tom.

"On count one do you find the defendant guilty or not guilty of attempted murder?"

Salma leaned forward as if she could will the man into speaking. A preemptive rage welled in her chest because it was *not* okay that Tom would be set free. It *wouldn't* offer her closure and she *couldn't* just get on with life. It would open a gash so deep and wide that it could never be healed. She glared at the foreman, wanting to slap the words from his lips. Finally, he spoke.

"Guilty."

"You find the defendant guilty and that is the verdict of you all?"

"Yes."

The word was like a pendulum swinging in her brain. *Guilty. Guilty. Guilty.* She collapsed against Bil, weak with relief. He closed an arm around her and she felt the rhythm of the breath in his chest, jittery with his own relief.

"Mr. Hutton, you will be remanded in custody until sentencing," the judge was saying. "Thank you, members of the jury."

Salma was overwhelmed. These twelve strangers had made sure that Tom would pay for what he did. They had stood up for justice, and their solidarity filled her with something close to joy. She turned by instinct and saw that Jamie was folded over his knees, trying not to cry. Next to him, Willa was as still as a statue, completely unruffled. Salma reached for Bil's hand. They didn't need to stay here any longer. They could leave. They could bring Zain home and start to rebuild their lives as Tom and Willa's fell apart. She realized how much strain she had felt living next to Tom. The pressure seemed to bulge in the walls and permeate the air. Now a purifying force swept through, clearing out the poison and allowing her—finally, freely—to breathe.

THE COURTROOM JANGLED WITH UNNATURAL sounds: the high, bright ping of a tuning fork, the alarming clash of cymbals—a cruel and demonic orchestra that played only for Willa. Jamie next to her bent forward like a rag doll. Through the gaps in his fingers, his skin was turning puce. She couldn't bring herself to comfort him, too weighed with grief for Tom. As she sat there, inert, Salma in the front row looked over at her. Willa registered sympathy there and it made her bristle with anger. Yet again, Salma was taking the high road. A perverse part of Willa was glad she would never know what really happened to her son. The verdict offered closure, but surely there would always be doubt. *What if?*

"This can't happen," said Jamie. "Dad can't go to prison."

She gripped his arm. "Jamie, it's okay." She realized that her nails were digging into flesh.

He shook her off. "I need to talk to him, Mum. I need to—"

"You will but not now." She pulled him back. "You're in too much of a state, Jamie." She gripped his face between her hands. "We can't let him see you like this."

"But—"

"Jamie," she said sharply. "Your father is stronger than anyone I know. He can handle this." She pressed harder as if to squeeze agreement out of him. Jamie nodded but tears leaked from his eyes. She released him and wiped them away with a thumb. Beneath her show of resolve, however, she felt a roiling nausea. She was sickened by the thought of Tom in prison, but more than that, she was sickened to learn who she really was, for in that moment it wasn't Tom who weighed on her mind most heavily but how she would explain this to friends and relatives. She pictured them clucking their sympathies and physically recoiled. Willa could bear anything but pity. She cursed Tom for igniting this wretched war, for pulling her and Jamie into it, and, most of all, for starting something he couldn't finish.

PART III

The April breeze blew through the classroom and out through the open door. Salma breathed in the scent: lavender or wisteria—she never could tell which was which. She heard a knock and knew who it was without looking. Haroon walked in and slid a white envelope across the table.

"Miss," he said shyly, "I got an offer from Westminster."

Salma snatched up the letter with a shriek. Westminster City was one of the best schools in the country. It stood in the shadow of Buckingham Palace, the Houses of Parliament, and Westminster Abbey—a far cry from Seven Kings. She scanned the letter. "Haroon, this is unbelievable." She fixed her gaze on him. "I'm so bloody proud of you."

He coughed, embarrassed. "Thanks for your help, miss."

"You come and see me, okay?" she said. "Don't swan off and forget where you came from."

He laughed—a bright, harsh sound designed to mask emotion. "I live down the road, miss. That's hardly likely."

"I mean it, Haroon. You come and see me, and you keep me in the loop of what's happening."

"I will," he promised, his jaw rigid with composure.

She stood and hugged him, then gave him a gentle shove. "Now go and celebrate."

He laughed again and slunk shyly to the door. There, he paused and looked back. "Thanks, miss."

"It was my pleasure, Haroon." She watched him leave with a new ache in her heart. She remembered sharing this milestone with Zain, how hopeful he had been starting his A levels. Five months had passed since the verdict, nearly eleven since his fall, and though there were signs of improvement—a fluttering of his eyelids, a new rhythm to his breathing—there hadn't yet been words. Still, the doctors remained hopeful, and as long as they had hope, Salma would cling on too.

She opened her metal filing cabinet and took out her own white envelope, tugging it free from the joint in the drawer. She reread the letter inside it. "HM Prison & Probation Service" was printed along the top next to the royal crest.

Your visit has been confirmed for Friday, 21st April.

She swallowed the dry clot in her throat and slid the letter into her bag. She checked her watch for the hundredth time and finally headed out the door. The drive was an hour but on a late Friday afternoon, took her almost two. She approached the sprawling complex, passed industrial fencing that had long faded to gray. She had spent nearly her entire adult life working in institutions, but none so claustrophobic. Everything about this place was designed to hew and flatten: the featureless walls, the alphanumerical labels, the grids and lines saying, *Welcome to the system.*

She entered the visitors' room and tensed when she saw him. Tom Hutton wore a buzz cut and a bright orange bib over a cheap gray tracksuit. In the five months since she had seen him last, he had bulked up even more.

"Thank you for coming," he said as she tentatively sat down opposite. "I didn't think you would."

Salma hadn't either. She had ignored his first few letters, begging her to visit him. It was the fifth one, handwritten and desperate, to which she had finally responded.

"I heard that you're letting Jamie see Zain." His gaze cut away from her. "Thank you. You didn't have to do that." He waited a beat. "How is he?"

"You don't get to ask that," said Salma.

Tom was unfazed. "I heard he's home now."

"He turned nineteen last week," she said. "I spent it changing his diaper, patching up his sores, giving him a bed bath. He—" She swallowed. "He smells and I just can't get rid of it no matter what I try. It's like he's dying in my living room." She exhaled. "So *that's* how my son is."

Tom's expression grew dark. "I'm sorry."

"You're not sorry. If you were sorry, you would admit what you did."

Tom clasped his hands together. "I didn't do it, Salma. I tried to save him. I swear."

"Don't. *Just don't.*"

Tom persevered. "That's why I wanted to see you: to look you in the eye and tell you. I should have done it months ago. I shouldn't have been so cocky, but I swear to god, it wasn't me."

Salma made a sharp, derisive sound. "Tom, if you're searching for redemption, then there's one way to get it. Tell the truth. You've already been found guilty. What do you have to lose? Tell me what happened to him." She laid her hands flat on the table. "Tell me the truth and I'll find some way to forgive you."

"I *am* telling the truth, Salma. Please believe me."

"Why did you ask me here?"

"Because no one believes me. The jury was *wrong*."

"Why tell me? Go and whine to your wife about it."

Tom looked as if she had slapped him. "Willa's divorcing me."

Salma was surprised. Had she misjudged Willa after all? All this time, she thought that Willa condoned his actions, but if she was divorcing him, then maybe she did have a moral backbone. "Perhaps your police buddies can help," Salma told him coolly. "Shall I find out who's on duty?"

"I deserve that," he said quietly.

"Can I ask you something, Tom?"

He tensed, bracing for a salvo.

"If my family and I weren't Asian, would you have knocked down our banner?"

He started to answer but then faltered. "I don't know," he said, a hint of awe in his voice as if realizing this for the first time himself.

"I think you do know."

The doubt in his features clarified into a shocked honesty, a private revelation.

"I thought so," said Salma. She scraped her chair away from the table.

"Wait, Salma, don't go."

She shook her head. She had thought she would enjoy seeing him like this—his sleek suits swapped for that pathetic bib—but it left her with a cawing sorrow. This, whatever this was, offered a paltry closure.

"Please don't go, Salma. Please just listen."

She stood and folded her jacket over her arm.

"*Please*, Salma."

"Good-bye, Tom," she said, not unkindly. She didn't look back when he called to her even in his desperate tenor. The door slammed behind her, breaking him off mid-plea.

WILLA SAT IN THE RESTAURANT and listened to her friends dissect her life. After Tom's conviction, Sato, Sophia, and Amelia had pressured her into leaving—whatever that meant when your husband would spend a decade in prison. She hadn't wanted to leave, told herself she could wait for him.

But you can't be with a con, said Sato.

You deserve better, said Sophia.

Amelia chimed in with *Remember Nick? Steven's friend from Goldman? He was obsessed with you. He's divorced, so won't mind that you come with baggage.*

Willa had been swept along by this aggressive loyalty. She agreed that, yes, she deserved better, and no, she couldn't possibly stay married to a con, whether he was guilty or not.

"And Jamie?" Amelia cut into her thoughts. "How's he getting on with his A level exams?"

Willa nodded brightly. "He's doing well." She shifted uncomfortably. "He spends a lot of time with Zain."

Amelia frowned. "And you're letting him? Why?"

Willa traced the stem of her wineglass. "It feels petty to forbid him."

Sato spoke now. "That family fucked up your entire life and it's 'petty' to keep them away from your son?"

"Look . . ." Willa paused to modulate her voice. "Maybe I've been unfair to Salma."

Her friends fell silent. For months, they had freely maligned Salma and now Willa was claiming that this was "unfair."

She looked at them in turn. "I mean, what did *she* actually do? It was Tom and Zain—the men. She and I were just caught in the middle."

Sato narrowed her gaze on her. "I don't know, Willa. I think you should be careful. What if she's after revenge of some sort?"

"What? A son for a son?" Willa scoffed.

"Precisely."

Sophia touched her arm. "Honey, please be careful. You don't know what those people are like."

Willa shrugged her off. "Neither do you, Sophia."

Her friend stared at her. "I'm only looking out for you." The warmth in her voice was gone.

"Like when you told me to walk out on Tom?"

Sophia blinked. "We didn't *tell* you to do anything."

"Really?" Willa asked coolly. She quoted their words back at them.

Sato cut in. "Listen, you're angry—we get it—but try not to be a bitch, Willa."

"You could try it yourself sometime," Willa shot back.

Sato winked at her. "But, honey, being a bitch is my brand." She raised her wine in a toast.

Willa lost her patience. "Okay, you know what?" She scraped her chair back. "I'm going home."

A chorus went up at the table. Amelia caught the sleeve of her blouse. "You're not leaving. Come on, sit down." She spoke to Willa gently. "I don't know where all of this about Tom is coming from, but be honest, Willa. You *know* he's not good enough for you. He never has been and now you get to start afresh."

Afresh, meaning what? A string of first dates with divorcés? Playing stepmum to a litter of kids? Willa recoiled at the thought, and in her dismay, she found a shard of clarity. She would go to Tom and confess the truth to him. *I'm sorry. Forgive me. I love you*. She would promise to wait for him. Their lives had fallen apart but if Willa held her nerve and Tom was willing to listen, they could both rebuild.

"You're right," she told Amelia. "It's time to be honest." She followed Sato's lead and raised her glass to her lips.

SALMA FLINCHED AS THE SMALL red cricket ball whizzed by Zain's bed. She let her breath out and urged herself to relax. This was her first Eid with family since Zain had come home in January. Bil and Salma's brother, Samir, had wheeled the bed to the garden while Salma looked on and berated herself for not daring to do this sooner. Zain deserved more than confinement to their living room. His presence was always heavy there, affecting every sense: the constant beep of his monitor; the dank, hormonal smell; the slash of cold air from the open window. Here, in the garden, they were one step closer to normal.

Salma's nephews had built a makeshift cricket pitch and were scrupulously keeping score. The youngest, Junaid, stood by Zain's bed and narrated the match to him.

"Ahmed runs in and delivers a full toss as Arif drives the ball through the covers. That should go all the way to the boundary . . . and it does. Four runs!"

The ball skittered across the grass and knocked into the fence, slipping through the sole loose board into Willa's garden. Salma groaned guiltily. After all these months, they still hadn't fixed it. Molly pelted into Willa's garden and returned with the ball triumphantly.

"Excellent fielding by Molly Khatun," said Junaid in the dulcet tone of a cricket commentator.

The sight of him with Zain filled Salma with rare joy, briefly ceasing the undertow of sorrow. She watched her family chatter and laugh and occasionally pause by Zain to give him the latest news. Her house no longer felt like a funeral parlor with guests paying respects by the coffin of his bed. Today, they treated him like he was awake, but it didn't seem a contrivance nor a perverse delusion. Instead, it felt easy and light: her family in its newest iteration.

Molly ran back and forth with the batsman, making Salma laugh. She loved that dog. She loved these people. Things felt calm.

Bil stood next to her and touched his fingertips to hers. "Are you okay?"

She smiled, wistful but warm. "Yeah. I think I really am."

He squeezed her hand and she saw her nephews exchange a look. Public displays of affection weren't etiquette in their culture. She kissed Bil's cheek, raising a chorus of protest.

"Zain *bhai*, you need to sort your parents out!" cried Junaid.

"*Siss*," said Ahmed, borrowing an expression of disapproval from the elder generation.

Salma and Bil laughed, and together they joined the cricket pitch, taking opposite sides. The evening was long and pleasant, the sun hanging low for hours before it yielded to dark. Salma insisted that her family stay for dinner but was relieved when they refused. All her emotion from the day was just below the surface and threatened to break through.

Bil and Samir wheeled Zain back to the living room and she watched her family say good-bye. There was no sadness, just their own ways of showing they loved him—a peck on the cheek, a ruffle of the hair, a light punch on the shoulder—before they filed out in a raucous bundle.

Bil closed the door behind them and sat on the bottom stair. *Woo*, he made a relieved sound. Salma sat down next to him and slung her arms around his neck. "Thank you for putting up with them."

He turned his head to kiss her. "You know I love them."

"Still. They're a lot."

"Yeah, but . . ." He let out a weary sigh. "Having them here shows me how lonely we've been."

Salma was taken aback by his choice of word but now that he had said it, she could feel it keenly. Without Zain, or family nearby, or neighbors they could trust, the two of them were indeed lonely. She laced her fingers with his and brought them to her lips. "Things will get better," she promised.

Molly padded into the hallway and looked at them expectantly.

The two of them laughed and Salma disentangled herself. "I'll walk her tonight," she said.

"You sure?"

"Yeah. I need to decompress."

"Okay. I might jump in the shower first." He glanced across at Zain. Though he was perfectly safe there, they were both wary of leaving him. "I'll be quick," said Bil, already unbuttoning his shirt as he headed upstairs.

Salma strolled to the garden to wait and breathed in the scent of something sweet. She tipped her head to the sky and watched the first stars emerge. The light went on in her bedroom and she watched Bil's silhouette move through his routine: bending to take off his trousers, never failing to make her giggle as he stood in his shirt and socks. In the bathroom, he would splash his face with water, ignoring the cleanser and moisturizer she had bought him last year after he complained about looking old. She smiled as she watched him inspect a gray hair.

She heard a bark behind her and turned in a full circle. She groaned when she realized that Molly had escaped into Willa's garden. She crouched by the loose plank and called for her to come back. She scanned the length of the garden but couldn't see any sign of the dog. After a few minutes of this, she squeezed through the space herself. She stayed low and called out discreetly. The last thing she wanted was to be caught in Willa's garden.

"Molly," she whispered. "Come on, girl." She heard her snuffling behind the shed. "Molly, come *on*." Salma advanced toward her but froze when a light came on in the kitchen. She turned toward it and saw Willa bending over a counter. The act seemed deliberately sensual. God, even when she wasn't being watched, Willa moved like a dancer.

Salma wasn't sure if she should stand and wave to make it obvious what she was doing, or try to skulk back undetected. She decided on the latter and approached Molly quietly. She knelt and held her collar. "Come on, sweetheart," she said. She peeked out from behind the shed and saw that Willa had her back to her. "Come on, Molly," she said more firmly. She tugged her and led her back to the fencing, praying that she wouldn't bark. She steered her back through the gap and hurried behind her.

As she did, a glint caught her eye. It was a strip of gold wedged between the two panels that ran beneath the fencing. She crouched closer to inspect it, then slid her fingers between the panels and tried to wiggle it free. It was wedged in there tightly and she sawed it back and forth to try to release it. Finally, it popped free and up onto the grass. Salma's blood turned to ice when she saw what it was. An old Nokia phone with two stickers on the back: a marijuana leaf and a golden skull and crossbones. She mapped the phone to its owner: Rich, the squatter who stole Molly. Her dread rose quiet and slow, something not computing. Had Rich dropped his phone on the day that he stole Molly?

No, because Salma saw him with the phone *after* that. He must have come back to . . . what? Steal Molly again? An appalling thought occurred to her: Could Zain have seen Rich taking her? He would have confronted him—there was no doubt about that—and Salma already knew that Rich could be violent. Was it *Rich* who had hurt Zain that day? Salma's pulse grew fast and erratic. She snatched up the phone and flipped it open. The screen was blank—out of battery. She pressed the ON button three times compulsively. To her surprise, it blinked to life, a purple-blue square in the night. Molly barked at it and Salma's attention snapped to the window, checking if Willa had heard. She pulled Molly close to soothe her. Then, with clumsy fingers, she opened the text messages on the old phone. There was only one.

TOM'S GONE AND JAMIE JUST LEFT.
GIVE IT HALF AN HOUR TO BE SAFE.

Salma stared at the message, stuck in a panicked pause. The clamor of her thoughts was too fast and violent for her to understand them. *Tom's gone and Jamie just left*—sent on the day of Zain's fall. She looked up at Willa in the kitchen window and was hit with a dreadful clarity. *Willa* had sent that message. *Willa* had sent Rich to the house.

You took my child, so I'll take yours.

Salma rocked back on her heels, hitting the ground with a jolt. It seemed to tilt beneath her, skewing the night around her. Willa couldn't have meant for Rich to hurt Zain. She *couldn't* have, because what would that make her?

You took my child, so I'll take yours.

Salma scrabbled away from the fence, needing to put some distance between them. Her instincts told her to stand up, to back off, to get far away from Willa—but a stronger force fixed her there, a compulsive need to *know*. Her fingers trembled as she thumbed the phone, careful not to drop it. She pressed the green button to call the sender and held the phone to her ear. The sweat on her skin cooled, making her shiver compulsively. She held her breath as the connection clicked in her ear. At first, she didn't think it would work, but then she heard the ringing. Willa snapped off the kitchen tap and hurried out of view. Salma could hear her phone ringing from here. She waited, heart revving, the ringtone trilling on. Willa came back into view at the window. In her hands she carried a microwave meal, the steam rising off in waves. She dropped it onto the counter, and at that very second, the phone call was answered.

"Hello?"

The voice in her ear was a shotgun, making the air vibrate. Horror snaked in her veins as she turned her gaze up to the second story.

"Bil?" The word was small and breathless.

His silhouette paused in the window, phone pressed to his ear. He ripped apart the curtains and their eyes met like a bolt of lightning. Every nerve in her body registered alarm, her mind lighting up with panic. The ferocity on his face was shocking and when he pelted out of the room, Salma felt impelled to move. She ran inside the house, Molly at her heels, and spun around in search for—what? Bil crashed into the living room and the two of them locked eyes, caught in a vacuum.

"Salma," Bil said calmly. "Give me the phone."

She withdrew it instinctively. "Bil." She looked at the phone in her palm. "What is this?"

"Salma, give me the phone," he repeated.

She charted the distance between them, then darted to Zain's bed, needing something solid by her side. "Bil." Her voice shook. "What's happening?"

"Give me the phone and then we'll talk." He approached her slowly, his hands held out in a non-threat.

She moved away from him, around to the other side of the bed.

His voice grew hard. "Come on, Salma. Just give me the fucking phone."

She held it up. "Bil, what the hell is this message?"

He lunged for her and she leaped away with a short, sharp yelp.

"Bil, stop it!" Salma backed into the kitchen, her voice high and panicked. "What are you doing?"

He slapped the railing and followed. "Give me the fucking phone, Salma." He lunged again and Salma lost her grip on it. It flew across the floor and skidded beneath the fridge.

Bil growled in frustration. "This fucking thing." He crouched by the fridge, sliding his fingers underneath. "For fuck's sake!" He sprang back to his feet and shimmied the fridge forward but only managed to move it a few inches. He smacked it with his hand. "Jesus fucking Christ!"

Molly bounded away, frightened by this novel rage.

Salma watched from across the room. "Bil." Her voice labored to keep its ease. "You're scaring me. What's happening?"

"What's happening is that fucking junkie couldn't do *one* thing right!"

A tentacle of dread closed around her chest. "What did you do?" She watched his face contract with rage as her own filled with heat. "Bil, what did you do?"

He bellowed in frustration. "I asked him to do one fucking thing!"

"What did you do?" Her voice was a whisper.

"It wasn't meant to happen like this." There was a slight give in his shoulders. "He was just meant to mess things up."

"Rich?" she asked.

Bil nodded.

Salma struggled to fit the pieces. "How?"

"I paid him to get Molly back. When I went to see him." Bil bared his teeth in a garish smile. "I gave him a hundred quid."

Salma blinked. "But you said they'd left her there."

"I paid them to leave. I didn't want you to know that. It's just so fucking *pathetic.*" He made a bitter sound, disgusted with himself.

"And then?"

"Then the police raided our house and I was just so fucking *angry.* Were we just meant to accept this, what they did to our son? To our home?" Bil grit his teeth. "I gave the junkie money to fuck up their house, told him to use our side passage to get into our garden and through the loose board into theirs. Zain's usually on Twitch at that time. How could I know he'd be in their house?"

Salma stared at him. "You," she said breathlessly. "You did this?"

"Zain surprised him. There was a tussle . . . It was an accident. He was only meant to mess things up."

"You." Her mind fell blank with shock.

"Rich panicked. He was about to escape when Tom came home. He ran back upstairs and hopped across onto Zain's balcony."

"Zain's balcony?" she asked dumbly.

Bil choked on his next words. "He was still here when we got home. I hid him in Zain's bathroom. I panicked, Salma. I didn't know what to do."

Horror churned inside her. Bil had harbored Zain's assailant in their very home. "You knew," she said with a note of wonder. "All this time you knew. You watched me at his hospital bed. You watched me cry and pray and *beg* to understand, and you *knew* all this time. The trial. The evidence you gave. All of it was lies." She bent forward, gripped by a crippling rage.

"*They* did this, Salma. Not me."

"They didn't do this!" She slapped the counter. "They didn't nearly kill my son!"

Bil pled for understanding. "These people. They want to break us and they push and they push and they push. Well, I broke, Salma." His voice cracked. "They broke me."

His despair compounded Salma's own. Her husband—a man who followed the rules, who tried to keep calm and carry on— had been driven to an act of . . . What? Revenge? Defiance? Insanity?

"Salma, *please*," he begged, tender but urgent. "It was an accident."

"You lied to me."

"How was I supposed to tell you?"

"You let me think that Tom hurt our son. Our *son*."

"What else could I do? You never would have forgiven me."

"I never *will* forgive you."

"Don't say that." He clasped his hands together. "Salma, please don't say that."

"You made me think it was Tom." Guilt scraped inside her. Tom had been wrongly convicted. "You have to tell the police," she said.

Bil stared at her. "No." There was no argument in his tone, just plain, simple refusal.

"Bil, you *have* to."

"I'm not going to prison, Salma."

"You'd have Tom rot there instead?"

There wasn't even a flicker of guilt. "Yes," he said. "I would."

"No, Bil. You wouldn't."

"I would, Salma, and I will." To punctuate the point, he knelt by the fridge and reached for the phone, grunting with the effort. "I searched for this fucking thing everywhere. The junkie said he dropped it and I searched and searched for it." Bil briefly straightened to pluck a large knife from the block. He slid it beneath the fridge and swept it back and forth. There was a dull thunk, and slowly, carefully, Bil retrieved the phone.

"Bil, you have to tell the police."

"We can't do that, Salma," he said calmly. "We've come too far. I organized it, I lied in court, I . . ." A shadow moved over his face.

Salma felt her hackles rise, sensing something awful. "Oh god, Bil, what did you do?" Salma thought of Willa, then Tom, then Jamie, searching for a secret injury. Then her gaze fixed on the phone and she was hit by a sick possibility. "Rich." His name died in her throat.

Bil didn't respond. He knelt by the sink and retrieved a hammer from the cupboard beneath it. He wrapped the phone in a tea towel and raised the hammer above it.

"Bil, did you hurt that boy?" Salma asked him urgently. The hammer trembled in his hand. "Bil, you didn't . . . Did you kill that boy?"

His breathing grew labored and Salma watched a bead of sweat drip off his forehead. "No," he said in a choke.

She studied him carefully. "But you know who did?"

"I didn't kill him." He lowered the hammer. "But I was there." The shock was like tin in her mouth. "Why?" she whispered.

"He was blackmailing me, taunting me, saying he'd tell the police. I ignored it at first because why would he admit to a crime, but then he started using *you*. He threatened to tell you and started demanding money. He lorded it over me, calling and texting at all hours of the evening. I went to see him one day to give him some cash and he'd clearly taken something. He was barely conscious, doing this weird side-to-side motion. His skin looked like old meat—all gray and clammy—and then he just . . . fell asleep."

"And?"

"And I didn't know what to do. I got my phone out to call the police, but how could I explain what I was doing there? I didn't touch him in case I left a trace, so I just . . . left."

Fresh horror welled inside her. "Did you know that he was dying?"

It took him a moment to answer. "I suspected."

"And you walked away?"

"He would have died either way."

Salma felt a rush of nausea, making her eyes water. "I have no idea who you are."

He took a step toward her. He must have seen her flinch because he swiftly set down the hammer. "Salma, come on. It's me."

"Bil, you're not going to get away with this. They'll catch you."

"Not if we both keep quiet."

She shook her head wildly. "You can't let Tom rot in jail."

"Why not?"

"Because—" Salma froze when she heard a creak by the garden door. They both looked up in unison to see Jamie in the doorway. The air seemed to contract—tense and electric. Bil moved toward him, slowly so not to startle his prey. Salma cut in urgently. "Bil, he can't hear."

Bil studied Jamie, who looked like a deer in headlights. The alarm on his face was clear and wild. "He can hear well enough."

"He can't." Salma raised a palm at Jamie to tell him to stay calm. For a moment, it seemed he would obey but a primal instinct got the best of him and he turned on his heel and fled.

"Jamie, no!"

Bil vaulted after him, seizing him by the shoulders just as he reached the threshold. Jamie thrashed against him, crying out in panic.

"Stop moving," shouted Bil, failing to restrain him. He pushed him into the wall but Jamie bucked wildly. "Stop moving!" Bil pinned an arm against his neck. Jamie resisted and Bil pressed more firmly.

Salma looked on in horror. "Bil, you'll hurt him!"

He pushed harder on Jamie's windpipe. "Maybe I mean to," he grunted.

Salma watched Jamie struggle to breathe. His skin grew pallid and his eyes seemed to lose focus, his pupils lying slack against the whites. Galvanized by panic, she barreled forward to try to free him. Bil blocked her with his body. She clawed at him but lost her footing in the tussle. She flailed backward and crashed into the granite counter with an ugly crack. Her vision exploded in a blinding, blackout pain. As the room folded into darkness, she sensed that Jamie wasn't moving. In her stupor, she thought she saw a figure in white standing behind Bil. It lifted something silver and heavy—but then the image faded and her body gave in to the pain.

CHAPTER 23

Salma's mouth was dry and the air was milky warm. There was a scent in the air: baby formula or something subtle and sweet. She opened her eyes, blinking away the glue. She saw a vase of flowers by her bed, one green sprig spilling toward her, spindly like an insect leg. She shrunk away from it and grunted in pain—a low, mannish sound. She tried to sit up but stilled when she saw who was in the chair opposite.

"You're awake," said Willa. She smoothed a fold in her white dress.

Salma sat up too quickly and winced from the pain. "Where's my son?" she asked croakily.

"He's okay. He's here. The doctors are checking him over."

Salma closed her eyes, seasick from the motion of the room. She pawed her neck to loosen whatever was there but found only her skin. She felt hurried, panicked, choked with everything she wanted to say. "It was Bil," she managed.

"Yes, I know."

Salma remembered the figure in white lifting the silver hammer. A cold, sink-away feeling opened in her stomach. "Is he . . . ?"

"He's okay," said Willa gently. "He confessed. The officers took him in."

Salma made a helpless bleat of a sound. She felt the sting of tears and covered her face to hide them.

"It's okay," said Willa.

On hearing this tiny kindness, Salma began to weep. Her sobs were low and pathetic: the cry of something spineless, depleted. She cried to soothe the nerves that still jangled in her body. She cried for her son whose life was thwarted so early. And she cried for her husband, for the man she thought he was, the man he had tried to be, the man who had failed so catastrophically. She had given twenty years of her life to him and everything they had built was gone. She closed her eyes but violence played on beneath her lids: Bil choking Jamie, his skin turning blue; her futile attempt to free him; the sound of bone on granite.

She looked across at Willa. "Jamie?" she asked, remembering those last few moments.

Willa cleared her throat. "He's okay." She pleated a section of her dress. "I saw you, Salma. I saw you try to save him." Her voice was thick with emotion. "I've been such a witch to you. Why would you help me?"

Salma couldn't articulate what she wanted to say. Saving Jamie was a basic human instinct, one that her husband had lost. "What could I do?" she asked. "Let this fight go on? Where would it stop?"

Willa grimaced. "I wish you and I could have been friends."

Salma's expression soured, her grief turning bitter.

"I really do," said Willa. "And I think we *could* have been if we hadn't got off on the wrong foot."

"I don't think so, Willa."

Willa ignored the edge in her tone. "Things could have been different, Salma. If you hadn't assumed the worst of Tom and we hadn't—"

"Excuse me?" Salma cut in.

"If you hadn't . . ." Willa registered the look on her face.

Salma was angered by her own naivete for thinking this a truce. "Do you think Bil's confession completely absolves Tom?"

Willa answered carefully as if it was a trick question. "No."

"Tom targeted my family—maliciously and repeatedly. He's not entirely innocent."

Willa considered this and it seemed to dislodge something: a tiny flake of honesty. She exhaled slowly, as if building her nerve. "I need to tell you something, Salma." She fiddled with the diamond on her ring finger. "I scratched your car—not Tom."

Salma was disoriented, caught off guard by Willa's confession. She remembered seeing the curtains move and assuming it was Tom behind them. "Why?" she asked her.

Willa's gaze flitted away. "I was angry at you for posting that video when you told me you wouldn't. I offered you money and you made me feel like shit for it."

Salma gripped her blanket as if it might lend her patience.

"There's more," said Willa. "It was me that sent the squatters to your restaurant. Rich was dropping off some weed for Tom and I mentioned that your place was empty."

"You?" Salma was incredulous. "Why would you do that?"

Willa spoke quickly, as if she might escape judgment by sheer force of speed. "I was the one who took Molly but I swear I didn't plan it. She kept lumbering into our garden and it was a spur-of-the-moment thing. I was angry that you'd cost Tom his job. I wanted to teach you a lesson, so I gave her to Rich. It was only meant to be for a day."

Salma felt a vinegar-jump in her throat, the acid taste of shock. She stared at Willa, unable to compute her cruelty.

"And it was me who reported the knives," she finished. "I'm sorry. I didn't think it through."

The words removed the air from the room. Salma tried to speak but could only make a choke of a sound.

Willa watched her soberly.

"You're a psycho," managed Salma.

Willa tipped her head in concession. "Okay, I deserve that."

"I need you to leave." Salma's heart rate spiked on the monitor.

"Look, can we discuss this calmly?"

"I need you to leave." Salma pressed the call button.

"Salma, you're not listening." Willa leaned on the bed, forcing intimacy. "I'm trying to say I'm sorry."

"You need to get away from me, Willa."

"Jesus, you *like* being angry, don't you?" She made a bark of laughter but there was no mirth in it, just a precise cruelty. "I come here hat in hand to say sorry and you just . . ." She moved a hand in front of her face, miming a blank screen. "You're not the only person who lost something, Salma. I lost my baby and they *blamed* me for it in court, but you don't *know* why she died. If you hadn't come round that day, she might still be here."

Salma had run dry of sympathy. "You need to leave," she repeated.

"Ah yes, how stupid of me to have expected your sympathy."

"Oh, fuck off, Willa."

"Don't be so rude." The retort was so sharp and instinctive that it made Salma seethe. "Get out," she said, her voice low and dangerous. "Get. Out." When Willa didn't move, Salma lost her temper. "Get out!" She swiped at a jug of water, which flew across the room and bounced off the wall in a plastic clatter.

Willa sprang to her feet, her eyes doe wide. She ran into the corridor. "Can we have some help, please? My friend is having a panic attack."

On hearing this, Salma began to shout—not coherent sounds but ugly threats and expletives.

Willa flagged down a nurse. "Please help her."

Salma writhed away from the woman, her temper at full tilt. When she pulled back, she knocked over the vase. It smashed on the floor and glass skittered everywhere.

"Can't you give her something?" cried Willa. "She'll hurt someone."

"No!" cried Salma.

"Just calm down," said the nurse. She reached for her but Salma batted her hand away.

"Please give her something," repeated Willa.

"No!" screamed Salma, but the nurse was already pushing a needle into her IV. The cloud closed in around her and her head swung back to the pillow. She saw Willa by the door, her features dark with worry. But there was something else there too: a rapt curiosity as if observing something improbable, a gorgon, a faun, or centaur. Something human but also half savage.

JAMIE TRIED TO SLOW THE dart of his heart to match Zain's own on the monitor. He was jittery with relief, buoyant with a great weight lifted. All these months he had blamed himself for leaving Zain alone that day. He had never believed that a random intruder was responsible for his injuries. In truth, Jamie secretly wondered if his father was in fact guilty. He could picture the scene: his dad confronting Zain; Zain mouthing back; his dad grabbing him, intending only to scare him; Zain fighting back.

Jamie had studied his father a hundred times looking for signs of guilt, always coming up empty—and now he knew why. Because Bil was the one who was guilty. How would Zain cope when he woke up to the truth?

If he wakes up, thought Jamie.

"I wish I could change things," he said to Zain, reaching out to touch his hand but hovering just above it. "I wish I'd just punched you that day." He made a small, bitter sound. "Maybe then you would've gone home and none of this would've happened. Instead, I did what I always do." He felt a remnant of shame whenever he thought of that day.

He remembered how Zain had enjoyed goading him. He had pushed at Jamie's chest and laughed when he raised his fists because it was so humiliatingly clear that he had no idea what to do with them. Jamie had a history of backing out of fights: with schoolmates who were cruel about his bulky hearing aids, or those older boys at the bus stop who were lewd about his mum that day. The fact that Zain had forced him into the same cowardice was a sorrow he couldn't bear. He stood there, lit up with shame, desperately trying to blink back tears.

Zain tensed, coiled for attack, but the threat in his face ebbed away. At first, Jamie didn't understand what was happening but in seeing Zain's pained expression, realized that *he* was fighting tears as well. The shame lifted off Jamie—as light as a bird off a wire.

Zain, however, grew angrier. He smacked the wall and swore.

It took a moment for Jamie to react. "Zain, are you . . ." He stepped toward him carefully. "Do you need help?"

Zain closed his eyes, his features in a wince. He took several short, sharp breaths, as if waiting for his anger to cool. Jamie watched on nervously. "I have to go," said Zain and turned toward the balcony.

"No, wait." Jamie groped for the words that would make him stay. He knew that if Zain left now, their friendship might never recover. "I talked to Camilla," he said quickly. "It was only for a minute but *she* came up to *me*."

Zain was disoriented, briefly snatched from his mood. "Camilla?" he said. "The girl you like?"

Jamie smiled crookedly. "Yeah." He barreled on, worried that the moment would separate: In this one, Zain would stay; in the other, he would leave and break off their friendship for good. He talked and talked until he saw Zain relax. Then, gently, he asked, "Are you okay?"

Zain slumped on the bed and scrubbed a palm across his face. "Fuck. I'm such an arsehole." He looked across at Jamie. "I'm sorry, man."

Jamie knew that Zain had reasons to be angry—getting kicked out of school, Molly going missing, the raid by the police—but this felt like something darker. He shifted uneasily. "But are you okay?" Before Zain could answer, an alarm interrupted them. Jamie glanced at the time. "Shit, I've got to get to tutoring." He looked at Zain with a question. "We've still got to upload the demo."

Zain stood up. "I'll get it done."

Jamie heaved his bag on one shoulder, the weight pulling it low. "You'll be all right?"

"Yeah, course."

Jamie paused in the doorway. "Listen, use my computer. It'll be quicker."

Zain made a face. "What about your parents?"

"They're out."

"And what if they come home and find me here?" He sliced a finger across his throat.

Jamie laughed. "Don't worry. I'll be back in an hour." He motioned at his watch. "We only have till six, mate. You better get on with it."

And with that, Zain's fate was sealed.

CHAPTER 24

Bil watched her uneasily from his seat in the prison hall. His hair was salt-and-pepper, and Salma marveled at how a mere four months could age someone dramatically. He had lost his natural ease and seemed to constantly second-guess himself. He would reach to fix his hair but then lower his hand again. He would speak in halting sentences that faded to ellipses, or immediately undermine himself with *although, but, however, that said.*

It made her think of a friend of hers whose home had been burgled last year. The husband had been beaten and emerged from the attack a different person. Once funny and gregarious, he grew meek and obedient. Salma had wondered then if she could stand such a version of Bil. Now she wondered if she could fix the one in front of her. Could they rewind through the different iterations, from this beaten version past the vengeful, angry one, back to the one she knew? She hadn't forgiven him, but a loud and beating part of her was still in love with him. The man she had married was *real* and worthy of the life she had shared with him. He had to pay this penance but she didn't want him broken, so when he reached out but then paused, she leaned across and took his hand. It was strangely bony in hers, his body already foreign. How would he look at the end of his sentence? Three long years at Pentonville for perverting the course of justice.

"Will you ever forgive me?" he asked her.

Salma tried hard to hold on to kindness. "I need Zain to wake up," she said. "Until that happens . . ." She didn't need to finish.

Bil turned his hand beneath hers and laced their fingers together. "I can't do this alone, Salma. What happened to Zain, to us. I can't be by myself and deal with that."

Salma saw the sunken look in his eyes, the new gauntness around his jowls, and swallowed the choke in her voice. "I don't know what to say to you."

"That you won't give up on me."

Salma couldn't answer and the silence stretched between them. She released his hand. "If I were in your position, what would you do?"

Bil didn't hesitate. "I would forgive you. *Of course* I would."

In her heart, Salma knew that this was true. "I need more time," she said.

"Do you still love me?"

"That's not fair, Bil."

"Do you?"

"Of course I do. I can't just switch it off."

"Then wait for me, Salma. Please."

She closed her eyes, tipping hot tears onto her cheek. "I don't know how to rebuild."

"Together," he said urgently. "We rebuild together."

A klaxon signaled the end of visiting hours. Bil stood and pulled her into a hug. She closed her arms around him, but her body was stiff and unyielding. This man did not feel or smell like her husband. There was a wiriness in his body and his clothes smelled of industrial detergent instead of the lemon-grass they used at home. When he kissed her hair, she tensed.

"I should go," she said, chasing away a tear. She pulled free and left without kissing him, losing the battle this time between kindness and cruelty. She fled from the prison, her skin itching as it always did after a visit there. The first thing she did when she got home was take a steamy shower, scrubbing herself free of prison lest news of it reached Zain. She checked on him, switched on his baby monitor, and gave him a kiss on the cheek. "We'll be back in thirty," she told him. She pulled on a heavy coat and clipped on Molly's leash. They stepped outside, where the air was cool with the first signs of autumn.

She spotted a large moving van parked outside the house next door. A man and a woman were halfway across the lawn, heaving a large gray sofa. Salma locked eyes with the man.

"Hi!" he called. He was in his early forties with muscular shoulders and a cartoonishly square jaw. He said something to the woman and they both set down the sofa. They walked over and introduced themselves as Matthew and Jenny Law.

"This is such a lovely street," said Jenny.

"It is," said Salma. "You'll be very happy here."

Jenny looked up at Matthew. "I hope so," she said, eyes shining. Then she glanced around and leaned in conspiratorially. "I'm so pleased we met you. Everyone else seems retired and we were starting to worry!"

Salma chuckled politely.

Jenny gestured toward their house. "It's a shame that Tom and Willa moved out. They seemed like such a nice couple."

Salma nodded. "A shame."

"Did you know them well?"

"Well enough," she said with a brittle smile.

Jenny took Matthew's hand and lifted it sportingly. "Well, I hope we can fill their boots."

"I'm sure," said Salma. Next to her, Molly barked, making the three of them laugh. "His master's voice," said Salma, indicating the leash.

"Well, it was lovely to meet you," said Jenny.

"You too." She nodded at Matthew. "Welcome to Blenheim." She raised her hand in a wave, then headed up the street with Molly. She enjoyed the crunch of leaves underfoot. More than spring, this was a time of renewal: some things dying and clearing away, making space for new. The air was crisp and cool and Salma felt a weight lift off her. For the first time that year, she felt hopeful about the future.

Molly tugged at her leash and Salma coaxed her along. A few steps farther, she stopped with a cluck of impatience. "Molly, I forgot your bags." She turned and lightly jogged back home, shushing Molly's whine. She let herself into the house and grabbed two, then three, plastic bags from the dresser and tucked them into her pocket. When she stepped out again, something caught her eye: a small red-and-white flag stuck in her new neighbors' plant pot. She tensed at the sight of the St. George's Cross. She watched it for a moment, fluttering in the breeze. Gingerly, she approached it and lightly touched the fabric. Then she tugged it from the soil. The tiny flagpole was unduly heavy. She traced a fingertip along the seams. Then she folded it neatly and tossed it onto their lawn. She and Molly headed to the park without a backward glance.

ACKNOWLEDGMENTS

I wrote *Perfectly Nice Neighbors* in the deep pandemic and could not have done it without Peter Watson, who listened to me fret and whine on our long and rambling walks. Thank you for never letting me feel sorry for myself.

Jessica Faust, you are the sort of woman that I aspire to be: tough and efficient but somehow also kind and patient. Thank you for everything.

Thank you to Mark Tavani, who fine-tuned this book with such grace and skill. It has been a delight working with you. I will cherish those notes that you added to the manuscript.

Thank you to Aranya Jain, Sally Kim, and the team at Putnam. It's an honor to join your stable of writers.

Thank you to those who have championed my work outside the United States: Manpreet Grewal at HQ, without whom I would not have a career. You're a street fighter and I'm so bloody grateful to have you in my corner. Thank you to Peter Borcsok and the team at HarperCollins Canada. Your words about my work have meant so much.

Thank you to Lucy Stille, Mary Alice Kier, James McGowan, and the BookEnds team. Thank you, also, to Eldes Tran for sorting my tidbits from my titbits and generally making me look good.

I am indebted to so many who helped me with their time and expertise. Thank you, Graham Bartlett, Dina Begum, Matthew Butt QC, Kelly Corp, Sairish Hussain, Hiren Joshi, Nadine Matheson, Dr. Daniel Wilbor, Dr. Claire Windeatt, and Dr. Michael Yoong. As ever, I hope you will forgive me for any errors I've made or creative license I've taken with your meticulous advice.

Thank you to all my fellow authors who have championed my work. There are so many of you who have done so much. I dare not try to name you all but I hope you know that I'm so incredibly grateful that you have taken the time to read and share my work.

A special thank-you to all the booksellers, librarians, reviewers, and bloggers who have shared my books with readers. Historically, there's been debate about whether names like mine on a cover can sell. Every time you have sold, loaned, shared, or recommended my book, you have made a difference and for that I am deeply grateful.

Thank you, as ever, to my sisters, Reena, Jay, Shopna, Forida, and Shafia. I won't harp on about you, especially as that's one thing you tend to enjoy: when I stop harping on.

Photograph © Ewelina Stechnij

KIA ABDULLAH is a bestselling author and travel writer. Her novels include *Take It Back*, which was a *Guardian* and *Telegraph* thriller of the year; *Truth Be Told*, which was shortlisted for the Diverse Book Awards; and *Next of Kin*, which was longlisted for the CWA Gold Dagger Award. Abdullah has written for *The New York Times*, *The Guardian*, the *Financial Times*, *The Times* (London), and the BBC, and is the founder of Asian Booklist, a nonprofit that advocates for diversity in publishing and helps readers discover new books by British Asian authors.

VISIT KIA ABDULLAH ONLINE

kiaabdullah.com
🐦 kiaabdullah
📷 kiaabdullah